# SWALLOWTAIL

SHERI MESHAL

*For Dad, my storytelling mentor, my hero and my best friend.*

There are hundreds of paths up the mountain, all leading in the same direction, so it doesn't matter which path you take. The only one wasting time is the one who runs around and around the mountain, telling everyone that his or her path is wrong.
Hindu teaching

# CHAPTER 1

PATTY THE TELLER SUPERVISOR, stopped dead in her tracks. Her mouth hung agape as steaming coffee ran from her mug onto the cool pavement, splashing her worn loafers.

Unease pooled in the pit of Claire's stomach. As she approached her, she ran her hands over her pants in a quick self-check. *Fabric softener? Panty liner?*

No, nothing horrifying was stuck to her, as far as she could tell. She was wearing her new cream-colored suit. *Winter whites —hardly anything to spill your coffee over,* she thought as she hurried past Patty and the tattered plastic smoking tent outside the bank's employee entrance.

Claire relaxed when she saw the back of George's bald head in the security booth. "Patty's a little off this morning." She flashed her bank ID and reached for the heavy electronic door.

George spun away from the security monitors. "I—I don't know." His ears seemed especially pink as he rushed up to the window.

Claire couldn't help wondering what he'd been watching and tried to get a peek over his shoulder.

George stepped to the side, blocking her view. He gave her

an overly-toothy smile, and buzzed her in as he reached for the phone.

Claire frowned and continued down the hall. She heard Marilyn from Human Resources snap at George through his speaker phone, "What is it now?"

She thought she heard George whisper, "She's here!" just as the heavy door latched shut behind her. *Me? I'm always here... like they'd notice if I wasn't.*

The Human Resources receptionist walked out of her office, engrossed in paperwork.

"Morning, Sue," Claire called out, noting Sue's usual sleek straight hair and flawless makeup.

"Claire?" Sue breathed, as she did a double take. A file slipped from her hand sending half-a-dozen sheets of paper floating to the floor.

"Sorry, didn't mean to startle you," Claire apologized as she crouched down to help her pick up the papers.

"Thanks, I..." Sue cut herself off. Her face flushed as she grabbed the papers from Claire's hand.

"How are the fertility treatments going?"

Sue blew at her bangs to keep them from sticking to her forehead. "I can't talk. I mean, I've got a million emails." She stood up and backed into the office door, clutching the folder to her chest.

"Don't remind me. I'll catch up with you later. Who's running the meeting this morning?"

"I don't know. Actually, I think it's canceled."

"Canceled? They never cancel. Even when we had the fire drill they let us sear a bit while they went over goals. What's going on?"

"Yeah, right," Sue half-answered. Blinking as she fumbled for the knob, she backed through the office door and quickly shut it.

Claire shook her head, adjusted her purse on her shoulder and continued down the hall.

She couldn't help pausing at the doorway to the boardroom. It was empty, but all the lights were on and the blinds were closed. No pastries, just coffee cups strewn about—one with blood-red lipstick tattooed on the rim. The leather chairs were in complete disarray. Claire's stomach knotted.

She detected the faint scent of Burberry cologne—Oren, their CEO. The blood-red lipstick was Marilyn's, head of HR.

Venturing inside, Claire spotted several pads of paper bearing Union Allied's logo. She stepped back over to the door, glanced up and down the hallway and slipped back to the table for a closer look. She picked up one of the blank pads and tried to decipher the impressions left behind. There was a list of names. Her heart seized when she spotted her own.

She hadn't noticed it before, but now the unmistakable odor of WD-40 permeated the air. Voices trailed in from down the hall. Claire tossed the pad back onto the table. She peeked out the door and saw two tellers paging through a magazine near the associate's entrance. Hurrying out of the boardroom, she glanced back one more time to make sure they hadn't seen her.

Her phone vibrated inside her purse as she approached her cubicle. She bit her lip and crumpled into her chair when she saw Julia's office directly across the hall was empty. In the seven years they'd worked together, Julia had never been late.

She fingered the little silver filigree tube of ashes she wore on a long chain, before she pulled her phone from her purse.

A text from Collin, "Suits everywhere. Stay put."

"Why?" she responded as she removed her coat and draped it over the file cabinet.

"Dont know yet cant get 2 dad."

Oren Redfield, Collin's father, had reluctantly placed his

younger son in charge of investments shortly after his eldest son's death nine years earlier.

Claire decided to give Julia a heads-up. Collin never would. It went straight to voicemail. She whispered, "Hey Jules, Something major is going down here. Not a good day to be late. Where are you?"

A commotion in the hallway. Two heavy-set older men in dark suits. A tall one with a thin white horseshoe of hair above his ears grumbled obscenities as they rushed into Julia's cubicle and began digging through drawers.

*I told her not to make fudge in there. Fire code violation. Never should have brought the hot plate in. Shit, I think my initials are on it.*

Claire didn't recognize the men, which instantly made things seem worse. *Don't really look like Fire Marshals. What does a Fire Marshal look like?* Luckily, as usual her presence went unnoticed.

Seated in her chair, she rolled herself over to the wall of her cubicle. The fabric-covered partition felt itchy against her cheek as she listened to the men. She couldn't make out what they were saying. Her fingers cramped. She glanced down to see she still had her phone clenched tightly in her hand.

She relaxed her grip and was slipping the phone into her pocket when she heard a crash. She held her breath and peered around the edge of the partition. They were tearing Julia's office apart. Files and papers lay everywhere. One man left the cubicle with Julia's computer. Another stood on her desk, removing tiles from the ceiling. Claire jerked her head back so fast her chair nearly slipped out from under her.

She peeked around the edge of the partition again and saw another older man in a gray suit and thick glasses racing down the corridor toward them.

Claire ducked back and tried to quiet her breathing. *Oh my God. My password. She's been using it for months.*

*Be rational. It's just a password.*

Yet, she couldn't forget Patty, Susan and George's strange behavior.

She also couldn't bear to take another look, but she couldn't resist either, and found herself inching toward the edge of the partition.

Two younger men were talking to the man with the thick glasses. They were scribbling everything he said in little notepads.

Claire rolled her chair back into the corner, realizing how ridiculous and guilty she'd look if someone walked in. It felt like it was a hundred degrees in her cubicle. Her brown silk blouse clung to her skin. She peeled off her jacket and hung it over the back of her chair. Fanning herself with her hand didn't help. She only managed to knock her favorite photograph of Paul and the girls off her desk. She froze and hoped the noise hadn't attracted any attention. *God, I wish I could reach Paul, but he's already in surgery by now, anesthetizing some lucky soul.*

*Get a grip. You want to be conscious for this.*

She set the silver frame back on her desk. Her gaze drifted to her own face next to her husband's—*plain Jane. If you haven't blossomed by thirty-three it ain't happening. Thank God the girls take after Paul. Anna's already stunning at fourteen; she just doesn't know it yet, and there's never been a cuter kindergartner than Em.* Tears welled up, but with a few deep breaths she forced them back. *Focus. Julia's in trouble.*

Claire's mind still refused to believe what her eyes had seen. *Said something she shouldn't have in an email. IRS? Please don't let it be an accident.*

Yet she knew deep down, none of that made sense considering what was happening just a few feet away.

Tears spilled down her cheeks as she pulled her phone out and texted Collin, then Julia, then Collin again—the same message each time: "CALL ME!"

*What should I do?*

*Get out of the damn corner, Claire, and sit at your desk like a normal human being. Someone is probably on their way to explain the whole situation to you. You spend every Thanksgiving with the CEO and his son. Collin's your best friend, for God's sake. I'm sure Oren is on his way down here right now. Calm down.*

She put on her jacket and rolled herself back along the length of her desk. Then she leaned back to see what the suits were up to.

The older men pulled the rest of the files from Julia's cabinets and threw them in boxes along with her personal belongings. Everyone was talking at once.

Claire tucked loose tendrils of what she considered mousy-brown hair behind her ears and wished she'd worn a little makeup. Some heavy hitters were on site.

Marilyn from HR appeared in the corridor between Claire's cubicle and Julia's office and stood there for a moment, staring at Claire. Marilyn was the tallest, thinnest suit of them all. She wore her hair cropped short and dyed blue-black along with her eyebrows, which resided too high on her forehead, given her age. She was clutching a file folder to her chest so tightly her fingers had turned white—*Julia's? Wonder what's in my file or if anyone's ever bothered to open the thing.*

Claire swallowed hard, afraid she might cry if she opened her mouth.

Marilyn remained stone-faced.

The two women had disagreed on more than one occasion. There had been little policy squabbles about parking, personal emails, and breaks, but there was one big battle *everyone* knew about. Marilyn had confiscated Michael Vanesko's turkey baster when she'd known it was his only means of calming himself.

———

Michael was quiet, autistic, in his late 20's and well liked by everyone despite his limited social skills. His attention to detail and affinity for routines made him an excellent employee. Like Claire, Michael had never missed a day of work. He was always in proper uniform with his nametag in place, and his dark hair neatly combed. He was meticulous when it came to his janitorial duties, and he was more reliable than the old bank clock. There was just one small quirk that posed a problem, for Marilyn, anyway—his turkey baster.

*Win/Win Staffing Solutions,* a non-profit organization that arranged employment for individuals such as Michael, had been perfectly clear with Marilyn about the turkey baster. They had also assured her Michael would be a wonderful asset to the institution, as he had a knack for noticing anything out of the ordinary. They even went so far as to suggest it would be like having a second security system, but the turkey baster was part of the package. There was no getting around it.

It was immediately clear to Claire how much Michael depended on those little puffs of air to get through his day. Rattled, he'd hold the long plastic baster by its gold bulb and squeeze it into his hand. Anyone could see it provided him with a soothing sensation whenever he felt the frustrated or upset. If someone moved something—a desk, a wastebasket or even a credit card application holder, Michael was quick to notice. He'd remain with the item for a few minutes repeatedly squeezing the baster until he'd made peace with the new arrangement.

Marilyn had agreed to the baster stipulation, but had confiscated the thing in less than a week.

"This is cruel," Claire had told her, after watching Michael pace and pull at his hair when he couldn't get his hands on his baster. "He's not hurting anyone and you knew he needed it when you hired him."

"We have an image to uphold and turkey basters are far from acceptable. He's not stupid. I've seen him fix complex machinery. He doesn't need that ridiculous thing."

"His *intelligence* has nothing to do with this. We're talking about his emotional well-being. Does Oren know you're doing this?"

Marilyn had scoffed. "I assure you, Mr. Redfield has more important matters to tend to."

"Has it even occurred to you that this is very bad for morale? I know Oren. If he finds out you're doing something so many of his associates consider cruel, you'll have a much bigger problem than a turkey baster."

"Fine," Marilyn had huffed. "Let's not make a federal case of this. I'm placing you personally in charge of this matter, since you're obviously so passionate about it. But get this straight, I don't want to see that thing in the lobby. You find a way for him to be discreet, and he can keep it." She'd pulled the baster from her desk drawer and slapped it into Claire's hand.

━━━

Finally, The Baster Nazi spoke. "Michael should be arriving

shortly. I want you to keep him here in your office until I tell you otherwise."

"You know how agitated he gets if we alter our routine," Claire reminded her.

"That's not my concern. I want the two of you to remain right here."

"What's happening?" Claire rose from her chair, trying to keep her voice steady.

"I'm not at liberty to discuss this with you. I would appreciate it if you would just see to Michael."

"Alright, but Marilyn... please, can't you just tell me... is she all right? Has something happened to Julia?" Claire heard her voice crack, as she discreetly slipped her phone into her pants pocket.

Marilyn turned her back on Claire, and entered Julia's office without another word.

Claire blinked in disbelief and leaned against her desk. She slowly turned to see about a dozen associates staring at her over the tops of their cubicles. When she attempted to make eye contact with the people she knew and spoke to everyday, they averted their eyes and sat down.

Her thoughts turned to Michael. At least, she could count on him to treat her the same way he always had. He needed more protecting than usual today with Marilyn on the war path. He always arrived right at eight. She still had fifteen minutes. Claire figured she could either sit at her desk pretending to check her email like an idiot, or she could find a good hiding place and try to phone Collin to get some answers.

Marilyn and all of the men in Julia's office were deep in conversation when she slipped out of her cubicle, but to her surprise, one man noticed her. There was no denying it. He looked like a detective. Their eyes met and he scribbled something in his pad.

Claire hurried down the hall to the ladies room near the drinking fountain. She paused outside the door when she noticed something odd. One of the security officers had stepped in front of the emergency exit at the end of the hall.

*He's just waiting for someone. You're being paranoid.*

She gave him a strained smile, which he ignored. Confused, she slowly pressed her hand against the restroom door.

Hushed voices echoed off the tiles. She cracked the door open further to take a quick peek inside. Two young women dressed in navy blue teller uniforms stood at the sinks. One applied lipstick while the other popped a piece of gum in her mouth.

"I can't believe she's here, like nothing ever happened," long hair said.

"Are you sure?" pixie cut asked.

"Hello. Didn't you see her old Slug Bug in the lot?" long hair snapped.

"That's nuts. Someone like her would never do that. Too goody-goody—no balls. I don't think it's true," pixie cut said.

"Oh, it's true. Patty's wigging out. Love it, love it, love it," long hair declared.

"Really?"

"Yeah, she told Marge we shouldn't even be open today–duh. Everybody's flipping out all over the place. It's the perfect time to walk off with a bunch more. Think about it. They probably don't even have the cameras on while they're going over all the tapes," long hair reasoned.

"I don't know. I think that's all digital. I'm sure they can record and play at the same time," pixie cut said.

"Still, you have to admit, they've never been as distracted as they are today."

Panic gripped Claire by the throat. Her hands began to shake. *This isn't happening. This isn't my life.* She turned to see the security guard eyeing her. She couldn't remember his name. There was that WD-40 smell again. A rivulet of sweat traveled down the side of her nose. She wiped it away and pushed the restroom door open. A deafening silence filled the air, punctuated by the swift click of her heels as she blew past the two girls to the last stall. She slipped inside and locked the door behind her.

"Holy shit," she heard one whisper.

Claire pulled her phone out to see if she'd missed any messages. "WHERE R U?" she texted Collin. The phone buzzed in her hand and she almost dropped it. It was Collin calling.

"You okay, Claire?"

"No," she whispered, trying to stifle tears.

The tellers were listening.

"Shhh... wait a second," Claire told him.

She waited.

The girls waited.

It was a stand-off.

*Come on, you can't stay in here forever.*

Then she distinctly heard one pair of heels slowly walk toward her stall. Claire's chest, neck and shoulders cinched up like someone had pulled a drawstring at the base of her skull. She backed away from the door to the cool marble wall. Bending down, she saw two feet clad in navy blue pumps.

*Go away. Please, just leave me alone.*

"Claire, are you there?" Collin asked.

Claire placed her thumb over the phone's speaker.

She heard the other girl whisper, "Come on, I'm gonna be late. I've already got two write-ups."

The pumps turned away from the door. Claire listened to their heels click across the tiles, before the door shut behind them.

"Okay," Claire gasped, "I'm alone. What's going on!?"

"Julia's disappeared with close to three million dollars."

"What? That's impossible! I—I knew something had happened to her, but... Jesus, Collin! Everybody is looking at me like *I* did it!"

"Breathe, Claire. Everything's going to be fine. You haven't done anything wrong."

"What if she's implicated us somehow?" Claire cried.

"How? Why would she do that?"

"I don't know! Why would she steal three million dollars? Collin, they're tearing her office apart. You'd better wipe those Mr. Leather pics off your computer."

"Don't be ridiculous."

"I'm not being ridiculous. We had lunch with her everyday. She's been using my password for months—since last spring when she forgot hers and expense reports were due. What if she set us up? What if we go to prison for this?"

"Oh, no. I'm not wearing an orange jumpsuit for anyone. Now those chambray shirts they wore in Shawshank, those were... "

"Knock it off. This isn't funny. I have the girls to think of and Paul. I could lose everything."

"Claire, seriously, calm down. You sound like Tommy Lee Jones is after you. Where are you? A hen house or an outhouse?"

"Outhouse," she whimpered as she stared at the toilet and humiliation sunk its teeth into her. She walked over to the toilet paper dispenser and tore off a few squares to wipe her nose.

"Stay there. Our meeting just broke. I'll come get you," Collin advised her.

"Don't. They've got security posted everywhere. I'm sure everyone knows exactly where I am, and besides, I've got to get Michael and take him to my office. Marilyn practically ordered me to keep him busy this morning. *She's* even acting like I had something to do with it. *Me.* I've never even been late. She's lost her mind." She shook her head and tossed the crumpled tissue into the toilet.

"No kidding?" Collin whispered.

"I'm telling you, she was absolutely awful to me this morning."

"No, I mean *Michael*. He's here?"

"He will be, like clockwork. You know Michael."

"Claire, he helped her."

"What!?"

"Julia conned Denny from Security into leaving the keys with her last night. Then she filled a bunch of printer paper boxes and had Michael carry them out to her car. Supposedly, it's all on camera."

"She did not! She *never* would have..." Claire sputtered in protest as she slid down the wall and squatted on the floor with her head in her hand. "Oh my God! What has she done? What was she thinking? She's never said *anything* that would make me think she was capable of... poor Michael."

"I know it's crazy. Obviously Michael had no idea what he was doing. He'll be okay. Everything is so chaotic this morning they're calling his dad. Sal's coming to take him home. Go find Michael and meet me in my office as soon as you can."

"But he'll have his bag of change to count, and I'm not supposed to let him do it today. He'll already be upset. I have to count that change three times every morning, no exceptions. You know that."

"Tell him he can feed my fish. He loves that."

"No, he loves feeding your fish *after* he's had his change counted three times, but I'll try."

———

Claire found Michael fidgeting by the time clock.

He held up a Ziplock bag full of change and made a beeline for her, his turkey baster puffing away.

*Help him. Save him. Think!*

# CHAPTER 2

"IXNAY ON THE ULIA-JAY," Collin suggested as he pointed to Michael's baster furiously puffing away.

"Right. Okay, we'll give it a minute," Claire agreed with a sigh. She pried Michael's other hand open and put the container of fish food in it. Space was the one thing she could give him that she knew he always appreciated.

Collin loosened his tie. "The meeting was all PR—damage control. I can't get much more out of anyone right now. It's too hot. Dad isn't returning my calls, not that he usually does. Still, I think I've already been cut out of the loop. Don't worry though, I've got a few friends at corporate," Collin reassured her.

"Thanks," Claire said and left the two of them standing at the fish tank. She walked across the room, leaned against Collin's desk and folded her arms.

The aroma of freshly-brewed coffee seeped beneath the door as Claire stared at one of Collin's paintings. It was part of her morning routine, drinking coffee with Collin in his office, and a little Irish coffee on their days off, but today caffeine was the last thing she needed.

The painting was a prison made entirely of stained-glass. In his spare time, Collin painted haunting images of stained-glass lit from within.

"Everybody's alive this morning. It's a miracle," he announced as he crouched down in front of his built-in aquarium for a second head count.

Michael placed the can of fish food on top of the tank.

Collin stood up and straightened an Ansel Adams print of Denali National Park before walking over to his desk. He glanced back at Michael for a second to gauge his anxiety level via the baster, before sitting down behind his desk.

Collin looked Claire up and down. "Fabulous suit—new?"

"Yeah. You don't think the pants are too long?"

"No, they're perfect with those shoes."

Claire remembered dressing for work and thinking this exchange would be more fun.

Collin's phone rang and he reached for it. "Hi, Marty," he said as he checked his email. "I know. I'm still working on it. I'll call you as soon as I talk to Sherman, get his input. Okay, super." Collin hung up. "Why today? As if it weren't crazy enough with the Dallas deal closing."

"Maybe that's why she did it last night. She knew it would be nuts around here, today," Claire replied, raking her fingers through her hair. She pulled her phone out.

"Who are you calling?"

"Paul."

"I'd wait 'til we know more."

"Voicemail. He's still in surgery."

"Any good ones today?"

"I don't know. I can't remember. I think he might have said something about a rotator cuff." She picked up Collin's Alaskan snow globe with the moose inside, gave it a good shake and set it back down.

"I was hoping for something gorier," Collin replied.

"Sorry to disappoint. Why did I have to give her my password?"

Collin lowered his voice. "She had a way of making everything seem simple. Hey, has he ever been there when they found something really freakish, like a partially-developed fetus in somebody's chest, or something?"

"Good God, Collin. Do you mind? My life is falling apart here."

"With teeth, and hair, and tiny little..." he continued, wriggling his fingers like spiders.

"Just stop. It's not going to work this time. I'm going to obsess about the crisis at hand and you can't stop me."

"You underestimate me. What about a foreign object like some bizarre alien implant?"

"Not today." She considered texting Julia again, but decided it was futile.

"Can't you just try your dad again real quick?" she pleaded.

"He knows we tell each other everything. He won't let me near this. We can't do anything but wait. Unfortunately, it's their move. Let's just play it cool. So what about removing deformities? You know, extra appendages and stuff?"

"How long ago did you talk to Manal at corporate?"

"Right before you came in. Surely he's seen an extra nipple or toe at some point."

Claire let out a sigh as she paced. "He's smart enough to leave those stories at work. Besides, he's just the anesthesiologist."

"Still, I bet he's seen some crazy shit. Does he still whisper encouraging things to the patients during surgery?" Collin asked as he stood up and cinched his tie.

Claire massaged her temples, looked up at Collin and smiled. "Basters' cooling off," she whispered and walked over to Michael. "Are you going to be Chef Boyardee again for the Halloween breakfast tomorrow? That was a fun costume."

Michael didn't answer. He hummed along with the filtration system, his eyes fixed on a bright yellow fish.

"Michael, did you work late with Julia last night?"

"Dad says it's dangerous to ride my bike at night." He abruptly turned, strode over to Collin's desk and grabbed his bag of coins, announcing, "Time to count my change." His hand was turning the door knob in a flash.

"Oh, I forgot," Claire said as she reached him and gently closed the door.

Michael reminded her, "First, feed the fish and then the money machine."

"You're right, I did say that, but I forgot the change counter is broken, hon."

"The money machine is broken. It's broken," he repeated, amping up the baster again.

"It's okay, Michael. I bet you have $3.78 in there. You worked late last night, so you probably didn't find any more change since yesterday's count."

"It's broken. It's broken," Michael chanted as he paced around the room.

There was a knock at the door. It was Marilyn. She pretended to pick a piece of lint off her blazer to avoid making eye contact with Claire and Collin. "Time to go home, Michael," she said in a sickly sweet tone as she motioned for him to follow her.

"I have to work," Michael protested.

Claire attempted to comfort Michael as she followed them down the hall to HR. "I think your dad is going to take you to the grocery store to count your change. Then you can ride your bike the rest of the day and maybe find some more. We can count it tomorrow."

Marilyn stopped and turned. She shot Claire a look that said, 'Don't count on it.' "I'll take it from here, Claire."

Stunned, Claire stopped following them.

Marilyn and Michael continued down the hall to Human Resources where Claire imagined Sal Vanesko anxiously waiting in one of the plastic reception chairs. She wanted to talk to him, to reassure him this would all get straightened out. Sal and Michael were like family.

Claire's face felt hot. She turned toward Collin's office. He stood in the doorway and motioned for her to come back. He looked like a 1940's Hollywood film star in his classic black suit with his slicked-back hair and dark eyes.

Her hand reached for her necklace, again. She was twisting the silver tube, seeking comfort, when a memory struck her so hard her chest ached. Fuming, she stormed back to Collin's office.

He gave her plenty of leeway and closed the door behind her. "What? Not the Crypt Keeper. Don't let her get to you. You know they removed her humanity during her last facelift."

"Not Marilyn, Julia! She planned it, Collin. I mean, I think Julia may have been planning this for a very long time. I'm going to be sick," she said and looked around for a wastebasket.

"Sit down," Collin urged her as he pulled his chair over to her. "Breathe, Claire." He pulled a wastebasket out from under his desk and placed it at her feet.

"My necklace..." she said as she sat down. "She used it."

"What are you talking about?" Collin crouched down beside her.

"The first week she was here she asked me about it. She said she'd seen me touching it. I was kind of hesitant, but I told her it contained some of my grandmother's ashes. You know how some people get creeped-out, when I tell them what it is, but Julia asked me to follow her to her office. She pulled this white, ceramic, heart-shaped box off her bookshelf and handed it to me."

"I remember that box. I assumed it held condoms."

Claire rolled her eyes and continued, "She told me to open it. Inside were these burgundy-black, dried-up rose petals. She told me this story about her dad giving her a single rose on the day of her first piano recital. She said he'd always wanted to play, that despite being unemployed he'd somehow managed to get her this old piano and even bartered firewood for some lessons. Anyway, she said he died a few weeks later."

"Complete crap," Collin replied.

"I totally bought it. I am such an idiot."

"Nah, I think most people would've fallen for that one. It's pretty good."

"It's just so devious I can barely wrap my mind around it. She suspected my necklace was a deeply personal memento and created one of her own just to get close to me. How creepy is that?"

"Uber-creepy. She was entertaining. I'll give her that, with her tramp-wear, travel adventures, and sex-capades. But God knows every girl needs a real girlfriend, with ovaries and every-thing, so I just stepped back and let the two of you do your thing."

"Your claws were always out whenever she was around. I just took it with a grain of salt. I thought you were jealous."

"Of what? Ovaries?"

Claire cringed, "I'm sorry."

"Don't be. Sometimes I'm catty just for the fun of it, but think about it. She always had too much cash, too many extrava-gances. Married people always assume anyone who's single has money to burn. It's simply not true. Her background, what little we were able to glean, didn't match her accessories, and you know it."

"Coming from Vegas, somehow it seemed entirely possible she had plenty of money."

"She probably did, but not from an honest day's work."

Claire chewed on her lower lip and frowned. "I've got to go. I can't keep hiding in here. I've got work to do. I'm going back to my office. Do you think you can find out any more while I run the morning reports?"

"If they *let* you run them," Collin gently reminded her.

"I can't believe this is happening."

"I know. She's probably choking on a dirt casserole somewhere in a cornfield in Dekalb."

"Collin!"

"Well, I don't think she was bright enough to pull it off by herself."

"I can't even think about that. Do you know how many times she's been in my home—how many gifts she's given the girls—mostly inappropriate, I might add?"

"Like what?" Collin's feathers ruffled.

"Oh, let's see... she gave Em a gun that shot disappearing ink. That one made it to the garbage in record time. Luckily, Anna wouldn't be caught dead in a leather corset. She's into goth, not domination. Where on earth is a fourteen-year-old girl supposed to wear something like that?"

"Hell's Angels' Renaissance Fair?"

Claire rolled her eyes and shook her head. "She stayed with us when her condo was remodeled. She used to pick Em up from school for me sometimes, and bring her back to the bank until I finished work."

"Ahem, I recall volunteering for that detail." Collin acted as if he were picking something off his tie.

"I know, but she was sort of a surrogate aunt for the girls."

"*I* wanted to be the surrogate aunt," he said, looking Claire in the eye and folding his arms.

"You were. You are. The girls love you. The girls... Collin, I could go to prison if she...."

"Seriously, Claire. We're going to get you an excellent attorney. Frank and I have several friends who can handle this. I've already told him to make some calls. He's on it." He placed his hands on her shoulders. "Come on, everything is going to be fine. You haven't done anything wrong. You've got to relax. They're going to move very slowly and very carefully. I guarantee it."

"Okay," Claire said with a sniffle, "I just wish everyone would stop looking at me like I drove the getaway car."

"Buck up, Buttercup. You look stunning in that suit and they're putting up the new smoking tent today," he said as he followed her to the door.

"We don't smoke."

"Yeah, but we could start. It'll be fun. We can take smoke breaks and gossip."

"Since when do you need a smoke break to gossip?"

"Well, just say a little prayer that it's a hot young crew of Latino men putting up the tent today."

"I already said my hot-young-Latino-men prayer first thing this morning."

"Now, there's the old Claire," Collin said as his phone rang. "I've got to get that. Hang in there. I promise I'll tell you as soon as I hear anything."

Claire's mouth was so dry she could barely swallow. She wanted to stop in the break room for a Diet Coke, but the thought of sharing such close quarters with any other associates made her uneasy.

*What if they start asking me questions? What I should say? I don't know anything more than anyone else—probably less. What if I say something I'll regret later? What if they just stare at me and whisper and no one even speaks to me?*

Her mind could barely finish one awful scenario before it raced on to the next. Claire kept her head down, making eye contact with no one. She slipped into her cubicle, sat down at her desk and tried to shake off the excess adrenaline through her hands before she began to type.

Within seconds her company email was open and right at the top of her inbox was an email marked 'Urgent' from her manager, Inez.

It read: "I've run the morning reports. You are not to interact with clients until further notice per Marilyn McFarland." The tone made Claire more nauseas than the content. Inez's emails were normally so chatty and unprofessional, often mentioning her kids and her plans for the weekend.

Claire shivered and began an email to Collin, as she struggled with the knowledge that someone in the bank was probably reading every word. She couldn't help herself. She felt desperate not to endure the insanity of the situation alone. Email and instant messaging were so much quicker and easier than texting. She'd risk it until she absolutely couldn't.

"Did you reach Manal?" she typed in the instant message box, went back and deleted "Manal", replaced it with "her" and waited.

Within seconds her phone vibrated in her pants pocket. Collin. "They think J is in S. America."

"No way," Claire texted back.

"Never find her if this was group effort," Collin replied.

"Group effort!?" Claire texted back.

"U R OK. Hang tight. Got a meeting," Collin ended.

Claire's stomach dropped. *How long will the meeting last? Is it about Julia?*

There seemed to be only one thing she was sure of. She was adrift now—shark food.

"Mrs. Cummings?"

Claire turned in her chair to see two security officers. It was George and Arvin. George was holding a printer paper box just like the ones Julia had supposedly used. Everything went into a slow motion skid. She could see George's mouth moving apologetically and Arvin looking like he'd rather be anywhere else on the planet, but she couldn't hear a thing. In her mind, she played her own little dream-soundtrack.

"It's all been a big mistake. We're so sorry. We've got the money and the boxes right here, see? The rest is right in the safe. She was just moving it. She's on vacation. Punta Del Estes, I think. Marilyn has the time-off request right on her desk. She just forgot. Michael's fine. Everything is fine. It was all just a big misunderstanding," George's part went.

"We feel so badly. Marilyn has given you the rest of the day off with pay. Would you like us to walk you to your car?" Arvin's part went.

But Claire knew what the box was for—her personal belongings. She watched dumbfounded as Arvin and George walked toward her.

Arvin took her coat from the top of the file cabinet and held it up for her like a gentleman. Claire stood and slipped her arms inside like an obedient child. She watched George set the box on her desk and remove the lid. He paused for a moment and looked at her. She was still in a daze.

George reached for a framed photo of her daughters at the beach and handed it to her. He motioned to the box.

Claire picked up her things and placed them inside one at a time. "Am I being fired?"

"No, Mrs. Cummings. I said you're suspended pending further investigation," George whispered.

Arvin said nothing and stared at the floor with his hands clasped in front of him.

"Oh," was all Claire could think to say, at first. "But no one's even asked me anything. You didn't even file a report. Mary sliced her finger open trying to cut a bagel, and you filled out a report for that," Claire reasoned.

"This is different. The authorities are involved. They'll be the ones doing the questioning," George answered.

"I didn't do anything, George," she whispered as she dropped a fistful of pens in the box and burst into tears.

George let out an exasperated sigh and handed her a box of tissues from her desk. "I can't discuss this with you, Claire. Please don't make this any harder. Do you have everything?"

"I think so," she said as she tucked a wisp of hair behind her ear, wiped her tears and closed her desk drawers.

"Let's go then," George put the lid on the box, tucked it under his arm and motioned for her to exit the cubicle ahead of them.

Reality sunk in like a knife. She turned to the two officers and managed to squeak, "Everyone is going to see us."

"I'm really sorry, Claire. We have to go to HR so you can fill out your suspension paperwork and give them your ID, before we walk you to your car," George explained.

"My purse, it's under my desk," she said, touching her necklace.

━━

Claire wiped her eyes and nose as she pulled her car in and pressed her thumb against the garage door button. Her limbs felt as heavy as lead the instant she killed the engine. Her fingers found their way to the door handle, but she didn't have the strength to get out. *Just go inside. You made it this far.*

*Okay, just a little nap,* she conceded, but when she leaned back and closed her eyes, the chatter inside her head was deafening.

Claire opened her eyes. The garage light went out and darkness engulfed her. There was no lighted makeup mirror in the old Beetle, but she flipped the visor down anyway. It was still too dark. Her fingers fumbled along the upholstered roof until she located the switch for the dome light, flicked it on and peered into the visor's little mirror.

*My nose is so red. I look like Bozo.* She flipped the visor back up. She'd cried all the way home, unable to reach Paul on his cell. She didn't want to call the hospital. *No need to upset him at work,* but she needed him. The sooner the better.

Claire reached for her necklace and rolled the delicate silver tube between her thumb and finger, desperate for the comfort of someone strong and steady, like her grandmother.

"I wish you were here. If you could ever help me, wherever you are...." She felt half-silly, half-crazy for asking aloud, but sighed and leaned her head back against the seat.

*WD-40—strong, like someone just sprayed it.*

At first, she thought she was so tired she was hallucinating.

*No, what would it be? Halluci-smelling?*

She even checked the back seat for a can, but there was nothing there.

"Nana?"

Nothing. Just the lingering pungent scent. Claire laughed at herself and covered her face with her hands. When she dropped them back into her lap, her eyes lit upon the maple bench next to the back door.

They called it the boot bench, because it was perfect for pulling your boots on, or taking them off before going into the house. The whole family kept their snow boots lined up beneath it year-round. There was a storage compartment in the seat. Claire's heart leapt at the memory of what was inside. It had been several years since she'd even thought about it.

With a rush of fresh adrenaline, Claire got out of the car and closed the door behind her. She hurried over to the bench where she knelt down on an old carpet sample and raised the lid. There it was, the note still attached to the black garbage bag with a twist-tie. It read: "Do not throw this away! -Claire". She grabbed the bag and clutched it to her chest, before she closed the lid and went in the house.

A bark came from upstairs. "Hey, Shadow. It's just Mom," she called out as she kicked her shoes off, knowing the dog had no intention of coming downstairs to greet her. She'd always met her at the door of their first apartment. Once Anna was born, and they moved into the house, it happened less and less. Anna was Shadow's unabashed favorite. The Irish Setter had taken up permanent residence in the girl's bedroom. Paul had even moved her food and water dishes up there.

Claire headed upstairs and walked down the hall. She poked her head in Anna's room, "Hi, girl. She feed you?"

Shadow looked up and wagged her tail. She was chewing on something.

Claire walked over, bent down and held out her hand. "Give it." When Shadow didn't comply, Claire balanced the garbage bag on her leg while she pried the dog's mouth open. "Another barrette. Way to go."

She stood up and decided this one had been mauled beyond recognition and threw it in the wastebasket, remembering why they'd bought the kind with the lid.

"That's a new one, huh?" she mumbled, still clutching the bag to her chest as she studied a large poster of an Arabian show horse on Anna's closet door. The walls of Anna's room had been covered with pictures of horses since she was six years old. In the past year, it had reached the point of looking like wallpaper. Claire bent down and scratched Shadow behind her ear for a moment, remembered the bag under her arm and took it to her room.

When she reached her bedroom, she threw her coat over a chair and sat down on the edge of the bed. The twist-tie broke apart in her fingers as she unwound it from the bag. She closed her eyes, raised the opening of the bag to her face, and inhaled. Something between a whimper and a groan of delight escaped her lips.

It was Nana's old chore coat and coveralls. After eleven years, all of her favorite scents were still intact: Lava soap, oil and gasoline for the tractor, hay from the barn, burning leaves and WD-40. It was a magical combination that drew Claire's thoughts back to the old farmhouse.

For Claire, the farm had always been the safest place on earth. She could close her eyes and see Nana on the porch, humming as she sewed pearl seed beads on a wedding veil for a neighbor. Nana had been a gifted seamstress having sewn more than fifty wedding dresses, by the time she died. She'd also kept the farm up all by herself after Claire's grandfather had died, crushed in a ravine when his tractor tipped over.

Claire reached into the bag and pulled the stiff coat out a bit. She'd hugged her grandmother in the old coat hundreds of times. Now it felt like Nana had given her one more hug when she'd needed it most.

"Thank you," she whispered, as she kissed the collar and tucked the coat back inside the bag. She couldn't bear to put it back down in the boot bench. She wanted it, *needed* it near her tonight. Claire leaned over, lifted the bed skirt and slid the bag under the bed.

She felt sleepy again as she stood up and walked across the

hall to the bathroom. She ran cold water on a washcloth, washed her face and was slathering on some moisturizer, when her wedding ring caught her eye in the mirror. *Needs a good scrubbing with a toothbrush.*

She removed the ring and was setting it on the edge of the sink, when a catch in her back made her gasp. Every muscle in her body seemed to ache from being so tense all morning. *Clean it later.*

Claire shuffled back to the bedroom, took her necklace off and set it on the nightstand. She managed to pull the covers back just enough to crawl beneath them. It was the last thing she remembered until she awoke from a nightmare, nearly five hours later.

# CHAPTER 3

PAUL STOOD in the doorway with a toolbox in his hand. He was still in his scrubs, his face lined with concern. "You okay, honey?"

"Something was chasing me." Claire sat up in bed, her heart still racing.

Paul frowned. "You're home early. You were sleeping so soundly. I didn't want to wake you."

He looked so handsome, still tan from summer. His dark curly hair was turning more salt and pepper. Claire found it incredibly sexy, and kept meaning to tell him, but she always forgot. After fourteen years, she was slacking when it came to compliments.

"Paul..." Claire began, suddenly remembering her morning at the bank.

"I got a letter for you, Mom!" Em shouted, brushing past Paul. A small blue note was folded in half and safety-pinned to her Little Mermaid sweatshirt. She had a rumpled macaroni jack-o-lantern glued to orange construction paper clenched in one fist, and a half-eaten Pop-Tart in the other.

Claire grinned and held her arms out, letting her hair fall across her face, hoping to hide her puffy eyes.

Em climbed up on the white down comforter and fell into Claire's arms. "Are you sick?"

"Just a cold, I think," Claire sniffled and rubbed her nose. I could use some snuggle time. I think I need a popcorn night."

"Yeah, popcorn," Em agreed.

"I'm on it," Paul said with a wink, and headed downstairs before Claire had a chance to tell him anything, or even ask him what he'd been doing with the toolbox.

"Movie night!" Em shouted. She was wearing her red mermaid wig cocked to one side. Her Pop-Tart was crumbling all over the bed, but Claire didn't care.

"Want some?" Em asked.

"Mmm, yeah." Claire realized she hadn't eaten a thing all day and was surprised when it didn't taste half-bad. "Nice jack-o-lantern. Should we hang it up?"

"I don't care. It's dumb. I wanted to make bats. The boys got to make bats. It's not fair."

"Aw, I'll make bats with you. We can do it right here on the bed tonight while we watch movies. What's the note say?"

"No bampires, I fink."

"No bampires? Why not?" Claire asked, removing the note from Em's shirt.

"Because bampires drink blood, and we can't wear a costume wif any blood and no weapons."

The note read: "Dear Mrs. Cummings, With your permission, I would like to have a speech therapist work with Emmy on Tuesdays and Thursdays after school. Please give me a call. –Mrs. Meyer"

"Well, I like bampires," Claire said, wadding-up the note and tossing it in the wastebasket next to the nightstand.

"Me too, but I like mermaids better."

"I love you, Em. Give Mommy another hug," she said, tearing up as she kissed Em's cheek and squeezed her too hard.

"Mom! You're choking me," Em squealed with laughter and dropped the rest of her Pop-Tart.

Shadow swooped in like a hawk out of nowhere and inhaled the pastry the second it hit the floor.

"You wouldn't have had room for dinner, anyway... even if it is just popcorn. Daddy let you get into the Pop-Tarts right after school, again?"

"No, Anna," Em whispered.

"Guilty," Anna confessed from the doorway. She dropped her bulging graffiti-covered backpack at her feet. She wore black Converse hi-tops, black jeans and a faded black Edgar Allan Poe T-shirt. Dying her chestnut-brown hair black was where they had drawn the line, "Not until you turn sixteen," Claire and Paul had agreed, hoping against all odds, the phase would pass by then.

Much to Claire's chagrin, the pretty fourteen-year-old still topped off her goth look with thick black eyeliner. It made her feel like a failure in the parenting department, but they'd tried everything from hypnosis to taping her fingertips to get her to stop pulling her eyelashes out. Nothing had worked. Truth be told, she was partially proud of Anna for coming up with her own novel solution for her trichotillomania, and partially sad that she hadn't come up with a better solution herself. The only upside was that Claire knew whenever Anna was feeling stressed. She'd either be working on her eyelashes or sitting on her right hand to keep from doing so.

Anna had always been a little high-strung and Claire would never forget how the kid had cried almost non-stop for the first six months of her life. Claire blamed herself, having read numerous articles in parenting magazines over the years, suggesting the child absorbed all of the mother's stress in utero.

———

Claire and Paul had still been in college and living together in a fifth-floor walk-up. She'd worried all through the pregnancy about money, finishing school, falling down all those stairs, squeezing into her teller uniform and her wedding dress, but everything had worked out. Anna had been the most beautiful baby, non-stop crying and all, and she had never stopped being beautiful, even with her death-warmed-over look. As a mother, Claire could always see her daughter's beauty right through all the layers of goth. That wasn't Anna at all, just a disguise for her eyes.

———

"You sick?" Anna asked, frowning and folding her arms.

"Just a cold," Claire said, grimacing and motioning for her to come in and sit on the bed with them.

"I've got a ton of homework."

"Just for a minute?"

"I still have to finish my costume for the dance. Dad's helping me make false teeth out of corn. Remember my English teacher, Mr. Hanify"

Claire gave her oldest daughter her best understanding smile, and let it go.

———

*I've got to tell him about work before we settle in to watch movies.*

Claire walked into the bathroom, distracted, pajamas in hand. Memories of Julia lurked in every room.

*She stood right here,* she caught herself thinking several times. It was hard not to obsess over the fact that she'd invited Julia to stay with them for several weeks while her condo had been remodeled the previous spring. *How could I have let her get so close to them?*

She flicked the bathroom light on, grabbed her toothbrush from the cup on the counter and reached for the faucet.

Five or six strips of duct tape were stretched across the sink. A note was taped to the faucet, which simply read: "No!"

"What on earth? Paul?" After a few moments, she heard Paul clear his throat, followed by the familiar creak of the bottom step.

"Did you need something, honey?" he called up the stairs a little too sweetly.

"Is this a crime scene or what?" She set her toothbrush down and thought she heard him mumble "maybe" as he tromped up the stairs. When he reached the doorway, he just stood there and stared at her, scratching the stubble on his chin.

"What happened? Is it clogged?" Claire asked, pointing to the sink.

Paul shook his head slowly and seemed to cringe a little.

"What? Why are you acting so...." Claire spun around. Her eyes darted to the empty spot next to the faucet where she'd left her wedding ring. "You didn't!"

Paul immediately wrapped his arms around her from behind and held her tightly, as if he were putting out flames. "I'm sure I can get it out. It's got to be sitting right down there in the gooseneck where it'll stay as long as nobody runs the faucet. I'll get right to work on it. It'll be back on your finger within the hour," he assured her, resting his chin on her shoulder.

Claire groaned and turned in his arms to face him. She placed her hands on his cheeks and smiled. "I love you, but this is no job for the wrench-impaired. I'll call a plumber tomorrow. Nice job with the tape, though."

"It's not a big deal. I'm sure I can...."

Claire placed her index finger against his lips. "You're an incredible father, a damn fine anesthesiologist from what I hear, and a phenomenal lover, but you are the world's shittiest plumber. Remember the garbage disposal? I'm begging you. Stick to what you know."

"Nobody can sugarcoat it like you, hon," he whispered with a sly smile.

Claire reached up and ran her fingers through his dark curls. "I need to talk to you about work."

"Sure, what's up?

*Now... tell him now.* Claire cleared her throat. "That note on Em's shirt—her teacher thinks she needs a speech therapist, but I can't stand the thought of correcting her all the time. Remember when she stopped saying 'swing-ded' and 'play-ded'? I know the baby talk can't last forever, but I still think we should let her straighten it out on her own."

"Really? A speech therapist? Well, we don't want kids making fun of her, and honestly I'm kind of surprised we haven't run into that yet. We could talk to her about it, about talking like a big girl," Paul reasoned.

"I guess so, but I really don't want to. She's such a confident kid. I don't want anyone or anything to start chipping away at her self-esteem, you know?" Claire argued.

"We can wait a while, see what happens."

*Now, chicken. Just tell him.*

"Are you still going to help Anna with her corn teeth for her costume?"

"Yeah, I promised." Paul smiled at the mention of his stellar idea. "Come on, what's really on your mind? You seem kind of... I don't know... sad tonight. What is it? Or did you want to talk about global warming first? How about the economy? Or maybe your mom?"

"Alright, alright. I just..."

Paul's phone rang. He reached into his pocket, checked the number and held it up for Claire to see. It was the hospital.

Claire sighed and sat down on the edge of the tub. *Great.*

"Hello... yeah... Who's operating? Be there in twenty," he said and slipped it back in his pocket. "Head-on collision. Three surgeries. Don't wait up." He gave her a quick kiss, before running out of the bathroom.

"Okay." She whispered and rubbed her forehead. She'd blown it.

"Paul?" Claire called out, but it was too late. She'd heard the creak. He'd already reached the bottom of the stairs.

"Mom, phone," Anna appeared in the doorway holding Claire's cell phone, "Collin."

"Thanks," Claire said, taking it from her. "I'll be out in a minute," she whispered, as Anna turned, walked down the hall to her room and shut her door. Claire added under her breath, "In case you suddenly need to share your deepest, innermost thoughts and secrets." She sighed, shut the bathroom door and leaned against it.

"Hi."

"Hi, yourself. How ya doin', sugar-puddin'?"

"I've had better days. Did you find a good lawyer?"

"I *so* did. Alex is a real pit bull. So don't worry. Hey,

wouldn't it be funny if you showed up at work tomorrow like nothing ever happened?"

"Yeah, a real riot. Marilyn would probably tackle me to the ground."

"What about the Halloween breakfast?" Collin asked.

"What about it?"

"Well, you won't get to see everybody's costumes this year."

"I'll live."

"Meet me for coffee."

"Before *you* go to work? Are you mad? Seriously Collin, that's like 5:00 A.M."

"You're meeting me for coffee at Starbucks... *in* costume."

"Not a chance."

"Come on. You know I have to wear a costume to work, so don't let me be the only guy buying espresso in a silver lame jumpsuit. I just found you a vicious lawyer."

Claire fiddled with the belt of her bathrobe, which hung from a hook on the back of the door. Anna always got Em and herself ready for school and Collin knew it. She couldn't use it as an excuse. "I don't know why you bothered. You'll never top last year's costume."

"True and sewing a skeleton to the side of a lime-green leisure suit is harder than you think."

Claire laughed. "Marilyn was livid. Who would've guessed The Crypt Keeper loved The Carpenters."

"I'm waiting," Collin said in a sing-song voice.

"I don't have a costume. Remember? Julia and I were going as the witches from *Wicked*. There's no way in hell I'm going to put on a wicked witch costume now. Out of the two of us, *I* was clearly the good witch. She must've thought that was going to be so damn funny, the last laugh. Well, she's not going to get it."

"So wear something else—anything, but you have to make me laugh."

"I can't believe you're still trying to talk me into this."

"You need to get out tomorrow. What were you planning to do? Spend the day under the covers worrying yourself to death?"

"Something like that."

⸻

Claire awoke just after 11:00 P.M., her body curled around Em's. Beneath the heavy down comforter, they'd found a cocoon of peace and succumbed to it. The TV screen bathed the room in blue light and hummed a soft electric lullaby. Claire realized what had awakened her. Em had been talking in her sleep again.

"Kitty food..." Em mumbled.

"Sorry, no kitties. One doggy's enough, my little mermaid." Claire sat up in bed and lifted Em onto her lap. She used her legs to pull herself to the edge. As she stood up she felt a sudden inexplicable need to savor the moment—Em curled up in her arms—for a split second, she was her baby again.

Claire held her daughter snuggly against her chest, and carried her down the hall to her bedroom. She tucked her in and fluffed her pink ruffled pillows. Claire loved Em's big white canopy bed. She'd discovered the treasure at a garage sale, badly in need of refinishing. Her mother, Lynn, had made a new canopy. She'd even sewn white eyelet curtains to match.

*I can't keep avoiding Mom,* Claire berated herself, as she admired the canopy. *We're well into October. She's probably been in a Seasonal-Affective-funk for weeks, now. I've got to check on her. Maybe tomorrow.*

She bent down and arranged four or five stuffed animals around her daughter's head the way Em liked. Then she kissed her goodnight and turned off her lamp.

Claire paused in the hallway. A swath of amber light spilled from beneath Anna's door.

An overwhelming sense of déjà vu held Claire in its grip. She tried to rationalize that she'd seen Anna's bedroom door countless times from this vantage point, even with the same lighting and at the same time of night. Yet there was something so eerily familiar, as if she'd once stood right there and even thought the same thoughts, her heart beating the same staccato rhythm, her nostrils relishing the same scents of dog, crayons and fabric softener. Her mind struggled with what the significance of the moment could be.

Claire had experienced déjà vu many times, and with each episode had come a strange sense of knowing from some faraway, long forgotten place.

*Hold onto this puzzle piece,* it seemed to advise her.

Claire shivered at the thought and forced it from her mind, as she approached Anna's room. She pressed her ear to the door, but could only hear Shadow lapping water from her dish inside. Claire tapped lightly on the yellow plastic sign which read: "Don't Even Think About It", but Anna didn't answer. She considered opening the door just a crack to see if she'd fallen asleep studying.

The truth was that she often wondered if Anna snuck out at night. The porch roof was just outside her window. She was nearing that age when the temptation would become irresistible, but Claire always managed to convince herself it wasn't Anna's style. She talked the talk, but she didn't walk the walk. Beneath all that eyeliner, she was still a bookish girl who loved horses.

Claire didn't get to tell her oldest daughter 'goodnight' as often as she used to. The ritual was dying a quiet death as Anna became more independent.

*We don't have a bad relationship,* Claire argued with herself. *She's just discovering who she is. She needs some space. I've just got to respect that space a little while longer and she'll come around. We'll be close again. It's just temporary. Blah, blah, blah... shit, I miss her.*

She felt if she pushed her, crowded her, Anna would grow even more distant. Claire couldn't afford to take that risk. She'd barely been privy to a bully-texting-fiasco Anna had apparently been on the wrong end of at the beginning of the school year. She'd noticed since then she never seemed to use her phone. Claire tried to remind her to keep it with her for safety's sake. But she suspected it wasn't even charged when Anna would roll her eyes, sigh and toss it in her backpack. Claire suggested they get her a new phone, but when Anna declined Claire worried she was isolating herself too much.

She rested her forehead against the door. *Hope you come around soon, Anna-Banana. I'd like to know the person you're becoming.*

She walked back to her bedroom and considered turning off the white noise on the television, but changed her mind. Lying in bed, her thoughts wandered to Julia, again and again. *I wonder where she is. What's she doing? Who was she really? Why did she do it? Was anything she ever told me true?*

When she awoke, Paul was snoring next to her. Claire performed her combination backrub-roll, and eased him onto his side away from her. As she stared at the ceiling, she considered waking him and telling him everything. Another opportunity was slipping through her fingers. *He was in surgery all night. He's got to be exhausted. I have to meet Collin in a couple of hours. Damn, I still need a stupid costume.*

She couldn't think of anything other than a pair of Paul's scrubs and Em's Little Mermaid wig. Em would need that for her parade at school, and Claire knew she'd never hear the end of it if she showed up for coffee with Collin in such a half-assed affair.

She rolled over and stared at the digital clock. She tried to come up with a better costume, between thoughts of canceling altogether and sweet things Julia had done for her, which she couldn't seem to reconcile.

Julia had forgone her afternoon cigarette more than once to run across the street to buy an emergency pair of pantyhose for Claire. It had been Julia who'd bought her all the books on Seasonal Affective Disorder when Claire's mother Lynn, had admitted to barely leaving her bed one particularly gray January. The ever-growing list of suspect kindnesses made her skin crawl—encouraging little notes, unexpected peppermint mochas, scarves and earrings from every imaginable exotic locale—was it all just to grease the wheels?

Collin would've simply arched his perfectly groomed eyebrows in response to such a stupid question. *Collin.*

She knew she'd have plenty of time to get back home and see the girls off to school. She was out of excuses.

The clock's glowing red numbers taunted her. She grimaced, reached out and turned it away from her, but the glow only intensified as it bounced off the wall.

She'd set the alarm on her phone anyway, so she reached beneath the bed and jerked the plug from the socket. Her hand brushed against the bag containing Nana's chore coat and coveralls. She'd forgotten all about them.

Slipping out of bed, she carried the bag into the bathroom. She took off her pajamas, kept her underwear on and pulled on a pair of pantyhose that had been hanging over the shower rod along with a bra. She pulled the grease-stained coveralls on, zipped them up and put on the filthy old chore coat.

*This is nuts.* She stared at her reflection in the bathroom mirror. *No,* she finally countered as she zipped up the old coat, *I'm a farmer keeping my end of the bargain.*

She crept down the stairs, careful to skip the bottom step. The hall closet was a mess, but after some digging she found an old forest-green stocking cap.

Torn between elation and disgust, she discovered a mouse had chewed a hole in the side of it. She headed for the white board that hung on the refrigerator, grabbed the marker which dangled from a red piece of yarn and quickly scribbled "Mouse-traps!" in large red letters. Feeling more herself again, she shuffled through the kitchen, opened the bathroom door and flipped the light on.

She inspected the stocking cap once more, put it on with the hole front and center and began stuffing her hair up inside. She stared at the stranger in the mirror. *Not bad, except... you look nothing like a farmer. You look homeless. Oh, well. Still needs something, though.* She snapped her fingers.

Claire knelt down in front of the living room fireplace. She scooped up a handful of ashes and rubbed them over her face and hands.

Back in the bathroom, she smiled into the mirror. She barely recognized herself, which somehow made her happy. For the next few hours, she was going to be someone else entirely and not the dimwit who'd been completely snowed by one of her closest friends.

Claire returned to the hall closet and found one of several pairs of combat boots Anna owned. They were a little snug but they'd be fine for drinking coffee and crying on Collin's shoulder.

She returned to the bathroom mirror one last time. She felt half-crazy for reveling in the adventure, but she needed to escape her real life, even if just for a few hours. She'd never done anything like this. *Maybe I can still change, become more interesting.*

Barely making a sound, Claire grabbed her purse and keys and slipped into the darkness of the garage. She'd managed to keep her little secret. Everyone was still asleep. She couldn't wait to tell Paul about this. It would be easier to break the rest of it to him with this as a punch line. She made a mental note to have Collin take a few pictures with her phone. She couldn't wait to see the look on his face.

*No costume party for Michael today, either. I need to give Sal a call later and see how they're doing. There's got to be something I can do to help him. Maybe I can take some change over there this afternoon, pick up a little change counter at Walgreens or something.*

Claire opened the car door. She got in, tossed her purse onto the passenger's seat, and noticed a photo sticking out of the pocket. She pulled on the corner of it. It was a picture of herself and Julia making a margarita toast at Mucho Gusto after Claire had been looked over for yet another promotion. "Let it go. Let it *all* go," Claire grumbled as she tore it into little pieces and stuffed them in the ashtray.

She slipped the key into the ignition, but didn't turn it. The brake pedal felt odd beneath her newly acquired combat boots, and she wondered if she could drive as well in them. She wiggled her toes for a moment, then reached for the keys.

"Oh, no," she groaned as she repeatedly turned the key in the ignition and nothing happened. "Shit," she exhaled as she glanced up at the dome light and flipped the switch back.

She snatched her purse off the passenger's seat, catching it on the gear shift. Its contents spilled across the floor mats.

"Doesn't match anyway," she huffed. She slipped a few bills out of her wallet, tossed it back on the floor mat and stuffed them into her pocket, forgetting her phone in the process.

Heart thumping, she carefully latched the car door shut and leaned against it. She closed her eyes, rolled her head back and felt a shift within as she released a deep breath and embraced a new plan. She'd take the train, like in the old days before they'd had two cars.

She smiled at the thought of being purse-free for the first time in God knew how long and slipped back into the house. As the front door latched behind her, she realized she'd just locked herself out, but she wasn't about to lose a minute more. *I'll just use the spare key when I get back. Hope it doesn't snow. I can never find that heart-shaped rock when it snows. We need a better hiding place—a good project for this afternoon.*

She sprinted into the darkness and felt so light, so free she didn't stop running until she reached the train station nine blocks later. Claire wiped the sweat from her forehead, smearing her charcoal. She'd arrived with a few minutes to spare.

*I'll die if I see anyone I know.* Panicked at the thought, she descended the stairs into the foul stench of the old El station.

The urine odor was worse than she remembered. Claire held her breath, her stomach fluttering as she walked onto the platform. She hadn't expected to feel so self-conscious amongst the pre-dawn movers and shakers in their tailored suits and expensive shoes. It wasn't so much their attire that made her nervous, but their dismissive looks. They clearly assumed she smelled as bad as she looked.

With her eyes cast downward, she made her way to a bench in the center of the platform.

*Why couldn't there be a newspaper lying around, something to hide behind?*

By the time she'd reached her stop, she'd never felt like such an outcast. *What was I thinking? This must be what it really feels like to be invisible.*

Descending the stairs, Claire thought she saw a rabbit dart through the foggy ditch to her left.

The wind was cold and damp. She was glad she'd gone with the ratty stocking cap. Turning the collar of the chore coat up, she wished she'd found a ratty scarf to match. The fog was so thick she couldn't even make out the bank at the end of the parking lot. She'd made it three-quarters of the way when she heard a hungry yowl. Claire stopped and turned back toward the expressway. She stuffed her hands into her pockets and wondered if she'd imagined it. Then she heard it again—a tiny, ragged, heartbreaking meow coming from the expressway.

Em had been relentless in her campaign for a cat over the past few months. She'd drawn pictures and laid out all the doll clothes she planned to dress him in. She'd even pilfered a couple of cereal bowls, so she could have a food and water dish in her room, just like Anna did for Shadow. Claire hoped he wasn't wild as sin. Regardless, she couldn't bear the thought of him being killed out there.

"Hang on little guy," Claire murmured as she pulled her hands from her pockets and broke into a run. *Shoot, there's a fence. It's only waist-high. I think I can climb over.*

Even in her baggy coveralls, she was able to hoist herself up onto the bar of the chain-link fence and swing her legs over. The sleeve of her coat caught and ripped as she jumped down.

She heard another mew and spotted the scrawny gray thing

a good three lanes in, headed right for the CTA's cement barrier. She couldn't let him cross those tracks. He'd die for sure. The fog was so thick she'd lose him if he went any further. "No! Here, kitty!" She was stunned when he actually paused and looked right at her.

A car flew past. The cat tensed and crouched. In a second, he'd dart back into traffic or onto those tracks.

Claire slipped on the grass and caught herself as she tried to make her way up out of the frost-covered ditch. She reached the shoulder on the third try and glanced down the expressway to her left and back at the cat. He still had his eye on her.

The fog wasn't as thick up on the expressway, but she couldn't make out the office buildings on the other side, only headlights just before the cars passed her. Traffic was still light. She saw a good break coming up and waited for a hotel shuttle to blow past, then sprinted across the first lane.

She saw the cat turn and leap for the barrier. "No!"

The feline froze.

She'd cleared the second lane and was well into the third when she saw sky, concrete, metal and glass overlapping like spinning fragments in a kaleidoscope. Her stomach lurched into her throat. Searing pain shot through her neck and seized her breath.

# CHAPTER 4

CLAIRE SAT up in the ditch and looked around.

*Where's my phone?* She rubbed the inside of her ring finger with her thumb. *Where's my wedding ring? Was I mugged?*

She checked her pockets for her phone, determined it was gone but that she was essentially okay, and got to her feet. *Nana's chore coat? Oh, no. The little cat, I lost him. Wait, I was over there. What time is it?*

She searched the ditch for her wedding ring, and remembered the tape across the bathroom sink. *Oh yeah, Paul's got it. Paul. I've got to find a phone. I feel funny.*

Claire shook her head and started walking. She shielded her eyes from the rising sun, and squinted to see if the little cat was still out there, but the traffic had grown heavier and it looked like there was a big accident up the road. Cars were pulled over and a crowd was gathering. The sky had turned a bright pink behind the thick gray smoke. Claire heard sirens in the distance and felt torn between looking for the cat and heading toward the accident.

*Collin! He'll be in the worst mood if I'm late.*

"Claire! Over here!"

Claire turned to see Nana standing about a hundred feet away wearing the very coat and coveralls she was wearing.

Nana was waving her arms and grinning ear to ear. "Careful, don't trip over your nightie, hon."

Claire obediently reached down to hike up her nightgown, although she couldn't remember changing and discovered she was now barefoot, as well. *I put this nightgown in our attic with Nana's sewing basket after her funeral.*

She ran to Nana. Tears streamed down her cheeks as she threw her arms around the woman so hard she nearly knocked her down.

"What are you doing here?"

"Come spend the night," Nana insisted, kissing her forehead and brushing her hair out of her eyes.

"But...."

"I've got a good fire going in the cook stove. There's beans and ham stewing and a pan of cornbread in the oven, but we've got to skedaddle," Nana said, as she placed an arm around Claire's shoulders and steered her in the other direction, toward the sun.

Claire couldn't get over Nana's radiant smile. It was hypnotic. *Those must be her real teeth and her eyes are as green as apples.*

She reached out to touch Nana's face. *I'm dreaming.*

Nana took Claire's hand, kissed it and pressed it against her cheek to prove she was real.

She'd been eighty-two when she died. Claire searched her face for a single wrinkle. Logic told her Nana shouldn't look at all like herself without her deep laugh lines and furrows of worry creasing her forehead. She'd had coffee-stained dentures and thick white hair she'd worn in a bun, for as long as Claire could remember. Only her hair remained the same, yet it was clearly Nana.

Every color appeared warm and inviting. Even the mud, which covered Nana's work boots, was the shade of Hershey's cocoa.

Sirens blared from up the road as Claire stopped to face Nana. She looked her up and down. The sirens seemed to twist and melt into horns and party favors, which made them both giggle. The sky was growing brighter by the second, brighter than she could ever remember. It was intoxicating. Something inside her wanted to laugh, soak up every ounce of light and melt into her grandmother's arms for a long nap. Yet a little nagging feeling lingered in the back of her mind—bittersweet, like riding to the top of the world's most magnificent ferris wheel and spotting your wallet lying open on the ground below.

"Wait, everything is happening too fast. I think I'm forgetting something."

"I've got everything you need back at the house, even your pink toothbrush with your name taped on the handle," Nana said, as she grabbed Claire's hand and took off running like a teenager, "Trust me. The cornbread's going to to burn if we don't get a move-on."

They continued running in the direction of the sun. There was an enormous flash of color. The sky filled with gems, the sun shining through them like a brilliant stained glass mosaic until it was too bright to bear.

When Claire opened her eyes, they were standing in the guest bedroom upstairs in Nana's farmhouse. She wasn't out of breath or even sweating, but she knew it was summertime, because the old wooden box fan her grandfather had made was wedged in the open window. Her eyes sleepily followed the blades as they turned in the breeze.

The sun was setting as Nana pulled the white chenille

bedspread back to reveal crisp sheets with yellow daisies. Claire smiled dreamily as Nana guided her over to the bed, tucked her in and turned on the fan.

"You've had a long day, kiddo," Nana said, as she walked toward the door, "You're not going to believe the fun you're going to have. Welcome home."

———

Claire awoke to the lilac wallpaper and old familiar furniture. The dark oak chair and dresser still stood against the far wall. The enormous braided rag rug Nana had made felt solid and cool beneath her bare feet as she stood up. At the end of the bed was a quilt she'd made too, from Claire's father's boyhood clothes. She remembered how she used to crawl to the end of the bed after Nana had tucked her in and trace the worn squares with her finger. She found her favorite square, a pretty blue silk swatch from the tie he'd worn to his high school graduation. Touching that piece had always made her feel closer to him.

"Always planned to give that to you," Nana said from the doorway, hands on her hips.

"What happened to it? We never found it."

"My sister-in-law swiped it before the estate sale, sold it and took a little trip to Vegas.

"Beverly? Are you serious?"

"As a heart attack."

"Not funny, Nana."

"Sure it is. Doesn't matter now. It's here in your hands just like I intended, so Beverly and I both got what we wanted.

Besides, I made sure she went home three-hundred dollars in the hole."

Claire sat down on the bed, frowned and pulled the quilt onto her lap. "Where's Ben?"

Nana whistled and Claire soon heard the sweet sound of the old Blue Heeler's claws clicking up the stairs. He loped into the room, tail wagging.

"Benny!" Claire cried as she patted the bed. He jumped right up and licked her face.

Nana grinned and leaned against the door jam, folding her arms.

The words, "Partners in crime, together again," filled Claire's head and made her laugh. Seeing Ben, Claire had to hear the story again.

"Tell it," Claire whispered, "Come on."

"You've heard it a thousand times."

"Tell it."

Nana smiled and crossed the room to join them on the bed. She stroked Ben's black and white coat as she spoke, "Your father was driving a load of cattle to Texas when he ran into an ice storm just outside of Kankakee. Freak storm—not in the forecast or he would've waited a day. 'Black ice,' they said. The rig slid and hit a utility pole, your father and Ben were both thrown from the cab and the cattle stampeded. They said your father crawled over to Ben and laid on top of him."

"Ben was always proof," Claire whispered.

"Proof?"

"Proof that Dad was a good man right up to the very last second of his life."

"He sure was. You were just four and you knew he made every run with him, so it took you the longest time to accept that Ben was going to live with us, but your daddy wasn't coming back."

"Why did you take Ben? I lost my dad and my best friend in the same day."

"Oh, honey. I know. It was awful, but your mother refused to take him home, said she couldn't stand the sight of him. She was convinced your dad could've outrun the cattle if he wouldn't have been so concerned with Ben. Me? I just wanted to help both of you through it the best I could. So I took Ben, and I took you every chance I got because your mother, well... you know your mother."

"Yeah," Claire said, looking out the window.

"She never really recovered."

"But he was your son, your only child."

"True, but I had the farm and animals to help me through it and your mother just shut herself off from everyone. I gave her space, as long as she let me take you whenever her blues got real bad."

"This was the safest place on earth," Claire said, tears spilling down her cheeks.

"I tried real hard," Nana said as she brushed the tears away and tucked a wisp of Claire's dark hair behind her ear.

"Is he here with you? My dad? Here?" Claire asked looking around the room, which felt as it were beginning to spin. "Here," she repeated as she touched the bedspread, the quilt, Ben... anything she could to ground her.

"Claire, it's okay," Nana took her hand.

"Not here, Nana. Not yet. My God, the girls. I need my girls... and Paul!" Claire cried, grabbing her grandmother by her arms.

"Breathe, Claire. No one is gone. They're closer than ever," Nana insisted, nudging Ben off the bed. She pulled Claire close to her, letting her bury her face in her neck as she sobbed.

"Tell me what Em's room smells like," Nana whispered, stroking Claire's hair.

Claire sniffled and gasped. "Play-Doh and crayons—she's a coloring machine."

"Good," Nana whispered.

"Anna's room always smells like something's burning. She's got that straightening iron going twenty-four-seven... watermelon gum, that awful black nail polish... and dog. It's Anna and Shadow's room. They're inseparable. Even when Anna isn't there, Shadow sleeps in her dirty clothes until she gets home, you know?" Claire rambled as she cried.

"Sure, hon. I see them everyday just like you did—just like you're still going to. I want you to focus, Claire. Smell the Play-Doh. Breathe in the baby shampoo from Em's pink pillows and just focus on her precious little essence," Nana whispered.

Claire did as she was told. "I feel a little better," she whispered and opened her eyes. They were sitting on Em's canopy bed. She gasped and covered her mouth, as Nana rubbed her back.

Em and Anna were seated at Em's little table coloring. Em was scribbling away, and Anna sat on her right hand, fighting the urge to pull her eyelashes.

A well-worn Crayola sixty-four pack sat on the table with various crayons and sheets of construction paper strewn about.

"I promised to buy her that crazy crayon tower—a hundred and fifty crayons—at the end of the year. She reminds me almost everyday," Claire sniffled, crawling across the bed to see what they were drawing.

Shadow was sprawled out on the floor next to Anna, secretly chewing on a Cornflower Blue crayon. Anna was working on a scribble picture, filling in the nooks and crannies with different colors as she sat on a little chair with her long legs sprawled beneath the table.

"How long do we have to stay up here?" Em asked as she drew a lush, green tree.

"Until Dad's company leaves, I guess," Anna replied, trying to feign indifference.

"Deyre not compny, deyre police. I saw da police car from da bafroom window," Em said without looking up.

"Alrighty then," Anna sighed, "They're police—no biggie. Dad probably stole some candy or something and they're just having a talk with him," Anna said, smirking.

Em looked up wide-eyed, "He'll have to give it back. *I* did and I had to 'pologize too, member? Wait 'til Mom finds out!"

"Em, I was kidding. Dad would never steal anything, but sometimes he forgets to put on his seatbelt, right?" Anna said, sounding pleased with herself.

Claire shook her head and smiled at Nana.

Anna glanced at Em's picture and frowned. "Why is Dad wearing a skirt? Or is that a kilt?"

"It's a blanket for his all-timer's, like Grandpa," Em answered matter-of-factly.

Anna shook her head. "Dad doesn't have Alzheimer's."

"He forgot lots of stuff today. Maybe tomorrow he'll forget our names like Grandpa," Em argued.

"Um, I don't think that's going to happen."

"He forgot to tell me Mom wasn't gonna pick me up from school and I wasn't going to swim lessons and Mom was taking a trip for her work," Em babbled as she scribbled harder.

Claire looked at Nana. "He'll have to tell them the truth," she whispered, tears welling up.

"In time, hon, but *their* truth is that you're missing. You left a thousand questions behind and very few answers. It's a blessing though, a more graduated grieving process for Paul and the girls and everyone, in its own peculiar way. That's why you chose it," Nana reminded her. She left Claire sitting on the bed and walked over to Anna.

"I don't remember choosing any of this," Claire said, aching to hold her girls, but afraid she could never let go.

"You will," Nana assured her as she stood behind Anna and placed her hands on her shoulders.

The teenager sat staring into space as her little sister worked on another picture.

"Anna can sense something's wrong. She's dreading the moment when the police leave and Paul sits her down for a talk. She knows Em's right. Too many routines were broken today. She knows this isn't like you. You always had a schedule and you tried to keep all of them on it, but the rest of the family's easy-going nature helped you keep a better balance," Nana said, as if interpreting a foreign language.

"True, but what can I do for them now? Show me how to help them," Claire pleaded.

"It's okay, Claire. She's kind of laughing to herself about the way she used to tease you. She used to tell you that you had chronic Obsessive Compulsive Disorder. She knows you're not on a trip, because your luggage is still in the hall closet. Your make-up and hairbrushes are still in the bathroom drawer. She's checked. She hasn't seen your purse though and this is giving her hope."

"Oh, God. I can't take this. Nana please, how can I help them?"

"Watch me." Nana winked at Claire as she ran her fingers through Anna's hair. Anna took a deep breath and slowly let it out.

Then Nana reached across the little table and tapped Em on the shoulder.

Em stood right up, walked over to her clock radio and turned it on.

Shawn Mullin's soulful voice visibly soothed Anna as he sang, "Everything's gonna be all right... rock-a-bye, rock-a-bye."

Nana wrapped her arms tightly around Anna's body and rocked her from side to side. "Em is going to be easy, but you'll have to work harder to reach this one. Feel this trance-like energy she's giving off right now? It's like a window you can reach through sometimes," she said, as Anna whispered to herself "Everything's gonna be all right."

Claire nodded and looked down to see Shadow staring directly up at her.

Shadow gave a loud bark and wagged her tail as she jumped up and put her front paws in Claire's lap.

Claire laughed and hugged her. "Why didn't she see me before?"

"Because you're learning to focus your energy. She can feel that. Shadow will sense you most of the time, unless she's working on a particularly tasty crayon."

Em laughed, pointing at the Irish Setter.

Shadow was pawing at the air above the bed and barking.

"You think she's got bees again?" Em asked, turning the radio off.

"Fleas, Em—maybe," Anna said with a sniffle and shivered. She looked toward the door. "Gonna wear your seatbelt from now on?" she asked, her voice a little shaky.

Claire's heart leapt into her throat at the site of Paul. His eyes were red and puffy as he raised his left hand and placed his right one on a Captain Underpants book on the shelf. He gave Anna a painful smile. "From now on, I promise."

Claire sensed the two of them would be a team from that moment on.

She tensed as Paul walked over to the bed and lay down under the canopy next to her, letting out a long sigh.

He eyed Shadow for a moment. The dog appeared to be lost in her own world, rolled over on her back. Paul closed his eyes.

Claire reached out to touch his cheek. They wouldn't be

lying next to one another tonight like they had thousands of nights before. They wouldn't be sharing their day's events and she had so much to share. He looked exhausted. She just wanted to take him in her arms and tell him everything. Instead, she crawled up to the head of the bed and shook with grief as she replayed all of their *lasts* in her mind. *We didn't know. It's so unfair we didn't know.*

Nana joined her on the bed, rubbing her back again. "You can still lie next to Paul and the girls. You can still comfort them. They *will* sense it. You just watched me do it. You can do anything you want, hon," she whispered.

Paul scratched Shadow behind her ears, as the girls climbed onto the bed and snuggled up next to him.

Claire turned to Nana. "What are they going to do?"

"Make you proud. Astonish and amaze you with their strength and resilience. You've been an incredible influence on each one of them. You just wait and see," she said taking Claire's hand and pressing it to her lips.

Paul sat up and hugged the girls tightly. "Let's not mess up mom's kitchen tonight. Whaddya say?"

"Wapple Stomp!" Em shouted as she pulled free and jumped on the bed.

"Waffle Stop?" he asked Anna, squeezing her shoulder.

"Yeah," she agreed, wrapping her arm around his waist.

Paul scooped Em up, and the three of them left the room with Shadow in tow.

"Leave something for Em," Nana said, "She's coming back for her jacket."

"How?"

"It's easier than you think. Concentrate your mind into a focused beam of light and sort of make a wish like you're blowing out birthday candles. Quick, think of something just the two of you did."

Claire thought for a moment, "Sometimes we had to go back to the bank after I picked her up from school—pretty boring. She never complained though. She'd make jewelry for me out of paper clips."

"Good one!" Nana clapped her hands. "Now focus that thought into a beam of light, wish for a paper clip and blow!"

Claire gave the ridiculous instructions a shot and opened her eyes. Lying on the bedspread between them was one silver paper clip.

"Nice work!" Nana cheered as Em came running into the room. She grabbed her red jacket from the floor and ran toward the door.

"Em!" Nana whispered.

Em stopped and turned. She stood motionless for a second. Then she walked toward the bed, brushing her curly brown hair from her eyes and picked up the paper clip with her pudgy little fingers. She silently studied it until she heard her father yell, "All ashore that's goin' ashore!" Then she stuffed it in her pants pocket and ran out of the room.

⊏────⊐

Claire and Nana swung back and forth on the porch swing while Ben slept at their feet, his paws occasionally twitching. The farm was still the most relaxing place she'd ever known, when she wasn't trying to retrace her steps, or figure out exactly what had happened to her.

"I think I got gypped on my clichés," Claire said, staring off into the bean field where the emerald leaves rolled in the wind like rippling water.

"How so?" Nana laughed, as she finished darning a sock,

and held it up on her hand for inspection.

"The way I went... it wasn't even close to what I expected."

"We see what we need to see," Nana said, smiling and closing the lid on her sewing basket.

"So, you're saying I didn't need to see white light, Morgan Freeman in a tunnel or anything? Just you?"

"I know, talk about your ultimate compliment." Nana grinned and patted Claire's knee. The socks and sewing basket had vanished.

"You make it sound like I'm controlling all of this, but I don't feel like I'm in control of a single thing."

"You're just a little out of sorts right now. That's part of the process. It's kind of like the way some dry-out clinics give alcoholics pills to ease their shakes."

"I'm detoxing from my life?"

"Yeah, kind of."

"Look Nana, you know how much I love you and this... *trip* has been so incredible, but I need to go back, now."

"Going back isn't an option, hon. Sorry."

"Never!?" Panic and anger clawed their way to the surface as she turned to face Nana.

"Didn't say *never*, but that body can't hold your spirit anymore. I guess if you'd seen it, you'd understand. I *did* kind of decide that for you by calling you to me. I'm not really supposed to do that. Hope I don't get in trouble."

"Could I have stayed if you hadn't called me?" Claire cried. Stunned by the possibility.

"Oh, gosh no, honey. We're responsible for our own births and deaths, plan them out very carefully, long before we go back to the earth plane. Your passing was quick, which is good, but it can be a tad rough when you're young like that. I know what you were doing, though."

"Glad someone does," Claire said running her fingers

through her hair, half-believing Nana, half-thinking she'd lost her mind and was imagining the whole thing.

A lone goose wandered up to the porch, pecking at unseen morsels. Claire eyed him suspiciously as she began to grasp that nothing was as simple as it seemed, anymore. For all she knew, that goose was God.

"Don't get your undies in a bunch. That's not him. He's got better things to do," Nana assured her with a knowing smile.

"You can read my mind? Anytime you want?" Claire asked, trying not to sound upset, again.

"I'm here to help you, to make this as easy as possible, hon. This is how you'll talk to everyone after a while," Nana moved closer and wrapped her arm around her.

Claire's fears melted in the warmth and strength of Nana's embrace. *She would never hurt me.*

"*Never,*" Nana agreed, crossing her heart. "You can still see your body if you need to. Sometimes it helps."

"Really?" Claire asked, perplexed by the prospect. "Is that a good idea? I think I must have been hit by a car trying to catch that cat."

"'I'm afraid so. Drunk, going seventy. No headlights and all that fog."

"Is he okay?"

"Not exactly."

"So, I'm road kill and you're suggesting I go check this out for myself?" Claire asked, as she rested her bare foot on Ben's furry stomach, his heartbeat beneath her toes an unexpected comfort.

Ben lifted his head and wagged his tail, before returning to his nap.

"Road kill? Nah, it wasn't that bad. Your neck snapped. You weren't mangled or squashed like a possum pancake. Still, not one of your better looks."

# CHAPTER 5

CLAIRE TRIED to imagine what it would be like to see her own lifeless body. She wore jeans and a white T-shirt, and watched Nana fiddle with the buttons of her red housedress, the one with the little white polka dots.

"I always loved that dress on you."

"I know. That's why you put me in it—you know, with your thoughts," Nana said, smoothing the dress over her knees and tucking it under her legs.

"I always felt bad about burning the sleeve with the iron."

"Don't be silly. I'd had the thing for a coon's age, and now it's good as new."

"I definitely don't remember choosing your dress. Are you sure? I mean, it's nice to see things I've forgotten about, but I should at least remember making that decision shouldn't I?"

Nana squinted in the direction of the rabbit hutch and turned back to Claire when she had the answer. "You know how scientists are always saying we only use ten percent of our brain? Well, here you're using the whole kit 'n kaboodle. Now your soul's running the show."

Claire gave her a confused look.

"Okay, let me see... I watched you work at the bank quite a bit with you always rubbing that necklace full of ashes like it was Aladdin's lamp or something," she said with a smirk. "Maybe I can make this a little easier to understand. You know all those computers you knew how to run?"

"Sure," Claire answered, astonished by the fact that Nana had often come to her when she'd thought about her or touched her necklace.

"Well, your mind's like all of those computers put together, like some giant super-computer and it's going to be running a lot of um... *programs* by itself to help you feel better in the beginning.

"Okay," Claire responded, mulling it over. "Makes sense, so far."

"Actually, think of yourself as running a program called *Comfort Mode,* for now. That program is running while you're also in *Sorting Mode,* which is kind of like defragging, as I understand it. So you're sorting and organizing your whole soul without even thinking about it." Nana raised her eyebrows, pleased with her translation. "You'll be doing that for a while. Enjoy it. *Comfort Mode* can make you as happy as a cow in clover."

"So, I don't need to worry about what I've planned for myself, just trust that it's good?"

"Bull's eye," Nana said, leaning in closer. "A touch of the blues is normal. There's are an awful lot of change to accept in the beginning."

"I do feel a little sad. It's like I'm drifting back and forth between what I've lost and what I've gained, and I can't stay focused on either one long enough to weigh them against each other. On the other hand, I don't ever have to wear shoes again, do I? Claire asked, smiling and wiggling her toes."

Nana laughed. "Pretty good trade-off, if you ask me."

"Still, there's this underlying sense of loss I can't seem to reconcile."

A gust of wind ruffled her hair and played with the hem of Nana's dress. Gentle pings of raindrops fell on the porch's tin roof. The scent of freshly cut hay came wafting up onto the porch, and Claire felt as if she'd been bathed in safety and unconditional love.

"Wow, that's nice."

"See? You'll find new ways to comfort yourself. You haven't lost a thing. Your perspective is just a little out of whack, right now. I'm a Spirit Teacher, here. Um... let me see. I'm like those Corporate Trainers showing folks the ropes. This is my work here until I go back again—love it," she said, smiling to herself and leaning down to scratch Ben's ear. Then, she sat up, closed her eyes and took a deep breath.

Nana had a bowl of green beans in her lap and an empty bowl had appeared between them. She started snapping, tossing the ends into the yard for the ducks and geese and the rest into the other bowl. About a dozen birds came pattering up to the porch, flapping their wings.

"I can teach you little things but just wait until your reunion," Nana said.

"What reunion?"

"Ahma's going to take you to see your Collective."

"Who's Ahma?" An identical bowl of green beans appeared in Claire's lap. She picked one up without even thinking, snapped the ends off and threw them to a runt of a duck excluded from the feast.

"Ahma's your Spirit Guide. She's like your bank's Regional Manager—a real big wig. Nice lady with major connections. Smart. You'll want to watch your P's and Q's around her."

"Good to know."

"Your Collective is so excited to see you they can hardly stand it."

"What are they like... in banking terms?"

"Hmmm... I'd say they're kind of like that Safety Committee you were on."

"The Safety Committee?" Claire asked as she popped a bean into her mouth and savored its sweetness.

"Collectives want to make things better for everyone, basically. I know, that's kind of vague, but they're your group, your council, like a collective conscience. There's a central Collective, which every living thing is a part of—God, himself, heads that committee, if you want to call it that... and him that, but after that comes your personal Collective. You've got your group karma through your Collective and then you also have your personal karma. With me so far?"

Claire squinted at Nana. "So far, yeah. What do I do with my Collective?"

"You've got a lot of projects and goals you've worked on as a group and there'll be a lot more."

Claire shook her head. "I feel like it's the first day of college and I forgot to buy my text books."

"Oh, I know, hon. Everything's going to seem so peculiar and random at first, but then you'll start to see the bigger picture. It's like the insides of one of those giant clocks, gears of all sizes clicking and turning, all working together. By the way, your Collective can't see you until your vibration's right. Just like they didn't expect you to do one of those fancy Powerpoint thingies for your co-workers your first week at the bank."

"Okay, I get it," Claire said as she dropped a few beans into the bowl between them.

Claire turned and looked at Nana, who was holding a glass of lemonade in each hand.

"See? It's going to be fun," she said, handing one to her.

Claire stared at it doubtfully for a moment then lifted it to her lips. The most perfect balance of sweet and tart filled her mouth like pure liquid pleasure.

Claire shook her head again as she licked her lips. "Okay, I admit all of this does seem vaguely familiar at times, like maybe I dreamt bits and pieces of it, but I'm really having a hard time believing I planned any of this. Are you saying that I planned my whole life out, from birth to death?"

Nana swirled the ice around in her glass and set it down on the porch. "Nah, not every second, but you made a sort of blueprint before each trip back to the earth plane. You carefully chose all of your lessons with Ahma and your Collective."

"Sorry, I keep thinking of things like buying socks at Wal-Mart or balancing my checkbook. It's hard to believe I had any grand plan going on."

Nana laughed and waved her hand. "Oh, that's just life. There has to be an ebb and flow to things. You know that Chinese Checker board on the bookshelf in the living room? Well, picture a gigantic one with the dots all connected by all of those lines. There are bunches of... what do they call them... variables, so many different chances to learn the same lessons... as many as the stars. It's kind of like math equations. Certain combinations of people and situations make for perfect opportunities for certain kinds of lessons. Like, you picked your parents, for instance. They were a huge part of your life equation."

"I chose a father who would die before I even got to know him and a mother with a completely debilitating case of Seasonal Affective Disorder? Why would anyone do that?" Claire asked, as she noticed the number of beans in the bowls didn't seem to change at all, no matter how many they snapped.

"But look at how you turned out."

"Dead?"

"Smarty-pants, look at what an incredible wife, mother and friend you were."

*Were,* the word stung, but she had to admit what Nana was saying made sense.

"You also planned out a departure with maximum growth in mind for everyone: yourself, Paul, your mother and the girls, all the way down to total strangers. There are so many forks in the road all over our blueprints. The order of your lessons was always flexible. We all tend to put the toughest ones off until the end."

"Julia," Claire whispered to herself, as she bent down and set her empty glass on the porch. The sky clouded over. Tree branches began to sway as a chilly breeze blew through the yard, creating dust devils in the driveway.

"There's always a bit of free will. I guess that kind of works like the tension knob on that exercise bike you had in your basement, the one you hung your blouses on to dry."

"Ahem, I know the one. Your point being?" Claire asked, glad she'd never have to see the thing, again.

Nana grinned. "Well, if you wanted to suffer through a lesson, fighting it all the way or giving up on it, only to have to deal with the darn thing again, later—you could. You always controlled the difficulty of the lesson. You could roll with the punches, or you could struggle against them. Struggles build strength, but attitude's everything," Nana said, as she reached over and brushed a wisp of Claire's hair out of her eyes, tucking it behind her ear.

"I made some things so incredibly hard," Claire said, remembering useless battles with her mother when she tried to get her to move from her cabin to the city.

"We all make things harder than they have to be sometimes. We're designed to do that. If we skated right through, we'd never learn a thing."

"True," Claire agreed, as the sun peeked out from behind the clouds. Nana's shirts were pinned to the clothesline. Claire watched them dance in the afternoon breeze.

*Nothing is random.*

"You visited this place in your dreams plenty of times, kind of like HR and your performance reviews at the bank," Nana explained.

Claire thought of Marilyn and shuddered.

"In a *good* way," Nana clarified, "To figure out the best win-win outcomes. Sometimes you came here in your dreams just to be social or to get messages from friends and family. That's where you're drawing memories of this place from now, but soon you'll visit the Hall of Records and it'll all be right there at your fingertips, every memory, every lesson, every thought and feeling you've ever had."

"No way. Every single one? That sounds horribly overwhelming."

"Don't worry. Every one of your memories and the reasons behind them will be crystal clear to you. It's dazzling. Savor your visit to The Hall of Records, Claire. It's one of the best dips in the whole roller coaster." She'd finished snapping her beans and stood up to stretch.

"You remember the last time you had déjà vu?" Nana asked. She hadn't gone inside, but the bowls of green beans had disappeared. She now held a basket under her arm and handed Claire a pair of knitting needles, some purple yarn and a partially finished potholder. Claire vaguely remembered that multi-colored potholder she'd started when she was around ten years old.

Nana sat down and took up her own pair of needles and some yarn.

Claire reached for her glass of lemonade, but discovered it had vanished.

As Nana continued talking and knitting, Claire focused on her own stitches. She hadn't knitted in years, but soon found herself gazing off in the direction of the barn, her fingers still working away.

"So... Déjà vu?" Nana repeated.

"Yeah, actually a few nights ago, I had it in the hallway outside Anna's door, and I used to have it at work sometimes." She remembered Collin and missed him. *I've got to try to find him.*

"Déjà vu's important," Nana continued. "They're like signposts you set up all over your life when you make your blueprint. They're to let you know when you're right on track with your plans."

Claire shook her head. "Sometimes, I had déjà vu during really scary experiences, though, like when Anna fell out of the tree at the old apartment. It was such a vivid memory I experienced, right as it was happening," Claire insisted, the skeptic in her still intact.

"Of course, because it was a very important letting-go-lesson you wanted to learn, so you arranged reminders for yourself to ride it out and learn it well," Nana answered without missing a beat.

Claire glanced down and noticed she now had a ridiculously long scarf instead of a potholder. "What's this?" she asked as she held it up, a frown creasing her brow.

"Not magic, just a little environmental hypnosis," Nana assured her.

The sun was setting. They'd knitted up a storm, but Claire felt they'd only been talking for about an hour.

"Time is strange here."

"True," Nana said with a smile and held up the better part of a sweater. "I promised Ahma I'd help you stretch your meditative muscles. You experienced time gaps on the earth plane too. Remember?"

"I guess so. Sometimes driving home from work I'd space-out and before I knew it, I'd be pulling into the garage."

"Exactly. It's the same thing. Relaxing things we tend to do on auto-pilot, take us into that same meditative or hypnotic state and time just slips away. Prayer can take you there, too."

"What's the point, though?" Claire asked.

"Well, it's healing and it's also the same state of mind you'll need to communicate with your Collective and everyone eventually."

"Always the clever teacher, Katherine," said a woman's voice from behind them. Claire was stunned to discover she was empty-handed and waist-deep in a meadow full of purple wild-flowers with Nana and this mysterious woman. An over-whelming sense of love coursed through her body. The sky, the trees, everything around them glowed so brightly as if electri-fied. Yet the light didn't hurt her eyes. It felt incredibly soothing, like a warm bath.

Claire turned to face the woman who had spoken, and found herself in awe of her beauty. She had thick black braids down to her knees and deep set amber eyes with skin as black as coffee. Claire sensed the woman was ancient, although she appeared to be no more than fifty. She wore a simple, elegant white gown, and whilst the woman's features were striking, it was as if her beauty emanated from her heart. She possessed an air of holiness like a shaman or a monk, yet she felt as intimately familiar to Claire as a sister might.

She also sensed the woman knew everything about her, about the world, in fact. This figure before her was more than a woman. She was a celestial being, some sort of angel who possessed the best attributes of men and women everywhere, flawlessly pooled together. She took her breath away.

Claire felt Nana kiss her cheek and drift away. Her instinct was to beg her to stay, but she couldn't pry her eyes away from the angelic being.

The woman's mouth didn't move, but Claire heard a deep rich voice inside her mind say, "I am Ahma." She then took Claire by the hand and they began to walk. "You're adapting very well. I'm proud of you," Ahma said out loud.

"Thank you, but I don't feel like I've really done anything," Claire replied, reaching out to touch the flower petals as they walked. The plants appeared to grow taller by the minute, their fragrance an oddly intoxicating combination of spring rain and freshly-bathed babies.

Claire's stomach fluttered, as if she and Ahma were in a little rollercoaster car creeping up a steep incline. When she reached for her stomach her hand swept right through it. She was still wearing jeans and a white T-shirt but when she glanced down, her entire body was transparent. She could see the flowers behind her. She felt lighter too, but more focused and sure of who she was than she could ever remember feeling. Her pulse quickened. She felt Ahma squeeze her hand.

"Just try it on for size," Ahma reassured her with a smile. "You've done some good work. You've kept yourself open, so your spirit is blossoming as fast as morning glories. I want you to remember that this is the most important thing you can do. Some souls don't progress for a very long time because they cannot get past their own expectations of this dimension. They know they're no longer on the earth plane. They all have ideas about heaven and the afterlife, but it's simply home. They remember that eventually. Yet, they still think they're not where they're supposed to be, and it keeps their spirit from evolving."

"I can see how someone might expect something else," Claire replied breathlessly as the wildflowers grew past their heads.

"Katherine's right. We see what we need to see, but we must remain open to new ideas and new ways of doing things. Progression of the spirit is the key to happiness, no matter where we are in the universe. One must develop one's soul and the spirit must grow, but we must seek growth. No one is going to force it upon us. A soul can remain a seed for as long as it wishes. It is entirely up to you," Ahma explained.

Claire suspected she was still a seed and changed the subject. "We've known each other a long time haven't we?"

"Forever. You can ask me anything. Right now, I feel you struggling to understand and accept everything. That's normal."

"Well, I know you want me to progress and move on and all that, but I feel so out of sorts, like I lost a mile-long to-do list, you know? I lost my body so fast. I think that's the problem. I feel like I need to say goodbye or something. I need to see my body, Ahma. Can you take me to it?"

"Of course, take a deep breath and mentally pull the violet light from the blossoms above you into your sixth chakra, your third eye, which is your ajna chakra in the center of your fore-head, just above your eyebrows," Ahma said as the flowers began to rustle above them.

Claire just decided to focus on the center of her forehead. She'd understood that much. She closed her eyes and tried her best to follow Ahma's instructions. When she opened them again, the emerald stems of the wildflowers parted, and she and Ahma stepped into a very small, gray, brightly-lit room.

The ceramic brick walls and tiled floor were dull from years of bleaching. One wall was a cooler. Rows of stainless steel shelves lined the other walls and hung above a large sink. On them sat electric saws and other bone-cutting tools Claire quickly relegated to the back of her mind.

A woman's body lay naked on a single stainless steel table clamped to the sink, the blood slowly draining from it.

"Oh my God, that's me?"

Covered with cuts and bruises, its eyes and mouth were open. Both hands had plastic bags taped over them with matching labels, which read: "Name: U/W/F, Ht.: 5'8", Wt: 136 lbs., D.O.D.: 10/31/08 T.O.D.: 05:00-06:00, Case: #0051163". There was a toe tag attached to the right foot with the same information. The skin was lavender-gray.

Claire didn't feel the sadness she'd expected. Instead, as she stood there in her celestial body staring at her earthly body, she felt more alive than ever. She crept closer to the table, reached out and ran the back of her hand along its arm. It felt foreign. It reminded her of a day not too long ago when she and Paul had driven past their first apartment. *Great memories, but that really isn't me anymore.*

"That smell... bleach and death...."

"Turn it down a notch, if you like," Ahma suggested.

"I can do that?"

"Exhale while focusing on your 5th chakra, the throat chakra. Continue dialing it down until it's tolerable."

"That's incredible," Claire remarked as she swiped her hand through her face, forgetting her lighter state again and giggling at the strangeness of it all.

Claire heard the doorknob turn. She'd never felt so exposed. She desperately wanted to cover the small pale breasts, the ugly appendix scar above the little towel, which lay just above her not-so-recently-shaved legs, but there was no time. Self-consciousness engulfed her as the door opened.

A lean dark-haired man in his mid-thirties appeared in scrubs, a clear, disposable face shield, a plastic apron and surgical gloves. He carried a large plastic bag with a label identical to the others.

Claire spotted Nana's chore coat inside the largest bag and wished she hadn't.

The man laid the bag on the counter next to some others containing her boots, coveralls, hose, bra, underwear and the ratty green stocking cap.

She noticed a digital camera sitting next to the plastic bags and was sickened by the realization that the last pictures taken of her had been less than flattering.

The man removed the bags from the hands and checked the labels against the toe tag and clipboard. He placed them in another bag on the counter. Next, he opened a large drawer filled with stainless steel instruments and little vials with lots of different color-coded caps. He then proceeded to cut the nails down to the quick, placing the clippings in more bags with matching labels.

Claire was fascinated by how focused and meticulous he was with his work. He combed wherever there was hair, and placed the samples in separate bags. He plucked hairs from the head, lots of them, and into paper envelopes they went. He even swabbed the mouth and placed the samples on glass slides, spraying them with some sort of fixative, then into bags they went.

She found the sheer number of bags intriguing, each labeled with all of her information, everything but her name. They all read: "U/W/F."

Another thing impressed her; throughout the entire process, the man was so respectful. He had muscular, rather beautiful hands and his touch seemed very tender and compassionate.

She remained on one side of the table while he stood on the other documenting every single one of her bodily flaws on a clipboard. She'd never been so glad she hadn't gone through with the *Cat in the Hat* tattoo she'd wanted on her ass, when she was seventeen.

"He's Tony Chism, right?" Claire asked Ahma, having no idea how she knew this.

Ahma, arms folded, nodded from the corner where she had been watching the two of them. "I'll leave you to your goodbyes now. Keep it simple. Don't stay too long. You can summon the flowers—the path back to me, the same way you summoned this place, just breathe them in again, right here," she said, tapping the spot just above her eyes.

The purple wildflowers instantly appeared and parted. Ahma turned and stepped into them before they faded away.

"She sure knows how to make an entrance... and an exit," Claire remarked, turning back to Tony, knowing he couldn't hear her, but longing for someone to share the experience with.

Tony glanced up.

# CHAPTER 6

STANDING PERFECTLY STILL, Tony finally exhaled. He set the clipboard on the counter and removed a hose from a hook over the sink. A forceful spray of water hit the body.

Claire studied his face. He grimaced when he returned the hose to its hook several minutes later and shook his head. He walked over to the counter and opened a second metal drawer. When he came back to the table, Claire saw a syringe in his hand. As he leaned in close to the face and positioned the needle near the right eye, Claire turned away.

When she felt it was safe, she glanced over to see him looking around the room, again. Frowning, he got back to work and deposited the fluid from the syringe onto a slide, which went into yet another labeled plastic bag. When she saw him move toward the other eye, Claire took a short walk to the other side of the room where several white boards hung on the wall. She studied the names on the board labeled "Today's Cases". Her eyes landed on the conspicuous "U/W/F" near the top.

She heard Tony pacing. Curious, she returned to the table. He was shaking his head again. He stopped at the foot of the table and stood there for a bit with his hands folded serenely in front of him.

Claire assumed he was meditating or praying, because she could feel that nice soothing energy coming from him, like Nana had described with Anna.

He ended his meditation with a shiver, and Claire thought it might be cold in the little room, but she couldn't feel it.

Tony then spoke to the body. "How about some music? We need to talk." He reached for a portable radio perched on a stainless steel shelf and flicked the power switch on. As he adjusted the tuner, the soft tinkling of jazz filled the air.

"I know it's a crummy little room. I got the regular caseload. Sorry, I'm low man on the totem pole—just a deaner. At least we have some peace and quiet. Everybody else is working in the big suites, packed in like sardines since the plane crash—two hundred seventy-nine fatalities. We got every one of them. O'Hare's our jurisdiction. Plus it's a high profile case—funding, you know. My boss is tearing the last of his hair out trying to round up refrigerated trucks from some poor local vendor who'll just have to kiss it off and hand it over. I wouldn't want a tuna sandwich off that truck a year from now, would you?" Tony laughed.

"Walter's a trip, but we didn't get off to such a great start." Tony moved a scale on the counter closer to him and pulled a small black case from his pocket. He lifted the lid and removed something from the case.

Claire bit her lower lip as she saw light reflect off of something shiny in his hand. It was a scalpel, his personal scalpel, apparently. "Okey-dokey, I'm outta here. I'd love to stay, but I'm not about to stand here and chit-chat while you scoop out my insides."

Claire's eyes grew wide as Tony's gaze shifted from the body on the table to her.

She waved her hand in front of his face, but Tony only took a deep breath and resumed his story.

"Had my shirt off when he came in the locker room to give me my first schedule. He saw my Reaper tattoo on my back and went off the deep end—gave me this ridiculous lecture about death not being cool, like I'm fourteen or something. Try thirty-eight. God, I can't wait for the guy to retire, just a few more weeks. I may be odd, but he's a real nut job. Crabby as hell, but obsessed with butterflies. Wants to start a butterfly farm down in Texas when he retires. Anytime he isn't chewing me up one side and down the other, he's talking about this crazy-assed butterfly farm. Did you know you can mail live butterflies anywhere you want for weddings and funerals and stuff?"

Tony continued talking as he made a clean diagonal incision from the top of the left shoulder down to the top of the breastbone.

Claire knew she should leave, but kept her eyes glued to his face instead, completely captivated by the fact that this man was so comfortable talking to her lifeless body.

"Anyway, I don't expect people to understand the Reaper tat. I got it years before I ever decided to do this for a living and it *is* huge, covers my whole back. In college, I guess it was a way for me to kind of make the best of my past, instead of feeling like a freak."

He began a second incision from the other shoulder to the top of the breastbone. "I was four when I found my parents dead in our basement—murder-suicide. That kind of thing really follows a guy. No escaping it, not until college anyway, and even then it eventually caught up with me. People look at you like you're a demon seed, or you could go postal any second. I've seen the inside of more psychologist's offices.... They either want to pick your brain or hear the gruesome details right from the horse's mouth— ghouls."

Claire felt more at ease the more Tony talked. She couldn't help glancing at the body, from time to time. It was getting easier to see it for what it was, a vehicle she no longer needed, yet not as plain-looking as she'd always thought. She also felt a twinge of admiration for Tony at times. The third incision, a continuation of the first two, swerved around the belly-button and ran all the way down to the pubic bone.

"All right, that's *my* big secret. Your turn. You can trust me. I promise. I'm here to help. I'm Tony and you look like a... Athena, goddess of wisdom," he whispered.

Tony hummed as he set down his scalpel and selected another stainless steel instrument from the drawer.

*Goddess of wisdom? Hardly.* Claire felt welded to the floor. He was really speaking to *her*. There was no denying it. *How can I leave now? Can he sense me? Hear me?*

She studied Tony's face as he worked, although it was more difficult to ignore the sound of bones being cut. He had a kind face with dark blue eyes and really seemed to care about her.

"You're keeping too many secrets, Athena," he coaxed, as he severed the ribs and chest plate with an electric tool that looked just like the woodcarver she'd bought Paul for Father's Day. It was even the same brand, a Dremel. "I know you can communicate with me if you really want to. My father did. He told me my mother had been ill, not to be angry with her or afraid, and that everything would be all right. I was really little, but I remember it." He turned the tool off and set it down.

"He *wants* me to communicate with him!"

"You are one big puzzle, lady." Tony leaned in and whispered, "Vagrants don't wear fancy push-up bras and pantyhose."

Embarrassed but excited, Claire laughed at first, until something about what he'd said struck her. "Vagrant—U/W/F. Oh my God! Unknown White Female... no one knows who I am! *That's* why Nana said I'm missing," Claire cried, breathlessly gaping at the body with a touch of sadness. It now had one friend in the world. At least it was one who really cared.

Panic obliterated her sadness. "Everyone is going to think I ran off with Julia! They have to know the truth. I don't want them to suffer even more, wondering where I am and maybe even thinking I abandoned them! Paul and the girls, Collin and Mom... it would be torture always having to wonder. I've got to do something."

Claire saw Tony place his hand on top of the head and study the face. The door knob turned with a loud click. Claire froze and Tony jerked his hand away.

The door opened and an older man's face appeared. "Chism!" he barked. "You're still on that vagrant? For Christ's sake, hurry up! You need to get a half-dozen of 'em in before you head home. You're doing the regular caseload by yourself, so move it."

"Yes, sir."

"We've got to keep them separate from the crash victims, so you're going to be in here all day. Actually, I'd prefer it if you stayed and just slept for a few hours, but I understand if you're still a little green for sleeping here."

"I can stay Mr. Rhinehardt. It's not a problem."

"Has Marnell stopped by yet? You know pathology is supposed to be in here, but she's got her hands full too."

"Yeah, she was here a while ago."

"Good. She tell ya not to post her? X-rays show a broken neck—straight to the cooler. Use the one in here since she's a Doe"

"Alright," Tony said in a quiet voice.

"I've gotta run. We've got to get these victims back to their families. The press is already calling, but we're still waiting on a shitload of dental records. Rick already take her photos?"

"Looks like it. That's his camera on the counter."

"Alright, get on with it then," Walter said sounding relieved, as he began to pull the door shut.

"Mr. Rhinehardt." Tony cleared his throat.

Walter poked his head back inside. "What?"

"You need to take a look at this one. I don't think she's a vagrant. She was wearing some pretty nice undergarments, has a pedicure and... well, look at her. She's beautiful," he said carefully.

*Beautiful?* Claire blushed and crossed her fingers. If the other man listened, they'd figure out who she was in no time.

"Prostitute. Some pretty ones come through here. Sometimes you think they could've been models if they'd known the right people, instead of the ones that got 'em here. Don't let 'em get to ya, kid. Finish her up and bag her. I want her in the cooler in thirty minutes."

Tony glanced at the clothing bagged and labeled on the counter: Victoria's Secret matching bra and underwear, coveralls, a stocking cap with a hole in it, a dirty old coat with a torn sleeve and combat boots...with pantyhose. "Yeah, she was really workin' it," Tony mumbled under his breath.

"What's that?" Walter said, looking up from his clipboard.

"Her skin's too soft. She shaved her legs and that wasn't dirt on her face. It was soot. Why would she have soot on her face?"

"I don't know and I don't care. I don't have time for this. Play Quincy when our load is back to normal. Right now, you'd better get on the stick and push her through. Grab a bite to eat before you start on that SIDS case, or better eat after him. I can't afford to send you home in the middle of this goddamn mess. Get busy," Walter growled and slammed the door.

"Athena, were you a chimney sweeping prostitute? I can just see you driving around town in your van full of sex toys with the broom and ladder mounted on the side. Nice little niche ya got there," Tony said reaching for a ladle just like one Claire had once seen Martha Stewart use for lobster bisque.

Claire looked around the tiny room. She zeroed in on the clipboard on the counter and effortlessly thought herself directly over it. More pleased each time by her newly discovered mode of transportation, she took a deep breath, focused and thought the clipboard to the floor with a clatter.

Tony jumped and stared down at it wide-eyed. He gave the body a wary look, slowly crouched down, and picked up the clipboard. He wore an expression of frustration as he set it on the counter and stared into the face. Then he smiled as he tenderly took the right hand in both of his.

"All right, what is it? You've got my attention. Tell me what I'm missing, Athena," he whispered.

Claire thought herself to the radio. She remembered Ahma had recommended a quick goodbye, 'keep it simple' she'd said... *but surely she'd want me to seize any opportunity to help my family.*

She focused her mind once again, into one of those concentrated beams of light, and the jazz faded into static.

Tony looked up at the radio, puzzled. He squinted and walked over to it, leaning in so close his nose practically touched the dial. He watched as it remained still along with the red needle, yet he could hear it skipping through stations and static until it stopped on a song loaded with meaning, if a guy was looking for it.

"I'll buy you a diamond ring, my friend, if it makes you feel all right," Paul McCartney sang.

"Ha-ha! I hear ya! Now *that's* what I'm talking about!" Tony shouted.

He ran around the table and grabbed the left hand. On the top it appeared normal, but when he lifted it up and examined the underside of her ring finger, he spotted the telltale marks.

There was an unmistakable groove accompanied by dry, flaky skin—the result of soap being trapped under a ring—a wedding ring.

He peered into the face and squeezed the hand, "You've worn a wedding ring for years. Somebody loved you and they deserve to know what happened to you. I won't let you down. Don't worry about Walter. We've got time on our side. I'll think of something, Athena," he whispered, excitedly.

Claire was so ecstatic she wrapped her arms around him and hugged him as hard as she could.

Tony gasped, ripping the mask from his face, his eyes darting around the room. He backed into the clipboard and knocked it off the counter. His breathing was shallow and rapid as he rubbed the center of his chest through his apron. "I need some air."

Claire watched him cross the room to the door and stop to rip off his apron, mask and gloves. He tossed everything into the large Hazmat container, whipped the door open, took one last quick look around and shut it behind him. Luckily, she was sure she'd also seen the beginning of a smile at the corner of his mouth.

There was a rustling sound behind her and Claire turned to see Ahma's tall purple flowers. *Do they do that on their own, or did she send for me?*

They swayed to and fro and parted, as if beckoning her from the corner of the little autopsy suite.

*Either way, I'm not going.* "Shoo! Go away!"

*I know I can help Paul and the girls, maybe even Mom and Collin. I've got to give them some answers... or at the very least, some peace.*

She turned her back on the flowers and crossed her arms. Out of the corner of her eye, she watched as the nagging blooms finally disappeared.

*I'd better make sure he's okay.*

Claire thought herself to the hall and noticed thinking herself from place to place seemed to be getting easier every time she tried it. She spotted Tony at a drinking fountain at the end of the corridor. She was about to think herself to him when she noticed a brilliant swath of blue light shining through a frosted glass door. Intrigued, Claire walked up to it and cracked the door open just enough to see a girl in a yellow tank top and jean shorts up on a ladder, reaching for a glass jar on a shelf.

"Well, get in here before the hummingbirds fly out," said the petite black teen with short pretty curls. She pulled the jar from the shelf, smiled and clutched it to her chest as she climbed down the ladder.

*She sees me!*

Claire slipped inside, looking around for any stray hummingbirds as she closed the door behind her. She thought the girl was close to Anna's age and instantly warmed to her.

"Hey, Newbie. I'm Wendy," the girl said as she set the jar on the counter. It gave off a bright lime green light and there was money inside, coins as well as bills.

"How did you know? I'm Claire," she said, extending her hand.

Wendy laughed as she took it in hers and gave it a firm shake. "You've got that frustrated, pissed-off at your Spirit Guide, confused-as-a-bumble-bee-shook-up-in-a-jar-look goin' on."

"Yeah, that's me," Claire said breathlessly as she walked the aisles, staring in awe at the hundreds of jars arranged on shelves all the way to the ceiling. "What is this place?"

"Shangri-la."

"No, really."

"Junk shop."

"It doesn't look like junk," Claire said, blinking.

Each jar gave off a different colored glow. Some had things moving around inside of them.

"I don't think it's junk either, but it depends on who you ask. Your Spirit Guide would tell you it's junk. Me? I say it's love."

"What do you mean?" Claire asked, reaching up and tapping a jar giving off an amber light. It contained five monarch butterflies. She instantly remembered how more than once, little blue butterflies had almost seemed to follow Em when she took her to the park to play.

"Look, you're here because you love your family and friends and you just want them to know you're okay. You're not hurting anyone. It's not like you're going to cause any trouble."

"Yes! Yes! Wendy, can you help me!?" Claire jumped up and down like a little girl.

"Like nobody else." Wendy placed her hands on her hips and a wide grin spread across her face.

"So these are like signs?"

"You know it, sister."

"I can send them to anyone I want, anytime?" Claire asked, barely able to believe her luck.

"Well, you can send them, but they don't always get them. Business is slow. People are really distracted these days with all their technology. Plus, some wouldn't know a sign if it bit 'em in the ass."

"Oh, right."

"Power surges are really popular now with every-body's faces glued to computers, but they still don't always get it. It helps if they're thinking about you right before you shoot 'em a sign."

"Oh sure, okay. How does the money in there work?" Claire asked pointing to the jar on the counter.

Wendy removed the glass lid and scooped out a

handful of coins. "The bills aren't as effective as the coins, but if you start leaving coins laying around everyday for someone, like everywhere they go... it's pretty tough for them to ignore it. And they're a fairly low-voltage sign, which means they don't take as much energy to manifest as say, butterflies or lightning."

"Lightning? Seriously?"

"Baby-steps, Claire."

"Right, gotcha."

"Now, the bills... people are usually so psyched to find money, they don't even care how it got there. Their mind's already spending it ten different ways and you're like, 'Hey, ya knucklehead, that was a high-voltage sign. I worked hard on that one.'" I mean, conditions aren't always optimal for sending signs. You've got a bit of electricity in you, but usually you'll have to pull it from another power source to send a decent sign that's going to get noticed.

"Oh. Well, what are some beginner signs you think I could do right away?"

"Take a look around. I've got rainbows, breezes, smoke detectors, ear buzzers..."

"Ear buzzers?"

"Yeah, you know when you get that eeeeee sound in one ear? That's a good one—hard to ignore."

"That's so true. Huh, I never knew that's what it was, though."

"Don't feel bad. Most people don't have a clue. You'll run into a few who actually look for signs, really keep their eyes peeled, but most are just too busy and preoccupied these days, not to mention jaded."

*Paul.* It was going to be nearly impossible to get his attention and then somehow convince him it was her. He'd never believed in any sort of afterlife. *He won't be looking for signs. He'll dismiss any he does see as coincidence.*

Claire thought of the girls and Collin instead. She felt giddy as she looked around, considering all the possibilities.

"Hey!" she said, pointing to a jar full of floating musical notes. "I think I just tried that one. I actually got a radio to pick up a song I was thinking about!"

"Awesome. Those can be really effective. Did it work?"

"Like a charm. He totally got it."

"See? You're a natural."

"So I just have to think about them? I don't have to come here to get them?"

"You got it. You just mentally pull the energy for them from light sockets, batteries, outlets, storms... power sources, basically." Wendy perched on a stool and swung her legs back and forth.

"What does it cost? I mean, I don't think I have any money or anything to offer you."

"Oh, I don't own them. I just collect them. People help me, too. When they find one that works really well, they usually tell me so I can stock it... the idea, that is. Think of my shop as a kind of traveling sign library. But instead of library books, you just borrow stuff with your mind. If you're ever stumped, just stop in and see me."

"Wendy, you're a saint. I'm so glad I found you."

"Actually, I found you. I look for souls like you with an awesome vibration—somebody who's not afraid to buck the system."

Claire grimaced and put her hands in her pockets. "I knew this was too good to be true."

"Aw, come on, Claire. Don't be chicken. It's like jaywalking. Everybody trolls a little now and then; sometimes it's just the smart thing to do. How incredible did it feel to see the look on that guy's face when he heard your song? Go on, take a look around. I've got perfumes, fireflies, shooting stars...."

Claire rubbed her arms, surprised she could still get goose bumps when she couldn't seem to feel heat or cold. The more she toyed with making contact with the living, the more heavy and solid her body felt—like climbing out of a pool after you'd been swimming all day. *If trolling was so bad, Nana never would have shown me how to do it.*

She walked the rows of jars, running her hands along the shelves, touching different signs and smiling at others as she made mental notes. A royal-blue glow caught her eye on a low shelf. Claire knelt down when she reached it. There was a can of WD-40 inside. *No wonder I smelled it at the bank all the time. I thought Maintenance was greasing everything in the place.*

She stopped in front of a jar full of cereal, tapped the glass and frowned at Wendy.

"Froot Loops," Wendy answered. When Claire's expression didn't change, Wendy added, "Psychics. Nobody seems to notice most of them have an excellent sense of humor. It was their idea, not mine."

The aisles grew darker as she neared the very back of the shop where older-looking jars gave off a murky glow in drab shades of brown, blue and gray. Claire pointed to the jars. "What are those?" she called out to Wendy who was back up on her ladder.

"Dark stuff," Wendy answered offhandedly, avoiding Claire's gaze.

"I can see that. What *are* they?"

Wendy lowered her head for a moment as if debating whether or not to tell her, and began backing down the ladder. She suddenly appeared at Claire's side.

Startled, Claire jumped and shook her head. "Sorry, still getting used to that."

Wendy smiled but then her expression turned

somber. "They can be useful; but you don't really need them. They're a little dangerous if you don't know what you're doing, and they can be habit-forming. You'll change... get kind of sick and confused."

Claire eyed the jars and took a step back. "If they're signs, how bad can they be?"

"Bad. Trust me. This dark blue one is Guilt. The muddy brown one is Pain. That black one, the darkest one, is Fear," Wendy explained with a hint of sadness in her voice.

Claire didn't want to pry, but she could tell Wendy had firsthand experience with these signs. They were intriguing nonetheless. Claire couldn't seem to pull herself away. The blue one Wendy had referred to as Guilt was crammed full of old black-and-white photos of miserable-looking children.

She could feel Wendy tugging on her hand the same way Em did at the grocery store whenever Claire lingered in the magazine aisle too long, but she had to get a closer look.

As Claire bent down and peered into the brown one Wendy had said was Pain, she discovered there were little things moving around inside. When she leaned in closer, she realized it was crawling with thousands of hornets.

Claire glanced at Wendy, who was looking impatiently at the floor and still tugging on her hand. She couldn't resist. She had to get a better look at the last jar.

Upon closer inspection, for a jar on a shelf, Fear had an impossible depth to it. The bizarre little black hole made Claire uncomfortable just looking at it. She began to back away. "Why would anyone—"

"Plenty of reasons, but it's a slippery slope into haunting and you don't wanna go there. It's too hard to find your way back. Come on. You like paper clips? I've got a whole section full of office supplies," Wendy said, as she pulled Claire out of the dark.

"I never saw the hummingbirds," Claire protested, knowing full well she hadn't seen every jar in the shop.

"They're just thoughts of hummingbirds and they're always around if you look hard enough—Contentment. Hurry up," she said brusquely, yanking on Claire's arm.

"On second thought, we'll save the office supplies for another day. There's a bunch of flowers outside and they're getting a little obnoxious. They'd love nothing more than to get in here and knock all my jars off their shelves. Git!" she shouted at them, as she opened the front door just enough for Claire to squeeze through.

The door slammed shut and Wendy waved goodbye apologetically through the frosted glass before it morphed into a janitor's closet.

# CHAPTER 7

CLAIRE PEEKED out of the flowers into an enormous meadow lit by tiny royal-blue wildflowers. She spotted Ahma beneath an ancient Oak, covered in something white.

*Snow?*

Ahma's intimidating voice filled Claire's head before she'd even emerged from the flowers. "Dear child, what have you been into? Your vibration is as heavy as marble. You cannot meet, let alone, communicate with your Collective in this state," Ahma scolded her.

Claire shuffled through the grass toward the tree. When she'd almost reached her, she blinked as clouds of little white butterflies flew out of Ahma's chest and she began doing some form of Tai Chi. Bright streams of pink light trailed from her fingertips like the afterglow of sparklers. The two of them stood beneath the tree in silence for what could have been several minutes or several days. Claire never knew, anymore.

Guilt finally got the best of her. "Tony needed help. I just gave him a hint and he got it."

"I'm sure he did, but he might have found it on his own had you exercised some self-control. Now we'll never know. That's his path you're manipulating. It's nothing to trifle with. You've altered his course."

The bright pink light trailing from Ahma's fingertips turned dark purple with her lecture, and was well on its way to a smoldering gray. Claire glowered and sat down in the grass. Shame turned to anger. Ahma wouldn't even *look* at her—an awfully passive-aggressive course for someone so enlightened.

"He was just so close. I need my friends and family to know what happened to me. I can help Tony piece it all together, get him to figure out who I am and contact them."

"Who you *were*, Claire."

"No Ahma, who I *am*. I'm still their mother. I'm still a wife, a friend and daughter."

Ahma sighed, dropped her hands to her sides and turned to Claire. "In the beginning, it is a form of comfort, but one can become quite ill hovering over loved ones, and before you know it, you're trying to control everyone and everything and completely obsessed with the past. You're haunting all the inhabitants of your former life."

*Inhabitants!? The people I love, the people who love me? My children, for God's sake!*

"Calm yourself, it was a poor choice of words. Even I am allowed a transgression now and then, but it is imperative that you understand. It only complicates their paths and slows your evolution, as well as theirs." Her voice was calm despite the darkening of the entire meadow.

"But I *am* helping them," Claire insisted. She got to her feet and folded her arms. Her jeans and T-shirt felt comfortingly real again. She nervously wound her big toe around a clump of grass and felt like a child for protesting, but it was the truth. She was not going to settle for being a memory, when she could still bring them some peace. She had to try, and she was willing to fight anyone now. Even Ahma.

"Back to the farm with you then."

With a wave of Ahma's hand, Claire was swept backward, and found herself standing in Nana's front yard. "Nice, Ahma! Am I grounded or what!?" Claire shouted. She raked her fingers through her hair, and wandered inside the old barn. The air felt cool as Claire climbed the ladder into the hayloft. A blanket lay on some bales of hay. She sprawled out on it, her thoughts gravitating to Paul. He would've seen her point. She missed talking to him about everything. She missed his touch and his laugh. She missed spooning with him, watching old movies in bed. Claire closed her eyes, and imagined herself spooned snuggly against his body.

———

"I know, Lynn," she heard Paul whisper.

He had the phone sandwiched between his face and the pillow, shivering as he pulled the covers up under his chin. "They're going to say all kinds of rotten things about her, but you and I know she would never do anything like that. We're talking about a woman who always put everything right back where she found it in the store—always put her cart away, said it was good Karma. They'll find her soon, and this whole nightmare will be over. I still say she might have had some sort of breakdown after Julia disappeared with all that money. They were close. Her office was right next to Claire's cubicle."

He paused, allowing Lynn to rant and sob, then continued when she stopped to catch her breath. "I know. I didn't care for her either, but she made Claire laugh and seemed like a good friend sometimes. Honestly? I don't know what they had in common. I think she must have served as entertainment more than anything."

Paul paused again, his eyes closed. "Come on, Lynn. You and I both know she had *nothing* to do with the embezzlement. We've got to hang in there and keep our heads on straight. I've got all kinds of contacts through the hospital. We're making hundreds of calls every day. I just know we'll find her recuperating somewhere. In the meantime, we have to stay sane for each other and for the girls. You've got to. Go easy on the sugar. You're making it harder on yourself being so emotionally up and down like this," he pleaded.

"Don't go there, Paul. I wouldn't wish this on anyone, ever," Lynn warned.

Claire felt weak for the first time since she'd left the earth plane, but it was more than that. She could feel them draining her energy with their hopelessness. She could still hear her mother sobbing on the other end of the line, and she thought her heart would break, but she couldn't think herself to her. *Not now. It's just too much to deal with.* She couldn't even bear to stay with Paul much longer. *One at a time. I need someone open, more hopeful.*

Paul hung up the phone, and Claire pulled herself up close to him again and held his face in her hand. The more she clung to him, the harder he cried and the weaker she felt. He shook with great heaving sobs until she couldn't take it, anymore. He wanted her mother to believe she was alive, to not give up hope of ever seeing her again, because *he* already had. *He's lost all hope.* She'd never seen him like this. It frightened her. She placed her hand over his heart in one last attempt to calm him.

Paul cried out.

Claire tore herself from him in anguish. *It's pointless. I can't reach him.* She had to find someone who *could* get through to him. There was only one other person Paul had always listened to, even when they disagreed—Gus.

Unfortunately, Paul's father, Gus, had slipped deeply into the clutches of Alzheimer's years ago. Claire thought of Gus's birthday party a few months earlier, how he had shrieked and clapped his hands like a little boy when they'd brought out the gifts and a chocolate cake loaded with candles. That had been one of his *good* days.

Gus had lived in a nursing home for several years; his wife, Lily, passed from pneumonia shortly after his diagnosis. He'd declined rapidly. Gus no longer knew Em or Anna or any of his friends, but he did still recognize Paul and Claire sometimes.

Claire was surprised by how easily she thought herself to Gus's bedside, through her memories of the party. He lay on his back, eyes open, staring at the ceiling. He was singing Moon River, but the same line over and over, like a skip in a record.

Claire sat and listened to him until his fifth time through. Then she telepathically interrupted. "Hi, Gus."

He stopped singing, then started up again.

Claire tried again, this time shouting the thought, "Hi, Gus!"

He paused and whispered, "Lily, darling?"

*Shit. Way to go.* She didn't want to make him more miserable, but she needed his help. *Maybe I can help Gus too, in ways I couldn't before.*

"No, that's Claire, silly," said a voice.

Claire whipped around to see her mother-in-law sitting in a rocking chair.

"We used to dance to Moon River all the time. It's my favorite."

"Lily!" Claire shrieked, reaching out to her.

Lily joined her on the bed and gave her a long hug.

"You sure are a sight for sore eyes! Did you see my little blue butterflies following Em in the park?" Lily asked excitedly.

"I did! That was you? Thank you!"

Gus moaned a response.

"I feel so bad for him," Claire said, looking at him.

"You needn't, dear. We'll be together again. I keep him company every day. He gets confused, but you can usually get a message through to comfort him when he becomes frightened. Of course, most of the nurses here think he's completely out to lunch

"I'm sorry. That can't be easy," Claire said, squeezing her hand. "How often does Paul come to see him now?"

"Such a good boy. Even with all of the stress he's under— worrying about you and taking care of the girls by himself—he still manages to see Gus every Wednesday around three o'clock."

"You really think I can get through to Paul?" Claire asked.

"It's worth a try, dear, but he's not a believer."

Claire knew she was right. Paul had never had any interest in the metaphysical. He had a great imagination unless it came to heaven or any kind of afterlife. He simply couldn't fathom it. She'd always attributed it to his being around too many surgeries. "You're here, and then you're not," he'd always say. He wouldn't even sit through a movie that hinted at such things, claiming it was wrong to play with people's emotions. Still, Claire knew she had to try.

"Would you meet me here at two o'clock every Wednesday and help me work with Gus, so I can try to reach Paul when he gets here?"

"I'm always here. You can count me in," Lily said with a grin.

Gus offered an impromptu recitation of *The Pledge of Alle-*

*giance.* When he reached "With liberty and justice for all" he added, "You're here and then you're *there.*"

Claire laughed and leaned down to kiss him goodbye. "I knew you were in there, Gus. I'm putting my faith in you. Together, I know we can do this. I'll be back tomorrow to give it a shot," she said, straightening the collar on his pajama shirt.

Suddenly, she felt a maternal tug in her chest, like when a toddler's been quiet for far too long. *Anna.*

Anna sat on her right hand at the end of her parents' bed, her stare cold and vacant as she twisted a lock of her hair.

Claire's heart nearly bled at the sight. *That poor hand's going to end up flat as a pancake for all the eyelashes it's plucked.*
Shocked by her appearance, Claire put her arms around her. "You look so tired, so different. You've stopped straightening your hair, and no more eyeliner by Crayola?" Claire spoke to her with ease, more freely than she had in months.

"Your eyes have always been so beautiful even with your sparse little lashes. And I always loved it when you let your hair go curly, even though you hated it. What's with the sweat pants and dirty T-shirt, Banana? Even when you aren't going anywhere, you make sure you're in full goth with stick-straight hair. It's like, your uniform. You look like you haven't slept in a week." Claire stroked her daughter's hair. Then she grasped Anna's hand and suddenly choked. The intensity of Anna's pain seemed to be concentrated in her hands and caught Claire by surprise. Heavy and bitter like soured milk, such a different sensation from when she'd touched Paul.

"Anna, I'm here. Can't you feel me?"

———

Anna heard a single tick in the air, but ignored it as the waning afternoon sun streamed through her parents' bedroom window. It shone through a rainbow sun-catcher, a Mother's Day gift. Ribbons of red, orange and yellow washed over her shoulder and across her cheek. Mesmerized by her image reflected in the large mirror on her parents' dresser, she touched the colors on her face.

*It's almost December. It's been a whole month. How does someone just vanish? Impossible. If Mom's alive and free, I never really knew her. I thought she was completely tied to us, heart and soul. She'd call if there was any way possible.*

"Then she's gone-gone?" Anna whispered to her reflection in the mirror. "Not *my* mom. *My* mom was smart, strong. How could *anyone* take her anywhere? Are they coming back for us? I don't care if they take me, as long as I can see her again. I've got to find that purse or I'm gonna lose my shit."

Anna was exhausted from tossing and turning all night, haunted by purse dreams. She'd dreamt about the brown leather purse almost every night since her mom had vanished. Sometimes, she dreamt it was sitting on the stairs. Her mom would simply walk out of the kitchen, as if she'd been home the entire time, like it had all been a colossal misunderstanding.

She loved seeing her mom in her dreams. The hellish downside was that each time she awoke she lost her all over again.

Anna approached the large mirror, and studied her eyes. She had her mom's eyes. Everyone had always said so. She frowned as a bit of her mom seemed to stare eerily out of her own reflection.

Anna placed her hands on the dresser, leaned in close to the glass and whispered, "Mom? Can you hear me? Where are you? Are you here?"

"Yes, I'm here! I'm here!" Claire grasped Anna's shoulders.

"Aaahhh!" Anna screamed, and jumped away from the dresser. "Dad! You scared the crap out of me!"

Just as startled, Paul slapped his hand against his chest. "Sorry! I was looking for Shadow." Paul reached for her. He wanted to hug her, but she backed away from him shaking and rubbing her arms.

"I think I'm going crazy. I'm like, not okay. I didn't even hear you come in," Anna warned.

"I should've said something. What do you mean you're not okay?"

"I can't stand this. I have to know everything. If you know more than I do, you have to tell me, right now. I mean it—everything," Anna demanded, her fists now clenched and trembling at her sides.

"We're falling apart here, aren't we, kiddo? Come here," he said, sitting down and patting the edge of the bed.

Anna walked past him to the head of the bed and yanked her mother's pillow out from under the comforter. She sat down next to him, hugging the pillow as she buried her face in it.

Paul put his arm around her, pulled her close to him and sighed as regret coursed through his veins. He'd been selfish with Claire's pillow, and now he wanted nothing more than a few gulps of her scent to be left for Anna, despite all the nights he'd fallen asleep clutching it. Claire's lavender bath soap had never been more of a comfort to him, and inhaling it directly from the bottle hadn't brought the same relief.

"She's still here," Anna said, lifting her face from the pillow, "Some little part of her, and as good as it feels to close my eyes and pretend she's standing right here, it still pisses me off."

"I know."

"We're just blowing in the wind. We don't know *anything*."

"Not much," Paul admitted.

"I can't take it anymore."

Paul squeezed her shoulder. "We all have questions, Ann. Tell me yours," he said, noticing for the first time that she seemed to have aged five years in the past month. The girl she'd been had disappeared along with Claire.

The funny thing was Em seemed to be okay. Em was holding her own. She never cried; just played with her dolls, went to school and swimming lessons and sat with Shadow in front of the television watching Little Mermaid Movies. She said she missed her mother on occasion, usually when Paul tucked her in for bed or laid out her clothes for school, but she never said those exact words. Instead, she'd say, "I wish Mommy was here, right now."

To which Paul would always respond, "Me too, honey." Clearly, Em was managing her marbles just fine. Better than anyone else.

"Where's her purse, Dad? You know she never went anywhere without it. I couldn't ask you before. I was too afraid, but I have to know. Just tell me," Anna pleaded.

Paul heard a whimper escape her lips, as he covered his face with his hands. He was about to pull his own daughter down into his bottomless pit. It felt so wrong, but it was too late. They were already tumbling down, down, down.

Only he and the detective had known about the purse. To the police, it was simply evidence. To him, it was the enormous stone tied to his ankle, dragging him down to the very bottom of his life.

"No," he heard Anna cry as she tugged on his sleeve. "Please, Dad. No!" she begged. "It's with her. It *has* to be."

He dropped his hands from his face and wiped his nose on his cuff. "I know," he answered, choking back tears and shaking his head.

Anna reasoned, "If someone took her from us, she would have died trying to reach us, and if that's not what happened, it's because she never had a chance. Nothing else makes sense. If Mom wandered off because she was sick or something, someone would have found her by now—the police, the neighbors —*someone*."

"You know your mother," Paul agreed, as he gathered his courage and looked into his daughter's eyes. For a moment, he caught a glimpse of Claire in her furrowed brow. It was the old 'You don't need a new lawn mower. There's nothing wrong with the old one' look.

Paul smiled and put his arm around her.

Claire sat at their feet, crying uncontrollably, her arms wrapped around her knees, as she rocked back and forth.

Anna's hand trembled as she handed Claire's pillow to him.

Paul lifted it to his face and inhaled, then set it down on the bed.

"The police have her purse."

"No," Anna argued.

"I'm sorry, honey. I found it in the Volkswagen. Everything was spilled out on the floor mats. I don't know what happened, but it wasn't like your mother to leave it all lying there like that."

*What the hell was I thinking!? If I had just taken the damn thing with me, I would've had my I.D. when they found me.*

"So when do we stop pretending?" Anna asked, her tone shifting from desperation back to anger.

"I don't know. There's no rule book. I guess I've been waiting for someone to tell me what comes next," Paul confessed. "The police are used to dealing with things like this, so I just follow their lead and wait for them to tell me the next step. That detective Robles doesn't seem to be able to come up with anything at all. She's relentless with her questions, but she almost seems embarrassed every time she calls or stops by for more. The purse is all we've got—no fingerprints, no witnesses, and your mom never showed up at the bank. Just vanished," he said, wiping his nose on his sleeve again.

Anna placed her hand on his back. "Let's take the next step. Let's do it on our own. I don't want to be told when to accept my own mom's gone. No one should be allowed to tell us that. We should have a memorial or something."

"Maybe." Paul took one more whiff of Claire's pillow, stood up and tucked it back under the comforter. He gave it a pat and smoothed the covers over it, knowing he couldn't even begin to think about a memorial.

"Makes me sick, you having to grow up so fast like this."

"I'm okay. I'd rather grow up too fast than be kept in the dark. Promise me you'll tell me everything they tell you," Anna insisted.

"I don't know, honey..." his voice trailed off.

"I'm serious, Dad. Even if they find...."

Paul walked across the room to the window and stared out into the street.

Claire followed him.

The neighbor kids were having a snowball fight, had no idea that the world within the Cummings' house had come to a screeching halt.

"All right. There's something else," he admitted, turning to her and folding his arms across his chest.

"What?" Anna asked as she joined him at the window.

The two of them turned and stared out onto the street, as if it would somehow make it easier.

"Dad?" Anna finally whispered.

Paul sighed. "You know they impounded the Volkswagen as evidence, and the battery was dead when they went to tow it. They thought she might have walked somewhere. They brought these dogs over, tracked her scent all the way to the train station, right down to the platform."

"Someone had to have seen her," she gasped.

"I know. They've posted fliers down there—still, nothing. Detective Robles said there were dozens of leads on women in suits with dark hair, but every one turned out to be someone else they were able to track down and identify. Plus, she said ten times as many people took the train that day because of the plane crash. The Kennedy was closed half the day."

"Shit," Anna whispered.

"Shit!" Claire echoed.

"The dogs weren't able to pick up her scent again on any of the rail cars. Detective Robles did say they might be able to pick it up again on land once the snow melts, but the odds are slim."

"This is nuts. Maybe she just snapped, or she hit her head and has amnesia or something. Maybe she was abducted by aliens."

"Your mom would never go to Mars without her purse."

"True," Anna smiled through her pain.

Claire pounded her fist against her leg. *There's got to be something I can do to help them.*

Struggling to remember some of the most intriguing jars in Wendy's shop, Claire jumped when she felt a tap on her shoulder. Before she could think, someone grabbed her and spun her around.

## CHAPTER 8

"NANA!"

"Hurry up! Let them know you're here. It's going take more energy now, but you can do it."

"You mean like, focus harder?"

"Not exactly, but that'll help. You need to siphon some extra energy to reach them, now. You were loaded with it when you first got here, but as your vibration changes, you're going to need more energy to connect with them. Everything is thicker, heavier and slower on the earth plane, kind of like running through mud. Pulling extra energy from things is like putting on monster truck tires—gives you more traction, more power."

"That's kind of what Wendy said. You know her, don't you?"

"You betcha—lots of spunk and cute as the dickens."

"I remember she said I could pull electricity from things, but how?"

"There's a light on in the bathroom across the hall. Pull some from the bulb. It's an easy one for beginners, but I still do it all the time."

Not having the first clue how to begin such a bizarre task, Claire gave Nana a worried look.

"Just pull the energy out of it any way you want. Use your instincts. Quit thinking so much and just try it," Nana advised, pointing her toward the bathroom.

Hesitant to play with electricity, Claire closed her eyes, held out her hands and took a deep breath. Finally she thought, *PUUULLLLLL!* The second she felt the pleasant tingle surge through her fingers all the way to her toes, she opened her eyes. She could actually see the electricity shooting across the room, her fingertips acting like lightning rods. Claire's entire body tingled, like a limb falling asleep—*Ironic, since I've definitely never been more awake!*

She turned and exhaled, enveloping Paul and Anna in a cloud of her lavender soap. She sprinkled it through their hair and into the creases of their clothing. She spun it around them like cotton candy, encircling them in a cool cocoon of her essence.

⊂⊐

Anna shivered and stared at her dad as the unmistakable scent of her mom's lavender bath soap filled her nostrils. She glanced around the room, but saw nothing unusual, except her dad shaking.

Their eyes met briefly. They both glanced toward the bed where her mom's pillow remained tucked beneath the comforter. Her dad turned to face her, took her by the hand and looked helplessly into her eyes. Something was happening, but she couldn't make sense of it, and from the confused look on his face, neither could he. She kept expecting him to say something —anything.

A loud pop came from the bathroom, which was dark by the time they turned to see what it was.

"What's going on?" Anna whispered as she latched onto her dad's arm, and craned her neck to try to see into the bathroom, unable to move.

"I think the bathroom light burned out," Paul mumbled.

⌑

"It's me! It's me!" Claire shouted, waving her arms between hugging and kissing them.

"Nice work, but they can't hear you very well. Sometimes they can, but your vibration is so much higher and faster that it'll just sound like a hum or a ring in their ear until you really holler at them. You've got their attention, though. So, go for it," Nana coached from over Claire's shoulder.

Claire shouted into Paul's ear, "Paul! Get the ring! The ring! Show her the ring!"

Nana joined in. "The ring! The ring!"

"Ring?" Paul finally muttered to himself.

"Yes! Oh my God! Yes!" Claire shouted.

"Dad?"

Claire knew the moment it clicked in his mind by the look on his face.

"Your mother bought you a ring for your birthday. I mean, it was going to be from both of us, but I forgot all about it. Your birthday's still a couple weeks away, but you want to open it now?"

"Oh my God. Yes!" Anna cried.

Positively giddy, Claire watched him walk over to her nightstand and open the top drawer.

Paul reached way in the back, dug around and pulled out a pink velvet box. He sat down on the bed and motioned for Anna to join him.

Tears spilled down Claire's cheeks when Anna took the box in her hand. She sat down next to her father and slowly opened it.

"Whoa, *real* jewelry," she whispered, slipping the ring on her pinky finger.

Paul sniffled and smiled.

Claire knelt at their feet clapping. She felt Nana crouch down next to her and pat her on the back.

"Look! I did it! She's wearing it!" Claire cried.

The ring was a dainty gold band with a pearl in the middle and a tiny diamond on either side of it. Claire had been to five different stores before she'd found exactly what she'd wanted.

"Yeah, real jewelry. You're not a kid anymore," Paul whispered.

Anna leaned over and hugged him. "Thanks, Dad," she said, holding her hand out to admire the ring. "Thanks, Mom," she whispered and looked up toward the ceiling.

Claire smiled, but the bitter sweetness hit her hard. "Great, she finally wants to talk and now we can't."

"There are lots of ways you can still communicate. Don't worry," Nana reassured her.

Claire looked up as Anna turned to say something to Paul, but he was already headed for the door.

"It's late. I've got to get over to see Grandpa. Can you watch Em?"

"Sure," Anna said cheerfully, but Claire knew that look.

Anna's face had dropped. She looked like she'd just missed the most important train of her life, as the entire experience shrank into the distance. She could tell Anna needed Paul to somehow acknowledge what had just happened, but he wasn't ready. He had literally run from the idea.

Claire watched her daughter intently as Anna stared at the ring on her finger. She flipped the box open and closed, open and closed. Anna held solid links to her, and nothing could change that.

"If I can just keep doing things like this, giving her tangible signs, eventually she'll understand that I'm okay, right?" Claire asked Nana.

"With a little luck," Nana answered, but Claire detected a hesitation.

"Are you sure this is okay? I'm not uh... ticking off anyone or anything, am I?" She stood up to straighten her favorite black-and-white family photo on the wall, the one where Em had cut her bangs down to the scalp. Claire cringed in anticipation of Nana's answer since she had no intention of stopping anyway. Still high from making direct contact and not wanting anyone to rain on her parade, Claire thought herself to Em's dollhouse, before Nana could reply. She'd been stopping by the dollhouse everyday since Nana had first taken her to Em's room. She'd hoped to find Em there, but the room was empty.

Nana laughed and shot her a wink when she caught up with her, like it was a game of tag.

Claire felt her watchful eyes as she knelt down in front of the dollhouse, reached inside and pulled out a tiny ceramic teapot with a hand-painted blue windmill on it. It was one of the few remaining pieces of a set Nana had given Claire for her sixth birthday.

"Tea party?" Nana wore a smile, but she had a mischievous look in her eye. It was clearly a loaded question.

Before Claire had a chance to answer, Nana took her by the

hand. The room went dark. Suddenly, the two of them were seated at the breakfast nook inside the old dollhouse.

Claire's heart raced. She couldn't speak or breathe. She grabbed the edge of the blue plastic table with both hands. It felt strange and flimsy, but at least it was something to hold onto.

"Have some chamomile. It'll help you relax." Nana winked as she poured steaming tea from the same pot Claire had just been holding between her thumb and forefinger. Now it was ridiculously over-sized, as were the teacups. They looked like mixing bowls.

Claire laughed nervously, "Slow down, Nana. I have no desire to meet any dolls today, got it?"

"They're as plastic as this table, Claire."

Claire watched her closely as Nana took a seat across from her, and shrunk her teacup down to a more manageable size simply by rubbing it. She nonchalantly sipped tea from it as Claire's cup began to shrink, too.

"Say when," Nana told her.

"When." Claire smiled weakly, nauseous but thankful the tea had shrunk right along with the cup. She tentatively raised it to her lips, blowing on it out of habit, when she noticed a yellow marshmallow Peep jammed behind the refrigerator. Claire laughed so hard she had to set her cup down to keep from spilling it. She'd thrown that Peep in the wastebasket twice, telling Em she couldn't keep it in there, that it would attract bugs. The last thing they needed was a roach-infested doll-house... especially from her new perspective.

"We've got company," Claire said, pointing to the Peep.

"He's never bothered me," Nana giggled.

"This—this is too weird," Claire stammered.

"Went too far, did I?"

"By about a mile," Claire replied. "Not Mt. Everest, not Paris, but the dollhouse."

"Oh, goodness, those places are too far. I've got chores—"

"Only because you want them," Claire cut her off.

"Sorry, I thought this would be fun. I just wanted to remind you that the possibilities are endless."

"Got it—loud and clear—all I want to do right now is see Paul and the girls... Collin, too."

It was uncomfortably dark inside the dollhouse since the windows were merely decals like the yellowing wallpaper, which also sported giant pieces of Scotch tape in a few places, tape Claire herself, had placed there when she was little. This simple fact now boggled her mind if she thought too hard about it.

Claire wished one of Em's little battery-powered lights were in the room, but she wasn't about to go searching for them. Instead, she continued to grumpily sip her tea.

"I really thought you'd like it here. You and this dollhouse go way back. For Pete's sake, you've played with it a million times."

"Not like this, I didn't. This has been... well, interesting I guess, but seriously, I'd like to go, now," Claire said, standing up. She flinched as something caught in her hair. When she looked up at the ceiling she discovered it was covered in neon smiley face stickers, but she rubbed her arms nervously, as if it had been a bat.

"You asked me if you were pissing off God," Nana reminded her.

"Something like that."

"He isn't the white-bearded judge in the sky we make him out to be."

"What a relief. Can we go now?" Claire muttered, walking to the edge of the kitchen and staring in wonder at the enormity of Em's room. It was unnerving at best.

"We feel him here all the time."

"In the dollhouse?" Claire responded dryly without turning to face her.

"Sheesh, you're about as pleasant as a rattlesnake with piles."

Claire didn't respond.

"Anyway, here, you'll finally start to get that he's actually something so amazing we don't even possess the words to describe him. You can't fully understand him until you grow and let go enough to join him in that egoless plane."

"Back up," Claire said, turning on her heel. "Did you just say I'll finally start to understand that I can't understand him?"

"Guess I did. Sorry, I just don't want you to be afraid of it, because it's the last thing it wants. What it *does* want is to flow through you. It's kind of like when you learned to do the back float down in the creek. It got a lot easier once you stopped struggling to float and just relaxed, but *you* were always more interested in chasing frogs, come to think of it."

Claire shook her head. "Stop making it sound so easy."

"It's true. You had to have faith that the water would support you, but first you had to have an interest in being supported."

Claire was in no mood for philosophy. She wondered what the other rooms in the dollhouse looked like up close, but didn't want to encourage Nana to take her on any more freaky field trips for a while. She just wanted to be with her family.

"The word 'he' isn't even close. I'm sure you've figured that out. That's just something we stick to him on the earth plane to try to make sense of it. Do you want a glimpse?"

Claire frowned and shook her head. "I wouldn't have a clue what to do or say."

"Well it's not a cheerleading tryout. You don't have to dazzle. It *knows* you. Every soul is connected to it in the same way—nobody is closer or farther. Doesn't matter what your beliefs were in that life or any of them. Only the soul can create distance between itself and what you call *God*... and almost every one of us does, at one time or another. Then we just have to learn how to bridge the distance and find our way home again. There are lots of different ways."

Nana propped her feet up on the chair across from her and poured herself another cup of tea. A bowl of sugar cubes appeared on the table. Nana picked up three, dropped two in her tea and popped the last one in her mouth.

"So what about past lives?" Claire ventured, folding her arms, almost afraid to ask.

"What about 'em?"

"Well, Ahma says I'm not ready to meet my Collective. That my vibration is all screwed-up. Honestly, I'm more interested in other things right now, but I do wonder about my past lives. I mean, you always hear about people thinking they were Cleopatra or Napoleon, but the reason I never once went to a psychic was because I was afraid they'd say something like, 'You? You fed the chickens.'"

Nana sprayed a mouthful of tea across the table in a fit of laughter.

Claire couldn't contain her own, as she looked around for a towel. She was about to try to manifest a dish rag, when Nana cleaned up the mess with a wave of her hand.

When their laughter had finally subsided, Nana resumed her tutorial. "Somebody had to feed the chickens, right? Chicken farmers have life lessons too, but I know what you're saying. We all fed the proverbial chickens at some point. There are quieter, resting lives, less eventful than others."

"Why?"

"People usually live a life like that after one spent in a whole lot of turmoil."

"Why doesn't everyone just stay here and learn their lessons?"

"Because the lessons you learn on the earth plane are so much more intense—painful and joyful to beat the band. They propel you further in your destiny over a shorter period of time —a speedboat instead of a rowboat. But you always have the option of remaining here to study, as long as you like."

Claire considered this as she walked back toward the table and stopped.

"What's the matter, hon?"

"Why don't you ever call it heaven? We *are* in heaven, right?"

"Well, as long as we're on the subject of chickens... the word 'heaven' is like saying 'chicken parts'—stirs up too many questions. Chicken parts gets people thinking beaks and gizzards and turning green. You say 'heaven' and you get people thinking pearly gates and streets paved in gold or whatever they were brought up on. It all gets in the way of the truth," Nana explained.

Claire gave her a pained expression and rubbed her sternum.

"What's the matter now?"

"It's that pulling sensation again. It's like someone's calling me, but instead of hearing it, I feel it."

"You mean like, oh, I don't know... say if someone were rubbing the heck out of a necklace with some of your ashes in it?"

Claire rolled her eyes. "Is it okay to answer it? Last time it was Anna, but it feels like Paul this time. I can't even tell you why. It just does."

"Of course, hon. Go ahead and answer it. Just don't stay too long. Make short visits at first, or things can get messy."

"Messy how?"

"Just good an' messy. Now, skedaddle."

———

Claire snuggled up next to Paul in his Honda as he pulled into the driveway of The Elms Nursing Home. He was clearly depressed, but she had to assume she didn't feel drained like before, because he was focused on Gus instead of her.

Paul killed the engine and rested his head against the back of the seat.

*Gearing up.* Claire had seen him do it in this parking lot too many times. He'd say, "That's not him—just a guy I look after now—make sure he's got everything he needs." It was a ritual, Paul's gearing up. Next he'd say, "I said my goodbyes that day I found him in the garage. He'd been out there all night—found him crying in the corner by the circular saw. He had grape popsicles from the old freezer all over his face. Couldn't remember how to get out of the garage. Jesus, how many engines did he rebuild in there?"

They both knew the story inside and out, but Claire suspected it was his conscience that made him repeat it every time. She waited for the recitation, but Paul remained silent.

Claire whispered, "I know," and touched his cheek with the back of her hand.

Paul dropped his head and fiddled with his wedding ring.

*Coincidence?*

"This is too much for one person." Claire spoke sternly into the air, hoping the words might reach someone in a position of power somewhere. "What has he done to deserve all of this?"

There was no response, not even Nana appeared, although Claire knew in her heart, she would have, had she persisted.

Finally, Paul wiped his eyes with his sleeve. "Get out," he

said to himself, "Get out of the damn car." His hand rested on the keys in the ignition for another minute. Finally he got out and grabbed a shopping bag from the passenger's seat, which contained several pairs of pajamas. When he closed the car door it didn't latch. He had to lean against it and bump it with his hip while he pressed his free hand against the door.

"Damn it to hell," he cursed. He beat the door with the shopping bag until he was holding nothing but the paper handles. "Nice."

He bent down, gathered up the pajamas and folded the bag around them, then dragged himself up to the double doors.

"This has got to work or he's going to come apart at the seams," Claire cried as she tore herself away from Paul and thought herself to Gus's side.

"First and foremost, he needs to know you're still in there, Gus," she instructed her father-in-law, patting his arm and turning his face toward hers by his chin.

Gus was strapped into a chair by the window with pillows propped up around him. His hair was damp and neatly combed.

Claire felt hope bubble up inside her as she watched Gus frown and touch his chin right where her thumb and finger rested.

She took a deep breath as she sensed Paul round the corner.

He paused in the doorway.

Anxious to get busy, Claire didn't realize what he was doing. Then she remembered.

He had once confessed that from the doorway, before he saw his father's eyes, he could pretend everything was fine for a minute or so. He could tell himself they were in Trinity Lutheran instead of a nursing home and Gus was just recovering from minor surgery. He'd imagine they were going to talk about lawnmowers, politics and Gus's jackass neighbor Bernie, spraying pesticides. He'd said as long as he stared at the back of his father's head everything was still okay, but once he caught sight of those vacant eyes, it all went to hell.

It was kind of a cruel game to play with one's self, but she wasn't about to rob him of this, if it helped him cope or eased his pain in the slightest way.

A pencil-thin young nurse in a Scooby-Doo smock, breezed past Paul and chirped, "We're all crisp and clean for you today Mr. Cummings."

"Super", Paul mumbled under his breath.

Claire thought she saw him mouth the words "Go away", but he quickly followed it up with an audible, "He looks nice. Thanks. We really appreciate all of you taking such great care of him. Here, I brought him some more pajamas." He held out the remains of the tattered bag.

"Oh, he has plenty of PJs. No worries, though. I'll just put them in the closet," she said, taking what was left of the bag and tossing it in a tall cupboard. "Buzz me if you need anything," she added and closed the door behind her.

Claire gave Gus's arm a squeeze as Paul wandered over to an empty chair next to him and collapsed into it.

"Hey Dad, it's me... Paul," he said, taking Gus's hand for a moment, then setting it down in his father's lap. "You look good —clean shave."

Gus's gaze remained fixed on the pond beyond the courtyard.

Claire grimaced and paced.

Paul sighed as he leaned back in his chair and stared at the same awful thing he always ended up staring at—the clock above the door.

"Come on Gus, I know you can do this," Claire pleaded. "Just tell him I said hi, or something." She repeated the words like a mantra, "Tell him I said hi. You can do it. Tell him I said hi." She even tried pulling energy directly from the wall socket, but she couldn't decide what to do with it. She let it go and watched it swirl in the air above them for a second, before it made a sound like a tick and winked out.

"It feels like there's nothing to connect with, Gus. Last time you were singing. Maybe you were giving off some kind of energy of your own," Claire reasoned.

Utterly frustrated, she retreated to think. She was so focused on the problem at hand, she didn't notice the space. She'd just created a quiet room out of necessity, and hadn't given it much thought until she heard the knock.

When she looked up, Claire found herself sitting on a white cushy sofa in a small room. She turned toward the knocking and saw a turquoise door. The rest of the room was as white as a fresh ream of paper. There was one small window on the opposite side of the room, about twelve feet away. A second knock came from the turquoise door.

"Claire?" said a voice from the other side.

"Oh my God," Claire breathed. She jumped up, ran to the door and whipped it open.

Gus was standing, arms outstretched, with a grin so big his eyes were little more than slits. "Ha-ha!" he shouted as he grabbed her face in his hands and kissed her cheek.

"Gus!" Claire cried, "How are you doing this?"

"*We're* doing this," he corrected her. "I was afraid I could only pull this off with Lily. It was a long shot, but I thought I might find you."

"Is Lily here too?" Claire asked.

"No, she decided it was best to let you figure this out on your own. She said it's hard for her not to interfere, but that's something she's working on."

"I understand." Claire closed the door, linked her arm through Gus's and led him to the sofa.

They'd barely sat down when Claire blurted out, "So how

do you take a message back for Paul?" She clasped her hands together beneath her chin and they migrated to her lips, as if in prayer.

"Oh geez, I sure want to, but it's a little tricky."

"Well, you made it here, which means you could hear me. Just tell him you've spoken to me, nothing fancy. Tell him to find a man named Tony Chism at the Cook County Morgue... as gently and lovingly as you can, Gus."

"Believe me, I want to help, but it's like I go through a spin cycle or something on the way back, and instead of losing a sock I lose everything *but* the sock. I'm not like you. Traveling between planes is different when you're still tied to your body. I'll give it my best, but I can't make any promises. You know I'd do anything for you and Paulie."

"I know, Gus," Claire said, her voice quivering, "But I really believe we can do this. We have to. Did you see how much pain he's in?"

"I can feel it." Gus looked troubled by this, as he adjusted the belt on his bathrobe.

Claire cracked her knuckles. "Between the two of us, we can make a believer out of him, help him get through this and find me. I know he heard my voice when he was with Anna," she continued, clutching at Gus's arm practically begging.

"All right then, let's give it a shot. Wish me luck," he said, getting up. He kissed her on the cheek again, and as he turned toward the door, Claire saw something odd. A ribbon-thin silver cord hung from between his shoulder blades and trailed along behind him like an oxygen hose. Claire couldn't believe she hadn't noticed it when he'd come in. It had been at their feet the entire time. She hoped she hadn't stepped on it.

"Gus?"

"Yeah?" he said, turning to face her.

"What's with the cord?"

"What, this?" he said lifting it with an index finger, which caused it to shimmer blue, purple and pink like an oily puddle in a parking lot.

Claire blinked and nodded.

"Helps me find my way back, that's all... and not stray too far I suppose."

"Oh, right." Claire smiled.

"Got to get back now."

"Okay then, just make it a good strong pow-of-a-message. Give it everything you've got, and let me know when you're ready so I can be there too."

"I'll try."

"I'm so happy you're able to come here and visit Lily, that this is your real life and not what we see there." Claire choked up. "Sorry, it's a lot to process."

"I know. Take your time. Say, there's a guy on his way to see you, so don't run off," Gus added, as he reached the turquoise door and placed his hand on the knob.

"Who would know I'm here? I don't even know where *here* is half the time."

Gus chuckled. "Mixed-up folks like me know you're here, double-timers," he replied before opening the door.

"Do I know any other double-timers?"

"Well, you have a unique relationship with this one." He grinned and gave her a wink as he closed the door behind him, one last loop of shimmering silver cord disappearing beneath it.

Claire flopped back against the white cushions. Now that she was alone, the room smelled like the ocean. She took a deep, savory breath.

She stood up and walked across the room to the small window, hoping with all her heart she'd see a pristine beach.

When her eyes lit upon the waves rushing up the shore, she pressed her hands against the glass, closed her eyes and thought, *When I turn around I want this room to be sunflower yellow with white trim. I want all of Collin's paintings hanging on the walls.*

When she turned away from the window and opened her eyes, she knew she was standing in a dream house just waiting to happen. The formerly plain white room had merely been a blank canvas.

# CHAPTER 9

*A BEACH HOUSE!* Claire ran from room to room, her mind painting and decorating as fast as she could think. She created crystal vases full of fresh tulips. She hung exquisite Moroccan luminaries. She created a room for every color of the rainbow and then some; a library, a guest room, a greenhouse.

She assembled skylights and shaped stained glass windows. She recalled her favorite family photos and scattered them throughout the house on walls, shelves and tabletops. She hung her favorite picture of her and Collin at their first company picnic, missing him fiercely. *Collin would love it here!*

In the photo, they had their arms slung around each other's neck, laughing despite the sweltering heat. An ice sculpture of the bank had just tipped over and crushed the kids' bunny cake. Paul had snapped the photo. Claire had always thought it captured her relationship with Collin perfectly. Through the biggest messes, they had always been able to laugh, as long as they were together.

Claire blew it up into a poster-sized black-and-white print for the entryway.

It seemed there was no limit to what she could create.

She graced the back of the house with a sprawling, white deck overlooking the beach. Then she lined the perimeter with giant white planters full of brightly-colored Zinnias.

She dreamt up an enormous kitchen with a breakfast nook like she'd always wanted, winced and stopped dead in her tracks. *Paul and the girls can't enjoy any of this with me. I could've made such neat rooms for the girls.*

Heartache engulfed her like a back draft. She blinked back tears, as she thought the kitchen down to a cramped dark galley before doing away with it altogether. *I don't even eat, now. What was I thinking?*

Claire wandered back into the first room and replaced the little window with French doors as she hiccuped through her sobs. It took her three tries to finish the doors just as a thunderstorm rolled in off the water. Lastly, billowing, white sheers were all she had the strength to muster. *I should just undo it all, go sit in the rain and cry my eyes out.*

A knock at the door startled her.

Claire tried to think herself to the turquoise door, but found she was so drained she could only make it halfway there and had to walk the rest of the way.

"Friend or foe?" She placed a hesitant hand on the knob as she rested her forehead against the door.

"Depends on how you look at it. Come on, Claire. Open up. I've already done the worst I can do."

*Why am I afraid? If he's an axe murderer, he's too late.* She stepped back and opened it.

She was surprised to find herself facing a man she still didn't recognize. They stood in silence, as she studied his face. There was something familiar about his eyes, but her gaze shifted down to his hospital gown.

"Of all the outfits you could choose here...." she said, raising an eyebrow.

"Not my choice," he replied with a weak smile.

"Sorry, that was rude of me. Please, come in. Would you like some coffee? Wait, can I do that?"

"Probably, but I'm okay. It's not really that kind of meeting."

*Meeting?* "Have a seat," she said, directing him to the sofa.

He moved toward it with one hand behind him, clutching at his gaping gown and the other pulling a shimmering silver cord alongside him, just like Gus's.

Claire cleared her throat and tried to avert her eyes. She could never stand anyone feeling uncomfortable or embarrassed. This had to take the cake.

He even smelled like a hospital, like Paul's scrubs.

The man sat down with her, and continued tugging to adjust his gown the best he could. He finally rolled his eyes and threw his hands up in disgust.

This time Claire couldn't contain her amusement or her anxiety, and she let out a nervous laugh. "Maybe I can help," she said as she closed her eyes and imagined him in a pair of worn Levis and a white T-shirt, just like hers.

"Thanks, much better. I spend most of my time off by myself, so it's usually not an issue," he said, clearly embarrassed by his own helplessness. His gaze shifted to the shears billowing around the open French doors. Then he stared down at his hands, which were resting on his thighs, palms up.

"I killed you."

"What?"

"On the expressway—I was driving the truck."

Claire tried to remember his face, but everything had happened too fast. One minute she'd been chasing the cat, and the next she'd been with Nana.

"I know I'm the last person to be asking you for anything, but it wasn't my idea, I swear. I'm Gerald McAllister. I was sent to you for guidance."

"Guidance? Sorry, Gerald. You lost me," Claire said, blinking.

"I was told you survived the crash. Do you have Alzheimer's too?"

"Alzheimer's? Oh, you mean because Gus—No, I just met him looking for you. I'm dealing with a completely different set of problems. I know this is strange, and I've got a lot of explaining to do, so just bear with me. I'm sorry," he said clearing his throat and covering his eyes, as he tried to swallow back tears. "I thought I'd be okay once we were face to face, but...."

"It's alright. It was an accident," Claire whispered.

"I've been shown a bit of the bigger picture, I understand why things had to happen the way they did. It's just that I'm still horribly aware of your loss. Maybe it's because I'm still tied to the earth plane and my body, and you're here...." His hands went to his face again, shaking.

*Nothing in life or death has prepared me for this.* Claire tried to look into his eyes and placed her hand on his shoulder. "Look at me, Gerald. I'm okay. I'm adjusting, and I've been told since I arrived that I *planned* for things to go the way they did. Please don't be so hard on yourself. You're not a murderer, if that's what you're thinking. It wasn't intentional."

Gerald abruptly wiped a hand over his face and folded his arms across his chest. "No, it wasn't intentional, but I'd decided to drink myself to death that morning. I'd say I screwed it up about as bad as a guy could. Here you are dead, and I'm in a coma."

Claire's mouth opened as she cocked her head to one side. Gerald's words hung in the air between them, twisted and strange. She pushed herself back into the over-stuffed cushions, pulled a large pillow onto her lap and pressed it against her mouth.

"Wanna punch me? Go ahead, I deserve it."

"No, thanks. The only thing I know for sure is that we're both where we're supposed to be. You said you were sent to me. I doubt it was so I could punch you. You mentioned guidance—regarding what?"

"I'm trying to decide whether or not to stay," Gerald said with a grimace.

"Stay here? You have a choice? What are you waiting for!?"

Gerald looked away. "This is too cruel," he said as he began to get up.

"Gerald, wait... please," Claire insisted as she grabbed his arm. "Let's try to figure this out. I think that's what they really want, whoever sent you. I don't think this is about punishment. That doesn't feel right. Punishment isn't something anyone here would want for us. They want us to grow and evolve. Forget about the accident. For whatever reason, I think we both chose this way to meet. Let's start by accepting that."

"Liane made me find you. She's my Spirit Guide."

"It's *your* life. Get back on the horse and get on with it."

"It's not that easy." Gerald stood up. His arms folded, he walked to the French doors. A storm was rolling in. "I'm paralyzed from the neck down."

"But you're alive. If you were supposed to die you'd be dead. You'd be here full-time like me, but you're not."

"But I feel so alive and free here," Gerald argued. "I've been dead for years back there... dead, drunk and numb. Now, the family I worked so hard to drink away won't let go. I don't deserve them. I run and hide as long as I can, but I always end up returning to my body to listen to my son read. I didn't think Kevin gave a rat's ass about me anymore."

"Teenager? They go through stages," Claire offered as she remembered Anna decked out in full goth gear, slamming her bedroom door.

"We barely spoke ten words to each other over the past two years, but there he sits by my bed, every miserable day. He reads all these miraculous recovery stories to me. I think I've heard every word ever written on spinal cord injuries."

Claire smiled, her eyes gently encouraging him to continue.

"My wife massages my arms and legs with peppermint oil. She even rubs it on my face. She's always talking about how it's going to wake me up. She never misses a day, not even the day of her own mother's funeral. All I can do is lay there like a giant Peppermint Pattie."

Claire laughed. "Maybe she's falling in love with you all over again."

"Nah, all I do is lie there."

"I bet it happens more than you think," she insisted, but Gerald shook his head.

He walked along the wall, studying the paintings of stained glass as he spoke.

"Sounds like a family worth fighting for." Claire stood up and joined him in his tour of her little gallery.

Gerald stopped in front of the painting of the snake swallowing its tail. "It's crazy, but the three of us have never been so close."

"I think there's a plan at work here, *your* plan. I think it's probably a good one, and you should just let it flow. I think God, your true self, your guides and your Collective are all trying to give you what you really want, but you're fighting it."

"Well, it's terrifying. Wouldn't you?"

"Trust them, or at least trust your original plan. There's a new life waiting for you. This has changed all three of you. Repeating history's impossible. You're going to have the love and support of the family you always wanted. There's nothing better."

Claire studied his face as a calmness spread across it.

"Kevin actually misses me," he whispered.

"He needs you. It's not too late to go back and be the best role model a boy could hope for. You'll be able to teach him things about courage no one else *ever* could," she said, reaching out to straighten the frame.

Claire sighed. "It's so much harder to guide them from here. I'd give anything for just five more minutes. I'm talking five minutes of the worst tantrum—anything," she said with a weak smile. "They sense me, but it's not the same."

Gerald grabbed her by the arm and pulled her close. "Ahma said you need balance. I'm here to be the fulcrum. I didn't have a choice. Don't be afraid, Claire," he said apologetically as he wrapped his cord around the two of them several times and cinched it tight.

"What are you doing?" Claire cried out and struggled to break free, as a gust of wind tore through the house with such force it blew the windows out and knocked them against the wall. Claire tried to raise her arms to shield her face from the rain, but she couldn't move them. Her back was against the wall, her body pressed against Gerald who held her with one arm and braced himself against the wall with the other, his eyes closed tightly as debris filled the air. Claire fought to keep her eyes open, but finally tucked her head into Gerald's chest. The house began to shake, and they were thrown to the floor.

Claire forced her eyes open. All she could see was sky. She heard shouting, a loud engine and firecrackers. *No... gunfire.*

She still couldn't move her arms, and her throat was on fire, yet strangely wet. A filthy, but handsome young man in a combat helmet and uniform appeared above her, just as she freed a hand and clawed at her throat. It came away drenched in blood. Claire coughed and tried to scream. All that came out was a horrific gurgling sound.

The man above her shouted and grabbed her hand, "No, Danny! Don't! Faster Vince! Come on!"

Claire managed to turn her head just enough to see another man in front of them, driving. She realized she was lying in the back of a jeep... dying again.

The man yelled and hovered over her. Then he tore his jacket off and pressed it against her throat. He cried and shouted obscenities.

*His eyes...* "What happened!?" she gurgled.

"Don't talk! You just yanked our chestnuts out of the fire again, you stupid sonofabitch!"

Claire couldn't remember a thing.

The man pressed harder on the jacket and the wound beneath it. "Sniper!—You kicked me down in the foxhole like a sack of potatoes and dragged Vince as fast your legs would go, but they nailed you. Only a few miles to the hospital. Just hold on! You hear me!?"

*His eyes... it's Collin!* She turned her head toward the man driving, as the jeep briefly jerked and jolted them into the air. They came down with a thud and bounced a few more times. Collin threw his body over hers to hold her in place. She gurgled in pain, but managed to turn her head again.

As Collin pulled back, he shouted to the driver, "Vince!"

The driver slowed down just enough to lean back between the seats, keeping his left hand on the wheel, glancing at the road every couple of seconds. "You're gonna be okay, Danny! We're almost there! You gotta hold on for Alaska, land o' the peacemakers! A real man never weasels out on a pact!"

*That's Gerald!*

Suddenly, images of a young woman's bruised and bloodied face flooded Claire's mind, along with a sense of terror and remorse. A deafening explosion wracked her body with excruciating pain and hurled the three of them into the air.

The acrid odor of campfire and soil clung to her clothing. Claire shuddered as she opened her eyes. She was back in the beach house, lying on the white sofa.

Ahma stood over her, emanating compassion as she swept her hands back and forth through the smoke-filled air.

Claire looked around the room. Nothing was out of place, the paintings were fine, no broken windows—not a single sign of the hurricane, or whatever it had been.

"Do you need anything?" Ahma asked, her fingertips billowing smoke Claire thought smelled a lot like a Cheap Trick concert from her high school days.

"No, it's sage, dear—it's restoring the peaceful energy to your little oasis."

Still dazed, Claire ran her hand over her throat and sighed with relief. "It was so real."

"Every minute of it." Ahma made her way around the room like a bee-keeper smoking hives to calm the drones.

"More...." Claire croaked. "Get that campfire smell out of here. No wonder I was such a nervous wreck whenever we went camping." Claire shook her head, sat up and perched herself on the edge of the sofa.

"Gerald said we had a pact."

"You were determined to become peacemakers when you returned home. You wanted to be a teacher. Vincent... now Gerald, would have been a musician and Christopher, now Collin, had his sights set on the priesthood.

"The priesthood," Claire mumbled as she looked around the room at all the paintings of stained glass.

"The three of you despised what you had become—trained killing machines and worst of all, you had grown to love the killing. That terrified you. You made the peacemaker pact to keep each other in check if one ever slipped into that mindset again—for eternity. I saw to that. Alaska was the first place you intended to go when the war was over. There you planned to cleanse your spirits, reconnect with nature and peace and rid your souls of the urge to kill. All excellent intentions, but your time had come."

"Well, that explains all of Collin's Alaskan cruises, but why is the pact for eternity?" Claire stood up and walked over to Collin's painting of the snake swallowing its tail, with a new understanding.

Ahma approached her and began smudging sage smoke over Claire's entire body. "Many soldiers circle directly back to the earth plane just as you three did. It is your God given right as political pawns. Your pact was anchored in time, because you left the earth plane together focused on a virtuous new life plan."

Claire waved the smoke away from her face and walked over to the French doors to open them. She remained there a moment, allowing the ocean breeze to fill the room.

"Gerald was just keeping me in check when he hit me on the expressway?"

"It was your one caveat in your life plan. He had to keep his word."

Claire turned to Ahma. "Julia's betrayal was going to consume me, wasn't it?"

Ahma nodded.

"To the point of killing again?" Claire asked incredulously.

"You were already descending into the mindset. That was enough. You had made it clear that was a person you never wished to become again. Especially where your daughters were concerned, but you wouldn't have been satisfied until you found her."

"Do you know why I came back as a woman?"

"You simply needed to be kinder, softer and more openly loving after such violence. You were desperate to give life instead of taking it."

"Are you sure I didn't want to experience the same vulnerability that German woman felt when I beat her half-to-death on her own kitchen floor?"

"Yes, that too."

"I can still smell the lye. Her hair was so soft and shiny. It smelled like lye. I was thinking about her when I died. I'd become a monster. I remember being scared to death as I took my last breath, knowing I'd pay for that."

"We've all been the murderer, the rapist, the sociopath— every one of us, Claire. We must evolve from something. Without darkness, there can be no light. Without war, there can be no peacemakers."

"You're in *favor* of war?"

"I'm in favor of conflict, for it breeds resolution, love and light… in time. Now go, your comrade needs you."

The room turned a blinding white, but like a hand grasping at a doorknob in the darkness, Claire managed to find herself in Gerald's hospital room amidst a sea of lab coats, scrubs and commotion.

"Pull the respirator!" she heard a doctor in pearl earrings shout.

A tired-looking woman in a baggy floral print dress stood in the corner weeping, a tall acne-scarred young man with a book in his hand, holding her close.

Claire pulled herself above the chaos to get a better look. Gerald was choking. She thought she heard him moan. The doctors and nurses exchanged surprised looks. The monitors attached to him were going wild, when one long beep rose above the rest.

"He's coding," a tall doctor with a cleft chin and wire-rimmed glasses shouted. Seconds later, he yelled, "Clear!" as Claire watched Gerald's body contort.

"Claire!" a voice shouted.

*Gus!?*

# CHAPTER 10

COLLIN SAT outside Claire's house in his black BMW, loathing another gray Chicago day. A bitter wind howled outside. He fiddled with his monogrammed keychain, a fifteenth anniversary gift from Frank, despite the fact they'd never officially tied the knot. *Six... no, seven mystery keys. How's that even possible? And what the hell does this one go to? Eight—fabulous.*

He stole glances at the two-story brick house, as he removed each useless key from the ring.

Things he'd ignored for years became urgent pressing matters whenever he pulled up in front of Claire's house. The week before he'd cleaned out the dashboard vents using a napkin wrapped around a chopstick. That first step inside Claire's front door was the worst, and it never got any easier.

Claire's house had always been a guaranteed good time, no exceptions. Now? Disney World during a power outage. Em always managed to liven it up a little, but without the girls, Collin feared the void in there would devour him. *Why did she have to be so hard on herself? She never thought she was good enough, pretty enough or exciting enough. God, I wish she just could've realized how easy she was to be with. She was safe. The world has enough beauty queens. She was so special. Why couldn't I ever tell her, just come out and say it without all the stupid jokes?*

Collin dabbed at his eyes with his coat sleeve. *This isn't helping anything. Go on inside.* He knew Paul needed all the support he could get. Collin had offered to watch the girls the first time he and Paul had spoken after Claire's disappearance. He'd gone on and on, insisting there had to be a logical explanation—that Claire would be home soon. Collin had been so sure of it.

He and Frank often discussed Paul's personal hell. One of their conversations now played over and over in his head.

"That poor guy is going to need some serious time away, because you know what's coming," Collin had predicted.

Frank had accused him of watching too much Lifetime—Television for Women.

"But the husband is *always* a suspect. Mark my words. Not even Paul can escape this." Unfortunately, he'd been right. Paul seemed more depressed and exhausted every time Collin saw him.

It was Paul who had decided Collin would come over on Wednesdays, so Anna could hang out with her friends after school, instead of watching Em.

There was an added perk for Collin. He'd discovered both the girls made him laugh, and brought back great memories of Claire. Minus the pain.

Em sounded like her mother at times with her determination, and Anna looked more like Claire every day, when you could see past her current resemblance to Lily Munster. Whenever he was with the girls, he knew the best parts of Claire would live on.

After weeks of sleepless nights, Collin had accepted she was gone. What he couldn't accept was never finding out what had happened to her. He'd been the last person to speak to her.

He suspected, hoped, Paul was attending a local grief support group for a few hours every Wednesday night. He never let on, though.

Collin always made it a point to get Em and get the heck out of the house, as soon as Paul left. He had to escape the emptiness as quickly as possible, and used it as an excuse for the two of them to eat terrible pizza and play skee ball for hours at a suburban Chuck E. Cheese.

He pulled back his sleeve to look at his watch. He'd been stalling for a good ten minutes. The wind kicked up, causing him to tug at his cashmere scarf as he pried himself out of the car and skulked up the sidewalk. He mustered a cheerful smile at the last second, just before Paul opened the door.

"Hey, thanks again," Paul said, shaking his hand. "Really appreciate it. This single parent stuff is a lot tougher than I...." His voice trailed off. Paul ran his hand through his hair, as he turned and walked back into the kitchen to finish unloading the dishwasher.

Collin followed him, removing his coat as he glanced around the kitchen. "To be honest, it's good for me too."

"I'm going to finish this up, and then I've got to get back to the hospital. Em's in her room watching TV."

Collin draped his scarf and long wool coat over a dining room chair. "Hey, is that the dog house she ordered online?" he asked, and pointed to the back yard.

"Oh, yeah. Nice, huh? Took so long to get here, she never even saw the damn thing."

"Sorry, I didn't mean to...."

"Naturally, Shadow won't go in it. Still naps under the deck. Actually, she stays inside a lot lately. She goes straight to our bed when I let her in. She always used to sleep in Ann's room. Now our bed's covered in dog hair."

"Lucky you."

"Yeah, Ann's going through an angry patch right now, and I think Shadow's keeping her distance or something. We're a sorry-assed bunch. Even the dog is depressed. All she does is sleep and bark at walls... mice. I've got to remember to get traps on the way home tonight." He stared at the "Mousetraps" Claire had scrawled across the white board on the fridge the day she disappeared.

He glanced at Collin and looked away, grabbing a towel to dry his hands. "Who says I have to erase it after I buy them? It was her last note. My last honey-do list. It's staying."

"Paul," Collin began with some trepidation.

"Yeah?" Paul answered, avoiding eye contact by busying himself with the drinking glasses in the cupboard.

"Has anyone talked about a memorial? You know, for the girls' sake. I mean, skipping Thanksgiving and taking them out of town was smart. It was way too soon to have to deal with a major holiday, but I just thought with Christmas and the New Year coming up. It might be good to ease into some closure for them, for everyone really. You know? Maybe you could start some new traditions. No, maybe it's better to keep the old ones. Oh, what the hell do I know? I've just been feeling like—"

"Yeah, I know, but I don't want to rush anybody—"

"Or force anyone to give up hope. I know," Collin agreed.

"I don't think anybody wants to be the guy who says it's time to move forward, but it's my job isn't it?" Paul asked him, gathering the nerve to look him straight in the eye.

"It's all you, but you know I'll help you in any way I can, whenever you're ready. It's what we do. We're good at that," Collin assured him.

"Bankers?"

"Queens, Paul," Collin said, straightening the centerpiece on the dining room table.

"Oh, right," Paul answered with a flustered nod.

"We're pros when it comes to support and throwing parties. Claire wouldn't want some dreary-assed memorial and you know it. Right now, I feel like she deserves more... more than us just waiting." Collin folded his arms and watched as Paul tried in vain to fit one last glass in the cupboard.

"I know, I just can't. Not yet," Paul said as he slammed the cupboard door shut and tossed the glass in the garbage. "I'm working on it. You know... her not coming back."

"You're right, I'm sorry. Take your time. I'm just saying, whenever you're ready to do something, let me know."

Paul was standing over the garbage can, hands on his hips, staring at the glass. "She could still come back couldn't she? It's not completely out of the realm of possibility, is it? It's only been a little over six weeks."

"You've known her longer than I have, but this isn't Claire," Collin whispered.

"I just had to put it out there. In case I dreamt the whole fucking thing," Paul said over his shoulder, as he walked to the front door and opened the coat closet.

Collin berated himself under his breath, mumbling what he wished he'd said, "She'll be back. Don't ever give up hope."

"I'll try to be back by ten," Paul said as he walked through the kitchen, pulling on his coat. He called up the stairs, "Em? I'm leaving now. Collin's here." There was no answer. "She might've fallen asleep. She hasn't eaten much today."

"No problem. She usually eats pretty good for me."

"I suck at this food pyramid thing. I hate to push them on anything right now. If they wanted tattoos, I'd let 'em," he said with a sigh, and slammed the door to the garage behind him.

Collin peeled a couple of stickers off of some

bananas sitting on the counter. Then he hurried upstairs and down the hallway, stopping to straighten a few family photos before he arrived at Em's door. "Hey Chiqui," he called out, as he plucked a purple feather boa from the doorknob and flung it around his neck.

"Collin!" She was lying on her bed with her chin resting on a stuffed elephant's butt. The Wiggles were dancing around on her little pink TV.

Collin plopped down on the bed next to her, pulled her hair back and stuck a banana sticker to each of her earlobes.

"Hey, where did you get a copy of last year's Mr. Leather?"

"He's not Mr. Wedder. He's Captain Feddersword," Em said, picking up the remote and turning off the TV. She sat up and brushed her tangled brown hair out of her eyes. The smile disappeared from her face, and she was quiet.

Collin sensed she was having a rough day, and left her tangles alone for a change. "A certain giant rat I know has a bunch of prizes he's just dying to get rid of," he coaxed.

"Are we going now?"

"Well, you're not wearing *that* are you?" he said, feigning horror. "Love the jewelry. It's timeless," he said, examining two paper clip necklaces she wore around her neck, "But you need a little something to make this outfit pop." He pulled the feather boa from his neck and draped it around hers. "Now what have you done with my favorite tiara?"

Em giggled as he picked up dirty clothes and dug through drawers. "Aha!" he said, pulling a rhinestone-covered plastic tiara from the attic of her dollhouse.

"Wanna play?" she asked, jumping off the bed and running to the dollhouse.

"Don't you want to go crack somebody in the head

with a skee ball, honey? Your aim is really coming along. I think that kid last week needed stitches."

"Uh-uh. I wanna stay here and play dolls. Only Mommy plays dolls wimme. You'll like it. I'm da mommy and you can be da baby, like when Mommy and me play." She gathered the dolls into a pile and handed him the baby.

Collin put a hand on her little back as it dawned on him that this was probably some self-made therapy. He sat down with her in front of the dollhouse to take inventory. The gravity of the situation suddenly hit him, and he set the baby down when Em wasn't looking. A purple pony was standing on the living room sofa. He picked it up instead and trotted it into the kitchen. "Your decorator, I presume? He'd better get to work. This kitchen wallpaper is an absolute nightmare," he said in an attempt to relax and lighten the mood, as he parked the pony next to the breakfast nook. "You want me to make you some new furniture?" he added, a little too excitedly.

"Okay, you can be da horsey. Den Mommy can still be da baby. Dis was her dollhouse when she was little like me," she said, as she put the mommy doll in the nursery and dropped the baby in the crib like an Alka-Seltzer.

Collin took a deep breath. "I don't think Mommy's going to play today, Chiqui."

"She comes ebryday," she said, sounding a little annoyed as she placed a plastic lion in the nursery next to the baby's crib. She looked at Collin, "It's okay, he doesn't bite."

"Oh... good," were the only words Collin could manage.

He watched her play for a while. She was the most unapologetic little girl he'd ever known, and he loved her for it. She didn't have a bit of that disease to please *he* did. He'd play. He'd do whatever she wanted, but he hated the thought of her missing Claire so much she'd make up stories. *Probably healthier than just shutting down, though.* He couldn't help but wonder how losing Claire would affect Em the rest of her life.

"Hey, you're not playing," Em scolded.

"Sorry." Collin snapped out of his daze and trotted the pony around the kitchen.

"Don't worry. Leo really, really won't bite. He never does. Mommy likes da lion. She says he's Leo da lion, and she's Leo da lion too cuz of her birfday."

"Horsey needs a martini," Collin mumbled, taking his tiara off. Something caught his eye. "Ooh fancy, you've got working lights in here. That's cool," he said, flicking a little switch connected to a yellow lamp in the living room.

"I know," Em replied, "But da udder one broke."

"Let me see," he said, and motioned for her to hand it to him. "I bet it just needs a new battery."

"It always needs a new battery. It's broke. Dad says no more toys, just batteries, but I know he's just joshin," she said with a smirk.

"Well, a girl can't live on batteries alone, most girls anyway," Collin answered with a smirk of his own.

"All my batteries are dead all da time 'cept da one in da yellow lamp. It always works. Mommy turns it on before I fall asleep to say g'night."

"Oh?" Collin replied, trying to maintain a casual tone, as every hair on the back of his neck stood up.

"Hey! Let's make 'em camping!" she shouted as she jumped up and grabbed a box of tissues from her art table. "Can you make a tent?" she asked, shoving the box into his hand.

"Um, sure. Hand me that sheet of orange construction paper. I think that'll work a little better," he said, quickly dismissing what he'd just heard, as he folded the paper in half and put the pony inside. "How's that?"

"Cool!" she answered and giggled.

"What? It's a pup tent. Were you expecting something a little more sophisticated, Madam?"

"Mommy says no smoking in da tent. She says to tell you it's *not* a smoking tent—no gossip."

"Smoking tent?" Collin stared at her in disbelief, before he choked on his own saliva and began to cough. "I need a drink of water," he gasped, covering his mouth and standing up in one swift move.

He rushed out the door and down the hall to the bathroom, coughing all the way. As he grabbed the bathroom doorknob, he distinctly heard Em say, "Why did you call it a smoking tent, Mommy? Da fire goes *outside*. Remember when we went camping?"

Collin shut the door behind him and leaned against it, trying to catch his breath. *Calm down. She's just playing dolls. Claire probably told Paul about the smoking tent at work. Em just overheard it.*

He stepped over to the sink and coughed a few more times to clear his throat. The cool metal faucet handle felt good beneath the palm of his hand, solid and real. Collin turned it and cupped his hand beneath the stream. Leaning against the vanity, he slurped a little water and wiped the rest over his face.

He looked into the mirror. Out of habit, he pressed the skin on his forehead up, then let it settle again, half-expecting to find a new wrinkle or a shock of white hair. *You're fine. Quit freakin' yourself out.*

He wanted to forget everything he'd just heard, but his heart was still racing as he looked around the bathroom.

Petrified by what he might see, he grabbed a yellow hand towel from the counter, telling himself it was to wipe his hands and face, but he pressed it to his mouth in hopes of muffling any screams. The idea of a blue-faced Claire appearing behind him in the mirror scared the shit out of him, even if he *was* missing her like crazy. "Claire, are you here?"

Not a sound. He had to laugh at himself as he lowered the towel. By the time he'd folded it and placed it on the towel rack next to the sink, he'd managed to convince himself the whole dollhouse episode was a simple misunderstanding. But as he turned to leave, a ringing sound grew so loud in his left ear, it completely overwhelmed him.

He was torn between wanting to turn around and face whatever was there, and throwing the door open, running and shrieking like Janet Leigh in *Psycho*, all the way to his car. He couldn't bring himself to do either. He couldn't move a muscle.

"Collin," Em called from the hallway, "Come play."

The ringing stopped and he gasped. He hadn't even realized he'd been holding his breath. "Just getting a drink."

The knob turned and Em pushed the door open. She held up a little red sock with the mommy doll sticking out of it.

"Look! A sleeping bag." She gave him an aren't-I-clever-grin.

"Cool," he said, scooping her up in his arms and carrying her back to her room.

They made a pit stop at her sock drawer. Then they sat down on the floor in front of the dollhouse, and put each doll in its own sleeping bag. When they were finished, Em placed the mommy and the baby inside the tent with the daddy.

"Dere's no room for Horsey. He has to sleep in da Barbie car."

"Oh, so that's how it is." Collin plunked the pony down behind the steering wheel of the pink convertible. "Fine."

Em began to giggle again. "Babies can't drink coffee."

"What?" Collin asked.

"Mommy says its morning, and da baby's crying cuz it wants eyelash coffee."

Collin turned to her as he felt beads of sweat form along his brow. "Eyelash coffee or... *Irish* coffee?

He wrapped his arms so tightly around himself, it felt like he was wearing a straight-jacket. "Em, do you hear Mommy talking, right now? Because I don't."

"Uh-huh," she answered, stuffing the mommy, daddy and baby doll back in the tent.

"How often does Mommy play dolls with you?"

"I told you, ebryday," she answered exasperated as she turned her attention back to the dollhouse and placed the lion on the kitchen table. "He's eating orange popsicles. I'm hungry."

Collin felt like his heart was going to beat right up his throat and bounce out onto the carpeting. "Can I ask Mommy a question?"

"I dunno. Can you make anudder tent for Horsey and Leo?" she asked.

"Okay," he said, suspecting they were bargaining, as he leaned over and grabbed a blue sheet of construction paper for the unlikely camping buddies. "Ask Mommy where she is, Em," he ventured as he pulled the pony from the pink convertible and placed him under the second pup tent.

"She's here, Cuckoo. Hear her?" she asked and knocked on the top of his head with her little fist, "Cuckoo, Cuckoo." She laughed at Collin and put the lion in the tent.

Collin laughed nervously. "So, she's talking in your head?"

"She says she's dressed up for Halloween. I was a mermaid, but we didn't go trick or treatin'. We went to da Wapple Stomp. Daddy let me wear my mermaid hair to bed and I didn't eben brush my teef."

"Wow," Collin said, struggling to sound casual, while barely able to swallow. He knew the information session could end at any second. His mind raced to come up with the best possible question. It might be the last one he'd ever get to ask Claire.

"Where was Mommy on Halloween, Em?" he finally managed, as he wiped his sweaty palms on his pants.

"On a train—woo-woo! Mommy says she was a bagan for Halloween. Dat sounds like bacon. Dat's funny! Shadow would eat her costume. She says to ask Tony Chicken at da mark."

*Holy shit.* Collin remembered Paul telling him they'd tracked her to the station. "Bacon or *bagan*? What *is* a bagan, honey?"

"I dunno. Uh-oh," she said, before he could ask who Tony Chicken was. "Look." She pointed to the little yellow lamp as it dimmed. "Mommy has to go."

"W-Where is she going?" Collin stammered.

"Back, Cuckoo."

"Tell her to wait," Collin cried out, as he tugged on Em's sleeve.

Em stood up and walked around the corner of the doll-house. She pulled it away from the wall and reached down behind it. "She went back."

"How do you know?" Collin whispered, glancing around the room.

"See?" she said, holding up a paper clip, "Da mail's here."

Collin crawled over and looked behind the dollhouse.

Em pointed to a tiny black mailbox to the right of the front door. The lid was open.

He looked down at the paper clip she was holding, "Can I see that?" he asked, and she dropped it in his hand. He studied her as she removed one of her paper clip necklaces from around her neck. Then he handed it back to her. Collin was speechless as Em worked two paper clips apart and attached the new one between them.

"How many do you have?" he finally asked.

"I dunno. It goes 'round and 'round. I can count to twenty, wanna hear?"

"Sure." Still stunned, Collin held his hand out for the completed necklace and motioned for her to give him the second one.

Em rattled off numbers as Collin slumped onto the bed and counted forty-seven paper clips. He glanced around the room and spotted a dolphin calendar hanging on the wall near her closet. In a flash, he pulled it off the nail and counted the days since Claire's disappearance. "My God," he mumbled, as he covered his mouth and blinked back tears. "Claire's been missing forty-seven days."

---

Downstairs, Anna slipped in the front door and set her backpack on the rug in the entryway. She tossed her coat on top of it and listened. Collin and Em were usually gone when she got home, but his car was out front and she could hear Em talking upstairs. She knew she had to move fast.

Anna crept through the foyer and into the kitchen. She spotted the business card on the refrigerator beneath the Oreo cookie magnet. Her eyes shifted to the mousetrap message on the white board next to it. She reached out and touched the M, then glanced at the clock on the stove, regaining her focus—the mission.

She slid the card out from under the magnet and rubbed her thumb over the raised black letters: *Jennifer Robles, Detective, Missing Persons Division, 16th District, C.P.D.*

Anna grabbed the cordless phone from the wall next to the fridge, unsure where her cell even was. She crossed the kitchen and eased the sliding glass door open, until she could slide through and close it again, without making a sound. Sleet and a vicious wind stung her face once she was out on the deck, but it was too late to go back inside for her coat. Her adrenaline-fueled plan was gaining momentum, and she wasn't about to let anything slow her down. She pulled the sleeves of her sweat-shirt over her chapped knuckles as she backed up against the bricks, and sat down to huddle where no one would see her. One more look around for any sign of saboteurs, followed by a quick kiss of her mother's ring, and she dialed the number.

A rustling sound came from under the deck, right beneath her. Panicked, Anna dropped the phone just as the call went through. "Shit!" She lunged for it and shut it off before anyone answered. Anna looked up to see a pair of sad, sheepish eyes staring back at her.

"Holy crap, Shadow! You scared me. She clutched the phone to her chest as the Irish Setter cowered on the steps. "Sorry. Come here, we'll keep each other warm."

Shadow wagged her tail and dropped the bicycle reflector she'd been chewing on as she slunk up the steps and licked Anna's face.

"Hungry?" A knot of guilt grew in the pit of Anna's stom-ach, as she pushed the dog's behind down and pulled her close. She knew she'd been a lousy friend, lately. She rubbed Shad-ow's cheeks with her thumbs, where the dog's fur had always been the silkiest. The gesture worked like a secret handshake and all was forgiven. Then she leaned over and kissed her on her head. "Good girl. Come on, we can't chicken out, now," Anna said, and hit the redial button.

"Missing Persons, Detective Robles," a voice on the other end answered.

Anna froze.

"Hello?" the voice asked.

Anna took a deep breath, looked down at her ring and let her have it. "I just wanted to let you know that you suck at this, and you might as well take a vacation, or maybe you already have. I bet that's what you did the very first day."

There was nothing but silence for a beat, followed by, "Okayyy... anything else?"

"Yeah, I've got something else. If she *was* okay, she probably isn't now, because you guys screwed around too long and let all the evidence slip away. I know there were dogs and they picked up her scent. They were on her trail. I know they could have found her if you would have done your job. Even if they found her... and, and it was too late, at least we'd have that, but now we've got nothing, nothing and I hate you! I hate you! You, stupid, worthless, asshole cops!" Anna cried and threw the phone. It hit the railing and broke into several pieces.

She crumpled on top of Shadow. Clenching the Irish Setter's fur in her fists, she buried her face and sobbed.

Shadow didn't make a sound. Her eyes were locked on Claire's.

"Be there for me," Claire told the dog as she knelt down to hug the two of them.

# CHAPTER 11

COLLIN WIPED AWAY his tears before turning from the calendar to face Em. *You will* not *cry in front of Em.* She was doing so well on her own, better than the rest of them, and now he knew why.

"I'm hungry," Em repeated.

"Me too, I could eat a rhino. Come on Chiqui, what's your poison?" He bent down on one knee, the signal for her to climb on his back.

"Poison Ivy?" she asked, as she climbed on and flung her arms around his neck.

"What do you want to eat?" he translated.

"No winos and no poison ivy. Octopus!"

Minutes later, they were in the kitchen. Collin backed up to the counter and set her down.

"Okay, where are the noodles?" he asked.

Em pointed to a cupboard next to the stove, and Collin pulled out a package of Ramen noodles. Then she jumped down off the counter and ran to the refrigerator. She opened the freezer door and grabbed a package of hotdogs, while Collin filled two pots with water and set them on the stove to boil.

He dropped a couple of hotdogs in one and the noodles and a few drops of green food coloring in the other. A smile flickered across his face as he remembered the last time he'd made the delicacy for her.

---

The dining room had erupted in laughter when he'd lifted the silver cover off Em's octopus dish. He'd never imagined it would be the last Thanksgiving he'd spend with Claire.

He'd cut the bottoms of the two hotdogs into quarters so they splayed out like octopus legs when he placed them on top of the Ramen *seaweed*.

Claire had remarked, "Maybe I don't like turkey so much either."

---

While the water came to a boil, Collin walked over to the table and pulled his phone from his coat pocket. Frank had called. He rolled his eyes as he listened to a lengthy message about the glass of beer he'd left on the coffee table the night before without a coaster and the subsequent water ring.

Em giggled as Collin made faces and poured her a glass of apple juice. He slipped his phone into his coat pocket and was walking back to the fridge when he spotted Anna's backpack in the entryway. His stomach sank. It wasn't like her not to come looking for them when she got home. "Call me when these start boiling Chiqui, and don't even *think* about touching them," he advised.

"I know. I'm not a baby," Em answered.

Just to be sure, he pulled a stool up to the sink, gave the bottle of dish soap a squeeze and turned on the faucet. He pulled some bowls down from the cupboard, dropped them in and said, "You're right. You're a big girl. Can you wash these for me?"

"Yeah!" she answered and climbed up on the stool.

He left the kitchen and searched the house for Anna, but something made him return to the sliding glass doors. Then he saw the cordless lying on the deck in pieces. Collin slid the door open and discovered Anna shivering, her body draped over Shadow's. When their eyes met, the dog let out a whimper.

"Anna! You're going to freeze out here!" She was half-asleep, her face red and swollen.

He carried her to the couch in the living room and bundled her up in an afghan. "What were you doing out there?"

"Nothing," she muttered and rolled over with her back to him, as Shadow whimpered next to her.

"I'm going to make you some soup. I'll split a can of tomato basil with you... grilled cheese on the side?" he asked, desperately trying not to dramatize the situation. She didn't answer. She looked so vulnerable with her goth make-up all smeared.

"Boiling!" Em shouted from the kitchen.

"Coming," Collin answered.

———

Collin was elated when he managed to get both girls to come to the table to eat. His nerves had been stretched to their limits over the past few hours, but he refused to let a depressing silence consume them.

"Anna," he began, "You know if you need to talk to someone outside of all this... what about a school counselor? Or I'm sure your dad could arrange for you to see someone."

"He tried to, but I don't want to talk to some stranger. How could they possibly understand any of this?" she said, crushing a bag of saltine crackers with her fist.

"Right, you're right. Well, I'm always here. You know that," he said.

"I know, but I don't want to *talk*. I want to *yell*."

"I wanna yell too," Em said, green noodles dangling from her mouth.

Collin laughed. "Oh my God, so do I! I'll start. Aaaaaaaaahhhhhh," he shouted at the top of his lungs and pounded his fists on the table. The girls went into hysterics. "Your turn," he said, spooning tomato soup into his mouth and pointing at Em.

They spent the entire meal taking turns yelling as loudly as they could and pounding on the table between fits of laughter.

When Claire took her turn, the light above the kitchen sink burned out.

---

Collin was washing the dishes with his eyes half-closed when Paul walked in.

"Long day?" Paul asked.

"Nah. How 'bout you?" Collin asked as he dried his hands on a dish towel.

"Yup. Did they eat for you? *Real* food?"

"Yeah, they did, actually. They were great. They're

in bed already. You need anything before I go?" Collin asked, slipping his coat on, tucking his scarf inside.

"No, thanks again for everything," Paul said, walking him to the door.

"No problem. Oh, before I forget, one of the kitchen lights burned out. I looked for another bulb, but I couldn't find any."

"Yeah, we're out. It's weird, can't seem to buy them fast enough lately. Old house. ComEd is coming out tomorrow to check the wiring again. Then I've got another round with that detective. I've already answered everything ten times over. When it rains, it pours."

"Get some rest, Paul. You look like shit." Collin smiled, as he turned to go down the steps.

"Don't sugarcoat it. Hey, don't forget about Ann's birthday dinner here at the house. Tomorrow night at seven," Paul reminded him. Collin nodded and waved back as Paul closed the door.

⊏⊐

Anna had been listening at the top of the stairs, and watched her dad return to the kitchen. Then she tiptoed back down the hall to her room. She felt lighter as she closed the bedroom door behind her and turned off the lights, like she had screamed and cried herself into a new state of mind.

*I wish I could have seen the look on that cop's face*, she thought as she crawled into bed and pulled the covers up to her chin. She was beyond tired, too tired to sleep. Anna took her ring off and held it up tothe moonlight streaming through her window. Even though logic told her that her mother had bought it for her before she disappeared, her heart would always believe she'd come back to give it to her.

She couldn't shake the sense that it was a special gift between them and maybe even a message, somehow. A thought struck her, and Anna gasped and sat straight up. She remembered something her mother had told her about getting messages from her father... *after* he died. She'd said that her mom, Grandma Lynn, used to lay her wedding ring on sheets of paper and trace around it, and sometimes her dad would move the ring from the circle during the night.

Anna jumped out of bed, flicked the light on and dumped the contents of her backpack on the floor. She found a sheet of notebook paper, grabbed a pencil and sat down at her desk. In a few seconds, she'd traced the outline of her ring. When she was finished, she picked it up and kissed it before she set it down and lined the ring up again.

Anna turned the light off and crawled back into bed, utterly pleased with herself.

Detective Jennifer Robles sat at her desk drinking cold coffee and staring into space until sunrise, when she could go out rowing to wash it all away, or try anyway. Two years in Missing Persons and she had never had a child confront her like that. The kid had balls. She really couldn't blame her either. It was a rotten case—reeked of something obvious and it was driving her batty. She could feel it there, something ridiculous just beneath the surface, a snag that would unravel the whole damn thing so fast your head would spin.

"Michael Anthony Vanesko, what would your mother say about you not eating?" Sal badgered his son, who still insisted on wearing his janitor's uniform.

The two of them sat at the kitchen table. Michael didn't meet Sal's stare or speak, but reached for his turkey baster.

"You've got to eat *something* or... or no more kittens... *and* I'll take away your coin collection," Sal bluffed. Threats had never worked with Michael, but he was at his wit's end. Michael had lost thirty pounds along with his lifelong interest in coin-collecting. It was more than that. He'd lost Claire, his personal coin counter and one true friend.

Luckily, a stray cat had given birth to a litter of kittens underneath their porch shortly after Michael lost his job. Afraid they'd freeze—if they hadn't already—Sal had brought them inside and lured the mother in with a can of tuna when she'd returned. The kittens had been the only things that held Michael's interest. Petting them seemed to calm him.

The worst part was that Michael was never going to talk about what was bothering him, or come right out and say that he missed Claire. It wasn't his way. Instead, he brooded, puffed away on his turkey baster, played with the kittens, and would only eat eggs. Sal had fixed them every way he knew how and that was plenty, having owned a restaurant for thirty years. He'd known Michael would grow tired of them eventually. A man could only eat so many eggs... and then what? Now he was lucky if he could get him into the kitchen for a hard boiled once a day.

*Mil would have a fit. She'd get him to eat somehow.* Sal sat with his head in his hands, elbows propped up on the yellow

Formica table where the three of them had always eaten together.

Sal stared at Michael as he sat on the other side of the table, playing with a gray kitten and a white one. *She'd have a fit over this too—cats all over the kitchen table—seventh sign of the Apocalypse.*

Michael held the white kitten up in the air, then brought it down and held it to his chest, petting it with long firm strokes.

Sal shook his head and reached for a sheet of paper sitting in the middle of the table. It was a Yellow Pages ad for an in-home healthcare agency specializing in developmentally disabled adults.

*Maybe someone else could get him to eat. A pretty girl perhaps?* Sal rubbed his aching eyes. *How can a guy sleep when his son was wasting away right in front of him?* "This can't go on, Michael. Should we give these folks a call? I know you don't like strangers in the house, but I think it's time."

"No strangers in the house," Michael echoed.

"I know that was one of Ma's rules, but Ma isn't here, and if she was she'd grab you by your ear and make you eat a salad. You can't help me shovel the drive tonight if you don't eat an omelet, or something pretty quick here. I mean it."

Michael offered no response.

"I bet they've got some pretty brown-eyed girl who could come over, and get you to eat something sensible, these folks," Sal said, shaking the paper at Michael "Come on, Mikey. Whaddya say?"

Michael frowned. He was looking at something on the floor, then above it, then back at the floor again.

Sal turned and looked behind him where a bowl of over-ripe fruit sat on the counter next to his deceased wife's dusty recipe box. "You want a banana!?" Sal shouted a little too excitedly, frightening the three remaining kittens off the table.

Michael stood up, holding the white one. Still frowning, he continued to glance from the floor to the counter then higher up near the cupboards.

"What is it?" Sal pushed his chair back, stood up and leaned over the table to see what was on the floor. It was a quarter—one Sal had never heard hit the floor.

He watched his son set the kitten down on the table and walked over to the coin. Michael crouched down and picked it up, then looked up at the cupboards again and laughed.

Sal was standing now, staring at the cupboards utterly perplexed. He hadn't heard Michael laugh for a good three weeks. It was a sound so sweet it brought tears to his eyes.

"Chicken Caesar salad... 1974," Michael said quietly, holding the coin up to the light as he turned to go down the hallway to his room, where he had jars full of coins on his nightstand. He didn't bother picking up the kitten *or* the baster.

"Well, all right then! Thank you, Jesus!" Sal exclaimed as he quickly crossed the kitchen, opened the freezer door and pulled out a package of chicken breasts.

———

Claire sniffled and smiled as she watched Sal toss the chicken back in the freezer, pick up the phone and order two Chicken Caesar salads and a pizza from the local Jewel Grocery. She missed them. She'd always been able to reason with Michael when no one else at work could. Some things hadn't changed.

Why had Michael seen her? Sal hadn't. She'd noticed Michael seemed to be buzzing with energy even though he was feeling down. Maybe that had something to do with it. She longed for a deeper connection with him, especially now that she'd grown to accept he'd been her father before he'd become Michael. There was no denying it. Her father—the man who had fed her, rocked her to sleep and loved her more than anything—so much so, he'd found his way back to her in his next life. He was surely part of her Collective, but would they ever be on the same plane again to really reconnect and talk? For some reason she doubted it. There was something about him, something so bright, almost electrifying... far more enlightened than her and her stubborn ways. Claire decided, in the meantime, she'd give him as much peace and comfort as possible. She'd talk to him whenever she could. *What if he doesn't have the coping skills to handle all this loss? Why did Julia have to involve him in the embezzlement? That was just plain mean.*

Claire's mood darkened. She noticed Sal shiver, as her thoughts turned to Julia. *What happened to me may have been my choice, although sometimes it's still hard to believe, but what's happened to Michael is just wrong. He was an innocent bystander if there ever was one, not to mention Sal... and Em and Anna and Paul... and I wonder where the hell Miss Money Bags is now?*

She'd not allowed her mind to go there even once—afraid it would bring out an ugly side of her that had no business in this plane. Now, she *had* to make Julia aware of all the suffering she'd caused. *Which little jar of fun would suit such a heartless back-stabber? First things first, can you even find her?*

A sudden rush of dark thoughts and images flooded her mind. Claire brushed aside the question of whether or not finding Julia was a good idea.

*What was so damn important that Julia had been willing to throw us all under the bus—even Michael? It had to be more than money, didn't it?*

Claire focused her mind into a tiny beam of light, as she

recalled a morning like so many others, when she'd approached the employee entrance to find Julia flirting with George, the balding Security supervisor. She'd never understood that friendship. Julia flirted with everyone, but she'd laid it on especially thick for George, the sweet, old, pot-bellied oaf... to the point it seemed they *had* to be sleeping together. It was still an absurd thought. Julia could've had just about anyone and did. Of course, now it made perfect sense when Claire tallied all the keys, codes and cameras George had access to. Difficult as it was, Claire focused hard on the memory of the two of them giggling, Julia's hand resting on George's thigh.

Claire squeezed her eyes shut.

*Shit shit shit—I shouldn't be doing this.*

*Shut up and focus or you'll never find her!*

—

Detective Jennifer Robles pulled her filthy Jeep Wrangler into the parking lot to unload her boat and oars. With that first whiff of rotting leaves and half-frozen goose droppings, the twisted cables of tension on either side of her neck began to relax.

*Once a sculler, always a sculler.*

She thanked God every day she'd been introduced to rowing in college. These days, it was the only thing that kept her among the sane. She only wished she had the water all to herself.

Years ago, she'd found a hell of a deal on a slick, red, straight pair Vespoli—a shell for two rowers. She'd always meant to find a rowing partner. Having read somewhere, that you have to make space in your life for special people to enter it, it had seemed like a healthy decision buying the bigger shell at the time. The problem was you needed help even loading and unloading the damn thing, let alone rowing it. She'd never found that rower to fill the extra seat. In fact, she'd never really looked.

In the meantime, she'd stored the Coxless shell, also known by rowers as 'the coffin' due to the difficulty involved in managing to escape in the event of a capsize, in her basement. She'd been forced to make do with an old, blue, single scull Janousek she'd found on Craigslist, but she still pined for the day when she could take that sweet, red Vespoli out on the water.

Jennifer shivered as she rushed through a few stretches of her quads, hamstrings and traps. *It's been a mild winter so far, and there's always someone around,* she rationalized. About one more week of good rowing, and then she'd have to settle for swimming laps at the gym until spring. Each winter, rowing was becoming harder to give up. *Gotta get while the gettin's good. It's as close as I'll ever get to meditation.*

"Need a hand?" A friendly-faced man in a black uni-suit and windbreaker called out and waved.

"Got it—thanks."

Jennifer hurried out to the dock in her sweats and fleece jacket, the shell on her hip. She'd set it down in the water, clicked her oars in place, stepped inside, sat down and pushed off, all in a matter of seconds. With more than twenty years of rowing under her belt, she never gave capsizing a thought anymore, but her pulse still quickened with excitement right before the scull hit the water. Then, with that first, long, luscious glide it began its long-awaited descent into the abyss of calm. *Never should have taken the promotion.*

As she rowed around the bend in the Chicago River, Jennifer ran her hand through the water to check for the familiar warm spot from the factories and smiled.

*Some things are always just as they should be.*

She sure as hell had never aspired to the self-torture and endless human tragedies she'd found in Missing Persons. No, patrolling Old Town had been the best deal going. She loved those people in her own way, knew the neighborhood inside and out—every store owner, vagrant, dog, cat and rat. It was where she'd felt wanted.

She was wanted in Missing Persons too, but to be super-human, psychic and stone-hearted. Jennifer Robles was none of those things, and it was killing her.

Her brother had just kept pushing her from his cushy high-rise advertising office on Wacker Drive, always asking her what she wanted to do with her life... like she was out flying kites. Finally, she'd caved and put in for Detective. *Biggest mistake of my life, complete with a new condo, ulcer and thinning hair.*

She'd solved cases, but they never brought the relief or satisfaction she craved. Most cases didn't end well, even if they were solved. Once in a blue moon, someone was found in rough shape, an addict or alcoholic, and by some miracle and the support of a few saintly friends and family, they would make it back to a somewhat normal life. She'd received cards from a few of them, or their family members, but it was the thinnest file in the cabinets.

Her brother continued to polish his awards for his brilliant breath mint commercials, while Jennifer marinated in human suffering.

His office building was coming up on the left. She rowed faster and stared off to her right at nothing in particular. It had become obvious that they were from different planets. For the life of her, she couldn't figure out how they could have possibly grown up in the same house. But their parents were gone, and with their passing, her big brother, Jay, had somehow become her measuring stick. The only path she could see out of their sick little story was a move—far away.

So, she spent most mornings daydreaming of faraway places on faraway continents, as she rowed her blood pressure back down to earth.

As soon as Anna had mentioned the search dogs, Jennifer had known which case she was talking about. The dogs weren't used downtown too often.

Claire Cumming's file was rapidly cooling. No reminder was needed, especially not from a furious, heartbroken child. Today, Jennifer couldn't muster any faraway places as she rowed. Her mind would only take her as far as the Cumming's house where she had first met Anna.

Jennifer remembered thinking, *It's going to be hard on that one.* She wasn't sure how she knew. Maybe it was just that Anna looked so much like her mother, with a classic, understated beauty you could see even through all that makeup. Maybe it was because fourteen is so damn hard to begin with. Add a missing parent, and it's a short road to overload.

Jennifer had been so blindsided by Anna's phone call, she'd barely managed a response, but the girl deserved some kind of answer. She'd have to pay her a visit. An all too familiar burning sensation in her stomach reared its ugly head at the thought.

She knew what it was like to lose a mother, but at least she had a grave to visit and a goodbye to hold onto. This girl had nothing, just like she'd said. It wasn't right. Why had she needed a fourteen-year-old to come out and say she sucked at her job? She didn't know. She was just glad she had. Detective Jennifer Robles had played by the rules long enough. In one swift stroke, she thought it might be a good idea to start coloring outside the lines.

*If I can't solve the case, at least I can help Anna.*

She felt a strange sort of kinship with the girl. *Aggressive...
like a sculler.*

⊏⊐

Claire found herself in the midst of a noisy street market
surrounded by fresh fruit and foreign conversations. Confused,
she made her way through the crowd as she searched for Julia's
long blonde hair.

*Damn. Where's a Garmin when you really need one?*

Claire was sure the blonde bombshell would be a cinch to
spot in the sea of raven-haired locals.

*Ouch! Shit!* Claire felt a shock, and everything went black
for a second as someone passed through her. She darted off to
the side and caught her breath, stunned. A village boy ran
on ahead.

*That would have been a nice little detail to know ahead of
time! Note to self: people passing through you—literally shocking.*

Claire waited for a gap in the crowd and merged with them.
She began jumping up to see over them, and realized she could
hover!

She rushed forward above the crowd, and unintentionally
slowed over another gap. Claire thought herself to the ground
and adopted the crowd's pace, but she still saw no sign of Julia.
This time, when she tried to rise above the crowd, focusing
everything she had on her memory of Julia flirting with George,
she got nowhere, like she was tethered to the ground. *I must be
caught on something!*

Frustrated, she was able to get a little higher on the next try,
but she still couldn't see Julia. She tried to see around a chubby

local in front of her in a gaudy mu-mu with a thick dark bun at the base of her neck.

Upon her third descent, Claire was yanked from the crowd and dragged about twenty feet before she realized what was happening.

# CHAPTER 12

"HEY!" Claire yelled.

"Hey, yourself! Let's go, sister," Wendy shouted with mock cheerfulness.

"What are you doing!?" Claire protested, trying to free herself from Wendy's grip, to no avail. Wendy dragged her beneath a vendor's table, and the world went black.

⸺

Claire winced and struggled to open her eyes as a spray of water hit her body. Fully clothed, she felt neither warm nor cold, but clearly annoyed as she stood facing Wendy. "Hey! Stop it!"

"Sorry, gotta get all those toxic particles off, girl. Hold still," Wendy ordered with that same strange cheerfulness.

"Get what off?" Claire shouted as the powerful spray moved further down her body, and she was finally able to keep her eyes open. They were standing in a community shower, the kind found in school locker rooms. Claire turned her head. She could see the glow from Wendy's shop just beyond the doorway. Somewhat relieved, she turned back to Wendy and gave her an exasperated look.

"It's really toxic. You don't want it to take hold—cause an infection. Almost done," Wendy assured her as she focused the spray on Claire's feet for several more minutes.

The humiliation was nearly intolerable. The only other time she could remember being hosed down was when she was four and, not wanting to interrupt her fun, had pooped her pants while playing outside.

Wendy giggled and quickly covered her mouth.

Claire shot her a glare for obviously intruding on her thoughts on top of everything else.

Wendy bit her lip as she shut the water off, and hung the hose on a hook behind her. Then she turned and waved her hand. A strange blast of air, neither warm nor cold, with no visible source, dried Claire's jeans and T-shirt.

"I'm sorry, but I had to," Wendy finally offered as the blast of air ceased.

Embarrassed, Claire looked down at her T-shirt and smoothed non-existent wrinkles as tears welled up in her throat.

"Come on," Wendy said, stopping her in mid-swipe, taking hold of her hand. Claire sulked all the way to the front of the shop where two white bean bag chairs awaited them up in the storefront window. Claire gave Wendy a questioning glance.

"After you," Wendy motioned for Claire to lead the way. The two of them plopped down. Claire folded her arms in defiance as she turned to see what now lay beyond Wendy's shop. The morgue was gone. It was a pasture of horses, Arabians, just like the one in the latest poster she'd discovered hanging in Anna's room. Claire's heart sank as she wished Anna was there to see them—then sank deeper as she realized what she'd inadvertently wished. *I've got to go.*

"Chillax, Claire. Rest a minute."

"Stop that. It's very rude to just pop into someone's head whenever you please."

"Sorry, but sometimes it's for your own good. You need to slow down for a little bit. It'll help restore your vibration. You're just starting to get a little color back," Wendy said softly as she crossed her legs.

Claire did a double take. Wendy was wearing something like a Hazmat suit.

"When did you put that on?"

"I've had it on."

"No, you didn't," Claire argued.

"I didn't want to scare you. I used a filter so you'd see me in my regular clothes, but I need to keep this on for a while, at least until your color's back," Wendy explained.

Claire looked down at her hands and arms. Her skin was dull gray. "Oh God, I'm sorry. I didn't realize...."

"No, my bad. I forgot to tell you about the uh, specials: use two or more signs and get one bailing-out-of-the-muck free." She winked at Claire.

Claire smiled weakly. "How did you know I was going to use the dark jars?"

"Guess I also forgot to mention the dark ones are kind of security tagged."

Embarrassed, Claire tried to explain. "I just needed to find her."

"And make her pay?"

"Why shouldn't she!? Why is everyone but her suffering as a result of her actions?"

"You don't know that." Wendy shook her head slowly.

"I *do*. I've seen Michael wasting away and Sal panicking.

I've seen my husband cry his eyes out, my girls lonely and confused. I've heard my mother absolutely beside herself with grief...." Claire cried, fresh tears rolling down her cheeks and throat.

"Their path is *their* path, Claire... the whole enchilada, beginning to end. I didn't think you'd dabble in the dark, so I just glossed over it, and didn't give you a fair warning. My mistake. Just so you know, you're going to be too low energy to produce any light-filled signs for a little while."

"Why?"

"That's the problem with the dark. Once you start dippin' into those signs, pretty soon it's all you have access to, and you just get more and more bogged-down in darkness. It's like you can't stop trying to fix and control things."

"I think you're overreacting. I didn't even find her," Claire said, as she angrily wiped away her tears.

"You were right on her. She was the woman in front of you, the one you couldn't see around. You zeroed in on her like a missile."

"The lady in the mu-mu? Yeah, right. Julia's blonde... and a stick. Her two favorite food groups are coffee and cigarettes. She wouldn't have been caught dead in that outfit. Besides, how do you know what I had in mind?"

"It was her. People change, and by the way, I ran into a friend of yours before he returned to the earth plane. He said *you* told *him* there's a plan at work. You forget all about that plan?"

Claire sighed.

"Well, consider this your one get-out-of-jail-free card. Now you're on your own... with great signs comes great responsibility."

"Very funny," Claire said with a smirk. "What about Michael?"

"Michael chose a wicked-hard path. Why would you think this wasn't part of it? You're messin' with his evolution. As an Egoless Teacher, his evolution is crazy-important to him. You're screwing up a plan he's worked hard on."

"But it's so painful to watch him suffer," Claire argued.

"So don't watch so dang much."

Claire grumbled and punched the bean bag with her fist.

Wendy laughed.

Claire finally had to laugh at herself. She heard a whinny and looked out the window. "They're so free. I always thought I'd be free here."

"You would be, if you'd just let go."

"And never use another sign?" Claire arched an eyebrow at Wendy.

"I didn't say that."

Claire closed her eyes and made a concerted effort to put the entire lecture behind them. "Why did my dad want to be autistic?"

"He's on his last trip back. He's closing in on this awesome plane of total light and love—the infinite."

"The Infinite," Claire whispered to herself. What do you guys mean when you call him an Egoless Teacher?"

"To make it to the highest level of enlightenment, you have to return to the earth plane, mentally disabled... by their standards. Your entire job is to teach empathy and patience to everybody around you, and girl, is it a bitch of a job. When you go back as an Egoless Teacher, there'll be days you wish your job was cleaning out the Porta-Potties after Taste of Chicago."

Claire made a face and rolled her eyes.

"Seriously, you go there knowing you'll get no recognition whatsoever for being such an important teacher. You might experience unbelievable love and care, or you might not, but you touch so many lives in ways no one else can. You reach people's souls and even transform some, but you have control over very little else."

"He seriously *chose* that?"

"Pretty cool, huh?"

"You live a hard life—sometimes stared at and teased. Totally misunderstood by most people, and only respected by a handful. You're preyed upon, and taken for an idiot by jerks who have no idea what a genius you are. It's the most frustrating existence, but also rewarding. The souls you do reach are healed in a way only one other energy is capable of."

"No kidding?"

"No kidding," Wendy nodded. "And chances are you won't have to deal with some of the other hassles in life, either."

"Like?"

"Money, sex and taxes," Wendy answered, running a hand over her pretty curls.

Claire laughed and clutched her stomach. "I always thought it was *death* and taxes." *Sex a hassle? How old is this girl, really?*

Claire felt heavy again and slow in her movements. She was tired, actually exhausted.

"We all have a trip back as an Egoless Teacher. I don't know about yours, but mine's a long ways off," Wendy added, looking around her shop, a glimmer of pride in her eye. "It'll keep."

Claire smiled at this. She was a feisty girl, but wise too. Claire admired her, and vowed not to abuse their friendship again, or the signs, if she could help it. An itch grew in her chest, and she tried to scratch it, but it persisted.

"Your mom's callin' you," Wendy said.

"What?"

"That's your mom callin' you."

"But it feels like an itch this time instead of a pull," Claire said.

"The way she's goin', it'll feel like a tickle pretty soon."

Wendy cocked her head to one side and smiled. "They'll all become tickles if you leave them to their own healin' like you have your mom, but man, it's hard."

"Why? What's happening? What is she doing?" Claire asked, suddenly concerned.

"She's revving up her vibration all by herself, right down there on the earth plane."

"How?"

"Go see for yourself."

"No, I can't. You don't understand. Our relationship—it's—I just can't."

"It's okay, Claire. She's not going to drag you down or drain your energy. She's not in that place anymore, nowhere near it, actually."

Claire wanted to believe her, but her mother had always been a bit of an energy vampire with her overwhelming bouts of seasonal depression. How could her mother have changed so much in the short time she'd been gone?

"Go on, you gotta see it to believe it."

Claire bit her bottom lip, closed her eyes and tried to recall her happiest memory of her mother, just to play it safe. She decided to imagine both her mom and dad, for extra protection. The three of them still together in the old house just down the road from Nana's farm. Her mother was bathing her in the tub, her father kneeling beside her, the two of them laughing as Claire giggled and soaked them with her blissful splashing.

When Claire opened her eyes, she was in her mother's cabin, the kitchen counter was covered with fruits and vegetables. Lynn was actually singing, as she pressed a pear down into a juicer. Gone were the cookie jar full of Nutter Butters and the loaf of white bread that had always sat on the counter.

"No way," Claire mumbled. The entire room felt positively

electrified with a light happy energy, and it was all coming from her mother, the energy vampire... in the dead of winter, no less.

⸻

Anna sat in her room studying her mom's face in a framed photo. *She was so pretty.* The corner of her mouth turned up as she remembered her mom usually lost at least two pairs of sunglasses on every vacation. *The camera! I bet there's pictures of her in there we've never even seen!*

Anna flung her bedroom door open, and raced down the hall to her parent's room. She knelt down in front of the night-stand and eased the drawer open, as if something magical might come fluttering out. To her disappointment, nothing but the scent of makeup and cherry Lifesavers escaped the dark drawer. She turned on the lamp and pawed through flowered thank you notes, batteries, expired dog food coupons and some tubes of lipstick she pocketed, not for their color, but because they'd touched her mother's lips. She paused on certain items, turning them over in her hands, letting memories spill out of them.

Anna reached for a book and flipped it over. She snorted when she read, "What to Do with a Dog That Eats Everything."

When she put the book back, she spotted the thin, gray, nylon strap of her mom's camera and pulled on it. *Yes!*

⸻

The following day, after school, Anna found a free monitor in the far corner of the computer lab, and inserted her flash drive. She wanted to do something special with the photos, but she wasn't sure exactly what. All she knew was that she wanted to do it secretly, and that right now she couldn't seem to get enough of her mother's face. The lab was almost empty since it was Friday. Everyone had bolted when the bell rang. Still, she was ready to minimize the screen in a heartbeat if anyone came near her. It would be all over school if anyone caught her looking at them.

"Pssst," came a noise from behind her. She minimized, turned and saw nothing. She brought the photos up again and resumed clicking through them. "Pssst," pierced the silence of the lab, once more.

The lab manager cleared her throat and glared in Anna's direction. Anna shook her head and shrugged her shoulders. Unconsciously raising her hand to her lashes, then quickly sitting on it, she swiveled in her chair to look around. A guy was staring at her from across the room. When their eyes met, he said, "Psss-tah!" over-emphasizing the "tah". The lab manager glared at both of them this time and slapped some papers down on her desk.

Anna looked around. There was no one sitting near her. She looked in his direction once more. Panic sprouted in her toes and wove its way up through her stomach and chest like wild vines. He wore a tight black T-shirt, the edges of the sleeves curling up against the tops of his bulging biceps. He had jet-black hair, brown eyes framed by thick black lashes and even thicker unruly eyebrows. They arched as a smirk spread across his face, and he pointed an index finger directly at her.

Anna thought she might throw-up for a second. She was used to being invisible to boys—counted on it. "Reject them before it's even occurred to them to reject you," had always been the name of the game. She'd had crushes, sure, but she'd always pushed them away the hardest. She was known for her gallows humor, so she joked with guys, but kept them at a safe distance. One boy named Brad Bennet, had even asked her once, "Hey, how come you joke with everybody but me? What did I ever do to you, anyway?" The answer was easy, he'd had the most potential to break her heart, and for that he'd been banished. She would have scooped her heart out with a spoon, before she'd admitted it to him. Instead, she'd only shot him a look, as if to say, "Are you smoking crack?" It was the last time he ever spoke to her.

Brad Bennet couldn't hold a candle to this olive-skinned Adonis. *God help me, if he has a brain and a sense of humor,* she thought as she went into banish mode and swiveled back to face her terminal. Her hand rose to her eyelashes, plucked one and held it up before she had a chance to think about it. She rolled the mascara-covered lash between her thumb and finger, savoring its arrival, staring at the tiny white tip. It had felt good to pull it, *really* good and now she felt bad —*really* bad.

⊏⊐

Between moving Anna's ring every night and the new photos, Claire felt she was dragging her daughter down more each day. She was desperate to give her a boost instead. It didn't help matters that Anna's best friend, Meg, had moved to Wisconsin two weeks earlier. Anna hadn't told a soul. Now she was blowing an eyelash from her fingertip.

Claire couldn't bear to watch her go on like this—going to the movies alone, walking home alone and even eating lunch alone, her face always buried in a book. *A new friend just might snap her back into the land of the living, but how can I make sure it doesn't turn serious and hurt her even more?* She looked at the guy watching Anna and tried to size him up from a distance.

*Too beautiful, but what if I don't get another chance? God, I don't want to do this, but she needs a friend in the worst way right now, and he's clearly interested. How do I do this? Can I? Should I? I've got to. Hope my energy's back up to par.*

Despite Anna's signature paler-than-pale-foundation, Claire watched her daughter's face turn a deeper shade of crimson with each passing minute. Beads of perspiration formed across the bridge of Anna's formerly-freckled nose. Claire knew she had to act fast, before Anna took off like a startled deer.

Claire thought herself to the boy's side. Expensive-looking sunglasses were nestled in his spiky hair, and he smelled fantastic. *So far, so good.*

He seemed gutsy, but he'd have to be to break through Anna's fortress by Maybelline. If she could just get him over to Anna, she knew how she'd handle it from there.

He was still watching her, but Claire knew his courage was fading when she heard him mutter, "Come on, Morticia."

Claire did a quick scan for telltale red flags. *I don't smell cigarettes, two points for you, buddy.*

He ran a hand through the back of his hair and eyed the door.

*No, no. Stay,* she pleaded as she caught a glimpse of something dark on the inside of his forearm. *Shit. A tattoo. Now you're in the hole ten points. Way to go, Slick.*

She moved in for a better look. It was a portrait of Bob Marley, a pretty good one, actually. *No Woman, No Cry... that's right. No teenage girls either. All right, ten points if you're a poet, minus twenty-five if you're in a band and minus fifty if you're into the ganja.*

She looked around for any other candidates—a boy with a shaved head engrossed in his chemistry, who kept sneezing, and a hippy-looking kid with one of those scary giant rings wedged in his earlobe—no way. The only other boy in the room had pink hair and was wearing more eyeliner than Anna. This Middle-eastern aspiring hair model would have to do, but he was a heartbreaker if she'd ever seen one. She couldn't set Anna up for even more pain. *Damn! I need time to follow him around for a while, but Anna's putting on her coat!*

Claire eyed the tattoo. Something was off. It was Marley's hair—his dreads. They weren't dreads, but electrical cords, cables and connectors. *Computer cables? Stereo cords?—Got to be a techno-geek either way. All right, it's on, Slick.*

He put on his jacket.

Claire glanced in Anna's direction. She was still on the computer, but she had her coat on, and had shoved her books inside her backpack.

Anna leaned down to remove her flash drive from the tower.

Claire gulped. "Looky, looky! Maiden in distress!" she coaxed as she popped back over to Anna. In a moment of sheer desperation, Claire shorted out her monitor by thinking *Push!* instead of *Pull!*

Boom—he was up.

"Yes! Good boy!" Claire clapped her hands.

He was at Anna's side in a matter of seconds, but Anna didn't know it. She was busy pushing every button she could find beneath the desk. "Oh my god. What did I do?" she breathed.

"Monitor's toast. Smell it?" he asked as he folded his arms and leaned against the counter.

*He even leans cool, for God's sake.* Claire cringed. She wanted to shake him, warn him not to break her daughter's heart, or even bruise it, because this was one girl who'd had more than her fair share of pain. At the same time, she knew she'd need to let go and let things unfold on their own, terrifying

as that might be. This teen energy was high-voltage, unpre-
dictable stuff, anyway. It felt hard to break through, and even
harder to steer once you did, but she wasn't finished. She
thought herself to an electrical outlet.

Startled, Anna jerked her head up. "What?"

"Kareem. Just moved from Des Moines—first day."

*Steady, steady, wait for it... wait.*

"I didn't think I'd seen you around," Anna answered in a
surprisingly cool tone.

"So, are you in mourning or do you always look like this?"
he joked.

"Actually, both."

Claire guffawed, *Nice one, Banana.*

"My mom."

"Shit!" Kareem said, as he covered his face with his hands.
"I'm such an asshole."

Anna laughed, and Claire recognized it at once as her
whose-got-the-upper-hand-now laugh. They were off to a halfway decent start.

"I'm surprised no one told you. I swear it's all anyone
around here talks about."

"Really? Why?"

"I can't believe this. The one person in the tri-state area who
doesn't have a clue what happened."

"You don't have to explain—really."

"At least one person in this stupid school should know what
really happened."

"Now!" Claire braced her feet against the wall, and pulled
every ounce of electricity she could from the socket.

# CHAPTER 13

THE LIGHTS FLICKERED, then went out.

"Whoa." Kareem laughed.

The lab manager shouted for everyone to remain seated until the back-up generator kicked-in. The few remaining students and teachers made a bee line for the door.

"Come on!" Kareem grabbed Anna's hand.

Claire sensed the two of them leave the room together. *I did it!*

The lab manager moved to block the door.

Claire thought *push!* And shot the electricity back into the socket. Sparks shot out, there was shouting and a fire alarm was pulled.

"Shit shit shit!" she cried as she panicked and thought herself to Anna's side in the parking lot. Students and faculty were trickling out of the school. Anna was okay, but Kareem was opening the passenger-side door of an old black Camaro.

*No, not the car. Wait! Anna! You just met him!*

Claire mentally shot herself into the back seat, just as the fire trucks came roaring up the hill. She stared in disbelief at the school, and tried to remind herself that they did drills all the time. Everyone would be okay. She hadn't meant to make such a mess, but she had to protect her daughter. For a second, she wondered if Wendy or Nana were watching, but decided it didn't matter. *What's done is done. Just don't screw it up anymore.*

"Let's get outta here." Kareem's knee hit an enormous plastic cup full of soda, ejecting it from the cup holder hanging from the door, but he caught it like a pro before he spilled a drop.

"Shit! I'm always doing that. It's a '77—no cup holders." He laughed, shook his head and took a drink before he offered it to Anna. "Where you wanna go? Hungry?"

She scrunched up her nose, shook her head and reached for the door handle. "I thought we were just getting in out of the cold. I have to get home. My dad's totally expecting me. He'll get all worried and shit, if I'm not home soon," Anna replied, as she adjusted her black pleated skirt. It was riding up, exposing several more inches of her opaque black tights now that she had her backpack between her feet.

Claire smiled to herself. Paul wasn't home. She knew Anna had the afternoon free. *She's always had good judgment. She's still Anna. So she's alone with a boy; she hasn't had a* lobotomy.

"Let me drive you then," Kareem answered as he punched the shifter into reverse, backed out of the space, pressed the gas pedal to the floor, and peeled out of the parking lot.

Anna braced herself.

"Just tell me where to turn. I don't know all the streets so great yet. Actually, I did manage to find this incredible forest preserve out a ways—looks just like Iowa. You wanna...."

"Yeah, I'd love to drive to a remote forest preserve with a complete stranger. Hey, let's stop at a gun shop —my treat."

Kareem threw his head back and laughed. "Says the Princess of Darkness!"

Claire could barely stay in the backseat, her frowning face right between them. Her eyes darted from Kareem's to Anna's, and back to Kareem's again.

"Says the serial killer who travels the world pretending to be the new kid in school. I have pepper spray," Anna said in a playful tone that surprised Claire. She might as well have said "Chap Stick."

"I have duct tape."

"I have a flamethrower," Anna replied, lips pursed, eyes staring straight ahead.

At that, Kareem laughed so hard he choked on his pop, and slapped his hand against the Camaro's dusty dashboard, until he'd caught his breath.

"Tell me you don't keep it next to the pepper spray, because that's an accident waiting to happen."

"Of course not, I keep it next to my herpes medication."

"All right, that's enough. We can stop this anytime," Claire shouted over their laughter.

"Holy crap! Does everybody in Iowa drive as shitty as you?" Anna asked, stabbing at the seatbelt mechanism with the metal disk at the end of her seatbelt, breathing a sigh of relief when it finally latched.

"Hey, I'm a pro. I learned to drive like this in Lebanon," he declared, "every summer at my Uncle Omar's. I was born here, though. Chill, would ya? I've been driving since I was ten."

Claire was acutely aware they were moving toward the expressway instead of their house. Maniacal driving aside, Kareem seemed to be a halfway decent kid, but she still hoped Anna really did have pepper spray.

Kareem wiped the back of his hand across his mouth. He had a stunning smile, teeth so white, one couldn't help but stare. He reached for the stereo and turned up Nickelback. "So?"

"Okay, but I have to be home by like, five. My dad took my sister to the dentist. Otherwise, I'd have to go straight home to baby sit."

"Anna Lynn Cummings! This is a bad idea! Use your head! You know better than this," Claire shouted, trying to shake her daughter's arm, but she was too weak.

"Cool, you're gonna love it," he said, speeding up again. "So... your mom?"

Anna leaned her head back against the seat and blew at her bangs. She looked down at her hands, straightened her ring and began picking at her blue-black nail polish.

"You really don't have to," he said.

"No, it's okay. I can talk about it. Just slow the hell down, would you?"

"Okay, okay." He let up on the gas and did a nearly-undetectable hair check in the rearview mirror.

Claire noticed a bead of sweat trickling down the back of his neck. Her mind was wandering to her first date with Paul, when she heard Anna utter those heart-wrenching words: "My mom."

"Are you sure you haven't like, seen anything on the news? Claire Cummings? Union Allied Bank?"

"Not in Iowa."

"Oh, yeah. Right. Okay, well my mom was basically kidnapped on Halloween."

"No shit?"

"Seriously, she like, just disappeared—left her purse, credit cards, everything—even her car. It's been total hell. I know she's like... you know, gone... I can't explain how I know it. I just do."

"Don't say that. You shouldn't give up hope. You don't know for sure. People disappear all the time and...."

To her relief, Claire could see Anna was biting her bottom lip to keep from telling him about the ring. "Keep it between us girls, Banana. Go with your gut. People won't understand."

"Besides," Kareem continued, "If it's been on the news so much, think about how many people are looking for her. That's gotta be a good thing, right?" He pulled his aviator-style sunglasses from his hair and put them on, as the speedometer approached eighty-five.

"Not exactly. I've got this vent in my room where I've been able to hear pretty much everything the cops have told my dad. They're looking for her because this woman, this like, unbelievably slutty woman she worked with—was friends with —she embezzled a shitload of money, the day before it happened. But there's no way on earth..."

"No shit?" Kareem slowed down for the exit, and floored it as soon as he cleared the turn.

Anna braced her right foot against the dash, and dug her nails into the armrest. "You had to know my mom. Anybody who knew her would tell you she was incapable of stealing even the tiniest thing. Like one time, the cashier didn't charge us for one of those packages of peanuts, the little ones..."

"Two for a dollar?"

"Yeah, those."

"Yeah, right."

"No, really. We'd just bought over two hundred dollars worth of groceries and we're about a block from our house, but she has to drive all the way back to the store and tell them. It was insane. Mom always said everything comes back to you ten times over. There's just no way she could have known anything about the money. She never would have let Julia go through with it. Sometimes I think like, that's why she's... gone. Maybe she tried to stop her."

"That's some heavy shit. What about your dad?"

"God, my dad. My dad is going to make it into the Guinness Book of World Records under "Most Interrogated Man in History." The stupid asshole cops have been on him like white on rice since day one. It's so unfair. They aren't even looking anywhere else, or for stupid Julia, I swear. God, it just makes me so mad."

"That sucks."

"Totally, but he's all going to work every day at the hospital and everything—anesthesiologist. I can hear him crying in their room sometimes, though," Anna said, in an almost inaudible squeak as she began to cry.

Kareem did a double-take and fumbled with the glove box latch. He dug around spilling fuses and screwdrivers onto the floor mat. He handed her a crumpled McDonald's napkin. "It's clean. I swear."

"Thanks," she whispered.

In the back seat, Claire stared at a half a dozen crumpled fast food bags on the floor, as she thought about Paul. She hadn't realized the police had focused all their attention on him like that. "How will I ever be able to look after all of them at once?"

"You need to get your mind off all this craziness, mellow out."

Anna sniffled while Kareem fished around in his pocket, driving upwards of ninety, one-handed. She reached for the wheel, but he mumbled, "Got it."

The sound of a lighter snapped Claire out of her daze. She glanced up to see him lighting a joint.

"Damn it! I knew it. Get out of the car, Anna. Make him pull over. Call Dad. Look for a gas station. Make him stop the car!" Claire shouted, but as she looked out the window her heart sank. They were too far out now, nothing but snow-covered trees and fields staring back at them.

The Camaro was flying down the blacktop at ninety-seven miles per hour. Kareem cranked Nickelback and passed the joint to Anna.

They drove for a good fifteen miles, laughing and singing.

Claire continued yelling at them to stop the car. She couldn't help but think of all the times she'd worried Anna might turn to drugs or drinking, and subsequently fall in with the wrong crowd trying to deal with her trichotillomania. She'd never imagined *she'd* be the reason Anna would do something like this, or that she'd be with her when it happened. Claire couldn't remember ever feeling so helpless. Then she saw it.

Anna was singing off-key at the top of her lungs and passing the joint back to Kareem, when a flicker of light in the distance caught Claire's eye. The sky glowed dark pink as if to highlight certain death, but Claire was the only one who ever saw it coming. It was moving fast—at least as fast as they were.

Her first instinct was to wrap herself around Anna to protect her, but she doubted it would do any good. It was too big a gamble. Claire ripped herself from the car, and hovered over the roof for a couple of seconds not knowing what she'd do or how she'd do it, only knowing she couldn't die twice. She had to save her daughter.

Her initial impact was so powerful it spun the car all the way around, sending the joint, the soda and Kareem's sunglasses flying through the air. They felt the second impact when the Camaro slammed into a snow bank in the shallow ditch on the other side of the road. Anna screamed from start to finish, and screamed again when the train roared past.

The two sat facing the road, trying to catch their breath.

Kareem was gripping the steering wheel so hard his hands had gone pale. The engine was running, but only their gasps for breath could be heard.

Anna cried, "What was that!?"

"I don't know—a deer I think. You okay?"

"I wanna go home. I wanna go home, right now!"

"Okay, okay. Just help me get it out of the ditch," he said, as he opened his door.

"I'm calling my dad!" Anna said as she looked around for her phone, wishing for once it was charged.

"Shit—the joint. Help me find it," Kareem said, turning in his seat.

"Oh my God, what if the car catches on fire?" Anna cried. They peered into the back seat.

"There it is," Kareem said, stretching as far as he could and emerging with the roach and tossing into the snow. "Get behind the wheel." He ordered then got out, slammed the door and waded through the snow, walking all the way around the Camaro. He kept frowning, bending down for closer inspection and frowning, again.

"What? What's wrong? Come on! We've gotta get out of here!" Anna yelled from inside, as she climbed into the slippery soda-soaked driver's seat.

Kareem ignored her, shivered and shook his head. He waded around to the back of the car and shouted for her to put it in drive and gun it.

"You're okay. Everything's going to be okay," Claire chanted over and over from the passenger's seat as she stroked her daughter's hair. Anna bawled. She looked absolutely terrified. Her black lipstick was smeared across her porcelain cheek and black mascara tears ran down her throat.

"I don't know how to drive!" she screamed at the top of her lungs. I'm all high and we're stuck out here in the middle of nowhere! Everything is all sticky... and it's getting dark... and I don't ever want to see you again!" she screamed.

"Good!" Kareem shouted, "Now, hit the fucking gas pedal."

"You're damn right it's good!" Claire shouted, shaking her fist at him.

Anna dropped her hands from the wheel and her foot from the gas. She covered her face with her hands and cried even harder, "I want my mom! I want my mommy!"

"Fuck!" Kareem shouted as he waded through the snow and opened the door. "Please stop crying. Would you stop fucking crying!?"

Claire wanted to slap him silly, but she was completely exhausted. She'd already decided what little energy she had left was going to be spent comforting Anna.

Kareem crouched down in the snow next to the door, shaking his head. "This is such bullshit."

"Ya think!?" Anna shouted in his face.

"I mean," he said, nearing the end of his patience, "Whatever hit us hard enough to spin us around like that... it didn't do any damage, not a scratch." He shivered again and looked around nervously. "Get over. Move! I—I need to warm up a minute."

"Jerk!" Anna said, sniffling and climbing into the passenger's seat.

"Shut up! Would you!?"

A pair of headlights shone through the car. A pick-up truck had slowed down.

"You folks okay? I got a tow strap in back," the driver called out.

"Yes, sir! That'd be great. I was starting to think we might freeze out here," Kareem said, his demeanor changing instantly as he got out of the car, slammed the door and plodded up the snow bank.

⊏⊐

Julia grimaced, as she sipped her herbal tea. "What I wouldn't give for just one little caramel macchiato. This crap tastes like furniture polish," she muttered to herself, and tossed the remainder of the tea over the railing of her small deck.

Enormous green fronds formed a virtual wall around the deck and a natural canopy as well. She loved it. The listing had described it as a "modest mountain house", but Julia felt she'd finally found the secret treetop hideaway she'd begged for as a girl. *I always knew I'd have to get it for myself.* She'd paid only forty thousand in cash through a friend, a year ago.

Julia shuddered as she remembered the small suburban library where she'd sat between a teenage girl picking scabs and an old man with a smoker's cough. She'd first drooled over the photos of her beloved bird's nest, on an old finger-smudged computer screen. It had seemed too good to be true, nestled in the mountainside of the eastern shore village of Santa Catarina, Brazil—minutes from the beach, an outdoor market and a few mom and pop stores.

When she'd arrived in the village, she'd fully expected to find a ramshackle cousin of the dreamy hideaway. Instead, she'd found it to be even better than the listing had indicated with pretty orange curtains, and not a single neighbor in sight. She was protected from the world. This was her reward for having the patience to carry out her complicated retirement plan over several years time.

Julia leaned back into the rustic wooden bench. She propped her swollen feet up on the matching sturdy table and looked around, trying to recapture the excitement she'd felt when she'd first arrived.

Inside, two rooms were simply furnished with more dark primitive furniture: a bed with a hand-woven fuschia spread, a nightstand, a set of floor-to-ceiling shelves which served as a closet, a table with two chairs, and a small kitchen area with a mini-stove and fridge.

Even though she'd lived in a spacious, luxury high-rise in Chicago's Gold Coast for the past few years, her heart had leapt at the sight of the simple décor. She'd found it soothing after her escape plan had grown inordinately complicated during the last few months of its execution. By the time she'd fled the country, she'd feared she'd keel over from a heart attack right on Signature's tarmac, and never even make it to her friend's Falcon.

She'd surrounded herself with the best of everything for years: designer clothing, furniture, jewelry, gadgets—you name it, she had it. Yet strangely, nothing had ever felt as liberating as walking away from it all, lock, stock and barrel. No more work bullshit and kissing ass. No more fucking for keys and favors, and no more people, period. English-speaking, anyway. Leaving the majority of her material possessions behind had been Julia's way of flushing all evidence of that hideous existence right down the toilet.

She'd reinvented herself before she'd even landed in Brazil. She loved speaking broken Portuguese and had no intention of improving. It provided a wonderful barrier between her and the locals, as well as the occasional tourist. Her Italian genes and her newly-dyed dark tresses helped her blend into the population, on the rare occasion she chose to be a part of it. She'd discovered early on that she could get just about anything delivered to her doorstep by hungry kids, for a few measly coins. She preferred dealing with the grimy little beggars over the rest of the locals any day. All you had to do was put a little money in their grubby hand, and they'd disappear. They didn't want to get to know her, and that had made them her favorites by a landslide.

It had been so long since anything in her life had been this clean, simple and uncomplicated. When she'd stepped over the threshold of her tiny cottage every cell in her body had shouted at once, "Welcome home!"

But several months had passed. She'd succeeded in leaving all the old hassles behind, as well as accumulating any new hassles... also known as relationships. Now she was bored. Julia had been playing people like pawns since she was a little girl. What did one do for fun, once one had flushed all the chess pieces? Her one true friend in life wouldn't arrive for three more months. Then she'd be fine, she told herself. Then she could handle anything.

In the meantime, she had sworn not to turn to the Internet to alleviate her boredom. She didn't trust herself to keep things simple and avoid temptation. Manipulating people, while often a pain in the ass, had proven to be the toughest addiction to kick, tougher than the caffeine and nicotine by a long shot.

Today, she couldn't stop thinking about the Internet. She'd already bought everything she could locally: the bassinet, blankets, baby clothes, diapers, toys and bottles. They were cute, albeit a little cheap, but they'd do until the two of them were settled in together, back in their little hideaway. Then she'd shop online like there was no tomorrow. Her baby was going to have the best of everything. *My baby*.

The thought always packed a wallop.

There was never supposed to be any *my baby*. All her life, she'd believed what she'd been told by a small town doctor. He'd said her endometriosis was far too advanced to conceive a child, one of the worst cases he'd ever seen. After treating her for another chronic infection, he'd mentioned how adoption could be a wonderful experience. Julia remembered snorting at him cynically. She'd been fifteen and relieved as hell that she'd never have to worry about birth control again.

That had been more than twenty-five years ago. She'd effortlessly pictured life without children. She'd been adopted, and she wasn't about to repeat the same bogus mistake. This, however, was no mistake. As far as Julia was concerned, she carried a miracle child who would have everything she'd been denied and more—the clothes, the toys, the travel... the *world*.

Lately, she'd been losing herself in daydreams of all the frilly baby things she could buy online from Bloomie's, Macy's and Baby Gap, not to mention all those gorgeous little high-end boutiques she'd begun perusing back in July, when the blue line had appeared on the sixth stick. The urge to cave in and shop online became harder to fight. Her friend Enrique had come through with her new identity, complete with new credit cards she'd yet to use.

Julia's head began to throb again at the thought. She massaged her temples and dismissed her daydreams. She still wasn't ready to take any big risks. So much more was riding on her anonymity now. She had someone else to think about for the first time in her life. Her mind drifted to the enormous hospital in Sao Paolo.

She knew she'd have to stay in a hotel near the hospital for the last few months of her pregnancy. Time was running out. She'd have to leave her safe little nest soon. There was no way in hell she'd be taking that god-awful boat ride, in addition to the six-hour bus ride, while nine months pregnant. There was no guarantee she'd even have a seat on the bus. The thought of doing this all at six months along, was daunting enough. She felt as big as a barn, having grown from a size two to a size ten. Admittedly, she'd been too vain to buy maternity clothes and regretted it. The rubber band looped through the buttonhole of her fat jeans had cut into her stomach more with each passing day, until she'd finally been forced to buy a few hideous, but ungodly comfortable mu-mus from the local market. *Maybe I should leave for Sao Paolo sooner. It would give me time to get some decent maternity clothes and see an eye doctor.*

She'd been experiencing blurred vision in her left eye for over a month. It had become quite annoying. Squinting all the time had given her a headache that never seemed to go away. She'd made peace with the fact that she probably needed glasses for now and laser surgery later, when the time came to relocate.

*Of course I need to get to Sao Paolo now. What was I thinking? The sooner the better. What am I so worried about? It's huge. I'll blend. Once I'm back here, I'll blend in even better with the baby. Besides, in Sao Paolo I can buy the rest of the baby's things and have them shipped!*

A parrot cawed behind her, jerking her back into the present. Annoyed by the intrusion, Julia swung her swollen feet off the table, pushed herself up until she regained her balance, and waddled inside. She stood by the table with her hands resting on her full hips. Today, the mere sight of the two chairs on either side of the little table pissed her off. She was lonely as hell, but she was succeeding at weaning herself from men, and in her current state, men didn't seem to mind.

Nearly positive she was carrying a baby girl, she had every intention of protecting her from the clueless, bumbling clods.

Technically, she'd quit men cold turkey once she'd left Chicago, but she still entertained bizarre fantasies which were anything but sexual. It wasn't men she fantasized about so much. It was *a* man—one man—Paul.

More than once, she'd imagined herself sitting at that crude little table with Paul, Claire's Paul—the end-all-be-all-father-of-fathers Paul, the two of them laughing about all the cute things the baby had said and done that day. The man was a natural with daughters.

Em and Anna were living testaments to the fact. They were polite, intelligent and downright clever—real treasures, not to mention beautiful. They'd never have to go to school smelling like a hog house, a day in their life. They'd never have to do a single chore involving an obstinate farm animal. They'd never be teased for being poor and wearing some other kid's hand-me-downs. They'd never have to baby-sit some smelly little brat just to escape it all, and they'd never have to accept advances from a creepy uncle just to get their hands on their first name-brand clothes. Who was she kidding? She missed the hell out of Claire's girls, but she wasn't going to waste any more time crying about it. She was going to forget them.

Paul was an aloof son-of-a-bitch. He'd never stolen a single glance at her cleavage. In fact, he'd rarely made eye contact with her, which drove Julia crazy, because it only made her respect him more. Respect him and hate him... and respect him more. *Fuck him. The only decent guy I've ever laid eyes on, and he wouldn't return so much as a glance. What made Claire, with her clean-scrubbed face and comfortable shoes, so fucking special, anyway?*

She'd never managed to unravel that mystery. Claire made so little effort, but she had it all—more love and perfection in her life than any woman deserved. Julia's head was really throbbing now.

She did not miss Claire, by God. She didn't give a rat's ass where she was or what she was doing either... in her perfect little house with her perfect little family. *Piss on her. I sure as hell don't care who or what went down in the aftermath, either.*

Yet she hoped the fallout had been ugly and that anyone

associated with her had gotten the axe, especially that little bitch, Collin. As much as his father loathed him, Julia took solace in the fact that this had surely been the last straw, and the painting princess had been thrown out on his ass.

It hadn't been easy weaseling her way between the two of them. Claire and Collin had been tight. It was some of her finest work to date. She'd naively counted on the lighthouse rule in the beginning—It being illegal in some states for three people to live in a lighthouse. Consumed by thoughts of the other two talking about him, one almost always lost his mind. Unfortunately, the bank had proven not to be isolating enough for the lighthouse rule, and Collin had turned out to be tougher than she'd antici-pated. *Gay men always are.*

She chastised herself for forgetting this rule of thumb. She would never allow herself to forget it again. Any gay man had surely been through at least as much hell as she had, growing up. They were notoriously formidable opponents, but they also heightened the stakes and made the game more interesting.

Collin had never liked her and that had been the only bone he'd thrown her. It had been easy to call Claire's attention to his tendency towards cattiness, as Julia naturally drew it out with little effort. Unfortunately, he'd spotted this trap early on. His cynicism had become so dark on several occasions he'd actu-ally repelled Claire, and driven her right to Julia. After that, Julia had to really keep an eye on him. She was astonished at times that he hadn't pieced enough of her plan together to blow it wide open. If anyone could have, it was Collin.

She had no doubt Collin and Claire were together again and tighter than ever, but at least it was in the unemployment line.

*What if my baby's gay?*

It hadn't occurred to her before. Whenever the thought had crept into her mind that she might be carrying a boy, she'd shuddered and resolved to raise a decent, proper, respectable man, if that were the case. A new breed was needed anyway. Aside from Paul, they could do away with the whole damn lot of them and start fresh from scratch. She'd never even caught him stealing a glance at her legs. She was invisible to no man, not even the fags. She dressed too impeccably. And Paul... Paul had simply been trying too hard to hide his attraction, she reasoned.

It didn't matter now. That was her old life, long since discarded. If she ended up having a gay little boy, she'd just mold him into someone so polished, cool and calculating even Collin would be impressed.

*You don't miss a damn one of them. So get over it and get back to your list of baby names. Maybe try writing them out—see how they look on paper.*

She searched for some paper and a pen, and nearly fell to her knees in pain when she bent over to look beneath the bed. Her head was pounding, as she pulled herself up and shuffled into the tiny bathroom with its simply-tiled walk-in shower. It was the only decadent feature in the place, and now she wished it were a claw-foot bathtub. She was sweating, and would have been able to sit in cool water up to her neck and soak all her frustrations away. She knew being upset wasn't good for the baby. *My baby.*

# CHAPTER 14

A LARGE MIRROR hung above the sink and since she had no medicine cabinet, odds and ends wound up in a wicker basket on the counter. Julia pawed through its contents until she found the nearly empty bottle of Excedrin. It hadn't seemed to help the past few days. She popped a couple in her mouth anyway, turned the faucet on and ran her hand beneath it, bringing long cool sips to her mouth until the chalky bitterness dissipated.

She lifted her head, frowned at her reflection. Her long dark hair was piled on top of her head with a clip, which used to look cute, but now her face was getting fat.

The local produce had posed a bit of a challenge when she'd first arrived. She'd never been much of a cook, more of a take-out connoisseur. She didn't dare venture into the more touristy part of town with its lovely restaurants down on the beach. It would be just her luck some vacationing little bikini-clad bitch would recognize her from the news. Or maybe she'd made it to the post office walls by now. The thought gave her a little rush, followed by a queasy feeling she tried to ignore.

The bottom line was that she was pregnant, and she

was going to get fat. So when she'd arrived in Brazil, she'd been ready to eat and eat *well*.

The only problem was this was a village brimming with locally grown fresh fruits and vegetables, and Jesus, were they proud of them. Everywhere you turned, there were mounds of fresh produce. Now that she was finally ready for a torrid affair with Ben and Jerry, the re-inventors of ice cream, they were nowhere to be found.

So she'd done the next best thing, and developed an addiction to sweet potatoes fried in butter. Sometimes, she indulged twice a day. She felt a little drugged once her stomach was full. She'd grown to love that feeling.

Julia grimaced and slowly turned as her gaze traveled down the reflection of her body, and stopped at her butt. She'd accepted the fact that her stomach was expanding, her waistline a distant memory, but why did her *ass* have to get fat? The thought sent her heart into a panic every time. Like, she could hear all her bargaining chips being sucked up by some giant cosmic vacuum cleaner... and it scared the shit out of her.

She'd have to remind herself that it wasn't like that anymore. She had the money now. She'd never have to screw anyone for anything again, and thank God, because who would ever touch an ass this wide?

Before she could shut her mind down—take a walk or something—it answered.

*George.*

He'd been the worst part of the whole plan, but being the Security supervisor, he'd been absolutely necessary. She felt nauseous at the thought of his age-spotted girly little hands unbuttoning her blouse, his bald head gleaming under the fluorescent lights of his office. It was almost as white as those damn gym socks he wore with his black shoes.

"Please God," she begged as she crumpled on the rug in

front of the toilet, grabbing the seat with both hands. *I can accept any of the others being the father of my baby—I promise.* "Not him," she cried just before she ejected that morning's fix of greasy sweet potatoes.

She sat there a while, and emptied her stomach, as she berated herself for crying. Then, she stood up and unsnapped her floral print, XL mu-mu. She let it drop to the floor, followed by her big, white, ugly underwear. She hadn't bothered with a bra lately since her implants seemed to ache all the time, now. She never had company, anyway.

She stepped into the shower with every intention of emptying the tiny hot water heater. Here, she allowed herself to cry, but nowhere else. She had broken that rule today, and this disgusted her. She was getting weak and emotional and she hated it. *It has to be the hormones, but it's got to stop.*

She cried almost daily, but from now on, she'd be damned if that was going to happen anywhere but in the shower. Even if she had to drag a chair in there to get it all out. Sitting on the floor was no longer an option. Gravity seemed to have the upper hand these days.

This baby had been the surprise of a lifetime, something she'd never even known she'd wanted. Its discovery had accelerated her plan, magnified its sheer brilliance. She would finally have all the money *and* love she deserved, and there wasn't a damn thing anyone could do about it.

As far as fathers went, there was a wide array of possibilities: pilots, dealers, drivers, lookouts... and security guards. It could've been just about any of them, Julia lied to herself. She hoped it was the delivery boy from Thai Palace—a tan, muscular thing working his way through pre-med, dealing a little coke with his Chicken Satay. A girl could hope, but she feared with all her heart it had been George, on his filthy desk.

When the water ran cold, Julia dragged herself from the

shower and stood in the doorway scanning the room once more, as she wrapped a small towel around her. Only the top corners met now. She tried to tuck one behind the other across her chest, but finally threw it on the floor, and squatted as low as she could to hook her moo-moo with a finger. She grudgingly slipped it over her head, and glanced about the room.

She spotted a triangle of something white against the dark wood floor. It was poking out from beneath the fuchsia bedspread. *I knew I had some paper.* She walked over and squatted down, holding her belly. When she pulled on the notebook, a snarled mess of light pink yarn came along with it. It was her old piss-poor attempt at knitting, which had also ended in tears. *Fuck that shit. Knitting's for masochists.*

She stuffed it back under the bed. Then she reached a little further beneath the bed to touch her old friend, the enormous black canvas duffle bag—*petted* it was more like it. It contained the entire, beloved, three mil. She smiled as she realized she actually thought of it like a pet. It was nice to know it was right beneath her as she fell asleep each night, and like a pet, it couldn't be left alone for long. It wouldn't piddle on the floor, but it might wander off. She felt a surge of love spread through her chest whenever she touched it—the same love she felt when she touched her bulging stomach. It was intoxicating. She felt better.

She slowly stood up and spotted a Union Allied pen atop the mini-fridge. Julia smiled to herself as she walked over and picked it up before heading back out to the deck to empty her head.

"Claire Elaine."

Claire recognized that tone. Although, she didn't think she'd heard it since the day she'd started a fire behind the barn to cook some mud pies. Odds were this was more serious, since it was Nana's first visit to the beach house. Claire rolled over and pulled the covers down to her chin.

Nana sat on the edge of the bed, arms folded across her chest. She wore an exasperated expression, but didn't say a word.

"Don't start. I feel rotten enough. I know I screwed up, but we're here to learn aren't we?"

"You kindled a relationship *and* a fire—talk about messing with people's paths."

"I just wanted to help her find a friend. Anna's so alone during the day. Em's the only one holding it together, and it's getting harder for me to get to her everyday to play. I'm spreading myself way too thin... wait, that's it!"

Claire sat up and grabbed Nana by the shoulders. "Show me how to be in more than one place at a time."

"Not a chance," Nana said with a laugh.

"Don't be a hypocrite. You're a die-hard troller. You didn't really come here to lecture me, did you?"

Nana looked away, as she ran a hand over her coarse white hair and checked her bun. She let out a long sigh. "Yes, I'm a die-hard troller, but you're a hard dog to keep under the porch."

"Who wants to be kept under the porch? Is that where I am?"

"I'm just saying you've got to ease up a bit, and start to think about exploring your new home. You're going to cause snags and tear up their paths, if you don't back off. I didn't come here to lecture you. I came here to warn you. You'll wind up having to answer to someone else if you keep this up."

"Like who?"

"I'm not sure, but they're going to let you know how much you're holding yourself back, and then there'll be rules to follow. That's no good. You want to stay free like you are now."

"Free? Ha!" Claire clenched a pillow to her chest, then lifted her head. "Holding myself back from what exactly?"

Nana leaned in and placed a hand on her arm. "There are so many souls here who want to see you again, but they can't because your vibration is as slow as molasses in January from all your trolling. You're all out of balance, because you're spending too much time with Paul and the girls."

"Like who? Who is so damn important that I'm supposed to walk away from my family during the worst time of their lives?"

"Hon, I'm not saying they're more important, but there are friends and family members who passed when you were young, even before you were born. There are people from your other lives, people you won't remember until you see them. They're folks you absolutely adored, but you can't even begin to remember any of that, because you're hanging onto your past like a tick on a dog, and have been since the moment I took you to the girls. I knew I should've waited, but you needed to see they were okay. It's my fault. I introduced you to trolling too soon, didn't give you time to explore."

"Nothing is your fault. I'm with my family where I belong. If it was such a bad thing, someone would have intervened by now."

"Claire, *I* am intervening before they do. Now, listen to me, please. Trying to protect everyone from everything is like trying to nail Jell-O to a tree."

"No, you're asking me to leave them and I won't. I can't. Not now. Don't ask me again."

Nana shook her head. "I'm on your side. I remember what it's like, but you leave me no choice. I have to ask for help now."

Claire pounded the pillow with her fist. "Don't you see? I've got to do everything I can to help them. I'll just be more careful. I promise."

"Come on," Nana said, extending a hand, "You need some fresh air."

Claire grudgingly took her hand and got out of bed. She wore a sleeveless, white, cotton nightgown, and thought herself back into her jeans and white T-shirt as she followed Nana down the hall into a flash of light.

"This is the road to the cabin."

"We're not going to your mother's cabin," Nana said as they stood in the road. "Look down there in the ditch and tell me what you see."

The rising sun shone brightly and at first Claire saw nothing unusual, but then a glint caught her eye. "My God, there must be hundreds of them," she said, pointing to the shimmering dew-covered spider webs.

"They've always been there," Nana assured her.

"No, I walked this road to the bus thousands of times."

"Cross my heart. There are always things at work all around us. Have some faith," Nana insisted.

"Oh! Oh no," Claire said as a magnificent black-and-yellow Swallowtail butterfly fluttered into the ditch, right for the webs.

"Don't worry. Nothing's going to keep her from tending her wildflowers. That's just her nature."

Sure enough, the butterfly lit on a milkweed pod, unharmed. Claire smiled at Nana and took her hand.

Nana then led Claire through another flash of light to the beach, down to the water's edge where a white blanket was spread out on the sand. She sat down. "Let's just lie down and rest our eyes for a bit. I won't mention trolling to you again. Just don't cut off the limb you're sitting on." Nana motioned for Claire to join her on the blanket.

Claire sensed a trick. She trusted Nana. Still, she knew she could have whipped up a breath of fresh air back in the bedroom easily enough without dragging her down to the beach. When Claire closed her eyes, she felt Nana squeeze her hand. When she let go, Claire's head felt heavy. Maybe it was the sun or the rhythmic lapping of the waves, but she couldn't think. She'd start to think of something, but she couldn't hang onto it. Finally, she let go, and sunk deeper into the calm blankness. It seemed like she'd been there in that wide open space for ages, when she heard someone.

A deep soothing voice whispered in her ear, "Well, look who's learned to levitate all by herself."

Claire struggled to open her eyes like, she was waking up from anesthesia. She could make out a tanned face with a deeply-lined forehead. His eyes were kind, Asian, dark chocolate-brown pools. His hair was Colgate-white, thick and long on top with the rest clipped short. He wore a cream-colored fisherman's sweater, which went rolling past her. Next, his worn and faded jeans and finally, their cuffs rolled up mid-calf were the last to cross her line of vision as she landed on the blanket with a thump.

Claire gasped. "How did you do that?"

"That was you," he said, as he sat down next to her on the blanket. He hugged his knees and sat facing her. "I'm Cal, your guardian."

Claire laughed. "Like, guardian angel?"

"That's me."

"Seriously?"

"Yeah."

"I didn't think I had one. Where have you been?"

Cal laughed and dusted the sand off his jeans. "The question is where have *you* been?" he asked, sprawling out on the blanket, then turning on his side to face her, resting his head in his hand.

"Here we go again. I've only been taking care of my family. They needed me," she said a little too defensively.

"It's nice to finally see each other again, don't you think?"

Claire shook her head. "Seriously, you're really my guardian angel? Like, you keep me out of trouble, that sort of thing?"

"Well, if I kept you out of trouble, I'd be denying you life experiences."

"Right."

"I'd say it's more like I give you nudges, you know, signs. Sometimes they're to keep you from repeating the same lessons over and over, but not always. Sometimes they're to steer you toward new ones you put in your manifest."

"My manifest?"

"Uh, you've been referring to it as your blueprint, I think, but you've got the general idea."

"You work with Wendy?"

"Among others."

"Do you work with... you know, God?"

"Yup," Cal said, scratching his chin.

Claire lay down, suddenly overwhelmed by thoughts of God. She rested her head in her hand to face Cal. The two of them gazed at one another in silence, until Claire felt her heart begin to race.

"You've been there from the beginning? Every minute? Every day?" she asked.

"I can be in several places at once, but yes. Don't worry, Claire. You're a good student. It's not very nice to toss your gum out the window. The birds will *not* eat it, but we're willing to let that slide," he joked, trying to lighten the mood.

She felt so exposed. "You know all my thoughts?"

"I know this is a little overwhelming, but trust me, it's a good thing. I know your thoughts, feelings and fears. Everything you experience, I experience with you. We're in this together."

"I must have bored you to death," she said, dropping her eyes, picking at the blanket, thoroughly embarrassed.

"Hardly, it was a good ride," he assured her.

"Does God think so?"

"Oh, yeah."

"You've been with me through *all* of my lives?"

"All forty-six. Obviously, you prefer to study on the earth plane. You've never spent too much time here, but I've spent *all* my time here. I've never been human. So you constantly amaze me. You're brave... and a tad stubborn," he added.

"Brave?" Claire snorted. "Try dull... we've probably had this conversation before, huh?"

"You are *anything,* but dull, and forty-five times, but I don't mind. I'm just happy to see you, and finally have you see me again."

"Telling me over and over again, every time like, it's the first time... that would drive me nuts."

"Comes with the job." He saw a flash of recognition in Claire's eyes.

"You had to have been there when I died... on the express-way. What was that like?"

"Meow."

"No."

"Cute little guy, wasn't I?" He gave her a wink.

"Why would you do such a thing?"

"Just following orders—*your* orders. Your manifest, your orders."

"It would be really nice to remember just one damn thing I put in there. At least I know you didn't get squashed," she said, shaking her head. "You must have all kinds of tricks up your sleeve."

A little blue-and-black butterfly lit on the back of her hand.

Cal smiled.

"Nice," Claire breathed. "I always believed in signs."

"I know. I want to thank you for that. Too many people don't believe in signs anymore, completely ignore them, and it makes their paths so much harder, so much needless suffering. Those are the guardians pulling their hair out," he said with a chuckle, as the butterfly took flight and disappeared over the ocean's waves.

"What's your favorite?" Claire asked.

"Oh gosh, there's too many. Let's see... I'd have to say déjà vu ranks right up there. The look on your face is always priceless."

Claire blushed.

Cal patted her leg reassuringly. "You know when you're playing fetch with a dog and you fake a throw, and he stands there for a second like, *Heyyy... wait a minute?*"

Claire threw her head back with a laugh.

"Same look," he said, laughing and slapping his leg. "Never get tired of that one."

"I experienced déjà vu a lot, now that I think about it," she said, trying to sound surly.

"Oh, it wasn't always me. Your loved ones over here have access to most of these signs too, and you also experience déjà vu when you're perfectly in-line with your manifesto," he added.

"Oh, right. I forgot."

"I've seen you pull a few good signs yourself, lately. You're lucky the big guy is lenient when it comes to stealing office supplies."

Claire's eyes grew wide.

"Kidding. You feel like a field trip?"

"Maybe. Where to?"

"Not far." He placed a hand on her forehead. It was warm, and he gently guided her to roll over and lie on her back."

Her pulse quickened. She wanted to tell him to stop. Despite everything he'd told her, he felt like someone she'd just met. She bit her lip and kept quiet as an image of herself as a girl, learning to back float in the creek popped into her mind, like part of a slideshow.

He kept his hand on her forehead as he spoke.

Claire was aware of a slight pulling sensation coming from his hand, as if it were a magnet literally extracting the worries from her mind. She was feeling much more relaxed, when she heard him say, "You're holding on to too much pain. Your vibration was so heavy I couldn't reach you to release it until now."

The next thing she knew, they were standing beneath an enormous green canopy of leaves extending from rows of trees on either side. At the same time, she sensed Cal was still sitting beside her on the beach. She could feel his palm resting on her forehead, but she could also feel the same hand holding hers at her side. It was like sleepwalking. Everything she was seeing and feeling in two completely different places overlapped. She became overwhelmed trying to separate them and finally gave up.

Only when she stopped trying to make sense of it, did they become firmly rooted in one place—the forest. A trellis covered in red roses lay ahead on the path. Just beyond it, Claire could see a brilliant purple light. She and Cal were now walking along the path hand-in-hand, although she couldn't remember setting out on a walk. As they walked beneath the rose-covered trellis, she could see the light was coming from a woman.

"Zahara. She guards the tapestry," Cal said, squeezing Claire's hand and nodding a greeting to the woman.

Behind the woman, hung a work of art so enormous Claire couldn't determine where it ended. She heard a gentle "hello" inside her head, and sent one back to Zahara.

The woman smiled at Claire and stepped aside, so she and Cal could approach the tapestry. It was so tall it brushed the treetops. Unable to see the edge, Claire thought it was easily forty feet tall, and it appeared to span the entire length of the tunnel, formed by the trees. She still couldn't tell what was holding it up. Claire searched her mind for a proper word to describe the dazzling spectacle, but nothing seemed adequate. The threads were metallic and brilliantly-colored. The tapestry shimmered as it moved, and was loaded with elaborate geometric designs.

At first glance, Claire thought there was a breeze blowing through the tunnel, moving the tapestry. As she stepped closer, she turned to Cal. "Can I touch it?" He nodded and Claire reached out to touch the fabric. She gasped and jerked her hand back, "It's alive!"

"Each thread is a life, a soul that affects all of humanity. Every event in history lies within the tapestry. It is a portrait of time."

Claire noticed other beings seated on the ground near the tapestry. They appeared to be studying this living work of art with their own guardians, guides and teachers. Some of them had silver cords like, Gerald and Gus.

"Look!"

Cal smiled. "We call them binaries. They visit the tapestry through astral travel... in their sleep. You did too, sometimes."

"So, my thread is here."

"Yes, your thread is here, and you can see how pulling on threads, snagging them, could affect the entire tapestry, don't you?"

Claire nodded, but a part of her now wished she'd never

seen it. That part of her wanted to leave, to think herself to Paul and the girls and never come back.

As if it heard her thoughts, threads sprung out of the tapestry, and lashed themselves to her wrists.

Claire screamed.

The threads grew in length and thickness, encircling her body, forming a cocoon from the top of her head, down to her toes, leaving only her face exposed.

Claire panicked and fought the thing with every ounce of strength she had. "Cal! Help me! What's happening!?" she screamed.

Cal slowly backed away. "Shhh... this is between you and the tapestry. I'm not allowed to interfere. It won't hurt you. Calm down. Breathe. Think. Are you in any pain?"

"No!" she shouted as she tried to catch her breath. "But I can't believe you did this! First, you lure me to my death, and then you feed me to this... this thing!? I knew I shouldn't have trusted you!"

Cal looked troubled but made no effort to help her, as Claire continued to buck and struggle against the threads. It was no use, like being subdued by a boa constrictor. She was terrified of what would happen next. The more frightened and angry she became, the more she fought. The more she fought, the tighter it cinched, until she was completely exhausted and could fight no more.

That was when the threads loosened a little.

"Can this thing leave here... or follow me?" Claire panted.

In response, the threads cinched tightly, once more.

Claire kicked, and cried out in frustration.

"No," Cal answered calmly, "But you're welcome to come back and study it as often as you like until...."

"Fat chance! Until what? Until I decide to go back?"

"Or continue your studies here," he answered.

"I'm never coming back here! You like having me here, don't you!? You like controlling me, don't you!?"

"No one is controlling you, but our visits *are* few and far between," he admitted.

"I still can't move. Why won't it let go? What does it want!?" Claire cried.

"How does it feel?"

"Horrible! Make it stop!"

"Come on, Claire. Horrible? Really? What if you could never control anyone or anything ever again? Wouldn't that be a relief in some small way?"

Claire sobbed. "I'm not hurting anyone." With that she threw one last tantrum. Her screams and cries turned so primal, Cal had to turn away, until she'd completely worn herself out.

"I didn't say you were hurting anyone," he finally answered, turning to face her. "Answer my question. What if you were no longer in a position to push and pull people along the paths you see fit?"

Claire cried out again as the threads lifted her into a horizontal position and cradled her up against the rest of the tapestry.

"Shhh... it's not so bad, is it?" Cal whispered.

Claire continued to cry and dropped her head against the tapestry in defeat. The fabric felt incredibly warm and soft against her face. The threads gently rocked her, and she could feel something patting her back. It was Cal.

"Shhh... you're okay."

Claire sighed, and grudgingly let her fear and anger slip away. New sensations flooded her mind and body. She began to feel warm and safe in the tapestry's embrace—the first warmth she'd felt since her death. All negative thoughts fell away. All fear and pain dissipated until she simply *was*. She could no longer sense *where* she was, or *when* it was, or even *who* she was.

She didn't care anymore, because it was bliss. Except she wasn't *feeling* bliss. She *was* bliss, pure and free—absolute ecstasy.

*Had anything ever felt so good?* The warm embrace, the gentle rocking, Cal's tender hushing—she was *inside* of love. She knew she had no conscious memory of these sensations, but somewhere deep inside, she remembered them. She knew that much. That was all the further she could think, all the further she wanted to think, until finally... she let go of that thought too, and just succumbed to the bliss.

She had no idea how much time had passed, when she felt herself being passed from the tapestry into Cal's arms. She tried to wake up. It was too hard. She had no choice but to trust him. He hadn't lied to her. He hadn't hurt her, and neither had the tapestry. She was okay, much better than okay.

"Try to remember. Too much interference disrupts the patterns. Just be careful," Cal whispered.

"I will," she mumbled.

"There's so much more out there. It's the vacation of a lifetime. Why waste it in the duty-free shop?"

"Okay," Claire whispered and smiled, a flutter passing through her eyelids, which were still too heavy to open.

"The tapestry *is* alive, and living things are not to be manipulated. You push nature, nature pushes back," Cal warned her. "I want you to stay home and rest for a while now."

"The beach house?" Claire struggled once more to open her eyes.

"Then you need to laugh and have some fun. Spend some time with a person who makes you laugh like no one else. That's an order," he said.

"Collin... love to... how?" she tried to lift her head, but it was still too heavy.

"Unless they're still feeling too emotional, missing you too much, they can visit you the same way they visit the tapestry, through astral travel. Wait until he's sleeping and pay him a visit. Don't push him or drag him anywhere. Just present yourself gently, lovingly like a living invitation, and see what happens."

"Okay," she said again, struggling once more to open her eyes, but finally giving up.

"He won't remember much of it when he wakes up, but he'll be happy. They take the healing with them," Cal explained.

"Miss him," Claire mumbled softly.

"I know."

"Thank you," she said, before he set her down. "When will I see you again?"

There was no answer, only the sound of waves lapping against the shore.

# CHAPTER 15

CLAIRE OPENED HER EYES. Cal was gone. She was lying on the couch in her beach house trying to make sense of the bizarre experience, but it wasn't something she could dissect. She simply had to let it be, accept it... cherish it. Then she remembered what he'd said about visiting Collin. She couldn't resist. She had to see him. *Gently, lovingly... like a living invitation.*

Claire closed her eyes, and pictured Frank and Collin's brownstone. She let her mind wander to the previous Thanksgiving, to the *octopus* dish Collin had prepared especially for Em. Then she focused her mind directly on the sound of Collin's laughter, and found herself at his bedside.

"Gently, lovingly... I have no idea what I'm doing," Claire whispered, as she walked to the foot of their bed.

Frank was snoring, and Collin had fallen asleep with a pillow clutched over his head.

Claire walked around to Collin's side of the bed, and knelt down beside him.

"Hey Collin, what are you doing?" she asked, experimenting. She was surprised when he responded.

"Stupid expense reports. Where the hell have you been?" He turned away from her and repositioned the pillow over his head.

Claire persisted. "Um, I—I was getting us lattes," she said, crossing her fingers.

"Thank God," he grumbled, rolling back toward her.

Claire didn't know how to get him back to the beach house, but she was sure there had to be a way. "You're in your office?" she hedged.

"No Claire, I've started going over the expense reports in the men's room. I've tried setting urinal cakes on my desk to achieve the same ambiance... of course I'm in my office. Get your bony ass in here, and help me. It's been crazy around here. Everyone's been saying you're dead," he ranted, like he had her on speaker phone.

Frank snorted and stirred next to him for a moment, but went back to sleep.

Claire giggled with relief. She focused on his desk, and was relieved when she opened her eyes to find him sitting across from her in his leather wingback chair.

"Well?" he said.

"Well what?"

"Well, where's my latte?"

She was about to answer when something scurried across the room. When she spun around to see what it was, it vanished into the darkness.

At first glance, it looked like Collin's office, but dimly lit and little things seemed to be shifting and changing. His deceased mother's crystal candy dish had sat on his desk, full of Frango Mints, for as long as Claire could remember. Now it held cuff-links. Before her eyes they turned into tubes of paint, then sleeping pills.

The window fixtures morphed back and forth from Roman

shades to plain ugly office blinds. The color of the walls and carpeting kept changing too, as if Collin were mentally redecorating his office every thirty seconds.

Claire's feet were wet. She looked down to discover the room was flooding. More creepy little critters could be heard splashing about the room. Claire pulled her feet up and tucked them beneath her, perching precariously on the chair just in time to see the walls moving in. They stopped abruptly, as if they'd been caught in the act.

Collin just typed, and occasionally kicked something away without so much as a glance.

Claire shuddered. Then she noticed Collin's paintings. There were two in his office, and at first, they appeared to be breathing like the tapestry had. Claire forced herself out of her chair to get a better look. She realized, as she stepped closer to the one behind his desk—the untitled one of the snake swallowing its tail—that it wasn't breathing. It was pulsating like a heartbeat. All the stained-glass pieces in the painting shifting slightly with each beat, practically begging her to touch them. She was too afraid and backed away.

"I'm waiting," Collin said curtly, without looking up.

Claire jumped, then laughed at herself. *Just like old times... the same snippy attitude he used to give me whenever he couldn't reach me for more than twenty-four hours.*

She recognized the familiar faint blue vein pulsing near his temple. It was, in fact, keeping perfect time with his paintings. A nervous giggle escaped her lips. "Your latte... right. I forgot."

She wanted to conjure up something decadent with whipped cream and chocolate shavings, but she didn't know how much time she had. If they were going to the beach house, she had to *gently, lovingly*... get him out of the office, before he woke up.

"I drank it. Come on, I'll get you another one," she said, still not having the faintest idea how she was going to transport him to the beach house.

"First you disappear. Then you drink my coffee."

Claire folded her arms. She'd come unprepared to deal with Collin's cranky side. She waded through the ankle-deep water, over to his massive fish tank, glancing over her shoulder a few times to make sure nothing was following her. This place gave her the creeps. She had to get him out of here.

He could be such a brat when his feelings were hurt, but she knew it was more than that. He was grieving the loss of their friendship. Out of the corner of her eye, she caught him staring at her. He looked away the moment she turned toward him.

Claire cracked her knuckles, walked over to Collin's desk and, in one sweep of her arm, cleared it.

"Have you lost your mind!? I've got to get these done!"

"Come on, let's go. I'm sorry you haven't been able to reach me but I'm here now, Pooker."

"Don't "Pooker" me. You didn't leave a note, an email, not even one measly text. Were you raised by wolves? Unless you're dead, you *always* send a note." He gathered his papers in a huff.

Claire was astonished. He'd just presented her with the perfect opportunity to broach the subject of her death, but then she remembered they were basically mucking around inside his mind. "Then you know where I am. I miss you too, but I'm still around. Remember the dollhouse?"

"I don't know what you're talking about."

"He's pretty pissed. I don't know if you'll be able to get anywhere with him tonight," a boy spoke from the doorway.

Claire jumped at the sound of the voice, and backed around behind Collin's desk. She hadn't expected anyone else to show up. *This is no co-worker cameo. It's a kid, a red-headed, freckle-faced, baseball mitt-toting kid.*

He casually tossed a tattered ball in the air and caught it.

Claire stared at him dumbfounded.

"Shut up, Doody-head," Collin muttered, and shot the boy a quick good-humored glance.

"You know each other?" Claire asked the boy.

"All our lives. Think, Claire—think hard. I'm not going to just give it to you. Forgive me, while I have a little fun with this. Collin's dreams aren't exactly chock full of intellectual stimulation, and he always makes me be ten years old."

"I beg your pardon, Death Breath?" Collin stuck his tongue out at at him, before he punched some figures into an adding machine.

Claire shook her head and wandered over to the black leather chairs in front of the aquarium. The water was drying up, revealing soggy grass instead of carpeting. She smacked the arm of the chair a few times to check for any funny business. To her relief the chairs were simply chairs.

She sat down with her elbows on her knees, resting her chin in her hands.

Eddie pushed each wall back about five feet, before he walked over and plopped down in the chair across from her, still tossing the ball in the air.

She could smell the oiled leather glove. She looked up to see him smiling sympathetically at her. "How old are you, really?" she whispered.

"I was thirty-two when I overdosed," he whispered back.

"Oh, Edward! You're his older brother. So, why ten?" Claire asked, as she studied his untied Converse high-tops, blue jeans and green striped shirt.

Collin stood up. "I'm going to feed some baby bunnies to the boa constrictor, so you two can talk about me freely," he announced, pulling a shoebox from a drawer and tucking it under his arm. He was sporting a silver cord just like Gus and Gerald.

Claire gave him a worried look, as she watched him leave the room with his box of bunnies. "Oh, God. I bet he means Marilyn, in HR."

"Lucky guess," Eddie replied, waving at Collin as he left the room.

"My guess is I'm ten because *he* always wanted to be the big brother. After footing the bill for all three of my trips through rehab, he's earned it."

"Why are you here?" Claire asked.

"Comfort and strength—I think I'm his symbol for doing what he really wants. He always envied me that, despite my life being a train wreck. I did what I wanted, when I wanted. Collin mostly does what others want him to, hates that about himself. You've seen him around our father."

"True." Claire propped her elbow on the arm of the chair and held her head again, as if it were heavy with new information. "He has your old job. He and Frank remodeled your brownstone, too."

"Case in point—he stepped right in to save the day, but he'll never live up to the legend. Dad's done a hell of a re-write. I get to be a martyr, instead of a junkie. He still insists I was kidnapped for ransom and murdered. Unbelievable, the lies people tell themselves. Try a hot dose in a flophouse. Just wanted out of my mess."

"Suicide?"

"Affirmative."

Claire suddenly forgot about getting Collin to the beach house. She'd stumbled onto something she had to investigate. For a second, it occurred to her that this could be the sort of thing everyone kept trying to tell her she was missing out on— the answers to all of the great questions.

"What's it like for you, you know... over *here*?"

"Well, as you can see, I'm not char-broiled," he said,

spreading his arms out for her to inspect his person, the ball in one hand, the glove on the other.

"Thank God," she laughed and covered her mouth.

"I did spend some time watching others make stupid mistakes, unable to stop them. Got a good taste of *that* kind of hell. I also had to deal with the aftermath, the horrific pain I caused my friends and family, especially Collin. That really sucked, to put it mildly. *That's* hell—custom made to fit like a glove." He smacked the ball into his mitt. "But what did I expect? Harps and angels?"

The floor had morphed into a perfectly manicured little baseball diamond. Claire nodded and touched her toe to home plate.

"Now I help. I'm a guardian and I'm not going back. I'm good at this. I specialize in breathing that little bit of hope into people, when they think they can't hold on another second, signs too—anything to snap them out of it, but it doesn't always work. It didn't for me."

"Do you know Wendy?"

"Oh yeah, I'm a regular."

"So, someone sent you a sign right before you died?"

"I was alone in the basement of this flophouse, no food or anything around, no reason for this rat to head my way, but he scurried straight up to the piss-soaked box spring I was sitting on. He looked old, kind of wise, you know?"

Claire nodded, her elbows perched on her knees, her hands folded beneath her chin.

"He actually sat up on his hind legs, like he was saying, "You're really going to do it?"

Claire shook her head, entranced.

"I saw *myself*, the rat *I'd* become. Maybe they should have sent a dove or a cat, something cuter."

"Cats can't be trusted," Claire advised him.

"Rats are ugly, but they're survivors. Guess I was unwilling to see that. I wanted out. I put the needle in my arm, and he sat there staring. He wasn't going to let me die alone. It's the last thing I remember."

"Your guardian?"

"You know it."

"So you're Collin's guardian?" Claire asked, taken with the notion, wondering what kind of resume landed him that job.

"Nah, I'm just a part-timer with Collin. I listen when he needs to talk, troll a bit, and try not to interfere too much. I have other souls to look out for, people I didn't know in that life."

"Even so, I'm glad you're looking out for him."

"I still want what's best for him. That's why you have to tell him."

"Tell him what?"

"Come on, Claire. Losing me was hard enough. Our mom died giving birth to him, so he lost her before he even got a chance to know her. He's buried too many friends. Now, he's lost you too. He'll get through this, but he needs to talk to you about it, so he can have some closure. As you can see, he's pretty torn over that. He wants to know what happened, but he doesn't. He knows you're gone, but he doesn't. Help him." Eddie tossed her the ball.

Claire surprised herself by catching it. "Okay, I get it." She stood up and tossed it back to him. "Will he remember anything when he wakes up?"

"A part of him will, like a little seed you're planting in his subconscious mind. That seed will help him work through it on his own, at his own pace. It's less jarring to the psyche."

"You're pretty smart for a death-breathed doody-head."

"Thanks. I'll see you around. You'd better get going. He goes to bed late and gets up early, the sick-o."

"Right," Claire said, walking away, suddenly wishing she

didn't have to say goodbye. She liked Eddie. He'd brightened up the place considerably in the short time he'd been there. She turned to tell him so, but he was gone.

Heading for the door, she stopped to take a closer look at one of Collin's paintings, the other untitled work—the stained-glass prison.

Claire's hand rose to touch the canvas. The moment her fingertips grazed the acrylics, a wave of passion rolled through her body. It wasn't like any kind of passion she'd ever felt for another human being. She'd only felt this as a small girl whenever she'd managed to be completely alone in nature. It was a feeling that had been asleep somewhere inside her for a long time, one she'd forgotten all about.

She lost herself. The colors swirled up around her and swallowed up the ugly fluorescent lighting and shape-shifting knick-knacks. She was lost in Collin's gorgeous painting, drunk with light and color.

Then suddenly, as if an invisible wall had sprung up, she was cut off from the passion. Even worse, she felt like it was gone forever, and she was being forced into a tiny box, where inescapable monotonous office images played over and over in front of her. She couldn't move. She couldn't breathe. Something grabbed her hand, and pulled on it with such force she thought her body would rip in half.

Claire forced her eyes open. She and Collin lay gasping on the floor of his office. Gone was the baseball diamond. It had become a Twister mat covered in big brightly-colored dots. The painting hung, undisturbed, on the wall. They stared at it, panting, hearts racing.

Collin broke the silence. "It's not really untitled. I call it, *Banker Murders Artist.* What do you think?"

"I think it's poison."

"Well, it feels like you're dying when you're always forcing your passion to shut up—only speak when it's spoken to so you can do the responsible thing and keep everyone else happy."

"Jesus, Collin."

"It's okay. I'll find a way out someday."

"I see feeding the boa constrictor has relaxed you," she joked, as she sat up.

"No, it just depresses me to the point where I don't have the strength to give anyone a hard time, not even you. I have this baby bunny dream all the time."

"There's more than one boa constrictor?"

"Marilyn and Dad," he answered, covering his face with his hands, "The bunnies scream sometimes."

"We are *not* staying here." There would never be a better time to show him what she'd done with his paintings. She didn't know how the idea came to her. She didn't care. Claire got to her feet and yanked Collin up with her. She grabbed a blue ball point pen from his desk and dragged him over to the prison painting. She drew a crude door as fast as she could, and prayed it wouldn't take her right back to the painful place she'd just been.

"Why did you do that!?" Collin yelped as if she'd carved it into his bare skin.

"I had to. You'll see," she said as she grabbed his hand, threw the pen down and pressed her other palm against the ugly drawing.

A brilliant indigo tunnel shot out of the painting and sucked them up inside its whirling light. Claire's skin prickled with an electric charge. Whenever she caught sight of Collin's face, his teeth were gritted, his eyes bulging.

They swam and flew through the glowing tunnel, locked hand in hand, until she saw the source of the indigo energy. *Yes!*

The indigo door to the beach house came up fast. As suddenly as the tunnel had appeared, it disappeared behind them, and dumped them on their feet. The last of the light rose up their backs, steadying them like loving cosmic hands, then disappeared into the evening breeze.

Claire reached for the door knob, and turned to Collin for a second, "Are you okay?"

"I didn't get any peanuts. Did you?"

*He's back.*

They broke into laughter as they opened the door and spilled into the entryway.

"Hey, I want one of those!" he said, pointing to the enormous black-and-white print of the two of them at the company picnic.

"That's nothing, consider it done." She laughed as she rushed to the middle of the room. "Welcome to my gallery!" Claire shouted as she threw her arms up with a flourish.

Collin gasped. He seemed to stumble about as if he were stoned, wandering from painting to painting, sometimes laughing, sometimes stopping to cry into his hands.

Claire gave him some space to take it all in, but she eventually walked over and linked her arm through his.

"Claire... you have *all* of them... even the ones from high school. You didn't even know me then. Where *are* we?" He was so overcome with joy he could barely get the words out. When he turned to her his face fell. He knew the answer to his question.

"No, you can't be," he pleaded, grabbing her by the shoulders.

"I'm sorry, but I am."

"Bullshit. What happened?"

"Come on," she said, pulling him through the French doors, out onto the deck. The moon was orange and full, showering them in a pale light as they walked to the steps and sat down.

The sound of the waves had a calming effect and Collin let out a long sigh.

Claire buried her feet in the sand, and closed her eyes as a cool breeze blew her hair out of her face.

"You made all this?" he asked.

"Yeah."

"Like, *I Dream of Jeannie* or *Bewitched?*"

"*Bewitched*, I guess. Jeannie never did a damn thing with that bottle."

"I know, right?—Just a new throw pillow once in a while, something. This is un-freakin-believable," Collin breathed.

"Thanks."

"Met anyone famous? Di? Freddy Mercury?"

Claire shook her head apologetically.

"No one?"

"You'll be the first to know. I promise."

"I damn well better be."

The unavoidable hung in the air between them.

"Alright, spill it."

"You sure?"

Collin took a deep breath and folded his arms. "Bring it."

"I was on my way to meet you at Starbucks when I was hit by a truck on the expressway. I was chasing a cat. You're never going to find me because I was in a stupid costume—thank you very much—with no ID. They think I'm homeless."

"Christ on a tricycle, Claire! I'm so sorry!"

"It's not your fault. It's the way things were supposed to go. Trust me."

He shook his head and patted her on the knee. "There are worse ways to go. Just ask Jayne Mansfield."

"Thanks."

"Sometimes I think I feel you around me. You were really

there with Em and I when we were playing with her dolls weren't you?"

"Absolutely, don't ever doubt it. Keep yourself open like you were that day."

"Are you kidding? I was terrified. Never needed a drink so bad in my life."

"Well, I'm glad you didn't have one, because I'd be willing to bet that makes it harder for me to reach you." Claire poured sand from one hand to the other and discovered a small piece of green sea glass.

"It's so incredible you can do that for Em," Collin added, picking up a stick.

"It's nothing compared to what I used to be able to do for her."

"That's not true. It's everything," he insisted, drawing a star in the sand and tossing the stick into the tall grass.

"What about Anna?" Collin asked, remembering how he'd found her clinging to Shadow on the deck that day.

"It's harder with her, but I get through."

Collin's gaze felt heavy, as Claire rubbed the silky-smooth sea glass with her thumb.

"And Paul?"

"So far? Next to impossible."

"Sorry." Collin reached down and gave her hand a squeeze.

"I'll get through to him. It's just going to take some time. What's that beeping?" Claire asked, looking around.

"Microwave."

"Uh, I don't eat. I don't even have a kitchen. I *know* I don't have a microwave."

"Smoke detector?"

"I don't think so," Claire replied, suspiciously.

"Fine, I tried to work it in. I don't want this to be over, but that's the alarm. We've still got a few minutes. Frank always hits the snooze at least three times."

"We've got less than that." She grabbed his hand. They stood and hugged each other until they cried.

Collin pulled back and wiped the tears from her cheeks. "How am I going to live without you?"

"I'm still around, just keep your eyes open," she whispered.

"It's not the same."

"I know," she said, hearing the beep again. "Give Frank a hug for me."

He rubbed his eyes and he was gone.

# CHAPTER 16

COLLIN REACHED past Frank for the dental floss, watching him shave in his old navy blue robe. He decided he'd throw it out the minute Frank left for work. Collin knew he was holding onto the thing for sentimental reasons. The robe had been the first gift he'd ever given Frank. He'd buy him a new one for Christmas, the thickest, whitest robe he could find.

"What?" Frank rinsed his razor in the sink.

"Nothing." Collin finished flossing and walked over to drop the floss in the wastebasket.

"Either tell me what it is, or stop thinking so loudly," Frank advised, as he patted his face dry on a hand towel. He walked over to the marble wastebasket, glared at Collin, picked the floss out and returned. He opened the cupboard below the sink and dropped the floss into the wicker wastebasket.

"It's nothing, really," Collin insisted.

"We are not getting a dog."

"It's not that."

"We are not going to Alaska a seventh time."

"Two strikes," Collin said, smiling to himself.

"We are not remodeling the kitchen."

"Losing your touch, Kreskin." Collin tossed his razor in the drawer, and lifted his forehead with the palm of his hand. He let it go with a shrug, not caring as much today that his face was heading south. "I'm just in a good mood, that's all."

"You're too quiet. That's rarely good." Frank straightened the still-straight towels on the rack, only to have Collin mess them up the second he walked away. "You're late too. Must be nice to be the boss's son."

"You're a fine one to talk, Mr. CEO. You could take as long as you like. I don't see why you always have to be the first one in the office. We built that place from the ground up," Collin reminded him as he walked over to the shower.

"You sure everything's okay?" Frank said, spraying Windex on the mirror and wiping it down.

"I had another dream about Claire."

"I'm only going to say this one more time..."

"Doubt that," Collin mumbled under his breath.

"I think you should see someone about a sleeping pill prescription. You should've done it a month ago. Have a little chat while you're at it, with a professional," Frank added.

"I'm okay," Collin insisted, running his fingers through the water, jerking them back and adjusting the knob. "It was a nice dream this time, what I remember, anyway. This one seemed so *real*. I think we were on vacation somewhere. There was a beach. I can't remember anything else, but I feel different. I feel like she's okay."

"You just needed time to process everything."

Collin turned the water off and walked over to Frank.

He was wiping down the counter with a lemon-scented disinfectant wipe. His eyes met Collin's in the mirror. "What?"

"I talked to Paul about a memorial service."

"In the spring," Frank stated more than asked, as he stopped mid-swipe.

"No, before the New Year."

Frank spun around to face him. "Have you lost your mind? You can't do that."

"Why not? She would've wanted us to," Collin insisted, walking back to the shower.

"No one else is thinking of her as being gone yet—just missing," Frank reminded him.

"Oh, for Christ's sake, why do we have to put on a charade?" Collin barked, as he grabbed a towel from the linen closet, and turned the faucet on again.

"These are far from normal circumstances. It's too soon. What did Paul say when you told him your bright idea?" Frank asked, as he dropped the wipe in the wastebasket under the sink, and pulled out a pair of yellow rubber gloves and a bottle of Pine-Sol.

"He kind of feels like it's time, too. He's got the girls to consider. They know she's not coming back. I think it's unhealthy for them to go on like this, just waiting for the inevitable."

"Now you're Dr.Phil?" Frank grabbed the toilet brush and scrubbed the toilet with a vengeance. "You can't micro-manage Claire's death like its some project for work. People need time. Besides, the villagers will talk if you rush it."

"The *villagers*," Collin repeated.

"The ones with the pitchforks and torches, who still think she *is* on a beach somewhere with Julia, working on her tan."

"Idiots." Collin jammed his robe on his hook next to the shower.

"I know, but I still think you've got to wait at least six months, maybe even a year." Frank returned to the cupboard beneath the sink and tossed the gloves in the wastebasket.

"A *year*? That's insane," Collin shouted from the shower.

"Google Amelia Earhart or Jimmy Hoffa. See when their families had memorials, because there's got to be a protocol."

"You did *not* just compare Claire to Jimmy Hoffa." Collin laughed, as he slammed down the shower handle.

"You need some time away. Why don't we go to a B-n-B for the weekend?" Frank suggested. He extracted the plastic bag from the wicker wastebasket, replaced it with a fresh one and walked to the door.

"No, they need us. The holidays are going to be hell. They'll have to deal with Claire's mom and her winter depression on top of all this."

"Forgot about that," Frank said, pausing in the doorway, tying a knot in the plastic bag.

"Let's spoil the girls rotten this year," Collin pleaded.

"No, this year I'm putting my foot down. Paul has enough on his plate without having to compete with Willie Wonka. Don't forget to squeegee," he said, as he turned to leave.

"I squeegee!" Collin called out.

"Don't go there. I check," Frank yelled back from the stairway.

Collin stepped out of the shower, grabbed his robe, and tied it as he hurried out the door and down the stairs. He found Frank in the entryway, putting on his coat. His briefcase was by the door, and Collin noticed he'd packed his lunch the night before. The two of them had created Queen Sweep in college. Frank had taken it over years earlier, when Collin took over his brother Edward's position at the bank. Frank now oversaw all nine branches between the suburbs and the city, and was stretched too thin to do lunch most days.

"Did you see the handmade thank-you note Anna sent us?" Collin asked.

"No, I still can't believe she's fifteen. What did we get her?"

Frank asked, grabbing his lunch and wrapping a camel-colored cashmere scarf around his neck.

"A fifty-dollar gift card from that little movie theater by their house and some fabulous shoes," Collin reminded him. "You're welcome."

"Thanks. Are you even going to work?" Frank asked, giving Collin a quick peck on the cheek.

"Doubt it."

"Good, take a break and think about what I said." He gave Collin a stern look. "I love you... and I'm worried about you," he added, the corners of his mouth turning up in a please-forgive-me-smile.

"Love you too," Collin said, and shut the front door. He opened it again and stuck his head out. "Meet me for lunch?" he pleaded.

"We've got four new buildings to set up and staff. Call me around eleven." He waved, closing the large iron security gate behind him.

Monday through Friday, Collin woke up dreading lunch—when he missed Claire the most. There wasn't another soul at the bank he could imagine lunching with. So he went out every-day, coercing Frank into meeting him whenever he could, but most days he settled for a sandwich by himself at a nearby book store.

Initially, he'd spent his lunch hour browsing magazines, but one day he'd noticed a book about World War II sitting on a table. It was full of haunting photos and veterans' chilling stories. Thumbing through the pages provided him with a strange, almost instant sense of comfort that he couldn't have explained to anyone if he'd tried. Even stranger, it somehow made him feel closer to Claire. He was well on his way to becoming a WWII history buff, with seven hardcover books hidden in his bottom desk drawers. He wasn't sure why he felt the need to hide them, but he did.

Collin considered Frank's relaxation advice over a cup of coffee and some leftover tiramisu. After making a call to the office to tell them he'd forgotten a dentist appointment, he wandered out to the sun porch. He hadn't picked up a paint-brush in months, but he spent the remainder of the morning nailing a frame together and stretching fresh canvas over it. He still preferred it to buying them ready-made. It took him back to his high school days, when he'd first begun painting and couldn't afford to buy them. His father hadn't coughed up a dime for them, hadn't recognized any value in nurturing creative talents, aside from Eddie's model airplanes—"Now that's art."

Collin's best work had always been on canvas he'd stretched himself. It was an old ritual, a cleansing of the mental palette.

By ten o'clock he'd stretched three canvases and was craving his lunchtime trek into the history stacks. Within fifteen minutes he was whistling in the car, on his way to the bookstore. He was pulling into a primo parking space, when he realized he'd forgotten to check with Frank regarding lunch. He pulled his cell out of his coat pocket to call Queen Sweep, but the answering service picked up. They'd already started their lunch breaks.

The guilt of not only skipping work, but also forgetting to check back with Frank, made it easy for Collin to skip the book store and head to the bank for a few hours.

He rehearsed his story about how his dentist's office had called that morning to remind him of his appointment... a bad filling. No one would bother to ask, but his conscience always got the best of him. When he pulled into the parking lot, he noticed two twenty-something tellers, go into the smoking tent.

Collin sat in his car, contemplating just how much longer he could continue the charade. He was no banker. His brother had been the banker's son his father had always wanted, and nothing Collin did could ever change that. Besides, if he decided to leave the business, Queen Sweep was making more than enough to see the two of them through. *If worse came to worse, I could always join Frank at the office again... but what if I started painting... I mean, really started painting and maybe even did a show?*

Simply laying his hands on his painting supplies had boosted his spirits. Never before had Collin allowed himself to daydream of a life as a serious painter, but ever since Claire had vanished without a trace, it had become harder to ignore just how quickly life could change... or disappear altogether. *How long can I last in banking? What's the point?*

His incessant need to prove his worthiness to his father was fading. A lifetime rotting at a job he hated suddenly seemed an outrageous price to pay for simply being who he was—*a gay painter, maybe even a good one.* For whatever reason, today he could easily picture his work hanging in a gallery. Collin could no longer ignore the overwhelming urge to be completely true to himself.

He glanced toward the tent again. His constant efforts to keep Claire's name out of the mud were failing. He had reason to believe those two were leading the pack. He'd even heard them gossip with customers about Claire. *As if Julia's embezzlement wasn't juicy enough, why do they insist on dragging Claire down with her?*

Collin locked the car and walked toward the tent, approaching it from the side, careful to remain out of sight. He sat on a bench next to one of the square, mesh screens with the secured Velcro flaps that rolled up for better ventilation during the sweltering summers. Collin pulled his scarf and collar up around his neck, adjusted his sunglasses and tilted his head back. At first, he could only discern the incessant whining of two spoiled brats.

———

"Assholes still haven't put my raise on my check," muttered Denise. Her face was long like a horse's. Her eyes were set too close together, but she had long, shiny, black hair which she had a habit of flipping to make a point. She and Stephanie were seated next to each other on the bench of a paint-chipped, green picnic table. They leaned back against the table, legs outstretched and crossed at the ankles.

"Get real. It took them four months to finally put Kate's on her check," Stephanie said between snaps and cracks. She'd already been written up twice for chewing gum on the clock. Unlike Denise, she'd managed to quit smoking and was now addicted to the nicotine gum. She was up to a pack a day. If she lost her job over chewing the stuff, she wouldn't be able to afford it, and now she couldn't function for more than a few hours without it. Stephanie had chewed herself into a corner.

She wore her hair short, and having nothing to flip, she fiddled with her nametag as she contemplated her dilemma. "Nine or nine-fifty an hour, what's the difference? It's never enough," Stephanie complained.

"Tell me about it. They give you no choice, but to help yourself a little. Really, you just about have to," Denise reasoned, dropping her head back and slowly exhaling a plume of smoke into the air.

"I can't believe my parents are making me pay for half my car insurance, and then they have the balls to insist on full coverage just because my Jeep is new. *They* bought it. It's such bullshit," she said with a flip of her mane. "If Julia and Claire had asked me to help them, I mean even hinted at it, I would've... in a heartbeat," Denise declared.

"Oh my God, no kidding. We could be on a fucking yacht somewhere right now. Can you imagine never having to work again? Where do you think they went? Mexico?" Stephanie asked, rubbing her jaw.

"No way. I heard Julia had this boyfriend in Costa Rica or something, the guy who bought her that gorgeous Mercedes. Remember how she was always taking trips? Did you ever see her office?"

"Oh yeah, she had tons of pictures all over the side of her file cabinet. Places I've never even heard of. They'll *so* never find them." Stephanie giggled with glee, stretching her gum from her mouth and twisting it around her index finger.

"Not a chance," agreed Denise, grinding out her cigarette in the ashtray.

"Do you think they were, you know, *into* each other?" Stephanie asked.

---

Collin rose from the bench and rounded the corner of the tent. As he passed the flimsy plastic door, he whipped it open, letting a blast of December air blow up their skirts. Without breaking stride, he smiled at their colorful string of expletives. Yet he quarreled with his conscience all the way to Marilyn's office. *They'll lose their jobs. It's almost Christmas.*

*They're stealing.*

*They're kids.*

*They're affecting the bottom line, as well as morale.*

*How will they afford Christmas gifts?*

*They can get jobs at the mall where they belong. This institution's suffered enough.*

Moments later, he poked his head into Marilyn's office. "We've got two tellers skimming, one for sure anyway," he said, popping a Tic Tac into his mouth and tossing the empty box in Marilyn's wastebasket.

"We'll have to tape them for now. I'll let Security know. We're already short for the holidays. We need the coverage," Marilyn replied without looking up.

"Sure. I'm just going to get them some coffee and a wheelbarrow. I'll be in the vault helping them shovel if you need me," he said tersely, and proceeded down the hallway to his office.

"Let Patty know," Marilyn called out, but he didn't answer.

Collin walked into his office and closed the door behind him. *God, I hate this place. Hate the numbers, hate the games, hate the bullshit—hate it, hate it, hate it.*

He removed his gloves and threw his coat and scarf over the back of a chair. As he turned, the painting by the door caught his eye. It looked different today. He felt a peculiar panicky sensation when he looked at it.

When he sat down at his desk, he noticed a small green rock sitting on his blotter. At first he thought it was a piece of jade and held it up to the light. Upon closer inspection, he realized it was actually sea glass, of all things. *Who's been on vacation? Wish I was on vacation.*

Collin dropped the sea glass into his shirt pocket and proceeded to check his email. He was relieved when he read Frank hadn't been able to make time for lunch with him. Collin clicked out of his email, leaned back in his chair and studied his paintings. *What if my best work is behind me?*

⸻

Tony Chism sat stewing on the bench in front of his locker at Cook County Morgue. He'd started to undress, but couldn't seem to get any further. Athena haunted him. He wound his T-shirt around his fist as he stared at the floor. *I can do this. I'm gonna figure this out, one way or another.*

His own investigation had begun with a few phone calls off the clock. After a long day of cleaning and preparing cadavers for autopsies, he'd shower, go home, crack a beer and call a few precincts. He'd contacted each of the CPD precinct's Missing Persons Departments, and left dozens of messages regarding the Jane Doe case.

When he'd contacted the 16<sup>th</sup> Precinct, a new desk officer had disconnected him three times, before Tony finally gave up and dialed the next precinct on his list.

He'd known it was a long shot. He couldn't give out his real name and credentials for fear of Walter finding out, and without his credentials, he was just another nosey civilian.

When Tony didn't hear back from any detectives, he started doing a little detective work of his own. He visited parks and homeless shelters at night. He showed them Polaroids of Athena's face, asking if anyone knew her or remembered seeing her, even though he couldn't imagine her ever being in those places.

One night, a van full of young men followed his car for more than twenty minutes, and eventually tried to run him off the road. That was when he realized rumors were spreading that he was a cop, and there was nothing he could do to change that. It had been the last time he'd ventured into the seediest parts of town asking questions.

He knew he was breaking rules left and right, and if Walter

ever caught wind of it, he was toast, but he couldn't stop. Athena and her family were counting on him, and if he didn't find out who she really was, maybe no one ever would. He slipped his work shoes on and tossed his boots into the bottom of his locker.

Tony had never been one to go along. He didn't own a television, a computer or even read the newspaper. Long ago, he'd become a sworn enemy of the rumor mills. *Discussing personal tragedies is bad enough, but broadcasting them to the masses for cocktail fodder... that's crossing the line. Maybe just the library, a little microfiche search...*he'd rationalize, but he couldn't bring himself to turn to what he'd long considered the dark side.

He kept close tabs on Claire's body, checking it daily for something he might've missed. *Luckily, we've still got time on our side.*

The body could remain in the morgue unclaimed for six months before it had to be buried. He'd discover Athena's true identity before that happened.

In the meantime, he encountered one dead end after another, searching for anyone who might have known her.

He felt a twinge of guilt, as he entered the big refrigerated room full of shelves. He hadn't checked on her in two days. Normally, he'd find an excuse to stop by work on his days off, usually claiming he was going to wash his scrubs, although anyone who worked there knew it was a moot point. That sweet noxious odor was always with you. Some said it was in your skin.

"What the hell?" Tony breathed, as he pulled the metal tray out a few inches. It was empty. He jerked the others out one by one. He grew frantic as he unzipped one body bag after another, only to discover Athena wasn't inside any of them. Sweat trickled down his back, and his heart thumped wildly. He whispered a desperate prayer to St. Anthony, as he unzipped the last body bag in the room. It was an elderly Asian man.

Tony closed his eyes and shouted, "Walter!" He ran to the phone and feverishly dialed.

"Walter Rhinedhardt," the voice on the other end answered with a hacking cough.

"You said we'd keep her here for six months."

"Who is this?" Walter demanded.

"Sorry, Walter. It's Tony. I went to check on my Jane Doe and she's gone. Did you guys move her over the weekend? You didn't bury her, did you?" he said, desperately trying to keep a casual tone.

"Nobody's been buried or moved around down there, and you'd best remember you don't own any of them."

"I know, sir. It's just that I was hoping someone might identify her before her six months is up." Tony clenched his eyes shut and ran his fingers through his hair.

"I told you, all we can do is hope for the best. Someone could still identify her," Walter reminded him.

"But she's definitely not down here. You said we had six months." Tony's heart was thumping so hard he could barely think.

"Midwestern Research doesn't pick up donated cadavers 'til the end of the month, but let me check the log. I'm sure she's still here," Walter grumbled.

As he paced back and forth, Tony could hear Walter rifling through papers and probably those damn butterfly books all over his desk.

The hum of the old fluorescent lights above him seemed louder than ever, as Tony waited for an answer.

"Shit," he finally heard Walter mutter on the other end of the line.

"What? What happened?"

"Midwestern was here Saturday," Walter answered.

"No." Tony slammed his fist on the stainless steel counter.

"Now, they were scheduled to pick up two males and a female shipped over from Evanston—they had a cooler go down, and I told them we had room, but that Jane Doe wasn't one of them. She was ours, and she was marked. We've got to get her back pronto, if they took her by mistake. Does can't be donated to science—state law."

"Right." Tony was biting the knuckle of his index finger to keep every foul word he knew from escaping.

"If somebody were to identify a Doe after a bunch of med students had been carving on her, well that'd be one hell of a law suit," Walter explained what Tony had already begun to imagine.

"Has it ever happened?"

"Probably, or they wouldn't have passed the law, but we've never had it happen here, not on my watch. That's the last thing I need with just three weeks to go. Jesus, Mary, Joseph! Nah, a mix-up isn't very likely. We'll track her down, but I don't want to see you getting so attached to your cadavers. You hear me?"

"Yes, sir," Tony replied and pressed a finger to the cradle, ending the conversation.

# CHAPTER 17

JENNIFER ROBLES GLANCED up from a pile of photos on her blotter.

A young desk officer, stood in the doorway, acting as if he were putting a curse on her, utilizing a variety of Italian hand gestures. "You've got company," he finally said, as he twirled his index finger near his temple and disappeared.

"Alice o'clock," Jennifer whispered to herself. They'd used psychics and mediums in the past, but these days it wasn't in the budget, or so the new chief said. Some still volunteered their services, and Alice Fiora was the last of a dying breed.

Jennifer had heard Alice had been a real asset in her day, beautiful too, but she was pushing ninety now and came across as a sweet, old flake. She was always losing her train of thought, which made it nearly impossible to extract anything of value from her. Yet, Jennifer suspected her work with CPD was probably the only work Alice still did, maybe the only social thing she did. It was probably good for her, gave her something to occupy her mind.

Jennifer had a soft spot for her and didn't want to hurt the old woman's feelings, but she'd wasted too many afternoons listening to disjointed tips from Alice, which inevitably led nowhere. She'd shamefully managed to hide from her the last few times, ducking into the lady's room. Her fellow detectives had taken to teasing her about it. Once they'd put a bottle of Pepto-Bismol on her desk in the middle of a Celtic cross of playing cards.

She hadn't been quick enough this time. The desk clerks were supposed to check with her first, to see if she was in.

Alice waved at her from across the room. Jennifer smiled and motioned to the old woman to come over. *To hell with them. It's good to see her.*

The old woman wore an elegant, long, black, wool coat with a bright orange and blue Bears stocking cap.

Jennifer spotted the familiar squirming lump in matching orange and blue beneath the woman's arm, her dog, Lucky.

As Alice crossed the room, Jennifer could feel the eyes of the other detectives on her, as well as the tension of their suppressed laughter. She wanted to heave a stapler at someone. She was feeling so depressed over her mountain of unsolved cases, that she found herself looking forward to a visit with Alice for a change, anything to dull the pain of frustration and defeat.

"Hi, Jen," Alice said, adjusting the wriggling, fat, apricot poodle. He was clearly excited to see Jennifer.

"Hi, Alice. Hey there, Lucky. Have a seat."

"Thank you, dear," Alice replied, as she set Lucky down on the floor, and handed the end of the leash to the detective.

Jennifer lifted the corner of her desk, looped the leash around its leg and set it down again. "Coffee?"

"No, thank you. We're on our way to the v-e-t, so we haven't got time."

"Everything okay?"

"We're getting old. That's all," Alice said, smiling down at Lucky, who'd left a puddle on the floor in his excitement.

Jennifer let him lick her hand, as she picked up some Subway napkins from her desk and tossed them onto the puddle with practiced ease.

"I got a message for you. At least I think it's for you," Alice said.

"Super. Let's hear it," Jennifer said, reaching for a pen and a yellow legal pad.

"A lady named Claire says to tell Anna she got the green balloon, and the answer is 'of course' and 'good girl, sending the note right away'... oh, and 'cute shoes'" Alice added. "You know I wear a size nine myself now. All my life I wore a size eight and now, all of a sudden, I'm wearing a nine," Alice continued, as Jennifer frowned at the message.

*Holy shit.* Jennifer pinched the bridge of her nose to stave off a tension headache with Anna's name written all over it. She'd convinced herself to let the angry teen's phone call go, chalk it up to experience. Now she was back at square one with this message.

"Hang on, Alice. Excuse me, Lucky," she said, getting up and stepping over him. Jennifer walked over to a gray file cabinet and pulled the top drawer out. She returned to her desk with a manila folder, flipped it open and added the note to it.

"I think she worked at a bank. At least I saw a bank for a second when I got the message."

Jennifer choked and reached for a bottle of water next to her phone. "Union Allied?" she sputtered.

"Not sure. You know they won't allow Lucky in our bank anymore," Alice said, shaking her head. "They used to always give me dog treats for him at the drive-thru when I could still drive, but now they've sure changed their tune. They told me I have to tie him up outside when I go in. Isn't that outrageous?"

"Yes," Jennifer managed to utter before she finally cleared her throat. "Anything else?" she asked, steering Alice back to the point of her visit.

"No, that's the most I've had in months. Wendy, my best guide, doesn't come through very clearly anymore," Alice said, slowly rising from her chair, acting as if she intended to pick up Lucky.

It was Jennifer's cue. She bent down, lifted the corner of her desk, scooped up the porky poodle and handed him to Alice. "I'll walk you out," she said, linking her arm through the fragile medium's. "You need a ride to the v-e-t's?"

"No, hon. It's just down the block."

When Jennifer returned to her desk, she pulled the multi-line phone onto her ink blotter. The call had to be made, but she hated making this kind of call. She didn't want to imply they did this sort of thing all the time. This was also a message specifically *for* someone, not just a tip. She couldn't keep it to herself, and just file it like she would any other tip. *It might lead to something bigger if I share it with them. It sounded so frivolous and just plain nuts, though.*

How could she call this poor, grieving man and give him a ridiculous message about balloons and shoes? It was unthinkable. She couldn't. *The message wasn't for Paul*, she reminded herself.

She had an idea. She'd bypass the grieving husband altogether, deliver the message directly to the daughter, and finally address the subject of Anna's phone call. *That'll work.*

She knew which high school Anna attended. It was the same one she'd gone to. *This is it, no turning back. I'm going against procedure. If I hurry, I can still catch her.*

She grabbed her jacket off the back of the chair and fished her keys out of the pocket.

Jennifer blew four stop signs, cringing each time, but she

made it with a few minutes to spare. She parked her jeep across from the school, climbed out and leaned against it. It was freezing, but she was sweating buckets. *Worst time of my life.*

*You're a cop now for Christ's sake. Let all that bully shit go. Little bastards are probably in prison anyway.*

She pulled her Cubs cap down snuggly, and folded her arms as she scoped out the parking lot and grounds.

The three o'clock bell rang and kids poured out of the building, scattering in every direction. She was afraid she'd miss Anna in the stampede. If she'd changed her look at all, reinvented herself, as teenage girls were known to do, Jennifer didn't stand a chance. She laughed at the notion the second she spotted the girl's raccoon eyes set against her alabaster skin and newly-dyed jet-black hair. Jennifer held a hand up as if to say, "I come in peace, don't make me call out your name."

---

Anna was walking toward the parking lot with Kareem, when she saw the detective wave. She stiffened, as their eyes met.

"Who's that?" Kareem asked shifting Anna's overloaded backpack to his other shoulder.

"That worthless detective I told you about. Hurry up," Anna whispered and kept walking.

"Great, here she comes. I still can't believe you yelled at a cop... worse than you yelled at me?" Kareem teased, moving closer to her and putting his arm around her shoulder.

Anna's heart leapt to double time.

"Anna," Jennifer said, as she reached them.

Anna stopped and turned to face her, but remained stoic. "Dunkin Donuts is a few blocks from here if you're lost."

Kareem coughed.

Jennifer smirked. "Original. Come on, Anna. I was hoping you had time to talk over a cappuccino or something. My treat."

Anna could see Jennifer was studying Kareem as he waved to some friends. Then she watched her study the friends. Jennifer's eyes met hers again, and Anna bit her cheek to keep herself from saying anything else. Her dad was taking Em to get a new winter coat, so she didn't have to be home for several hours. Yet she could think of a thousand ways she'd rather spend them. "Your treat or the taxpayers'?" Anna asked grudgingly.

"Mine," Jennifer replied with a wry smile adding, "The taxpayers can feed the meter."

"I've got a lot of homework." Anna turned her back to the detective and walked toward Kareem's Camaro.

Kareem looked from Jennifer to Anna, wide-eyed.

Anna glared at him, her hand on the door handle, but he didn't move.

"I have something for you," Jennifer persisted.

Anna did her best to remain nonchalant, "If it's a McGruff Crime Dog coloring book, I've got my hands full with Algebra."

"She got the green balloon, Anna," Jennifer offered.

Anna turned around. Her eyes met Jennifer's. She swallowed hard. "Later, Kareem," were the only words she could manage as she grabbed her backpack.

They walked in silence to the jeep, as Kareem jumped into his Camaro and made a hasty retreat.

Jennifer opened the passenger door for Anna. "I can put your bag in the back if you want."

"No, I've got it."

Jennifer walked around the back of the jeep, wiped her brow, climbed in and turned the key in the ignition.

Anna sat in the passenger's seat picking at a hole in her glove. "Is she dead? Just say it."

"The message was given to me by a medium we work with once in a while," Jennifer answered, pulling out of the parking space.

"What *exactly* did she say?"

"Four things: a lady named Claire told her to tell Anna she got the green balloon and then something like, of course, good job sending the note right away and cute shoes."

Anna covered her face with her hands and began to cry.

Jennifer pulled the jeep over and cut the engine. She opened the glove box, pushed her gun aside and handed her a package of tissues.

"I knew it," Anna cried softly as Jennifer looked out the window.

Jennifer continued when Anna stopped to blow her nose, "Does it make sense?"

Anna sniffled and let out a long sigh, as she leaned her head back against the seat and closed her eyes. "My sister gave me a balloon bouquet for my birthday. We had a little dinner at our house, just some friends and family. We were going to go to my favorite restaurant, but I didn't feel like it without my mom. It was her favorite too. After everyone went home and went to bed, I wrote a note to my mom and tied it to a green balloon. I snuck outside and let it go," Anna explained.

"No kidding?" Jennifer said, turning in her seat to face Anna.

"I swear it."

"What did the note say?"

"I asked her if she'd been there, at the party with us," Anna said, slowly rolling her head on the headrest, toward the detective.

"You got shoes?" Jennifer asked.

Anna placed her right foot on top of her left knee to reveal a shiny, black patent leather Sketcher with silver laces.

"Alice, old girl, you've still got it," Jennifer said, as she shook her head.

"What?"

"The medium, her name is Alice and she doesn't do much work with us anymore. She's older than dirt. We kind of take her for granted, but it looks like she was right on the mark this time. Maybe I can get something of substance out of her, something that will lead us..." Jennifer didn't finish.

"Oh," was all Anna could manage.

"Look, I can't imagine the hell you've been through these past few months. I know it's beyond frustrating, but I promise you, we've followed every lead as far as we could. There just weren't very many. The weather was a bad break with the dogs. It wasn't in the forecast, and it really screwed things up. You were right. That *was* partly my fault. At my age, I should know better than to trust a Chicago weather forecast."

"Can we go see this psychic?" Anna asked.

"Medium and no, that's not a good idea. I could lose my job. Besides, she's inconsistent at best. I wouldn't want you hanging on her every word. She tried to get me to contact Liberace's estate once, said she had a message for his wife. I think she gets her wires crossed more often than not."

"We have to try," Anna insisted, staring at the jeep's roof.

"Right, no you're right about talking to her again. Crazy not to. Just let me be the go-between. I promise I'll tell you if she has anything else to say about your mother."

"God, I can't even tell anyone, except maybe my Grandma Lynn, my mom's mom. You know? This is kind of out there," Anna said. *But not as far out as Mom moving my ring.*

"What about your dad?"

"You'd be sitting here with him right now, if you really

thought he'd buy this."

"True," Jennifer admitted. "Still, Christmas is in a few days. People tend to be more open-minded with the magic of the holidays and all that."

"I'm not gonna hold my breath. I don't want to ruin his Christmas. This is so final. Its good news, but also the worst news," Anna said, adding, "I have to wait for the right time."

"I know. How about a cappuccino?"

"You don't hate me?" Anna asked.

"Hardly, you've got guts." She started up the jeep again. "I was pretty mouthy when I was your age. You can turn that skill into something fairly useful, if you're smart about it."

Anna smiled to herself.

"You still like horses?"

She gave Jennifer a puzzled look.

"Sorry, I've been in your room, remember?"

"Right, horses. Yeah, I guess so. Just haven't thought about them for a while."

"I've got a friend you should meet. He's got a stable."

"I've got enough friends."

"Yeah? That one? If he gets caught with more than two and a half grams on him they'll haul his ass in. I don't think that's a phone call you really want to make."

Anna sighed and rolled her eyes. "Like you even remember how messed up high school is. It's not like I have the greatest pool to choose from. My mom was with some dork obsessed with her nose until she met my dad in college."

"Foster—the plastic surgeon."

"Ha, figures. You've talked to him?"

"I've talked to anyone who ever had any kind of relationship with your mom, Anna. If she were here, she'd agree. You can do better. Uh... hi, Dad? It's me, Anna. Can you come get me? I'm at the police—"

"All right, all right... so when are you going to call this medium?"

———

Claire breathed a sigh of relief from the back seat. This *is the kind of friend Anna needs, and bless their hearts, they managed to find each other on their own.*

Claire felt a tug in her chest, followed by a heavy sensation. It felt like Paul was sitting in the nursing home parking lot again, an unscheduled visit. She wanted to stay with Anna and Jennifer, but she couldn't afford to miss an opportunity with Paul. These decisions were becoming so much more difficult.

———

From a chair in the corner, Claire watched Paul turn on Gus's little television.

"Thought we'd watch the game today."

Claire knew this routine, too. She remembered Paul telling her sometimes he didn't have the strength to deal with his father's silence. She couldn't fault him for it. The two had always been able to talk for hours. Claire wasn't surprised the silence growing between Paul and his father had become too big for him to face alone. She'd been the buffer since Gus's Alzheimer's had progressed. It was painful to watch them struggle through communicating on their own.

"Cold out."

Gus didn't respond.

"You look good."

Gus still didn't respond. He was busy fiddling with the drawstring on his sweatpants.

"Hope we have snow for Christmas. It's been a damn dreary December so far. I haven't put up any of the decorations or lights. I can't even think about a tree," Paul said, now talking to himself more than his father. "We need some snow. We need some magic." He sat down with the remote and surfed the channels.

*I'll give you magic.* Claire thought herself to Paul, stroked his curly hair and kissed his cheek. Then she thought herself to Gus and knelt down next to his chair. Touching his arm, she whispered, "I have an idea." Then she closed her eyes and thought herself to the indigo door.

Claire pressed her eye to the peephole to see if Gus had arrived.

"Hey there, Sugar," Gus called out. He waved and made his way up the walk. Why she had a walk, she had no idea. It only led into an enormous empty green pasture.

"Gus! Come on in," Claire said, putting an arm around his shoulder and hurrying him into the house. "What took you so long?"

"It's getting harder to go back and forth."

"Oh, I'm sorry."

"I'm not. Means I'll be here with Lily full time pretty soon."

"You're not going to leave him *now*, are you?"

"I know, poor Paul. He's not doing so hot, is he?" Gus asked.

"No, and I can't even think about him losing you too. We've got to show him it's more than simply lights out, and something tells me we can get his attention today."

"I don't know. He's pretty set in his ways."

"No, really, if we can just get our foot in the door, get him thinking, questioning. I think we've got a chance. A person can only write so many things off to coincidence before they start to open their mind a smidge."

"Or start to think they're going crazy," Gus offered, looking around at the dozens of strange paintings covering the walls.

"No, this could work. There are things only a husband and wife know. I've been thinking about all those private conversations. We've had millions of them. Let's try that route."

"Sounds like a plan."

"Thank you so much for helping me with this," Claire whispered.

"Don't mention it. I need him to believe too, Claire," Gus said, clasping her hand in his.

---

"Dad!" Paul shouted as he struggled to lift Gus up off the floor. He let go of his father's arm and ran into the hallway. "Nurse! Hurry!" he yelled. As soon as he saw the white of a uniform round the corner, he darted back in the room. Paul crouched by Gus's side, and tried to lift him again.

"He just slumped over and slid onto the floor," Paul explained when the nurse entered the room.

An older heavy-set woman with wiry gray hair nodded and knelt down on the other side of Gus. "We've got to wait for the paramedics. We don't want to move him just yet." She began checking his vitals and as she lifted his left eyelid to shine her penlight in it, Gus's other eye flew open. He flinched, flailed his arm and clocked her in the jaw.

"Oh shit!" Paul said as the nurse sprawled backwards onto the linoleum.

"I'm okay," she said, getting to her knees and picking up her glasses.

"What was that? What's happened?" Paul asked.

"Well, he's back. Could've been a stroke, but probably a heart attack, and you didn't hear that from me. We'll send him to Resurrection for tests. The ambulance is on its way. You'll need to fill out some paperwork, Mr. Cummings."

"Glad I was with him," he said, staring at his father, who now seemed unusually alert.

"Me too, I'll be right back." She stood up and left the room, closing the door behind her.

"What's the score?" Gus asked.

"What's the score?" Paul repeated in disbelief. "Dad one, nurse zero," he bent closer to get a better look at Gus's eyes, as he slid his hand beneath his father's head.

"You really smacked her good, Dad. You scared the hell out of me. Are you in pain?"

Gus turned his head and stared at the TV screen. "Claire says 'hi'."

Paul grimaced. "I don't think so, Dad."

"Did you really brush your teeth with diaper rash cream?" Gus asked, turning to look directly into Paul's eyes for the first time in more than a year.

"What?"

"Claire says you brushed your teeth with Desitin right after Anna was born. How'd it taste? Minty?" Gus asked in a casual tone.

"Yeah, I—I guess," Paul said, laughing. "I was late for class and it was sitting on the bathroom counter. I had a mouthful before I figured it out."

"I would've gagged," Gus said, making a face.

*Conversation! We're having an actual conversation! Keep it coming, old man.* "Claire said she'd never tell anyone. She promised me, when I promised not to tell anyone about the time she got diarrhea canoeing. She told mom, didn't she? What in the world made you think of that, Dad?"

"Claire did, you jackass," Gus said, grabbing Paul by the wrist. "Wake up son. She's still with us... loving us, helping us. She was just here!"

Paul began to shake. He stared at his father, trying to make sense of what he was saying. *Claire's alive!*

"You saw Claire!? She came to see you?" *Stop it! This is insane. He doesn't know what he's saying.*

*But he hasn't been this coherent in more than a year.*

"Dad?" Paul said quietly.

"What's the score?" Gus repeated, his eyes glazing over as he looked back toward the TV and dropped Paul's wrist.

Paul was digging through the junk drawer, when Anna shuffled into the kitchen with Shadow.

"Morning," Paul said, looking up from his excavation.

"Morning," Anna mumbled. She wore one of Claire's old Cheap Trick T-shirts and a pair of sweat pants.

Paul watched her perform her morning ritual out of the corner of his eye. He smiled to himself. It was like a sleep-ballet. *Does it all with her eyes half-closed the same way Claire...*

Paul forced the memory of his wife from his mind as he untangled a pair of boot laces. Thoughts of Claire and her whereabouts were too much to handle after the crazy night he'd had with his father.*Christmas Eve. Why did he have to end up in the hospital on Christmas Eve?*

He pressed the dead batteries, dog collars and adaptors down into the overflowing drawer and jammed it shut.

Anna took a seat at the end of the counter and tossed a few Cheerios on the floor for Shadow.

Paul pulled a chair out from the dining room table, where he sat down and began removing the old laces from his boots.

"Ann, I'm afraid Grandma may be a little too much to handle this Christmas. You're not a kid anymore. I suspect you already know she gets really depressed during the winter. I have to admit, she usually perks up around Christmas, but like the rest of us, she's missing your mother something fierce."

"I know," Anna mumbled.

"She's her only child. I can't even begin to imagine what she's going through. It would kill me if..." he shook his head, unable to finish.

"She's still coming isn't she?"

"Of course. I'm just saying I'm not sure how she's holding up."

"I think she's doing okay, Dad." Anna appeared to blink her way to semi-consciousness.

Paul noticed her little pearl ring made her hands appear even more like her mother's. Her usual black nail polish was missing. *Maybe she's shedding her goth skin.*

He hadn't said a word the night she'd emerged from the bathroom with soaking wet, blue-black hair.

"She might be doing okay. Just don't let her get to you, if she's not," Paul quickly added. He finished tying his laces and sat back in the chair, his hands on his knees.

"I know. I get it. You love her. You're just trying to protect us. It's okay, Dad. That's like, your job," Anna groaned.

"Good. I'm glad we're clear on that," he said, putting on his coat. He walked over to her and wanted to kiss her on the forehead more than anything, but he squeezed her shoulder instead, adult to adult. "I'm going to dig out Santa." He nodded to himself encouragingly and disappeared into the garage.

## CHAPTER 18

THE KITCHEN PHONE RANG. Anna picked it up, tucking it between her cheek and her shoulder. "Hello?" She rinsed out her bowl in the sink and dried her hands on a dish towel. It was Grandma Lynn. She'd only visited them once since her mother's disappearance, at the end of the first week when things had been the craziest. She'd held Anna on her bed, rocked her like a baby for hours.

At the sound of her voice, Anna realized how much she'd missed her. "Grandma!"

"Hey, sweetheart."

"What time will you get here?"

"Oh, in a couple hours. I've still got some last minute wrapping to do."

"You should leave now and wrap the stuff here. We're getting snow... an ice storm, actually. Plus I've got a ton of stuff to tell you." She pulled a dog treat from the jar next to the sink and fed it to Shadow.

Shadow promptly spit it on the floor and chewed on a dish towel hanging from a drawer handle.

Anna pried her jaws open, took the towel from her and threw it in the sink.

"She's moving my ring every night," Anna whispered.

"Are you using a fresh sheet of paper and tracing a new outline every time? I still have every one of your Grandpa's."

"Yeah, but I haven't shown them to anyone."

"No, honey... best not to."

"I brought the Christmas tree up from the basement last night," Anna continued.

"Oh, good. You just do what you want and everyone else will follow suit. I'll be there shortly. Is your Dad around?"

"Yeah, he's in the garage trying to get the light-up Santa down for Em. He said he wants to set him outside the front door this year, though. Em keeps saying he *has* to go on the roof."

"Uh-oh."

"I feel bad for him. It's freezing out. Hurry up and get here —I can't wait for the peanut-butter balls."

"Oh hon, I didn't make them this year. I've been eating really healthy. I did make a raw pumpkin cheesecake for everyone to try though. It's so good. You're going to love it," Lynn insisted.

"Raw what? You make peanut-butter balls every year. I've been craving them. What about the Snickerdoodles?"

"Sorry, no junk this year, kiddo, but I did make a raw version of the peanut-butter balls with carob powder and raw nut butters."

Anna stuck out her tongue in disgust and frowned as she opened the oven door.

Shadow poked her head in and sniffed around, then licked something black encrusted on the oven door.

"No," Anna whispered and pointed toward the stairs. "We don't use the oven much. Dad put a bunch of pans in here. We pretty much nuke everything, but I can take the pans out to the garage so you can cook the stuff when you get here."

"Oh, I won't need to cook anything."

"But you said 'raw' as in salmonella," Anna said, closing the oven door.

"Yes, but that's how you eat it. You don't need to cook anything. I'm eating everything raw now: fruits, vegetables, nuts and seeds. I feel fantastic. You'd better hurry up and get your dad, so I can get going."

Anna rolled her eyes and opened the door to the garage. "Dad! Grandma's on the phone."

———

"Alright, just a minute," Paul said, as he slid the giant, plastic Santa down the ladder. A wave of shame rolled through him, having avoided Lynn so many times, but it had been a matter of self-preservation.

"She didn't make peanut-butter balls or *anything*," Anna whispered, covering the phone with her hand and warming one foot on top of the other, as the chill of the garage poured into the house.

"No peanut-butter balls?" Paul moaned taking the phone from her. "Go on, shut the door before you let all the heat out."

Paul hadn't even realized he'd been counting on Lynn's old recipes to get him through the holidays. Claire had introduced him to her mother's treats their very first Christmas together and he'd had them every Christmas since. He rubbed his neck and lifted the phone to his ear.

"Hi, Lynn."

"I'm not going to say Merry Christmas either, because it's not. I just want to make things as nice as possible for the girls. I went a little overboard on gifts this year. Don't be mad."

"No, that's okay. I'm slacking in that department, in all departments actually," he said, brushing cobwebs from his hair and wiping them on his sweatshirt as he sat down on the step. "I'm dragging. The girls have barely said a word about Christmas." Paul wiped the sweat from his forehead and stared at the six foot tall plastic Santa leaning against the used minivan he'd bought to replace Claire's beetle. No one would ever be driving that thing again, even if they did get it back.

"I've got just the thing for you—green smoothies," Lynn said.

"Whatever that is, it doesn't sound good. I need a double espresso with lots of sugar. I'm definitely not in the mood for anything green. If I ever needed peanut-butter balls, Lynn, it's now."

Paul tucked the phone in the crook of his neck. He stood up and opened the door to the kitchen, sized up the Santa, grabbed him and forced him through the doorway.

"Oh Paul, caffeine is so bad for you and sugar is the absolute worst."

"Who are you and what have you done with Lynn?" he said, before he realized that joke would never be funny again. Paul kicked the door shut behind him and dragged the Santa into the kitchen.

"I know, me? Sugar-free? I knew I'd never make it through this if... I've been eating nothing but raw foods for the past month. I don't know how I'd be getting through all this without them. Most days I miss her so bad I want to tear my hair out, but I'm surviving."

"Well, good. One of us needs to be in top form. Just

get yourself here as soon as you can, and help me pull this Christmas off," Paul pleaded.

"I'm on my way," Lynn assured him.

"Hey wait, I think it's great you're kicking sugar, but I don't think I have to tell you that you'd better not show up here without some kind of chocolate something. You said you wanted to make things nice for the girls. Don't even think of bringing them a bunch of asparagus. They're looking forward to their old favorites too," he reminded her.

"I suppose I could pick up some fudge and cookies," she said, "But they'll have to be from a store close to you. I don't completely trust myself to be alone in the car with sugar yet. I could care less about sugar right now, but I could backslide. I can't afford to fall back into the same mental state I was in before. With things the way they are... I might never pull out of it again."

"We'll eat the fudge under the deck if we have to. Just bring it."

Lynn laughed. "I'll see you soon," she said and hung up.

Paul stared at the phone in disbelief. *That's got to be the most normal conversation I've ever had with that woman.*

He heard something rustling in the living room. Paul set the phone down, closed his eyes and pretended it was Claire stringing the lights on their tree. *She'd be disappointed we waited so long to haul the decorations out.*

"Anna?" he called out.

He walked into the living room and caught Shadow nosing through a box. She lifted her head with a moose decoration clenched between her teeth.

"Drop it!"

Shadow bolted through the foyer and up the stairs.

"Anna," he called up the stairs after her.

"Yeah?"

"You'd better keep an eye on these decorations or Shadow's going to eat every last one of them. Find her, would you? She's got one."

Anna appeared at the top of the stairs in jeans and a red T-shirt, her hair pulled back in a ponytail and her face freshly scrubbed. She held up the slobbery remains of the ornament. "It's a gonner."

"Yeah, I'd say so. Hey, have we got any cookie mix or anything?" Paul asked.

"Yeah, there's a tube of those slice and bake ones in the fridge, but I think they're from Halloween."

"Hey, if it doesn't bother you, it doesn't bother me. You think you could toss those in the oven? This house doesn't smell like Christmas, and I'm afraid your grandma's gone tofu on us."

Em came running down the hall, stocking in hand and Shadow in tow. "Is he on the roof!?" she shouted, jumping up and down.

"Not yet, but I'm working on it," Paul said, running his hand through his hair.

"Catch me!" she said as she jumped from the top step, into Paul's arms.

"Whoa, a little warning, ya daredevil," he said, barely catching her and pulling her to him. He loved the energy he felt whenever the three of them were together. It was something he wished he could hold onto and spread out over the days to come like a safety net. *This is not the place to have this conversation.* He'd avoided it as long as he could. *Christmas is bearing down on us. There's no escaping it.*

Paul buried his face in Em's Rudolph sweater, put his free hand on the railing for support, then lifted his head. "How do you guys feel about Christmas?"

"Horrifically commercialized," Anna answered without missing a beat.

"I mean, how do you want to do this? Because we can do whatever you want. If you want to go away, not do Christmas without...."

"Mom," Anna finished.

Paul sighed. "Without Mom. I understand, and if you want to do everything the same, I understand. Either way, it's time we made a decision."

Anna sat down on the top step, but said nothing.

Em looked from Paul to Anna. "Ebry...." She huffed and began again. "*Evvvrythhing* the same, Dad," she said, struggling to produce the correct pronunciation, but with attitude like, it was a no-brainer.

"Yeah," Anna said, "Like she's still here."

"Yeah, she's still here," Em agreed, fingering her necklaces.

"All right. Let's do this up right, then. Let's decorate the tree." He grabbed Anna by the hand and pulled her down the stairs behind him.

Em clambered from his arms, jumped down the remainder of the stairs and was waiting by the tree before they reached the bottom step.

Paul had always left the decorating to Claire and the girls.

Anna put the tree together and strung the lights in record time.

Paul grabbed an ornament from the biggest box, a puppy in a basket, which he'd bought for Claire the year they got Shadow, and hung it on the tree.

"Not like that. Mommy does the candles and music first," Em scolded him.

Paul looked at Anna.

"She's right," Anna said with a shrug.

"Well, come on then, show me which ones," he said, clapping his hands together as he tried to ignore the sinking sensation in his stomach.

Em pulled several cds from one of the boxes and Anna grabbed a couple of candles from another. The girls laughed as Anna extracted some plastic mistletoe from Shadow's mouth.

"That's for kissing, not eating, Shadow!" Em giggled.

Paul watched Anna pick up her favorite ornament, a crystal snowflake with their wedding photo inside. She glanced up to see if he was looking, and he quickly averted his eyes. Then he watched as she carefully hung it on the back of the tree so he wouldn't have to face it. He used every ounce of strength he had not to cry while he lit the candles. *We're moving on.*

He collapsed on the couch to watch the girls' antics, as they sang off-key and dug through the boxes.

Claire curled up next to him. "Look at them. They're going to be okay."

———

"Did you get something for the mailman?" Frank asked Collin.

"Scotch."

"You didn't," Frank said, closing his eyes and clenching the steering wheel, as the car warmed up.

"Gift card. Relax," Collin said, scraping the frost off the outside of his window with a credit card.

"*Me* relax? That's going to melt in about five minutes so roll up the window and wait it out, Mary. And by the way, you don't have an ounce of proof that he's an alcoholic," Frank insisted.

"Well, he sure falls down a lot, and don't *Mary* me. Unlike some people, if I'm going to be broad-sided during an ice storm, I'd like to see it coming. Stunning Gay Couple Killed in Car Wreck Christmas Eve. Too tragic. I can't go out like that."

"Fine. We'll sit here and defrost for a minute, but only because we're *stunning* in your little headline. You ready for Lynn?" Frank asked, turning in his seat to face Collin.

"I don't know why that woman doesn't just bite the bullet and get some Wellbutrin or something. I couldn't go through that every winter. Claire said it used to be really bad when she was a kid, that Lynn's actually mellowed some."

"She holds it together pretty well around the kids. Just keep an eye on her. Don't let her drink anything. Remember that bottle of Port? I never should have brought it. Two tiny glasses and she was an absolute mess," Frank recalled.

"She's really sweet, though."

"Always the softy. I noticed you switched scarves. That really doesn't go," Frank said tugging at the hand-knit, purple scarf Collin had neatly tucked into his Burberry coat.

"Just pretend it does," Collin said smiling and tucking it back inside.

Frank removed his leather gloves to organize the items inside the armrest.

Collin opened the glove box and pretended to organize the Jiffy Lube receipts. "I'm just going to say this: A certain five-year-old knew a lot of things she couldn't possibly know when I baby-sat her last week. Em talks to Claire everyday... and Claire talks back."

"Collin, really." Frank shook his head.

"I know it sounds crazy, but a lot of strange things are going on in that little girl's room and nobody even knows it. When I asked her where her mom was, she said to ask Tony Chicken at the Mark."

"Are you saying you want to find this Tony Chicken?

If, by some miracle, he's an actual person, which I doubt. With a name like that a detective could find him in a matter of hours."

"There's a Mark Hotel in New York. Let's just make some calls," Collin pleaded.

"Now, don't go all Nancy Drew on me. Your first call is going to be to that detective with the huge traps," Frank said, turning out of their driveway, onto the street. It had begun to sleet and he turned on the windshield wipers.

"Her traps weren't that big."

"Like Lou Ferrigno's."

"I've got a thousand paintings running through my head right now." Collin closed his eyes.

"Really?"

"I swear it," Collin replied as his phone rang. "It's Paul," he said and answered it.

"Oh, no. Be there in about twenty minutes." Collin stuffed the phone in his coat pocket. "Shadow's really sick."

CHAPTER 19

PAUL SAT underneath the edge of the kitchen counter with his back against the cupboards. "We'll hear from the vet any minute, girls," he said, reading their tense faces as he stroked Shadow's back.

Anna sat on the other side of Shadow smoothing her long tail. Paul had moved the bar stools and spread out a blanket. There was dog food, water and even cookies nearby, but the dog wasn't moving, only her eyes showed any sign of life.

Em sat between Shadow's feet, brushing her.

Lynn bustled back and forth from the fridge to the table with platters of food, while Christmas music floated in from the living room.

"What do you think it was this time, Dad?" Anna asked.

"Honestly, honey? I have no idea." He stared straight ahead, his fingers rubbing his temple.

"But she's eaten all kinds of things before and she never got sick like this. She ate Mom's roses, your credit cards and Em's doll's shoes. Remember when she ate the Legos?"

"I know you don't want to leave her right now, but

what do you say we take turns searching the house and her usual hiding places? If we find part of what she ate, it might help the vet."

Em and Anna looked at each other as if they had an unspoken agreement. Between the two of them, they knew all of her hiding places, but they weren't about to leave Shadow's side.

Lynn joined them on the floor. She had a tray with four cups full of bright green liquid, a couple of notepads and some markers. "I'll search. You guys just write down all the hiding places." She handed Paul and Anna notepads and markers, and turned to Em, "You just tell Grandma the best places to look and I'll write them down."

"I can do it," Em argued, "I'm big. I can make pictures."

"You sure are. Green smoothie, anyone?" Lynn said, handing one to Paul.

"Are you trying to kill me?" Paul asked, making a face. "What, in God's name, is in there?" he asked, not moving to take the cup. He touched Shadow's nose hoping it would be moist again, but it was as dry as sandpaper.

"Funny you should mention God, its all stuff he grew. Spinach, bananas, mangos and a pear," she said, taking a drink from one of the cups. "Mmm... so good. You just taste the fruit, really," she insisted.

"It looks like pond scum," Paul said.

"Yeah, ponds gum," Em echoed.

"It does look kinda disgusting, Grandma," Anna weighed in.

"Just try a sip. I've been drinking a quart of this a day for the past month and I feel like Superman. I haven't had any junk food in a while. I don't even want it anymore."

"Seriously? All right, I'm game. Pass the pond scum," Paul said.

Em and Anna each took a cup from Lynn.

Lynn smiled as she stroked Shadow's ear.

"You do seem to have a lot of energy," Paul said, still eyeing the contents of the cup.

"I feel like I'm twenty. I couldn't think anymore. My mind was running in circles. I had to do something, control something. I organized the whole cabin and the storage shed, too. Last winter, it was a big accomplishment just to get out of bed each day and shower. I can't live like that anymore."

"It's good. Tastes like bananas," Em announced and licked her lips.

"Yeah, not bad," Anna agreed.

"I've tasted worse. I think it's great that you've finally found some relief, Lynn."

"Thanks, but it's more than relief. I feel like I'm getting younger. I've got to buy some new clothes before I go home. These are getting too baggy," she said, tugging at the waistband of her pants.

Shadow whimpered and everyone sat their cup down and moved closer to her, petting and consoling her.

Paul looked at his phone. "I can't believe the vet hasn't called back yet. It's still Dr. Hammond, right Ann?"

"Um... no dad, that would be mom's foot doctor."

"Aw, geez! What's the name of the vet!?"

"Dr. Handler. Mom's got it in her pho—I think it's on the emergency number list by the desk, but last time she just took her right to the animal hospital."

"Can you find the number? Did you guys finish your lists for Grandma?" he added, trying to stay calm.

"Here," Anna said, handing hers to Lynn, "Don't forget to look under the deck. Last year we found all the stakes and seed packets from the neighbor's gardens under there."

"Is this your bed?" Lynn asked, taking a drawing from Em's hand.

"Yup, under my bed and in my closet. She ate my Barbie's legs off in da-*the* closet," Em said, furrowing her brow.

"Oh dear," Lynn said, winking at Paul and taking the list from his hand.

"Good luck," Paul said grimly. He heard the front door open and Collin and Frank stomp the snow off their shoes in the entryway.

"Between the three of us, we'll find the smoking gun in no time," she said and headed off to brief them.

"I don't fink, th-*think* she could eat a gun," Em said, sitting a little taller after she'd corrected herself.

"No, I don't think so either, honey," Paul answered. He'd noticed Em correcting herself more lately, and while he knew it was a good thing, it made him a little sad to see her baby talk disappearing. But Claire had been right. Em was taking care of it on her own.

*Where are you, Claire? I need you.*

Claire had been sitting next to Paul from the moment they'd spread the blanket out on the floor. She'd always been Shadow's nurse. She was surprised to find herself more helpless than ever, except for picking up an occasional thought from Paul. She'd heard him say the words, "How could I mix up the doctors?" but his lips had never moved. She'd exercised some self-control, hadn't interfered and now she was *hearing* an occasional thought. *Interesting.*

Claire watched as Paul crossed his fingers, Anna crossed

hers and Em used her left hand to cross her fingers on her right hand. She listened for more thoughts and distinctly heard, "I love you," as Em lay down, pressed Shadow's coarse paw against her face and closed her eyes.

———

Collin watched Lynn and Frank disappear up the stairs with their lists. He hung his coat in the hall closet, as he scanned Paul's list of Shadow's hiding places: behind the couch, under the deck and behind the camping equipment in the basement.

He pulled a box of Fannie May chocolate covered cherries from the wicker basket full of gifts Frank had brought in from the car. *I should check on Paul and the girls, see if they need anything before I get started, maybe grab one of Lynn's cookies.*

It wasn't the cookies he craved so much, as the sense that everything would be all right, as if the Law of Nature stated that nothing bad could happen in the presence of freshly baked cookies.

"Well, I'm not kissing any of *you* under the mistletoe this year," Collin said, trying to lighten the mood as he entered the kitchen, opening the box of chocolates and handing it to Paul. His face went slack at the sight of Shadow, her breathing shallow, her eyes closed. He took a seat on the floor next to Em, who immediately sat up and hugged him.

Anna lifted her hand for a small wave, but she couldn't manage anything even close to a smile.

"What's going on?" Collin asked.

"I let Shadow out while the girls were decorating the tree. She didn't come when I called her, but she does that sometimes. Then Em started saying Shadow was sick down by the creek.

Don't ask me how she knew, but about a half hour later Mrs. Gleason called and said her kids had found Shadow down by the bridge. I went and got her."

"You called the vet?"

"No, apparently I called a foot doctor," Paul said, rubbing his forehead. "It's *Handler*, not Hammond, but even if I'd reached Dr. Handler right away, the weather's so bad... God, nothing's gone right. Thanks for the chocolates, by the way. Forgot to eat today," Paul said, as he shoved a second one into his mouth, and handed the box back to Collin.

"Shadow ate something bad again," Em translated for Collin, as she clung to his neck.

"She'll be okay," Collin assured her as he petted Shadow's head. Although he doubted it was true, and instantly regretted saying it. He decided to keep his mouth shut for a while and offered the girls chocolates instead.

"I don't like ones with guts," Em said.

"No, thanks," Anna said, making a face like he'd offered her a chocolate-covered cockroach.

The buzzer on the stove rang and Collin shouted, "I've got 'em, Lynn." He stood up with Em in his arms, set the chocolates on the counter and walked over to the oven. "Your necklaces sure are getting long. Maybe it's time to start a third one," he whispered. Collin lifted one necklace and rubbed his thumb over a paper clip, shaking his head and giving Em a wink.

She blinked both eyes in her attempt to wink back at him.

He set Em down on the counter by the bananas, and slipped on an oven mitt. When he'd set the cookies on the stovetop and turned the oven off, he looked at her. She had placed a banana sticker on each earlobe.

"You going to help me look or stay here?" he asked.

"Stay with Shadow," she answered and reached for

him. He helped her down off the counter and she ran back to her spot at Shadow's feet.

Collin broke off a piece of hot cookie, popped it into his mouth, and walked into the living room where Burl Ives was ordering everyone to "Have a Holly-Jolly Christmas." Collin cracked his stiff neck and turned the volume down. *Don't boss me, Burl. I'm in no mood.*

He'd barely begun searching behind the couch when he heard Frank shout, "Got it! I found it!" as he sped down the stairs with Lynn behind him.

Frank held up the remains of an old red and white cardboard package with tinsel dangling from it.

"Shit," Collin breathed. His eyes locked on Frank's for a second to convey his crystal-clear understanding, before Frank proceeded to the kitchen.

Lynn looked at Collin and mouthed "What?"

Collin just shook his head and motioned for her to follow Frank, as he mustered his best poker face for the girls.

"Is there enough room to lay her down in your minivan?" Frank asked.

"Where are we taking her? The animal hospital hasn't called back yet," Paul explained, getting to his feet and picking Em up in his arms.

"The tinsel... they can't digest it. It can get caught," Frank said. He threw the damp tinsel box into the garbage, and bent down to grab the edges of the blanket. "I've got her on this end. Paul, you get the other side."

"Our friend Bob's beagle—" Collin shut his mouth the second Frank glared at him.

Paul hurriedly set Em down, picked up the corners of the blanket, and together he and Frank slowly lifted Shadow off the linoleum.

Shadow's eyes opened a bit and she made a feeble attempt to wag her tail, but no effort to move.

Lynn, Collin, and the girls all huddled around the makeshift stretcher as they shuffled toward the garage.

When they reached the back door, the room fell silent for a second as all eyes shifted to the girls, their faces pale, tears streaming down their cheeks.

"Ann, grab my coat. I think the keys are in the pocket. Em, go get your coat and have Grandma help you with your gloves. You two wait out front and I'll pull the van out. Go on now, both of you, hurry up," Paul said, firmly.

"Our friend Jim is a vet," Frank whispered as the girls left the room. "I just talked to him yesterday. His choir's performing tonight at the Art Institute. If I call him, I know he'll do everything he can. We can pick him up and head straight to his clinic."

Lynn called over her shoulder, "Now, that's a plan. I'll pack everything up. We'll have Christmas Eve one way or another, wherever we are." She headed for the pantry where she found a wicker basket and began to pack it full of food from the table. In a matter of seconds, she'd grabbed another container of green smoothie from the fridge, a laundry basket from the desk, hooked her arm through her purse on the table and headed past Santa into the living room to pack up the gifts.

Collin held the door for Frank and Paul, and ran into the garage to slide the van's door open. "I'll be right back. I'm going to get our coats."

As Collin shut the door to the garage behind him, anger and sadness rolled through his chest. This was too much for one family. He tried to breathe through it. Finding their coats, he shut the closet door, but his knees weakened at the sight of the family photos hanging along the stairway. He imagined the stairway without all the photos of Claire and Shadow, and he fell backward and slid down the door. Tears fell onto his dress shirt, creating dark blue spots. *I can't fix any of this.*

He tried to stand up and pull himself together. He knew he had to, but he couldn't. Collin sat on the floor, coats piled on his lap, pressing the heels of his hands against his eyes.

He thought he was seeing spots when he pulled his hands away. His vision was a little blurred, but he was sure he'd seen a flash of red. As he looked around for the source, a swath of emerald green fabric beneath Frank's coat caught his eye. He'd grabbed someone's scarf along with the coats. Pinned to the scarf was a little plastic snowman.

Collin folded the scarf with the snowman on top and set it down next to him. *They're waiting. Get up.*

He suddenly wondered if Claire had managed to communicate something to Em about Shadow. Em had known where Shadow was. Amidst the commotion, no one had asked her how she knew.

The tears returned in full force. *If you can do that, Claire, why are you letting this happen!?*

The overhead light flickered and burned out.

Collin held his breath. The sound of his own heartbeat grew loud in his ears. He saw the faint red glow again and looked down. The snowman's eyes were lit up. Then they went dark.

Grabbing the scarf, Collin scrambled to his feet and shouted at the ceiling, "Do it again!"

He stood in the dark, panting, wanting to push all doubt from his mind, be grateful, be satisfied, but he needed more. *I have to know it's you!*

"Show me it's you, Claire," he whispered into the dark. "One more, Claire. I know you can do it. Give me three different signs and I'll know for sure, and I promise I won't ask for anything else ever again. I swear. I'm ready. Come on," he said, holding the snowman up to his face. He didn't dare move. *I've found the magic spot!*

Collin's chest heaved in anticipation. He could hear honking and Frank shouting his name, but he knew nothing short of an earthquake could tear him away. Not even the wrath of Frank.

He waited. He could hear the tick-ticking of the stove cooling down, the faint tinkling of a wind chime outside the kitchen window, a slow steady drip in the stainless steel sink, but nothing definitively *Claire*.

He dropped his hands to his sides in defeat. He was eyeing the van out on the street, through the long window pane next to the front door when his phone rang. It should've been Frank screaming his head off, but it wasn't.

With the scarf still clenched in his fist, Collin bent down and feverishly searched through the coats on the floor until he found his phone.

He inhaled so hard he choked. The screen read, "Claire." He pressed "Send", his heart about to burst, but the call wouldn't go through. He tried four more times, but it was no use. It was no longer in service. Paul had told him he'd canceled her service several weeks after the police had bagged it for evidence. So it had to be sitting in a box at the police station with a dead battery.

"That was three. Fair enough. You did it. Are you here? Are you here, now?" he asked, his voice quavering in the dark.

He held the snowman up to his face once more. "Once for yes, twice for no!"

The front door flew open, slamming against the stopper on the wall.

"What the hell are you *doing* in here?" Frank demanded, bending down to gather up the coats.

"I—I..." Collin stuttered.

"Should we go without you!? That dog is in real trouble, and you know it. Let's go!" Frank grabbed the door knob with the coats draped over his arm and stepped out the door.

"I don't think she's going to die," Collin said as he tried the light switch, flipping it up and down several times, smiling to himself.

"Bob's Beagle died from this very same thing, and in case you haven't noticed, this family seems to have the worst luck in the world," Frank replied.

"Claire won't let it happen. She's here."

"Knock it off. Get in the van."

"No, she showed me. She's made contact. I mean, *unmistakable* contact," Collin insisted, still flipping the switch.

"For Christ's sake, Collin," Frank said, swatting Collin's hand away from the switch. "You cannot carry on like this in front of the girls. I won't allow it. They're too vulnerable." He grabbed Collin's arm, pulled him out the door and slammed it behind them. He handed Collin his coat and put on his own. Then he checked to make sure the door was locked and yanked Collin down the icy steps as he clung to the railing.

"She was here! Look! She called me on my cell! She burned out that light and lit up this pin!" Collin cried, still carrying the scarf and trying to shove the snowman and phone in Frank's face.

Frank sighed, stopped on the sidewalk and grabbed Collin by the shoulders, freezing rain pelting their faces. "All right, all right, we'll talk about this later. I believe you, but *later* —got it?" he said, pulling Collin by the hand.

"Okay, *believe me*, believe me or shut-up-and-get-in-the-van believe me?"

"I *believe* you, believe you. Now shut up and get in the van!"

━━━

Claire looked around the animal hospital. "This isn't so bad."

Framed posters of puppies and kittens adorned the yellow walls. Two large bulletin boards overflowing with letters of gratitude hung on either side of the double doors. Pinned to them were dozens of colorful little Thank-you notes and photographs of happy pets and their owners. The boards exuded warm, undeniable reassurance. Claire made note of a small bare spot in the lower right hand corner, where their Thank-you note for saving Shadow would fit perfectly. *They should use that cute one of Shadow playing in the leaves with the girls.*

Instead of the standard plastic waiting room chairs, there were big blue comfy couches spotted with a few well-scrubbed and deodorized stains. Several brightly-colored bean bag chairs were nestled in a corner. An aquarium full of goldfish was situated next to a child-sized red table and matching chairs. Coloring books and crayons were scattered across the table. *Mmm... crayons, Shadow's favorite.*

Claire loved the big Christmas tree in the corner with its twinkling white lights and Snoopy decorations. If they couldn't spend Christmas Eve at home, this was the next best thing. In fact, maybe it was better. The important thing was that they were all together.

Janet, a female intern, was spending her Christmas Eve taking dogs with casts and plastic funnels around their necks, outside.

Dr. Roger Ellis, part owner in the small animal hospital with Jim, was also spending his holiday at the office.

The two of them had been eating pizza, watching *It's a Wonderful Life* starring Jimmy Stewart on a small television behind the desk, when they received the call from Jim to prep for a canine intestinal surgery.

Janet distracted the girls with a grand tour.

Collin and Lynn settled into one of the cushy couches, while the rest of the adults proceeded to the X-ray room. "Green smoothie?" Lynn asked, holding out a Rubbermaid container full of thick, bright green liquid.

Collin shuddered. "Linda Blair called. She wants that back."

"I promise, it's good for you."

"Be serious, Lynn. Hand me a Snickerdoodle before someone gets hurt." Collin held out his hand and waited.

Lynn handed him the basket. "Girls, are you hungry?" she called over her shoulder.

Janet held Em on her hip, letting her feed the fish, while Anna read Thank-you notes on one of the bulletin boards.

"You and I really need to talk," Lynn said, patting Collin's knee. "I'll be back in a minute."

"Take your time. I have a feeling we're going to be here a while," Collin replied, brushing crumbs from his lap.

Lynn walked over to the bulletin boards, and put her arm around Anna. "She'll be okay. You and I know that for sure," she whispered.

"Do you think they go there too? I mean, are you sure?"

"They have souls don't they?" Lynn reasoned.

"Yeah, they've got to."

"I wouldn't expect her to move things around like your mother, but there must be a doggy equivalent. Something distinctly Shadow, she'll surprise you with someday, but I think she's going to pull through. She always does."

"I've been hanging out with Detective Robles."

"I thought you hated her."

"I did," Anna confessed, staring out into the snowy parking lot. "But she came to see me at school. She had a message for me from a psychic or a medium, whatever you call them."

"Really?"

"It had to be mom," Anna insisted.

"What was the message?" Lynn asked, captivated.

"She said she got the balloon I let go in the backyard the night of my birthday. She knew the color and everything and she answered "yes" to the note I'd tied to it, asking her if she'd celebrated with us. She even knew about the shoes Frank and Collin gave me and the Thank-you note I sent them. I hadn't told *anyone* about the balloon. Dad and Em were asleep when I snuck outside."

"That's incredible, Ann. I knew she'd come through. We just have to keep our eyes peeled."

"Don't you think everybody else would be doing better if they knew the things we know?"

Lynn shook her head. "I'd be careful about that. Most people aren't ready to believe the things you and I have seen, and I don't want anyone convincing you that you've imagined it. You know better."

"Psst," Frank whispered from the hallway next to the intake desk, motioning to Collin.

Collin gave Lynn a quick glance of unease and crossed the room.

"Looks like there might be news," Lynn said, rubbing her hand over Anna's back. "I'd better see what's going on."

"Grandma?"

"Yeah, hon?"

"Thank you for being... you know, the way you are. Thank you for believing and for, you know... believing me."

"Thank *you* for keeping an open mind. Don't ever lose that Anna."

## CHAPTER 20

LYNN COULD HEAR Frank and Collin talking inside a little exam room. She opened the door to see pumpkin-orange paint with a Golden Retriever border near the ceiling.

Collin closed the door behind her. Their eyes met briefly, but Collin just shook his head.

Frank took a seat on the exam table, crossing his arms and his feet at the ankles. "Jim says they call it a linear foreign body, the tinsel," he said, rubbing an eyebrow with his forefinger, as if he could coax the correct terminology to the surface. "One end got stuck. The contractions caused the tinsel to saw through the intestine."

"How bad is that?" Collin asked.

Lynn sat down next to a little desk and put her head in her hands. "Help her, Claire," she whispered.

"They're going to open her up to repair the damaged intestine and remove any tinsel they find, but Jim said if an infection sets in, she's got an even slimmer chance of pulling through," Frank explained.

"Anna just turned fifteen. That makes Shadow twelve," Lynn interjected.

"I had no idea she was that old," Collin said, taking a seat next to Frank on the exam table.

Frank sighed. "Let's think positive, here. They're going to operate. They must think she's got a good chance of bouncing back, or they wouldn't put her through it."

"Where's Paul?" Collin asked.

"He was saying goodbye, except..." Frank's gaze dropped to the floor.

"What?" Lynn asked. She got up and walked over to him, placing her hand on his shoulder.

Frank shook, and Collin put an arm around him. He pushed himself away from Lynn and Collin, hopping down off the exam table. "I should have said something to let him know I was there. We'd all left the operating room to give him a few minutes alone with her. He didn't hear me. I was supposed to get him out of there. They needed to get started. I think he was telling her goodbye, but it was like he was saying goodbye to Claire, too. I heard him say Claire. He's all mixed up. It's too much."

"What should we do?" Collin whispered.

"Open gifts. I'll tell the girls Shadow's going to have an operation. Then I'll go get Paul. You two go out to my car and bring everything inside."

"Everybody's on edge. I don't think it's a good time," Collin argued.

"I *know* everyone is on edge. That's why there's never been a better time for a big distraction. Besides, he'll be relieved to shift his focus back to the girls and making sure they still have a nice holiday," she assured them. "I just need a minute alone."

"Okay," Collin said. He and Frank left the exam room and closed the door behind them.

Lynn had grown accustomed to a world of solitude and craved it when she needed to sort through her thoughts in search of clarity, but more than anything she wanted to talk to her daughter. "You and I both know there's nothing I can say to help him. He's got to find his own way through it just like you and I did after your Daddy's accident," Lynn said to Claire, looking around the room hopefully.

Claire wrapped her arms tightly around her mother. "Just bring your strength to the table. That's all he needs, someone to lean on, someone to count on. He forgets he's human," Claire assured her, hoping somehow a word or two might find it's way into her mother's mind.

There was a tiny ringing, like the buzz of a mosquito, in Lynn's right ear. As it faded the fluorescent light above her flickered. Lynn smiled as she looked up, "Help me with the words, Claire. I know you're here. If you could ever do anything to help me, give me the right words for Paul," she said, hesitating to leave the room, but sensing it was time. Lynn quickened her pace down the hallway as two simple words came to mind, like glass buoys bubbling to the surface of a pristine pond. "I know," she whispered to herself. "I know.

Paul stumbled down the hallway outside the operating

room. His head throbbed as an uncontrollable force rose up through him. Some shrinking part of him hoped it was only vomit. Shaking, gulping down deep breaths, he stopped to stare at a poster on the wall in an attempt to regain control. It had worked before. *Focus on something, anything. Breathe.*

He inhaled, his eyes still trying to focus on the ridiculous image of ferrets in pink sunglasses and rhinestone collars. His mind could no longer make sense of the shapes and colors before him. Not a single cell in his body found the image even remotely amusing. Rage ignited his pain and swept through his body. Every inch of sparkle, pink and fluff before him fed the blaze.

Paul knew he had to get out of the building fast. He tore down the hallway toward the glass door. He wrenched a large red-and-white striped umbrella from a stand, knocking it over, before he hit the glass door full speed, not caring whether it was unlocked or not.

Yelling like a madman through the slick, snow-covered back parking lot, he singled out the first thing in sight, a large old oak. He laid into it with everything he had, but the red-and-white striped umbrella made a cushioned thwack as it connected with the bark. It didn't matter. Again and again, he struck the tree, crying out in anguish, sweat and spittle flying. On the fourth blow, the umbrella bent in half and began to open, but Paul didn't stop. The aluminum rods sliced his fingers and forearms, but he didn't stop. His blood stained the moonlit snow, but he didn't stop. He couldn't stop.

When he'd smashed the umbrella into an unrecognizable tangle of metal skewers and nylon, he cast it aside, grabbed a large tree limb from the ground and resumed the beating. The ear-splitting crack of the limb was much more satisfying.

"Where *is* she?" he growled, sweat and blood trickling down his face and hands, seeping into the collar and cuffs of his pale gray oxford. The wind and snow whipped around his sweat-soaked hair, but cold was the last thing he felt.

He was soon holding nothing but a short, jagged stick and he stabbed at the trunk as if it were an enormous bear, rising up to crush him. Paul felt nothing but rage, screaming until his throat was raw.

He didn't hear the person behind him shouting his name. He didn't realize it was a person at all, grabbing him and knocking him to the ground. He hoped it was death, heavy and hungry, swallowing him whole into a gut of black silence... but he knew it was too small to be death.

Slivers of white light seeped through the crevices of a tall fence behind the tree, dancing about in the blur of Paul's pain and confusion.

There was the distinct sound of a sliding glass door opening and the tinkling sound of a party from inside. A man shouted something over the fence and the thing on top of Paul shouted back. Reality descended, bit by bit, word by word.

"It's okay," Lynn shouted. "Everything's under control. We don't need the police. Just give us a minute, please."

The fire inside him was burning out and the cold began to snake around his neck. The crackling sound was no longer within him, but beneath him. Paul shivered and vomited in the rotting, snow-covered leaves.

Lynn rolled him over. Her eyes and face were red and her nose was running, but she felt warm and strong as she whispered, "Shhh, I know." She cradled him like a child.

Paul curled himself into a ball and shook, snorted and sobbed until all but the last bit of energy had left his body.

Lynn rocked him until he caught his breath, and rubbed his arms fiercely when he began to shiver.

"Claire didn't die," he gasped, as he struggled to open his eyes and stare up into Lynn's face. "She was ripped from our lives and I don't know where she is. I don't know where she is. I can't believe I don't know what the hell happened to her."

"I know," was all Lynn said.

"I don't want to live," Paul cried.

"I know," she answered.

"I still have the girls, but I can't live like this," he cried.

"You won't live like *this* Paul. Things are going to get better. I promise. The girls will ground you. They're finding their way," Lynn assured him.

"If I didn't have the girls, I'd be dead already," Paul whispered.

"Let's get you inside and cleaned up before you freeze to death." Lynn got to her feet and hooked her arms beneath his. Together, they waded across the parking lot.

A Pepto-Bismol-colored restroom just inside the back door had been restored to its original 1950's splendor. Lynn pulled Paul inside and locked the door behind them.

Paul backed up against the wall and slid to the floor. He closed his eyes, as Lynn dampened brown paper towels with warm water and crouched down to dab at more than a dozen cuts on his face and hands.

"It's a miracle, but it doesn't look like you're going to need any stitches." Lynn gave him a weak smile and shook her head. "I'm going to pilfer some bandages, and you're going to sit here and think up a reasonable story for the girls." She stood up, tossed the paper towels in the trash and closed the door behind her.

Paul pulled himself to his feet to survey the damage. There was one rather large cut on his right cheek. He winced as he touched it. *You can't lose control like that ever again.*

"I guess I fell down some stairs," he said as Lynn opened the door with scrubs in one hand and alcohol swabs and bandages in the other.

She laughed. "Yeah, from the top of the Sears Tower, all the way down... must've been carrying a rosebush too." She knelt down on the floor and motioned for him to join her, as she tore open alcohol packets with her teeth and dabbed at the cuts.

"Ow, shit," Paul said, wincing as he cracked an embarrassed smile.

They remained silent for a long time as she bandaged him up and helped him change into the scrubs. Paul felt like a little boy being put back together after a bicycle wreck.

She pulled a little bottle of mouthwash from her pocket and handed it to him. "Always carry one in my purse."

Nearly ten minutes had passed before he spoke again. "I've been talking to her. Is that crazy?"

"No, so have I. You can feel her, can't you? The air or maybe it's the silence, it's different. It's like you can feel it, but with your ears, right?" Lynn asked, putting his wet clothes in a plastic bag.

━━

Claire felt dazed and hollow from screaming at Paul to stop before he really hurt himself. She sat on the floor across from them. Her mother's question felt like a rickety suspension bridge swaying between Claire and the love of her life, blowing in the wind, high above a bottomless chasm. *Will he slash through those ropes with his skepticism and destroy any chance we have of ever connecting again, or will he cling to them and make his way across to me?*

She studied their familiar faces and bodies. They were both thinner. However, her mother seemed to glow under the pressure of it all, and Claire felt proud of her for the first time in a very long time. "I love you, I love you..." Claire began to chant as she closed her eyes.

"I feel *something*," Paul said, after a long silence. "Okay? Just between you and me—yes, I feel or hear that *something* in the air sometimes. It's like that feeling you get when you know you're being watched, or when someone has walked into the room behind you."

"Exactly," Lynn agreed.

"You sense a change, maybe a change in the energy around you. I don't know, I'm no scientist, but I have no way of proving or even knowing it's really her."

"How much proof do you need? No matter what she offers, it'll never be enough. We'll always want to know, beyond a shadow of a doubt, and I don't think that's possible," Lynn reasoned.

"I feel like I'm grasping at straws or trying to wish things into reality, whenever I allow myself to think about it. Like, maybe I'll lose my mind. That scares the absolute shit out of me," Paul argued.

"Don't be scared. You're not going to lose your mind, but I know what you mean. I danced along that fine line between sanity and the abyss for years after I lost my husband. Just try to trust the feelings even if you don't understand them. Have some faith. Open up. We used to believe the world was flat."

"I can't accept that she's just gone, that she no longer exists. It doesn't feel like it. It feels like she's away somewhere. We were so close, so intertwined.

"Maybe it's like an antenna on a roof," Lynn offered. "The difference between mentally hooking your antenna up to receive a signal, or just letting it sit up there blowing in the wind."

Paul looked at her, considering the theory. His eyes narrowed. "You smell that?" he whispered.

Still chanting, Claire thought her way across the floor to them, placing her hands on their faces.

"Lavender. She's here," Lynn whispered.

"What does she want?" Paul asked, breathlessly, searching Lynn's eyes.

"Maybe just this, just acknowledgement... belief," Lynn answered, closing her eyes and inhaling deeply.

Paul closed his eyes and imagined a rusty old antenna atop their roof. He pictured himself clinging to the dark, steep shingles beneath an overcast sky. He was trying to keep his mind focused on his antenna, when a wave of warmth hit his throat and poured down over his shoulders and through his chest. It was the same feeling he used to get anytime Claire walked into the room.

Lynn's head rested against the wall. After several minutes, she opened her eyes and slowly turned to face Paul. "Wow," was the only word she could manage.

"This stays here," he warned her, raising a shaky finger.

"Okay," she agreed. "But please don't pretend it away. It was as real as it gets."

"I won't," he promised.

"We got our stories straight? You slipped, right? We're all going to open gifts now," Lynn said, as she grabbed the edge of the sink and pulled herself to her feet. "Come on," she said, hoisting Paul to his feet, as well.

Lynn led Paul back to the waiting room where the girls had deciphered the tags on the gifts and created piles near each person.

"My God, what happened?" Collin asked as he looked from Lynn to Paul, and back to Lynn again.

All eyes turned to Paul, and Em came running over.

"Daddy!"

"The good news is that it's still snowing!" Paul announced.

"The bad news is that's it's crazy-slippery out there," he said, laughing a bit too hard. "I went outside to get some fresh air and wiped out, knocked the wind right out of me, soaked my clothes," he added, tousling Em's hair. "It looks worse than it feels... rose bushes."

"*Ninja* rose bushes?" Collin asked.

Frank elbowed Collin.

Anna stood frowning and chewing on her lip until Paul winked at her. She gave him a small uncertain smile, but couldn't stop frowning. Her right hand brushed her face, but she quickly tucked it beneath her arm, sparing a lash or two.

"No worries," Paul assured everyone. "Grandma fixed me up good as new." He gave Lynn a kiss on the cheek and took Em by the hand, leading her over to the gifts.

---

"Is he okay?" Frank whispered.

Lynn nodded. "He had some things to work through, but he's going to be okay."

Janet looked stunned. "Do you need anything else? Does he?"

"No, but make sure you put the bandages and scrubs on our bill."

"No, don't worry about it. Um, Jim said to let you know the surgery seems to be going well. Merry Christmas," Janet said and hastily returned to her desk.

"Hear that everyone? Jim says the surgery's going well!" Lynn shouted.

An audible wave of relief swept through the room.

Paul beamed with pride as he watched Ann, fresh-faced in jeans and a T-shirt, cross the room and set a gift on the reception desk for Janet. He assumed it was the perfume set he'd bought for Lynn. Every year he found himself asking Ann to wrap his gifts at the last minute. This year she'd wrapped them without him even knowing.

Everyone settled in amongst the packages. In no time, they were chattering, laughing and knee-deep in a mosaic of bows and wrapping paper.

Frank pulled a thick white robe from a box. "I knew it. You *did* throw it out," he said, squinting at Collin. "I kept telling myself, *What would a cleaning lady want with my old robe? Myra's never stolen so much as a kleenex from us.* I knew it was you. Thank God I didn't say anything to her."

Collin gave him a sheepish grin and picked a piece of lint off the new robe. "That thing was ready for the Field Museum. I special ordered this one. Isn't it gorgeous?"

Frank shook his head as he examined it. "I liked the old one," he said stubbornly and stood up to pull it on. "It's going to take me years to break this in," he added, feigning exasperation as he knotted the thick belt around his waist.

"You poor thing," Collin said dryly.

"You're a pill."

"Yeah, Merry Christmas to you too," Collin said, as he pulled a pair of tickets from an ornate red-and-green foil envelope. "The Louvre!? Are you kidding!? I got you a robe, for crying out loud."

"Queen Sweep is going public. We've earned this and we're going to celebrate it properly."

"But I got you a *robe*. I stuck to the spending limit. *I* gave the rest to charity like we agreed."

"I thought you might find the Louvre inspiring. You don't really want to grow into a tragic old queen behind that desk at the bank, do you?" Frank asked, tossing a new pair of socks at him.

"You're too much. I don't deserve—"

"Shut it," Frank cut him off, sitting down next to him and patting his leg. "Look." He smiled and pointed to a mound of wrapping paper lit from within. It turned dark, then lit again.

"It's a... um... chandelier for the dollhouse," Collin said, covering his eyes.

"By all means. Every child should have a chandelier or two in their dollhouse," Frank replied.

"I got her Play-Doh and paints too."

Frank just shook his head and laughed. "You even remembered the batteries? Gay Uncle of the Year, I'm telling you."

"Actually, I completely forgot about the batteries. I meant to stop and get some."

They stared at each other, then back at Em beneath her pile of glowing paper.

Lynn went around the room draping newly-knitted scarves around everyone's necks, which brought about more laughter, as they each had several more just like them at home. When she reached Paul, he was extracting a large wooden picture frame from a box.

"Ann," Paul cried.

"It was in Mom's camera. Bet you forgot all about it."

The room grew quiet, as Paul dropped his bandaged hand from his forehead and turned the photo around for everyone to see.

"Our last picture with Mom... that's just the best, honey. Come here," he said, passing the photo to Frank and spreading his arms.

Anna tip toed through the piles of discarded paper and bows, and settled into her father's embrace with the ease of a toddler.

"There's bunches of them. I'll show you when we get home," Anna whispered and hugged him before she stood up and walked over to sit next to Collin.

Em ran up to Paul with a puzzled look, and handed him a clear plastic box full of colored paper clips.

Paul laughed and pulled her onto his lap. "I thought you might like to make some necklaces with these instead. Look at all the different colors."

"But these are from Mommy," she said, staring at him blankly, and fingering the strands of dull, silver paper clips around her neck.

"Okay, I'm sure Dr. Jim could use these colored ones here in the office then," Paul suggested.

"Okay," she said, hopping down and running off to give them to Janet at the desk.

Lynn curled up on a bean bag chair and covered herself with one of the afghans she'd made for the girls' beds.

Collin set down the new wine opener he'd been fiddling with and went over and sat on a bean bag next to her.

Claire snuggled up close to Lynn and rested her hand on Collin's arm. She'd never loved her mother more, and strangely, she'd never felt closer to her. Claire suddenly realized she was closer to all of them than she'd ever been while she was alive. *Now, I know their souls... they're breathtaking.*

Claire studied each of their faces, then turned back to Lynn and was surprised to see Nana sitting on the other side of her bean bag chair.

Nana reached across Lynn's lap and took Claire's hand. "Savor every second. They're hardly ever all together like this."

"For once, I'm not distracted by all the preparations. I can really enjoy everyone. I just wish they didn't have to have so much pain," Claire explained.

"But isn't it amazin' to watch 'em grow?" Nana asked.

Claire nodded.

Lynn's cell phone rang and she pulled it out of her pocket. "Merry Christmas, Sal. No, she's in surgery. How's Michael? Good. Yes, I'll be sure and call you as soon as we hear anything. You've got to stop by the house for your gifts before I leave. Okay, goodbye."

Claire winked at Nana, laid her head in her mother's lap and smiled to herself.

*Kiss my ass, Norman Rockwell.*

# CHAPTER 21

CLAIRE WANTED to hold the vet's hand or rub his back—whatever it took to give him the strength he needed. She could tell he was exhausted by the way he'd dragged himself into the waiting room.

Suddenly, she wanted to hold Paul's hand too.

"Paul," Jim whispered. He nudged Paul's arm and waited for some kind of response.

Paul stirred, mumbled something incoherent, and rolled onto his side away from the vet.

Jim bent over him with his hands on his knees for a moment. He dropped his head and stared at the floor, seeming to steel himself for the talk.

Claire didn't envy the poor guy. She could tell he'd done this many times and was probably even good at it. He possessed an especially comforting demeanor she felt she could trust. She softly encouraged him. "You did everything you could, Jim. He'll be okay. Just do what you do, and know that they'll all be okay."

She smiled as Jim's expression softened.

He straightened up, wrapped his arms around himself,

closed his eyes as if in prayer, then crouched down again to wake Paul.

Claire perched herself on the arm of the couch and waited, frustrated that she still couldn't determine which words made it through to their conscious mind, or how many. Yet she took solace in the fact that it was usually enough to bolster their spirits.

Jim cleared his throat, but Paul continued to snore. "Paul," he repeated, this time squeezing his shoulder.

"Huh?" Paul sat up and rubbed his eyes. "Guess I dozed off."

"It's okay. It's late."

Paul glanced around the room. The girls were nestled in bean bag chairs beneath their new afghans; Frank had nodded off in an office chair, his new robe draped over him; Collin slept on the other couch; and Lynn slept soundly on the floor between the girls, with her head next to Em's on a bean bag.

"It's 6:00 A.M.," Jim replied, straightening up and stretching his back, twisting from side to side. "We're snowed-in. Figured you all might as well get some rest. Janet says the plows are out, but you know how long it takes them to get to the side streets."

"You must be exhausted," Paul said.

"I'm okay." Jim sat down next to him.

"I was thinking I'd better get up and find you. That's the last thing I remember. We've been through a lot these past few months. Frank or Collin fill you in?" Paul asked. He busied himself by inspecting a small hole in the knee of his jeans, hoping the guys had spared him the task.

"Sounds like this Christmas was going to be hard enough."

Paul quickly steered the conversation back to Shadow. "Can I see her?"

Jim sighed and rubbed the back of his neck. "I thought we had a pretty good handle on things, but there were complications. I'm afraid they really threw a wrench into the works."

"What do you mean?" Paul's heart sank.

"Your wife collected antique Christmas tree ornaments?"

"No," Paul responded too quickly, as if it could erase the complications. He looked at his shoes as Jim waited in silence. "Not intentionally—auctions—you know how you buy a box of stuff for one item and there's a bunch of random crap in there?" He felt like he needed to defend Claire's actions, and keep Jim from saying what he knew was coming.

"It's no one's fault, Paul. The tinsel they make now is foil or plastic, and it can slice through an intestine, which is what happened. But that's about all the damage it'll do."

"But?" Paul braced himself.

"But the tinsel from the 40's and 50's was made with lead. Lead poisoning is a tough hand to draw on top of surgery and old age. I'm sorry."

Paul bent over and buried his face in his hands. "No," he whispered.

"You can see her," Jim offered, wringing his hands in his lap.

Paul stood up, wiped his eyes and nose on his shirt sleeve and slipped his feet into his shoes.

Jim led the way. The two of them walked across the waiting room, past the reception desk. Janet mouthed "Sorry," blew her nose and busied herself with paperwork.

When they reached the door to the operating room, Jim

turned to Paul. "Roger removed her breathing tube. I'll leave you two alone."

Too choked up to speak, Paul nodded, as Jim held the door open for him. *Oh, God. There she is.*

"Take as much time as you need."

Paul didn't answer and welcomed the sound of the door swinging closed behind him.

Shocked by the sight of her, he averted his gaze, mentally labeling anything familiar. *Towel clamps, needle holders, heart monitor... breathe. Flexible scope, scalpels, forceps... breathe. It's okay. You're okay.*

The similarities to the equipment he used almost everyday were undeniable, almost intriguing. So many familiar sights and scents, but none of them had provided him any kind of protection or advantage. It didn't seem fair.

He took a deep breath, placed a thumb and a finger against his eyelids. Spots formed before his eyes as he pulled his hand away, and a blurred image of Shadow's body emerged. *Oh God, here we go.*

Paul's knees felt weak, as he stepped forward and reached out for the edge of the operating table. Were it not for her subcutaneous sutures and an awful-smelling topical preparation around the incision, at first glance, she could have been sleeping across the foot of Anna's bed.

Thankfully, her eyes had been closed, but her dark pink tongue lolled out of the side of her mouth onto the table.

Hot tears leaked onto his cheeks as he pulled a candy wrapper from his pocket. He crinkled it loudly between his fingers, knowing she wouldn't respond. *She's really gone.*

He bit the inside of his cheek to quell the tears, and stuffed the wrapper back in his pocket.

Paul stroked her ear, out of habit. "You really did it this time, you old garbage-eating hound," he whispered, as he pulled his hand away to wipe a tear from the corner of his mouth. He felt a tingle in his other hand, and reflexively shook it out.

Reason and accountability slipped away as Paul draped himself over Shadow's body. He needed to rest his head on it one last time, block any evidence of surgery from view and pretend everything was fine for just a minute or two.

He rested his other hand on the table near her head, letting it dangle over the edge. The tingling sensation crept into his fingertips and spread to his palm, but he was too tired to care, and clenched his fist until it disappeared.

Shadow stood wiggling next to him. She licked his hand a third time, as she wagged her long copper tail. She whimpered when she got no response, and cocked her head to one side as she stared up at Claire.

"He's okay," Claire replied.

She bent down and lifted Shadow's muzzle to kiss the bridge of her nose, like she'd done since she was a pup. "Come on, let's go chase some seagulls." Claire wrapped her arms tightly around the dog and thought the two of them to the beach.

Paul managed to avoid all questions with a subtle shake of his head to each of the adults, as he entered the waiting room. *I can't lie to Anna*, he told himself, but when she searched his eyes, he held up crossed-fingers and managed a small hopeful white-lie-smile.

---

"Is Santa mad?" Em asked, as Anna fastened her seatbelt for her.

"Santa," Paul breathed. He threw Lynn a dread-filled glance, then shot another at Anna through the rearview mirror.

Anna's eyes met his and widened in silence as she shook her head.

"I got it," Lynn whispered from the passenger's seat. She pulled her phone from her coat pocket and mouthed, "Where?" as she listened for a ring on the other end.

Paul whispered as he turned on the wipers and cranked up Elvis singing *Silver Bells* on the radio. "Garage. In a bag of pool toys."

"Good one," Lynn answered with a wink.

"Mad about what, honey?" Paul asked, over his shoulder, as he turned the radio down.

"He didn't get milk and cookies at our house." Her voice was filled with genuine worry.

"Oh Em, Santa's been to our house so many times. He knows where we keep everything. I bet he just helped himself."

Paul took the scenic route home, giving Sal time to play Santa, while Frank and Collin stayed behind to take Jim, Roger and Janet out to breakfast.

---

"Hey, there's a wreath on our door. Look, Em! Santa's plugged in on the front steps! It's Michael and Sal," Anna said when she caught sight of their blue Oldsmobile in the driveway. "Too bad you didn't bring a turkey this year, Grandma. Michael could've basted it for you."

"He'd make a good chef with that thing, wouldn't he?" Lynn laughed.

"Did you know he lost his job at the bank?"

"Oh, no. That's too bad." Lynn's brow furrowed with concern.

"I bet Sal brought cannolis!" Anna whispered.

"Mmm... let's cross our fingers," Paul said, unfastening his seatbelt.

"Did you make scarves for them this year, Grandma?" Anna asked, jumping out of the van and waiting for Em to climb out of her car seat.

"Absolutely, got to take care of my boys," Lynn replied.

"Ho-Ho-Ho!" Sal shouted as he waved from their front door, wearing a red-and-white Santa hat. His face was gaunt, but his smile was genuine.

Inside, Michael paced throughout the house, turkey baster in one hand, kitten in the other.

"This is not our tree. Our tree has garland," Michael informed them, squeezing his baster.

"Have a seat on the couch, Michael. Introduce the girls to your little friend," Sal instructed him firmly.

"Sal, you're a lifesaver," Paul said, placing a hand on the old man's bony shoulder.

"Don't mention it. I put the key back under that heart-shaped rock. Speakin' of rocks... somebody throw a bunch at ya?"

"That's a story for another time," Paul answered.

Lynn kissed Sal on the cheek. "How have you been?" she asked, looking straight into his eyes.

"Tired. Damn chemo's kicking my old butt. We have a girl—Linda. She takes Michael out a couple times a week, petting zoo usually. Don't know what I'd do without her. I can't set him up somewhere else, but I can't do it by myself anymore either."

"What about you? Who's taking care of you, Sal?" Lynn asked.

Sal didn't answer. He closed the front door and followed everyone into the living room, where the girls were sitting on either side of Michael on the couch. He held the kitten against his chest, petting it with long, firm strokes.

"Can I hold him?" Em asked.

"He's not scared," Michael said, handing him to her.

"He's so cute. I love him. When Shadow gets home she can be his mommy."

Anna looked at Paul who sat in the armchair, staring at the thing from across the room. With her arms folded, she didn't seem quite as enthused. Her right hand reached for her lashes as if in protest to the new arrival, but she caught herself and promptly tucked her hand under her leg.

Paul avoided her gaze. He spotted the girl's stockings under the tree, spilling over with candy, DVDs and the flavored lip glosses he'd bought them. Next to the stockings sat a little white pastry sack filled with cannoli, he suspected.

Claire had been crazy for Sal's cannoli.

Paul was touched by the fact that the old man had brought some this Christmas, the same as he had so many before. The presence of the familiar little white sack beneath the tree made him feel like Claire was right there with them.

Lynn knelt down next to his recliner. "I gave the green light on the cat. I know it wasn't my place, but I had to go with my gut. Forgive me?"

"In a heartbeat," Paul replied.

———

"How 'bout a glass of holiday cheer?" Sal asked, as Paul walked into the kitchen.

"No, but thanks."

Sal lifted his glass. "Suit yourself. To Claire then," he said and brought it to his lips.

Paul smiled, relieved to be with someone who wasn't going to tip toe around her name. "Did you put those stars in their stockings?"

"Oh yeah, hope you don't mind. Mil always made sure Michael got a new ornament in his stocking. I've been doing the Santa thing over thirty years now. Got it down cold."

"Michael still...." Paul began to ask, then the comment sunk in.

"Yup, still believes. Although with Michael it's more about traditions and routines than the magic of Christmas. When Lynn called and asked me to haul my Santa expertise over here on the double, I just grabbed those," he said, taking another drink, his wedding ring clicking against the glass.

"Well, thanks. I can't tell you how much I appreciate you doing this," Paul said. "Santa was the furthest thing from my mind when we took off for the animal hospital last night."

Sal pulled up a stool and sat down. "Well, the bank officially shit-canned Michael, but finding quarters and raising kittens seems to be getting him through it. Fills his days, anyway," Sal said, briefly closing his eyes.

"I can't believe they fired him. Does Collin know?" Paul asked.

"This was out of Collin's hands. I imagine the powers that be realized someone who could be conned into just about anything, probably shouldn't be working in a bank. You can't really blame 'em. I bet they make sure Collin is the last to know. He'll give 'em hell, no doubt, but that's water under the bridge. I never expected that job to last as long as it did."

"Sorry," Paul replied.

"Ah, it's not so bad. I got him a little change machine so he could sort and roll all his coins himself. I just had no idea there'd be so many quarters."

"Quarters?"

"He's finding quarters all day long. I'm not talking one or two, mind you. He finds one every couple of hours. It doesn't matter where we are—the grocery store, the backyard or in our own kitchen, for Christ's sake. There'll be another one right there on the linoleum, plain as day. I shit you not. I may be old, but I know damn well *I'm* not dropping them. He averages around eight or ten a day and never, I mean *never,* an odd number, which would drive him nuts. Not even once," Sal insisted, setting his glass down on the counter.

Paul stared at the glass and asked, "These quarters? How long has he been finding them?"

"A while now, and it's like, wherever they're coming from *knows* how much an odd number would drive him up the wall. How's that for booby-hatch-thinkin'? It's true, though."

"Huh."

"I don't know, maybe this shit has spread from my prostate to my brain already, but you can't ignore those damn quarters. I've tried," Sal insisted, as he finished his drink. "I thank God for good friends like you folks," he added, brushing at the corner of his eye.

"You're family, Sal. You know that," Paul said quietly.

"No Paul, the way you people have always been with us is more than family. Lynn just invited us to stay with her out at the cabin... indefinitely. She thinks I can still beat this with health food or something. I don't know, but she rambled off a bunch of ideas, and I started saying to myself, 'Why the hell not?' You know?"

"Sure, absolutely."

"I never would've thought Michael could transition out of the bank. But if he can handle a change like that, I think he could handle being out at Lynn's for a while, and who's to say those quarters won't follow him? I used to take him fishing. I can't anymore, but nature has always had a calming effect on him, and he likes Lynn. She knows how to deal with him on his own terms. It could be a good thing for both of us."

"I think you're right—it'd probably be good for all three of you. You should go for it."

"Hell, I might even live and prove every one of those know-it-all doctors of mine wrong," Sal said, getting up from his stool.

"I'm always hearing stories like that around the hospital," Paul said.

"Lynn sure has perked up, eatin' all those fruits and veggies, a regular Pollyanna... bless her heart. I've got a shred of hope. I thought the well had pretty much run dry there. You know? But I still couldn't bring myself to make any arrangements with a home for Michael. I couldn't see that working out for him at all. Maybe this is why. Something better was just around the corner," Sal reasoned. "No matter where he ends up when I'm gone, you'll visit him. I know you will."

"Of course, it goes without saying." Paul reached for the gaunt old man and gave his shoulder a squeeze. "I saw my dad yesterday. He's back at the nursing home, but he's not doing too great."

Claire sat at the end of the counter, watching the two of them. She was sure Sal's hugs were few and far between these days, with Michael not being a big fan of physical affection. She shook her head, astonished by the way everyone seemed to patch each other's holes... without her help.

A message for Paul suddenly bombarded Claire's mind, crowding out any other thoughts. Sensing its importance, she didn't dare question where it came from or why, as she began to chant, "Say yes to grace. Say yes to grace."

CHAPTER 22

CLAIRE STOOD up in the sand, watching Shadow dig holes along the beach. *I wish there was a way to show Paul and the girls how happy you are. Come on, girl. Head back.*

*Hold on, I've almost got this little, crunchy, crawly guy,* Shadow answered back telepathically, as she stuck her nose down in the hole again. *Oh, all right.* Shadow ran back up to the house and jumped up on Claire, licking her face.

Claire sat back down in the sand, hugging and kissing her old friend. *Oh, go on back to your digging.* Claire laughed, feeling exhausted for the second time since the day she'd crossed. *Talking with animals must require more energy.*

Shadow came across as a hyper teenager. She had more than enough energy for both of them, running off to explore, while Claire rested.

She was leaning back on her elbows, thinking about Em's necklaces, Anna's ring and Michael's quarters, wondering how many signs she was capable of juggling at once, when she spotted something unusual out on the water, a long flickering blue light.

Claire sat up, craned her neck and squinted, but still

couldn't figure out what it was. She decided to get up to investigate. As she neared the water's edge, the light grew brighter. She was knee-deep in the surf, when she remembered she could think herself right to the source. *Oh my God! It's a cord!*

Jennifer Robles had sunk deep below the surface by the time Claire reached her.

Claire grabbed her by the arm, and shouted her name through the water.

The detective didn't respond.

Claire rushed her to the surface and continued to scream the woman's name, shaking her. She finally slapped her, as they bobbed up and down in the moonlit water.

A peaceful expression spread across the detective's face.

Another slap, and Jennifer's eyes fluttered open. She instinctively clung to Claire's neck, and began to gasp and cough.

The detective appeared completely disoriented. Claire watched her blink in disbelief, but she knew the instant Jennifer recognized her.

"Shit!" Jennifer gasped. "Oh, shit!" she yelled, and try to get away.

"Jennifer, wait!" Claire screamed. "I don't know what's happening, but I don't think you're crossing over. I think you still have a choice," Claire insisted.

"If I'm seeing you, this can't be good," Jennifer argued, and tried to break free.

"See this?" Claire shouted, raising the glowing, blue cord from the water. "If you were dead or dying, you wouldn't have it. I know that much. Usually they're silver, but maybe they start out blue."

Jennifer reached for the cord, trying to piece together what might've happened. "I think I flipped it. I ch-chucked, and the oar knocked me out of the b-boat," she said, her teeth chattering.

"You took a boat out in December?" Claire shouted.

"I knew I sh-shouldn't, but I did, and now it's over," Jennifer said as she began to panic.

"It's not over. You're going back."

"Can you do that? How?" Jennifer argued.

"I don't think the *how* is what you need to focus on. I have a feeling the *how* just happens and the *why* is the big one," Claire reasoned. "I think *how* will take care of itself, if you have the guts to stake your claim on a second chance."

"K-kay," Jennifer said, through tears. "How do I s-stake my claim?"

"What's worth going back for? Think perfect world. What would you go back and change?" Claire demanded, squeezing her shoulders as hard as she could, as the two of them tread water.

"I hate being a detective!" Jennifer cried. "I don't ever want to work on another case like yours again!" she screamed into Claire's face.

Claire cried with her. "I can't go back, but I think you can. What are you going to do?"

"Quit! Take Anna under my w-wing. I'll keep a c-close eye on her because I c-care about her, and I'm not just saying that because she's your d-daughter. She needs it."

"I know," Claire cried.

"Is that what you want? Is that why you're here?"

"I don't know why I'm here with you, but someone like you could make an enormous difference in Anna's life. Jennifer!? What's happening?"

"I feel lighter. Are... are you s-sure I'm g-going back?" Jennifer sputtered.

Claire didn't have any idea where the woman was going. "Keep thinking about your plans! Picture yourself doing them! Don't stop!" Claire shouted.

"Something's pulling my arm," Jennifer cried, as they watched the limb fade away. Black water spread through the detective's body.

Within seconds, Claire was bobbing on the surface alone. The light from her beach house flickered in the distance. Shadow's voice filled her head, calling out her name. Claire focused on the dog and thought herself back to the shore.

She threw her arms around Shadow's neck as she looked out at the water and saw nothing but blackness. Claire let go of Shadow, thought of the Jennifer's face and focused with every ounce of energy she had left.

When she opened her eyes a man below her was shouting for help, between chest compressions on the body of a blue-faced woman. It was Jennifer. She wasn't moving.

Claire spotted a surprisingly large flashlight lying next to the man's foot. She placed one hand on the flashlight and one hand over Jennifer's heart, right through the hands of the man trying to save her. With the next compression, Claire thought as hard as she could, *Pull!* with one hand and *Push!* with the other.

The detective convulsed, coughing up water, as she swung her arms at her rescuer, a gaunt jogger with a backpack full of bricks and dark circles beneath his eyes.

The man rolled the coughing detective onto her side as the ambulance pulled up.

———

"She's drooling down the back of your coat, Dad." Ann whispered, as she followed them up the stairs. "I knew she'd fall asleep in the van if you cranked the heat. Mom used to do that."

Paul stepped on a stuffed animal, stumbling and kicking it aside as he entered Em's room, but she didn't stir. "Help me get her out of her snowsuit." He lay Em down on her bed, and together they removed her damp hat, mittens and snowsuit.

Anna hung them over a chair to dry, while Paul lifted Em off the bed, and pulled her comforter back. *I've got to get rid of Shadow's stuff while the girls are out of the house. Maybe Collin can take them to the mall, but first, I have to tell them.*

Anna sat down at the little table.

Paul felt her gaze on him, watching him tuck Em in and kiss her on the forehead.

"When are they bringing the kitten back?" Anna folded her arms across her chest.

Paul reached up with both hands and grasped the canopy frame above his head. He rested his head against one arm and gave Anna an apologetic smile. "Tomorrow. I know, it's going to be a little strange having a cat around here, but Sal said he'd set us up with a litter box and the works. You okay with the kitten?"

"He's cute, but I don't want those white hairs all over my black stuff. He can sleep with Em. My room is off limits. There's no way Shadow's going to share my room with a cat. She's got seniority."

Paul bit his cheek, mentally preparing himself for the unavoidable, but Anna switched topics.

"Are Sal and Michael really going back to the cabin with Grandma?"

"Sure looks like it. That should be an adventure, huh?" Anna picked up a broken orange crayon Em had torn the paper from and rolled it between her fingers. "Don't forget, you have to buy Em the biggest thing of crayons at the end of the school year—that carousel thing. Mom promised."

Paul walked over to the table and gingerly sat down on the little chair across from her. "Right. Keep reminding me."

"Did you see the little chandelier Collin got her?" Anna asked, as she drew a horse on a scrap of paper.

Paul shook his head and smiled. "For the girl who has everything."

Abruptly, tossing the crayon down on the table, Anna blurted, "Let's cut the crap."

Paul held his breath and twisted his wedding ring around his finger.

"Shadow's gone, isn't she?"

Paul exhaled, reached across the table and took her hand. "I'm sorry, honey. I was waiting for the right time to tell you."

"I haven't been very nice to her since Mom.... things have been so different and I just sort of ..." Anna whispered, her voice trembling.

"Oh, honey. Come here," he said, standing up and pulling her into his arms.

"I ignored her," she cried, as she buried her face in his shirt.

He glanced at Em. She was still sound asleep. "Ann, Shadow knew how much you loved her."

"I hurt her feelings. That's why she started sleeping in your room," Anna argued, between gasps.

"You two have been inseparable since the day you met. You were always her best friend."

"I know. It's just hard," she said, wiping her nose on her sleeve.

"I think Shadow missed your mom just as much as the rest of us, and that's why she started sleeping on our bed."

"Come on, Dad."

"Hey, you and I aren't the only ones who've smelled

your mom's things. One day, I found Shadow in her closet smelling her shoes."

Ann laughed and covered her mouth, trying not to wake Em. Her somberness returned. "How do we bury Shadow? Everything's frozen."

"She's being cremated. Jim's going to give us the ashes. We can do whatever you want with them. We could bury some in the backyard or..."

"Could we take some to Pooch Park?"

"We'd have to be a little sneaky about it, but I think we can pull it off."

"Grandma thinks Shadow's going to be around, that she might give us a sign or something," Anna added in a quiet voice.

"We'll have to keep our eyes peeled." Paul rubbed her back and chased the thought from his mind.

"Shadow's at Mommy's house by da ocean," Em mumbled.

Startled, Paul responded before he turned around, thinking it was a question. "Yeah, honey. She is." He braced himself for another round of tears, but Em was still asleep.

He gave Anna a confused smile and shrugged.

Anna giggled. "She's talking in her sleep."

"Shadow could play wif Snowball if she was wif us," Em mumbled.

"I'm sure she would have," Paul responded and gave Anna a wink, wondering how long he could engage Em in conversation.

Intrigued, they stood by Em's bed, waiting for more.

Her eyes still closed, Em smiled. "She can run fast now."

"I'm sure she can," Paul said, making a face and shaking his head at his lame response.

"Mommy says she chases seals on the beach."

*Mommy? Mommy and Shadow are together? Of course! What else is Mommy saying!?*

Paul's eyes grew wide, his body stiffened and he felt Anna grab his sleeve, but he couldn't take his eyes off Em. He reached for the bedpost to steady himself as a memory of Shadow barking at the birds in their backyard, flashed through his mind. "Seals or seagulls?"

They stared at Em, as she curled her fingers around one of her paper clip necklaces.

"Yeah, seagulls," Em answered dreamily and puckered her lips as if she were kissing someone.

―――

"Yes! Tell them!" Claire was savoring the looks on their faces, when a desperate voice filled her head.

"Claire! Please! You've got to come now!" It had been months since she'd heard it, but the sound of Julia's voice was unmistakable.

# CHAPTER 23

AHMA APPEARED next to Claire in a pink robe. "She needs you."

"No."

Ahma could be intimidating, but Claire had reached her limit.

"Surely, you're not going to ignore a plea for help."

"She's why I'm here. Forget all that blueprint-manifesto business. The bottom line is Julia betrayed me. I could still be *with* them. I wouldn't have been crossing the expressway if she hadn't stabbed us all in the back." Claire knew her anger was about to boil over. *No, not with Ahma. Why is she pushing me?*

Claire crossed her arms and stared at her family with a defiant resolve.

"I can literally wait for an eternity. You, however, have some important decisions to make and rather quickly," Ahma patiently explained.

Claire still didn't answer when Ahma wrapped her arm around her and pulled her into her purple meadow, but her eyes were drawn to Ahma's hand. Another hand began to materialize, its fingers anchored between Ahma's. An arm appeared, bare feet, then the pregnant body of a woman, and finally, Julia's grief-stricken face.

Claire swallowed hard, crossed her arms and clenched her fists, trembling with anger. She looked incredulously from Ahma to Julia, and back to Ahma, again.

Julia mouthed the words, "Please help me, Claire."

Claire glared at Julia in her hospital gown with her protruding belly. She had a cord too. "You are unbelievable."

Claire tried to hide her shock. In all the years they'd been friends, she'd never seen Julia look so awful and helpless.

Julia didn't answer. She seemed to have difficulty speaking.

Nana materialized on the other side of Julia in a pale blue robe, and grasped Julia's other hand.

"Nana? Do you know who this is?"

Nana nodded somberly.

Cal appeared next to Nana, taking her hand in his. He wore a hopeful expression and a yellow robe similar to theirs.

"What is this? Choir practice? An intervention? I haven't done anything wrong, and I haven't been *forced* to do anything since I got here... aside from that tapestry, so why now and why *her*?" Claire demanded.

Ahma shook her head and gave Claire another smile of never-ending patience. "You're not being forced to do anything but consider your options. Come. Some things have changed. I think you're going to be very interested in a new opportunity." Ahma extended her hand to Claire.

"I can't trust her! How can you expect me to trust her!?"

"I don't. I expect you to trust *us*," Ahma said, her hand still extended.

Claire closed her eyes. She hated feeling so angry in their presence. It felt like she was breaking all the rules. She sensed she was ruining everything, but being asked to help Julia was too much. "You cost me my kids, my husband... my life!" she yelled at Julia.

Julia gave Ahma a hopeless look.

In one sweeping motion, Ahma ran her hand down the front of Julia's hospital gown, which wove itself into a peasant's blouse and a long wool skirt. A kerchief appeared over Julia's hair, which had turned a lighter shade of brown. Julia's features slipped and shifted to reveal a much younger, bruised and bloodied face.

Claire's heart sank as she recognized the woman from her journey with Gerald, into their past. Julia had been the German farm girl Claire had viciously beaten.

Claire looked down at her hands and wept, shaking her head. "That doesn't make it alright. What she's done to me, to all of us, was still...."

Ahma brushed her hand back over Julia's clothing, returning the woman to her previous state. Then she extended her hand once more. This time Claire took hold of it.

Cal took Claire's other hand and the moment he did, the room filled with a gale-force wind so strong, Claire was power-less to keep her eyes open.

When she closed her eyes she saw two people locked in battle, time and again. She tried to open her eyes to escape the pain, frustration and sadness, but it was impossible. She and Julia had been through many battles throughout many lifetimes, so many that Julia's final betrayal seemed almost miniscule. The group reviewed each heart-breaking conflict at mach speed. Even more surprising to Claire was the realization that *she* had been decidedly more calculating and violent, and far less merciful.

Julia shouted above the howling wind. "Why have we done all of this to each other?"

The wind died down, and Claire was finally able to open

her eyes.

The five of them stood in a circle, still holding hands on a cliff overlooking a tumultuous sea. Waves could be heard crashing on the rocks below. The air smelled fresh and clean. Rippling green grass covered miles of hills behind them.

"You have been each other's greatest teachers—brutal at times, to be sure, but loving as well. The two of you are right where you are supposed to be. Come along now," Ahma said as she walked between the two, grasping their hands.

With another tremendous gust of wind, Claire found herself seated at a round table facing Ahma, Julia, Nana and Cal.

Claire lowered her eyes, unable to face them after all of the ugliness she had no choice but to claim.

"Remember Claire, we are not here to judge you or anyone else, only to guide you," Cal reminded her.

Claire looked at Julia.

Julia responded by somberly staring at her pregnant belly, caressing it with both hands.

"I don't understand why we didn't immediately hate each other when we met again at the bank," Claire said to no one specifically.

Ahma sat back and folded her hands in her lap. "The intensity of the old emotions carry over from time to time, but rarely are you able to discern what those old emotions were. They could be the intense feelings of fear, sadness, anger, jealousy or love... or all of them combined. It is impossible to unravel such emotions. You each recognized something familiar in the other, and simply gravitated toward the familiar," Ahma explained. "There is a deep mutual love and respect that forms between two such formidable opponents. This is a very special day. It's taken you thousands of years to reach this point in your relationship."

Claire and Julia smiled uncomfortably at one another and everyone relaxed a little.

"Claire," Ahma began, "Julia has reached a critical point in her manifesto, or blueprint, as you call it. The two of you are, once again, at a crossroads. An opportunity has presented itself for you to end your self-appointed spiritual teaching obligations to one another. The proposal is Julia's. The decision will ultimately be yours. You have the benefit of having two members of your Collective here today to advise you, should you choose to seek their guidance."

Claire sensed an overwhelming surge of love and support rise up around her like a cloud. She glanced at Cal, who gave her a little salute.

Nana smiled and nodded, blinking back tears.

"Where would you like me to begin?" Julia asked.

Claire finally warmed a little to the sound of her voice. It was stronger now and Claire realized that she had, in fact, missed her. "Where are you on the earth plane? What's happened? From your cord, I gather you're still alive?"

"I'm in an intensive care unit in Sao Paolo, Brazil" Julia began. "I'm on life support, because I've had a cerebral aneurysm. I'm brain dead," she said with a frankness that caught Claire by surprise. No games, no coy calculations behind the eyes, just the stark truth.

"How?"

"I holed-up in a little coastal town, but I started getting these pains behind my eyes shortly after I arrived. At first I told myself it was stress, that it was psychosomatic. Then I told myself I needed glasses. Finally, I began to experience numbness on the left side of my face and the most horrific headaches of my life. I knew I was in trouble, and I had to get to Sao Paolo if I wanted to save my baby."

Claire's gaze fell upon Julia's swollen belly, a pang of

sympathy finally swimming to the surface.

"I was living by myself in a little cottage I'd bought in the hills. I never touched the bank's money, by the way."

Claire shot her a look of surprise.

"Actually, I take that back. I touched it a lot, fondled it is more like it, but I didn't spend a penny." Julia offered them a small embarrassed smile. "Anyway," she continued, "When the pain became intolerable, I knew my options were extremely limited, because of the embezzlement. My world became very small, very fast. I called a friend of mine in Venezuela—a lawyer. He wanted to fly me out of there—get me to an emergency room, but I refused. He finally agreed to come and stay with me in the cottage until we finished all the legal preparations. I had to protect my baby, and Miguel owed me a favor from way back."

"So you and the baby are both on life support?"

"Yes, he drew up the paperwork for me to be kept on life support if it came to that, and the expense would be covered, in addition to a generous donation to the hospital. The stipulation was that I would remain anonymous. No questions were to be asked. They would keep me on life support until I carried the baby to term, and then she'd be delivered."

"It's a girl," Claire responded, slowly taking it all in, unable to fathom where this was going, and what it could possibly have to do with her.

As if Julia had been silently cued, she broached a new subject. "Ahma said Gerald spoke to you before he returned to his body, about your tour of duty in Germany."

"Yes, he told me that he and Collin and I were stationed there together, and we had some sort of pact. Were you part of the pact? Why didn't he tell me? Why don't I remember everything and she does?" Claire asked, directing the last question to Ahma.

"It is crucial that Julia be the soul to relate certain pieces of your shared history. Trust the process, Claire. You may continue, Julia." Ahma motioned with her hand.

"The reason you had such difficulty trusting me when I entered your life at the bank was because I had tried to poison the three of you. I was the last surviving member of my family, when you found me hiding in the cellar. My brother and father had just been killed. I was still in shock. You took over our farmhouse. You made me cook for the three of you. You found whiskey in the cellar."

Claire's eyes were fixed on Julia's. She felt defensive—full of shame and remorse, but she fought hard to keep her head clear and free of judgment, and eventually found her inner student.

"You were very angry young men, fed up with the war and being so far from home for so long. And the drunker you got, the angrier you became," Julia explained.

It was becoming too difficult for Claire to separate her emotions. She exhaled loudly with regret and fear of what lay ahead.

Ahma reached for her hand. "No judgement. All souls take a turn at being every kind of person imaginable... and a few unimaginable, in the process of spiritual evolution."

Claire bit her lip and nodded.

"My father had been a veterinarian," Julia continued. "I found a bottle of horse tranquilizers in a drawer and tried to slip them into the stew, but Collin caught me—probably no small coincidence, he couldn't stand me this time around."

The two women actually laughed at that, and everyone around the table relaxed a little more.

"You were the most furious with me. I'd planned to drug all of you and burn the house to the ground. You beat it out of me in a drunken rage," Julia stated calmly, "You let Gerald to rape me."

"Your hair smelled like lye," Claire said, piecing fragmented memories together.

"There was a shotgun in the closet under the stairs. I shot myself. I'm the biggest reason Collin chose the life of a homosexual this time. He wanted to be an artist, a peacemaker, a mother, but after that day in the farmhouse, he simply couldn't reconcile those desires with the ultimate vulnerability of being a woman. It was a difficult decision for him, but in the end he found his compromise," Julia explained.

"God, the four of us must form one hideous knot in the tapestry," Claire whispered.

Ahma shook her head with certainty. "Your threads are no more ugly nor tangled than the rest."

Julia shook her head. "I felt you'd finally succeeded in taking absolutely everything from me, and that part of me recognized that part of you—that same vibration when we met at the bank, ready to go another round."

"Of course," Claire whispered, more to herself than anyone else.

"I became determined to take everything away from you, one way or another. I'm trying to evolve beyond these kinds of feelings, but my vibration is lower than yours. You're an older soul, more evolved, believe it or not," Julia said, teasing a little.

"I still have plenty of lessons ahead of me, but you chose a very different path this time. You're closing in on a new level in your progression, your evolution," Julia clarified and looked to Ahma for approval.

Ahma nodded for her to continue.

"Really?" Claire asked, looking at Nana and Cal, and finally at Ahma. "I'm not feeling very enlightened or even human right now."

"That's to be expected when sorting past lives," Ahma said, her ancient almond eyes calm and reassuring.

Julia shifted in her seat and straightened up as tall as her bulging stomach would allow. "I would like to propose that you and I end this cycle here, and begin a new one which will benefit us both."

"We've learned so much from one another. I have to warn you that this next phase will be much more complicated, should you choose to embrace it. I am nowhere near an undertaking of this magnitude on my own path, but I'll be with you every step of the way. Watching over you will play a large role in my own healing and progression to a higher vibration... not that I expect that to matter to you right now."

Claire felt a shift in the energy around them. This was big. She could see it in everyone's expressions. Nana looked like she was about to burst with pride and Cal clearly wanted her to accept. Ahma remained calm and cool as ever, but there was an undeniable twinkle in her eye.

A breeze rustled through some dead leaves on the ground, tossing them in the air before they went swirling over the edge of the cliff.

Julia placed her hands on the table. "I'm offering you the opportunity to your family."

"What? I can go back to Paul and the girls? Collin? My mom? How?" Claire cried, springing to her feet.

"Miguel, the lawyer who drew up the agreement for my life support, will be contacting Paul after my baby is delivered by C-section. I appointed you and Paul as her legal guardians, not knowing you'd been killed. Despite my jealousy, I always thought you were a good mother. The two of you were to raise her if she went to term. She will, if you accept. You'll return to Paul and the girls through my unborn child, Claire. In your next life, you'll be my daughter."

"No! That's not what you said. You said I could...." Claire

cried, searching the faces of Nana, Cal and Ahma, hoping
they'd stop Julia from continuing with her lunacy.

Nana looked as if she wanted to jump in and save her, but
Ahma raised a finger, signaling her to wait.

Cal's brow creased in what Claire could only read as frustration.

"Continue, Julia," Ahma said softly.

"Paul will be your adoptive father. He's the best father I
know. Your biological father is George from Security at the
bank, but he'll never know this, nor will anyone."

"George? No. No, no, no," Claire said, turning and walking
away from the table. The grass felt damp and cold beneath her
bare feet, jolting her to her senses. *Just leave. This is insane.
They've all gone crazy.*

"You'll be Em and Anna's little sister," Julia reminded her.

Claire's heart caught in her throat. She stopped and turned
toward them, speechless and heartsick with a mother's longing.

"Your name will be Grace."

Claire covered her face with her hands and wept
inconsolably, as her mind struggled to make sense of the outrageous proposal. "Say yes to Grace... Grace is a person!" Claire
cried, finally realizing the meaning behind the phrase she'd felt
so compelled to chant to Paul.

Claire's eyes met Nana's. "Is this really possible?"

Nana nodded, eagerly. "It's a whole new set of rules
though, hon. It'll be a tough row to hoe, but a good life—one to
be real proud of, and it'll propel your spirit right into the infinite
just like your father's."

"Why?"

Julia leaned forward with a sense of urgency. "My
body is being kept alive by machines, Claire. I'm being fed
through a g-tube. Grace is barely surviving. She's begun to
suffer from malnutrition, and she's not getting the oxygen she

needs. You'll have multiple birth defects, but technology has advanced enough that you'll survive, if you're a fighter... and I know you are."

"What kind of birth defects?"

Nana cut in, "You won't be able to walk or speak. You'll have a weak heart and lungs, and need a couple of surgeries to fix them, maybe even a heart transplant at some point."

Claire frowned, as fear rushed through her veins... *so strange to know this before you begin.*

"But," Nana said, raising her index finger, her face lighting up, "All of your past struggles with trust and control will be put to rest. You'll be healed by having to rely on others to take care of you. You're gonna be a world class teacher when it comes to patience, empathy and love."

"Come on, Nana. You don't seriously believe I can do this? It's too much."

"I know you can do it. Your father had his doubts too, but look at him go. He even found you. And there's one more thing. You'll hang onto most of your experiences you've had here. You're going to remember who you were before you were Grace. You'll cherish the gift of this reunion every day of your life, with all your heart," Nana explained, clasping her hands beneath her chin, her green eyes glistening.

"Of course Paul and the girls won't be aware of this," Cal chimed in. "And your relationship with Paul will have a whole new dynamic, but it won't be the first time. You and Paul have been just about everything two people can be to one another."

Somehow, Claire had known this, and nodded with a twinge of sadness. She hadn't accepted the fact that she'd never make love to Paul, again. It had been too painful to think about. But never talking and laughing with him the way they always had, was far more painful.

Ahma's lips straightened into a thin, straight line. "It will be exceptionally frustrating at times. However, the positive aspects far outweigh the negative. This is a very rare opportunity, Claire. Few souls return to the earth plane so swiftly. However, your father was also an exception. I want you to take your time. Consider every possible element of the equation."

Claire thought about everything that had been explained to her. "Was this in my blueprint?"

Ahma's eyes softened. "It was your most courageous dream. It will require you to set aside any remaining ego. This is one of the biggest sacrifices a soul can make and a broad path to the infinite."

Nana looked as if she wanted to add something, and Claire worried it was the catch to end all catches.

She took a deep breath. "What is it, Nana?"

"It's just that most people are going assume there's nobody home. And even more are going to speak to you, and treat you like you're incapable of anything at all. In some ways, you'll be a baby your whole life, totally relying on others, sometimes even strangers, for the most basic things like: food, warmth and most important of all... physical contact—love."

"Don't forget," Julia quickly added, "You'll also be in a much better position to heal your family: Paul, the girls, your mom, even Frank and Collin. Don't forget Michael and Sal, too. You'll be the one that holds them all together, and heals their hearts simply by being yourself. I'll be spending a lot of time with Cal, learning how to be a spirit guide, now that you and I have finally buried the hatchet. What do you think?"

"Sounds okay, except for having no control over a single thing. That's a hell of a price tag, wouldn't you say?" Claire sighed.

Nana slapped her hand on the table and laughed. "What better gift for a dyed-in-the-wool control-freak?"

# CHAPTER 24

DETECTIVE JENNIFER ROBLES opened her eyes to discover she was in a hospital bed, her lips and mouth as dry as dead wood. Her chest ached when she tried to sit up.

Aside from the dim green light of the heart monitor, the room was dark, but private. She was thankful for that.

*Where am I? Bleach... paper-thin hospital gown... drab room... damn—Cook County. I can't believe I chucked after more than twenty years rowing. Shit! Where the hell is my boat?*

Chucking was simply part of learning to row, but Jennifer was seasoned. Chucking happened when you lost your rhythm and caught the oar in the water on the backstroke. Sometimes the oar hit you in the stomach.

*Last time was at the NCAA finals senior year. Topped off the humiliation by throwing up. Cost us second place.*

*Shut up. Shut up. Shut up.*

There was a table on wheels on the other side of her bed, with a water pitcher, a Styrofoam cup and two flower arrangements.

*Water.*

Jennifer grabbed the cold metal railing to pull herself up. A flash of pain shot from her sternum to her toes, taking her breath away. *There's a button here somewhere.*

Her hands fumbled along the edges of the bed, sending ripples of pain through her chest. Seething, she tried to slow her painful breathing by studying the flowers. One was a holiday arrangement of red-and-white carnations with a big silver bow—definitely the department. The other was a monstrous bouquet of Stargazer Lilies, reeking of guilt. They really stunk up the room. She didn't need to see the card to know her brother had once again, sent some over-priced flowers to stand in while he tended to more important things.

*Wait, it must be Christmas. Don't be such a baby.*

Jennifer didn't like the feelings the room stirred in her. Dread sunk its teeth into her stomach for no apparent reason. She suddenly felt as if she were being left behind. *Calm down, maybe it's a reaction to some drug they've given you.*

Her eyes searched the room, taking inventory: *TV, clock, closet, chair, crooked calendar, ugly drapes, dusty blinds, marble windowsill with a big chip....*

*Impossible.*

She squinted at the chip in the marble windowsill. *I must be whacked-out on pain meds.* She blinked several times, waiting for the crack in the windowsill to disappear. The thing just seemed to get bigger. It was like making eye contact with an old acquaintance in the check-out line when she was in no mood to chat. She couldn't get away from it. It demanded she acknowledge its presence.

Years ago, Jennifer had sat in a wooden chair with orange cushions, just like the one at the foot of her bed, with her feet on that windowsill. She'd propped a foot on either side of that damn chip, stared out the window and listened to her mother's last ragged breaths for twenty-seven of the longest days of her life.

*How!? They've got six floors and four wings. How many rooms is that? It's impossible. I've never been hospitalized in my life and now I'm here?*

She couldn't get away. She couldn't even move. Only one explanation seemed to make sense. This had to be her mother's way of letting her know she wasn't alone.

*Not my mother, my mother doesn't do things like this. Anna's mother does.*

*Oh yeah? What about the Monarch butterflies?*

Jennifer had managed to spot a Monarch butterfly on her birthday, every single year since her mother had died. It never mattered where she was. She had seen one out on the water from the end of Navy Pier once, and another perched on the outside of the glass on the fourteenth floor of the Sheraton Towers.

*You were looking for them.*

*Oh yeah? Was I looking for the one that flew right in the bathroom window as I stepped out of the shower?*

She'd never told anyone about the butterflies because it was nuts.

Jennifer thought of the messages she'd given Anna from Claire. She was drawn to Anna's fiery spirit, even her smart mouth. *I don't want to mother anyone ever, I've got no business... but I think I could guide that kid in the right direction.*

Jennifer clenched her jaw and searched for the controls again. She finally found the small gray box and buzzed the nurse's station. Then she tried to mimic any Lamaze breathing she'd seen in movies, to chase away the waves of pain.

"Miss Robles?" a voice crackled from the box, sending a small vibration through her mattress.

"I need a number from my cell phone. Do you have it?"

"Sure do," the nurse answered.

Several minutes later, a tired-looking woman with a bleached-blonde beehive and what Jennifer assumed was a bad case of heel spurs, hobbled into the room. She handed her a blue plastic bag sealed at the top.

"President?" the nurse asked nonchalantly.

"Detective."

"All right. You've got one more chance before I call Psych in for a full evaluation."

"Best president we've ever had... canvassed for him myself... won a Grammy... Mary Todd Lincoln."

"I'll let Dr. Simmons know you're awake and a bred-in-the-bone smartass. We'll get you something to eat, but we'll still have to run a few tests."

"Can I have a glass of water?" Jennifer asked, as she extracted her cell phone from the bag.

"Sure, but let's get you sitting up. Then our next mission is a little trip to the bathroom."

Jennifer grimaced and readied herself, as the woman located the controls and raised the head of the bed. "Holy shit!"

"Sorry, CPR compressions leave some nasty bruises, but they worked and you're here." The woman handed her the cup of water and waited while Jennifer drank it.

"Thanks," she managed, and gave the Hollywood Lamaze breathing another try. *CPR? Really?*

The nurse smiled sympathetically.

Jennifer handed the bag and cup back to the woman.

"You'll have to use our phone to make the call. Dial nine to get out." She picked up the beige phone from the nightstand and set it on Jennifer's bed. "I'll be back in fifteen minutes for our little field trip."

Jennifer managed a weak smile, picked up the receiver and punched in the numbers. She hoped Paul wouldn't be the one to pick up.

"Hello?" a high-pitched voice answered.

"Hello, is Anna home?" Jennifer asked as she scratched at an irritated spot on her wrist beneath the plastic ID bracelet.

"Annaaa... phooone," Em shouted. "She's in the baf-*bath*-room. She's got diarrhea. Dad says she ate too many Hershey's kisses. He put my stocking on top of the frigerator, but I can still reach it if I stand on my tippy toes on the counter. I got a kitten for Christmas. He's Snowball."

"Oh," Jennifer said, trying not to laugh, because it hurt too much.

Anna finally picked up. "Hello?"

"Anna, its Jennifer... Detective Robles."

"Oh, hi. Em, hang up."

"I'm talking."

"Em... Daaad!"

"Okay, okay!"

They heard a lot of clunking, then a loud click.

"Sorry." Anna sighed.

"No problem. How was Christmas?"

"Not the greatest. My dog died."

"No. Oh, Anna. Oh, God." Jennifer covered her eyes, barely able to believe it. "How are you doing?" She wracked her brain, not knowing what to say after that.

"I'm okay. She was pretty old. She ate some tinsel and got really sick. We were actually at the animal hospital on Christmas Eve," Anna said, with a small humorless laugh.

"That sucks."

"Then Em got a kitten from some friends of ours. He's okay, but I miss Shadow."

"Always thought I should get a dog, just never got around to it. Anna?"

"Yeah?"

"You still like horses?" Jennifer asked hopefully.

"Yeah, sure."

"Well, a friend of mine owns a stable in Old Town. You know the carriage drivers you see sometimes over by the old Water Tower?"

"Yeah, we went on a carriage ride for Em's birthday last year. The drivers are so goth with their black capes and top hats."

"What would you say if I could get you a job working in the stables?" Jennifer asked, and held her breath.

"Really!?"

"Really," Jennifer exhaled and slowly relaxed into her pillows, wincing. "It's not as glamorous as it sounds. You'd be shoveling horse shit and lugging big buckets of feed and water. It's hard work. They'll pay you under the table until you turn sixteen. After you've put in some time, they'll show you the ropes. In a year, you could probably be a weekend driver."

"Oh my God, that would be so cool! You really think you can get me the job?"

"I'm ninety-nine percent sure. He owes me. I caught some kids trying to break in one night. I'll pick you up at your place Monday around noon, and we'll drive over there. Make sure it's okay with your dad though, and wear some old clothes and shoes you don't mind ruining. He might have you start right in."

"Yeah, okay. Oh my God. I can't believe this. Kareem is gonna freak when I tell him."

Jennifer took a deep painful breath. "Sorry, Anna. That's the trade-off. Trust me, that guy's trouble. He's had some scrapes already. I checked. We've talked about this. You know you can do better."

"You can't do that! You can't tell me who I can hang out with! What kind of scrapes?"

Jennifer twisted the phone cord around her finger for a second, and went out on another limb. "What's your dad think of him?"

"See ya Monday," Anna grumbled.

"See you Monday." Jennifer smiled and set the phone back in its cradle. It was the first conversation they'd had with no mention of Claire. She couldn't decide if that was good or bad. It was going to be hard to leave this case behind when she resigned. *Shit, I guess I've made up my mind. I'm quitting.*

It bothered her that she couldn't remember when she'd made the decision, but it didn't feel like she'd made it alone.

Jennifer's head ached and her throat hurt. She wished she'd asked for some Ibuprofen. She was about to call the nurse again when a knock startled her.

The door opened slowly and her chief walked in, smiling and shaking his head.

Now that she was sitting up, Jennifer noted the number on the door, two-thirty-three. *Unbelievable. It really is the same room.*

"When you said you had to give up rowing every winter and swim instead, I assumed you meant in a pool... not the Chicago River. Wanna talk?" He took a seat in the orange chair at the foot of her bed and pulled off his stocking cap and coat. He was wearing a sweatshirt and jeans. He'd come down to see her on his own time.

"Sure, why not?" Jennifer answered with her usual bravado.

"Before I start in with the ass-chewing, I've got some bad news. Your psychic died."

Jennifer closed her eyes and clenched her fists. "Medium, she was a medium. This is the crappiest Christmas I've had in a long time."

"I know. I would've waited a couple days to tell you, but she left instructions for you to take her dog."

"Yeah, right," Jennifer said, opening her eyes.

"No joke, Robles."

---

"Dad?" Anna followed a loud clanking sound into the bathroom and crouched down on the rug in front of the sink. "What are you doing?" Sticking out of the cupboard beneath the sink were her father's jean-clad legs and bare feet.

"Getting your mom's ring out. It might still be down in this goose neck. Almost got it loose."

Anna heard a grunt. The wrench clanked against the pipe again. "Why are you doing this now? Aren't you going to get ready?"

No answer.

Anna hoisted herself up on the counter, tucked her robe between her knees and turned to face the mirror. She set the tube of adhesive next to her. Then she removed a dainty brown false eyelash from a small plastic box and bit her lip in concentration, as she picked up the tube of glue and unscrewed the cap.

"Dad?"

A determined growl and another clank came from under the sink, followed by a splash.

Anna froze, a false eyelash pinched between her thumb and finger. She swung her legs over the edge of the counter and looked down. "Dad? Are you okay? What happened?"

"It's okay. The water's off. Ha! There it is! I got it!"

He wriggled out from under the sink. Running his hand over his wet face, he sat on his haunches and held the ring up in triumph.

Anna grinned back at him. She hadn't seen him so excited in ages.

He moved over, sat with his back against the wall and happily polished the ring with his faded flannel shirt. She watched his eyes fill with tears, while his smile remained intact.

Finally he looked up at her, then at the wreckage in the cupboard beneath the sink. "I had to try to get it out." He dropped his head unable to hold her gaze, and flipped the ring back and forth between his thumb and finger, the small diamond glinting in the light. "She'd be so happy."

He looked defeated, even with the ring in hand. His hair and shirt were soaked. She watched him remove his wedding band and press it against her mother's ring.

"She knows," Anna insisted.

He was smiling again, but the tears spilled down his cheeks.

Anna quickly turned back to the mirror and squeezed some glue across the band at the base of the false eyelash. The bathroom remained silent as she applied her new eyelashes and a little mascara. Finally, she uttered a, "Huh, there," and turned back to face him.

"What do you think?" she asked, batting them.

"I think you're beautiful no matter what, and I love you very much."

She gave him a half-smile. "I love you too, Dad. The funeral's at one. Are you going to get ready? Em's already got her dress and tights on. She's just looking for her shoes."

"Yeah, I'd better jump in the shower. Damn. We can't run the water until I get this fixed." Paul sighed. "Your mom would have told me to call a plumber *and* which suit to wear. Care to take a crack at that?"

"I like the gray one. She did too, but Grandpa would love it if you showed up like this," she said, hopping down off the counter. She opened a drawer, dropped everything inside and closed it. "He hated dressing up." She laughed. "We should bury him in his favorite greasy coveralls."

Paul smiled and got to his feet. He set the wrench on the counter, was going to set the rings down near the sink again and thought better of it. Instead, he slipped them on the end of his index finger.

"I saw your mom's cream-colored pants suit by the ironing board. Are you going to wear that?"

"Yeah. Is it okay? Anna asked, biting her lip again, afraid she'd overstepped her bounds. It was the last outfit her mother had worn. "It's a little big. I shortened the pants, just basted them. I can take the stitches out in a few seconds."

"No, no, it's better than okay. It's fantastic, but you're right. I'll never get away with jeans and a flannel now. Not with you two all dressed to the nines," he grinned as he wiped his grimy hand down the front of his shirt.

Em cried from down the hall.

Paul gave Anna a puzzled look.

Anna rolled her eyes. "Either she can't find her shoes or it's her tights. She doesn't like the way the seams feel on her toes. They have to be lined up just right or she freaks out." She headed toward Em's room with Paul behind her.

# CHAPTER 25

WHEN THEY WALKED into her room, Em was sitting in front of her dollhouse with her little battery-powered lights strewn all around her. She'd stuffed her tights into the dollhouse chimney. "They're all broken and there's no mail today!" she cried.

"Uh-oh. Come here," Paul said, crouching next to her. He wiped the tears from her face while Anna dug around in her closet for the shoes. "Our mailman doesn't come until this afternoon. We'll get you some new batteries for your lights on the way home, I promise. Then we'll get the mail and we'll make some popcorn and have a movie night. How does that sound?"

Em continued to cry.

"And ice cream?" Paul tried.

"Found 'em," Anna said, crawling out of the closet.

"There you go. See? Has she got some socks that would go with this?" Paul asked, smoothing Em's red dress. "You look so pretty," he said, touching her ever-growing paper clip necklaces and kissing her cheek.

"Yeah, here." Anna held up a pair of red socks. She

walked over and knelt down on the floor as she scrunched a sock up, readying it for Em's foot.

Paul set Em down on a little white chair. "Anna can help you while I get ready. Okay?"

"Okayyy," Em sniffled, rubbed her eyes and began to cry again.

Paul sighed, looked down at the rings on the end of his finger and twirled them a couple of times with his thumb. He kept twirling them as he walked back down the hall to his bedroom. Part of him felt like he wanted to keep her ring with him, but a bigger part of him was afraid of losing it again. He opened Claire's jewelry box and was carefully pressing it down between two pink velvet humps when her necklace caught his eye. It was odd she'd left the necklace containing her grand-mother's ashes on her nightstand that day, since she'd rarely left the house without it. He'd forgotten he'd put it in her jewelry box. It had been too painful a reminder to see it sitting on her nightstand day after day. *What do you do with something like this? Maybe I should ask Anna if she wants it.*

Paul got an idea. He unfastened the clasp of Claire's neck-lace, removed her wedding ring from the box and slipped it onto the sterling silver chain. His pulse quickened as he walked over to the chest of drawers where his own box sat with a few cuff-links inside, a watch that needed repairing and one ring. Without hesitation, he raised the lid and found his father's class ring. Paul slipped the second ring on the chain as well, fastened the clasp and slipped it over his head. He walked over to the bed and sat down, holding the silver filigree tube full of ashes and the two rings in the palm of his hand. Without thinking, he whispered, "Dad? Claire? I want the two of you to take care of each other. You too, Nana," he added as an afterthought, then smiled and scratched the stubble along his jaw.

"Are you thinking about Grandpa?" Anna stood in

the doorway, a vision of femininity. Gone were the black boots, lipstick and eyeliner. Her hair was still black, but she'd curled it and pulled it back in a barrette. She looked all grown up in her mother's suit. She'd found little pearl earrings to match the pearl ring Claire had bought for her.

Paul rubbed his eyes, as if he were seeing things, "Cindy Crawford? What are you doing here?"

"Cindy who?"

"Never mind, have you seen Em?" Paul asked.

"Yeah, she fell asleep on her bed."

"Seriously honey, you look like a super-model. What's the matter? Couldn't you find anything black?" he teased.

"Good one, Dad. I know you must be sad about losing Grandpa on top of everything else that's happened," she said, frowning and looking down at her stocking feet, unsure of what to say next.

Paul looked at the necklace. "Actually, no. I mean, I'm going to miss him, but I'm relieved too. Wherever he is, he's himself again, you know?"

"Yeah, I'm glad you're talking to them."

Paul blushed, realizing she *had* heard him talking to them. "You really think she hears us, Ann?"

"I *know* she does."

"Wherever we are? Wherever we go?"

"Definitely. Everywhere," Anna said, as she crossed the room and sat down on the bed next to him.

Paul blurted out, "Then let's go away for New Year's."

"Where?"

"I don't know. Some place pretty and quiet... some place we can just hop in the van and drive to."

"Milwaukee?" Anna asked, doubtfully.

"What about Galena?" Paul suggested.

"Any place is fine with me."

"We can do something special for your Mom on New Year's Eve, just the three of us."

"Yeah let's, but I have to be back by Monday," Anna said.

"For what?"

"Detective Robles is getting me a job at the stables where those carriage drivers work." She'd said it quickly, hoping he wouldn't say no.

"Detective Robles?"

"Really, she's been super-nice to me. Is it okay?"

"Uh... sounds interesting. Let's talk some more about it later," Paul said, shaking his head, trying to wrap his mind around the two of them hitting it off. *She's getting a job?*

"Awesome. Thanks. Come on, you've gotta get dressed. We're gonna be late."

Nana led Gus and Lily up the narrow farmhouse stairs. "It's like she's been paralyzed by the enormity of the decision. I've talked 'til I'm blue in the face. Maybe you can get some kind of response out of her. I hate to call on Ahma and Cal. She's supposed to sort this out on her own, but it's getting' down to the wire. They're getting Julia ready for her C-section and Claire won't even get out of bed. She hasn't been anywhere today."

"I just wanted to say hi, but we'll see what we can do," Gus assured her, squeezing Lily's hand as they reached the landing.

"Don't get me wrong," Nana whispered and turned

to them, her hand on the glass doorknob. "I couldn't do it. Not many can, but what an amazing opportunity for growth. I'm so afraid she's going to say no." She gave them a painful smile and turned to open the door.

———

Claire was sitting up in bed, looking out the window. "What were Ben and Shadow barking about?"

"Maybe they're in love," Gus offered.

Claire whipped around. "Gus! Lily! What are you doing here?"

"No, what are *you* doing here? This is no time to hide your head under the covers, Claire. Did you know *Paul* has been talking to you?"

"To both of you," Lily corrected him.

"Don't be jealous," Gus teased. "You turn's comin', dear." He patted Lily's hand. She walked around to the other side of the bed and sat down. Gus sat down on the side closest to the door and Nana stood at the end of the bed, wringing her hands and smoothing her quilt.

"You're just saying that to get me out of here, but I'm not ready to make a decision." She pulled her knees up to her chest beneath the covers.

"It's true. Paul's been talkin' to ya," Lily said as she put a hand on Claire's arm.

"Great. I didn't even play with Em today, but she's not going to understand if I just stop. I can't hurt her or Anna with her circles and her ring... or Michael. How can I do that to them? I've already abandoned them once. No one can ask me to do it twice."

Nana slapped her hands down on the footboard at the end of the bed. "Claire Elaine, you won't be *leaving* them! You'll be *joining* them!"

"But they won't even know it's me! And what if Paul doesn't want the baby? He'd be crazy to take that on."

"You always want to save 'em from everything. They're gonna save themselves no matter *what* body you're in, and Paul *will* say yes to Grace. I know he will," Nana argued.

"I'm not ready to be so powerless, so helpless. I'm not some Buddhist monk."

Nana laughed at that and threw her hands in the air. "I give up."

Claire hated arguing with Nana, but she was being so controlling and insistent when all she wanted was time and space. "What did Paul say, Gus?"

"He wants us to take care of each other. That's all I'm trying to do, Sugar."

"I know," Claire sighed, and looked him up and down. "Hey, where's your cord?"

"Traded it in on a much better deal," he said, winking at Lily and reaching across the bed to take her hand.

"Oh my God. They've lost me, Shadow and now you too? How could you leave them now?"

"It was time, Claire. And one way or another, they're going to heal each other's hearts, with or without you. You've seen them do it."

She had. It was so beautiful the way people created patches of love to keep each other from falling apart. Trolling was exhausting and she didn't think she'd ever really master it. She wanted to be everywhere, helping all of them but she just couldn't swing it.

"Because you haven't taken a single class," Nana answered Claire's thoughts out loud. "You never even had your reunion with your Collective, or visited The Hall of Records."

Claire shot her a 'no trespassing' glare.

"Well, you haven't. You can't tear yourself away from any of them long enough to evolve even the tiniest bit over here. Trolling doesn't count. You might as well be on the earth plane where you can help yourself, as well as them."

That made sense, actually. Nana was right on both counts. She hadn't even thought about taking any classes or working on her own spirit. Her friends and family came first, but there were probably thousands of classes.

"Billions," Nana corrected her.

"Okay," Claire said finally, covering her face with her hands. "Let's do this."

Jennifer Robles had taken a stand. "No more tests, needles, pills or anything until I get today's Trib."

Sylvia with the beehive produced a newspaper ten minutes later. She tossed it onto Jennifer's bed and promptly jammed a needle into her arm.

Jennifer didn't blink. She just opened the paper one-handed. A deal was a deal. Normally, she never bothered with the paper. She got all her news firsthand at the precinct; but here she was cut off from the world, and it was driving her batty. TV news was crap, and the god awful soap operas and talk shows were intolerable.

Sylvia removed the rubber band, and hobbled out of the room without a word.

Jennifer watched her go and turned to the police log. She

hadn't missed much. An article below it titled, *Angels in the ICU,* caught her eye. It was about a quadriplegic and former alcoholic named Gerald McAllister, who was writing a book with the help of his son. He claimed to have had a choice in whether or not he lived. Not only that, according to Gerald, a woman or angel, had actually convinced him to fight for his life while he was in a coma. The words sent shivers through her, as she shook the paper straight.

The entire incident seemed eerily familiar. She couldn't remember a thing that had happened once she'd hit the water. Still, she had a vague recollection of someone yelling at her or arguing with her, but she thought she'd been alone. There hadn't been another soul out on the water before she'd chucked.

She forced herself to let it go, as her eye was drawn to another article on the opposite page.

*Old Town Neighborhood Advisory Committee Looking For Replacement Vice Chair,* she read. *I know everybody on the board. Oh, Burt Miller had a stroke. Shit. Great job though. I could do that job with my eyes closed. No pay though. Still... nobody knows that neck of the woods like I do. Wonder if I could get another job in the neighborhood just to pay the bills. Tend bar at the Old Town Tavern or Second City. Why not? How much do I need to squeak by?*

She opened the drawer of the tray table and found a pen inside. She was scribbling figures on the edge of the newspaper when Sylvia hobbled in again.

"You were supposed to turn this off when you put it back in the bag. It's been going bananas for the last fifteen minutes. I was ready to write somebody up, thought one of my nurses had one on. Here," she said, and handed Jennifer's cell phone to her before she turned and called over her shoulder, "Meatloaf and carrots for lunch, Detective. Lime Jell-o if you're good."

Jennifer grimaced then eyed the screen as her phone rang.

She didn't recognize the number. "Detective Robles, Missing Persons."

"Morning Detective, this is Dave Kelly down at Midwestern Research. We've got a situation here. I was told to call you."

"I'm off duty right now. Let me give you Detective Moreland's number."

"No, I was told to call you specifically. We had a Dr. Jeff Foster from Miami teaching a surgical course here this morning —rhinoplasty. Unfortunately he knew one of the cadavers. I know this sounds crazy, but he insisted we call you. He kind of had a panic attack. I think he said her name was Claire."

"Holy shit! Where did that body come from!?" She threw the newspaper on the floor and pulled herself to the edge of the bed.

"Evanston, I think. Why?"

"She's a missing person—an active case." Jennifer was up, wincing and checking the closet for her clothes, but it was empty.

"Hold on, let me get her paperwork. I'll call you right back." Dave replied hastily.

When Jennifer closed the closet door, Sylvia was standing there.

"Jesus! You scared the shit out of me. Have you got my clothes in one of those blue bags?"

"Who wants to know?" Sylvia asked, folding her arms.

"You got kids, Sylvia?"

"Sure," Sylvia answered, as she backed up to the closed door and leaned against it, her arms still crossed for emphasis.

"What about grandkids?"

"Too many."

"Okay, so what if, God forbid, one of your kids was being dismantled in some surgical class in the name of science, by mistake. Would you want your grandkids to find out?" Jennifer asked, as she checked herself in the mirror, searched the drawers and gave Sylvia her best clock's-a-ticking stare.

Sylvia's stern face went slack.

"No? What about their spouse? Think that's something they'd like to have in their head the rest of their life?" Jennifer found a comb in one of the drawers and did her best to tame her short, curly hair. She gave up, threw the comb back in the drawer and looked at Sylvia again to gauge where they were in this little process. Sylvia's expression had softened.

The seasoned nurse looked at her watch and back at Jennifer. Then she smoothed the back of her hive, calmly hobbled over to the bed and picked up the controls. "Vickie, bring the detective's personal effects, some scrubs and an AMA form down here. She's got a work emergency."

"An AMA?" Vickie responded.

"That's right—Against Medical Advice. It's the yellow one way in the back of the bottom drawer... since we never use them."

There was a "Be right there," from the controls.

"I get it. Thank you," Jennifer said, and murmured, "Claire thanks you."

Jennifer's phone rang again as Sylvia hobbled across the room to wait by the door for the clothing. "You'll need scrubs. They had to cut your clothes off you."

"Robles," Jennifer answered, pacing the floor.

"It's Dave at Midwestern. We've got a problem."

"No shit, Dave."

"I mean a *bigger* problem. This definitely isn't an eighty-seven-year-old black male. Judging by the paperwork, one of our guys took the wrong body from Cook County Morgue. Do I call Walter Rhinehardt down there or do you?"

"Me. What's the number?"

"I'll text it when I hang up. Wait...uh, one more thing. She's in a couple different departments, if you catch my drift. Like I said, this was a rhinoplasty class so her head's here... shaved of course."

"Jesus, Dave. Severed the head and shaved it too? I've got a family to deal with, here. They still have to identify her. Get her together, *all of her*, and I mean *now* or this could be the biggest lawsuit Cook County's ever seen. You like court? Like taking time off work for court?"

She knew she'd seen bodies in far worse shape—unrecogniz-able bits and pieces in fact, but she had never allowed herself to get to know those families like she had Claire's.

"I understand. We'll do our best."

"*You'll* do your best. Don't tell *anyone*."

"Right, I'll just say I'm repossessing body parts on behalf of God," Dave answered.

"I'm on my way. Southeast entrance? I'm going to ride with her back to the morgue."

"You want to ride with the body in the van?" Dave balked.

"I'm not letting her out of my sight. Let's hope this Walter Rhinehardt can put me in touch with someone really skilled for reconstructive work."

"All right," he conceded and hung up.

Jennifer closed her phone and turned to Sylvia, who looked like somebody had just run over her dog a few times.

Sylvia held out the blue bag. "My sister has an electrolysis business. Pretty tight with the drag queens—best wigs money can buy. Want me to call her?"

"God, yes. Dark brown, shoulder-length."

"What—no highlights?"

Jennifer shot her a sheepish look, as she tied the drawstring on her pants. "Just trying to think."

"You can make it up to me by signing this release. I'm not responsible if you drop dead, while you're riding around town with your corpse." She held out a clipboard with a Paxil pen dangling from it by a string.

"Fair enough," Jennifer said, as she finished tying her shoe, grabbed the clipboard and scribbled her signature.

"I'd be out of here before Dr. Simmons and Jolene get back from *lunch*. At least, she'll have put him in a good mood," Sylvia advised.

## CHAPTER 26

"SORRY TO INTERRUPT YOUR LUNCH," Walter told a handsome young man sitting at a table as he and Jennifer entered the dingy little kitchen.

The man arched an eyebrow. "I could never eat in here," he said, closing his paperback and setting it on the morgue's lone lunch table. "You must be Kathie's replacement."

Jennifer shook her head and started to introduce herself, but Walter interrupted.

"No, this is Detective Robles. Detective, this is Tony Chism, the cleaner who worked on her," Walter said, motioning for her to take a seat at the table with Tony.

Jennifer saw Tony shoot Walter a look of concern, but Walter seemed to ignore it.

Tony stood up and shook her hand.

"Missing Persons," she said and pulled out a chair. She and Tony sat down and Jennifer set the vintage hat box she'd been carrying on another chair.

Walter wore a pained expression and put his hands on his hips. "Your Jane Doe was up at Midwestern Research, after all. The detective just brought her back. Hell of a mess, but I think we can tidy it up some without a bunch of folks losing their jobs. Although, their driver probably has it coming. I'll run upstairs and get her file. Can I get you some coffee, Detective?"

"No thanks, I'm good."

Tony collapsed against the back of his chair, closed his eyes and sighed. He ran his hands through his hair and shook his head. "I knew it. They swore they didn't have her when I called, but I knew it had to be Midwestern. How did you...wait... you know, don't you? Who *is* she?"

"I'm sorry, but I can't discuss the details of the case," Jennifer said, swiftly producing a notepad and a pen from the pocket of her pants. It was cold in the little kitchen, and her scrubs felt as thin as newspaper.

"No, you have to tell me. We don't even need her paperwork. Ask me anything. I know every word in that file," Tony insisted.

Jennifer shook her head. "You know I can't."

Tony stared at her with pleading eyes. "Come on. You have no idea how important this is to me."

She eyed his wrists. Two full-sleeve tattoos peeked out from beneath his cuffs. *For a tough guy, he's sure attached to her.*

"Christ, remind me to resign before they fire my ass."

"What?"

"Never mind. You first. Come on, I've got your *who*. I just need the when and where."

Tony leaned in conspiratorially. "She's *not* a vagrant."

"No, she's not."

"Definitely not a prostitute."

"Far from it."

"Married, right?"

"Yes."

"Kids."

"Yeah, two girls."

"A professional—a lawyer or something like that?"

"Bank exec. You need a job?" Jennifer dropped her no nonsense demeanor for a second and smiled.

"Nope. Like my job."

"You should be an M.E. You're good at this."

"Thanks, but everything about her seemed off. Still, I was ordered to push her through and ask questions later. I tried like hell to find out more when things calmed down, but then she disappeared. I called everybody who'd set foot in this place, trying to find her. I called every precinct trying to figure out who she was. I swear, your name sounds familiar."

"I'm in and out a lot and our desk clerks aren't the brightest crayons in the box. When did you get her?"

"October thirty-first—early. She was already here when I came in at six. Walter had called everybody he could get to come in for the plane crash. I mean everybody, even retirees. We were completely overrun with the plane crash. He had to get a refrigerated truck like they did during the heat wave."

"You still have her personal effects?"

"Yeah, bizarre clothing—coveralls and a parka—filthy, but you know I've been thinking... it *was* Halloween. The body was in pretty good shape for a vehicle versus pedestrian."

"I need those clothes. Where was she found?" Jennifer asked. Her mind shot back to the article about the quadriplegic. He'd said he'd struck a homeless woman.

"In the ditch. Westbound Kennedy, west of Cumberland before the O'Hare exit—broken neck, punctured lungs. Never knew what hit her."

*Right by the bank.* Jennifer scribbled a few notes. "Was it a pick-up truck?"

"I don't know, but I think the driver survived. We didn't get him. The accident was on the news, but I didn't hear anymore about it after that. Where was she going? Work?" Tony asked, rubbing his forehead.

"No, she was suspended the day before." Jennifer had let too much slip and sighed when Tony caught it. "She was supposed to meet a co-worker at Starbucks across the street. Never made it." Jennifer chewed on the end of her pen, then scribbled, "Gerald McAllister charged? Acquitted due to health issues?"

"Why was she suspended?" Tony asked, but he looked like he'd realized the answer before the last word left his mouth. "Union Allied—embezzlement."

Jennifer shook her head indicating she wasn't about to go there. That case wasn't even hers to blow.

"People couldn't stop talking about the embezzlement. They spent the afternoon taking turns squandering the three mil a dozen different ways while they worked on the crash victims. I know—sick, but I guess Walter had turned the news on in the big suites for more info on the crash. When they mentioned the embezzlement, I guess it kind of eased the tension and gave them something else to talk about in all that charred mess. So, she was in on it?" Tony asked, grimacing.

"No, but she knew the woman who pulled it. They were close. Real bad timing on Claire's part." Her eyes darted to the hat box, then from the hat box to Tony. "Shit."

Tony pounced on the name. "Claire what?"

Jennifer ran her hand over her face.

Tony smiled. "What's in the box?"

"Pictures and a wig. They put her back together the best they could over there, but she still needs some work before I can even think about asking her family to identify her. You know someone good?"

"I know the best—Kelly over at Van Hove."

"Good. Can you get her in here right away?"

"Yeah, she's asked me out for coffee a couple times."

"Good. Get her on the phone and get her over here. You sure she'll keep it quiet?"

Tony nodded.

"As soon as we've got the dental records and you've confirmed it's her, have your friend get started. I want her ready for the family to ID by tomorrow morning."

"God, this is such a relief. I can't believe she'll have a funeral and everything... but how do you make that call?" Tony asked.

"The dentist? It's a Dr. Link out in Oak Park. Went to him since she was a kid. I just ask him to send the records over," Jennifer replied, stuffing the notepad and pen back in her pocket.

"Not *that* call... the family."

Jennifer stood up. "I appreciate your help, but this conversation that never happened? It's over."

———

"I can't believe you let us see two movies back-to-back," Anna laughed, as she opened the silverware drawer.

"It was your idea. We could've headed straight home to figure out where we're going to put another sympathy casserole," Paul teased.

"No way. That was awesome. Two movies was *so* something Grandpa would've done. He never complained when we wanted to sit in the front row."

"Isn't it interesting how the neighbors feel so gosh darn bad about Grandpa?" Paul grumbled, staring into the refrigerator as if, given enough time, it would rearrange itself.

Anna didn't respond. When he glanced up he could see the disappointment in her eyes.

"Sorry, it's thoughtful. I appreciate it. I'm just tired."

"Me too," Em weighed in from her stool at the end of the counter.

"*You?* You slept through both movies." Paul laughed.

"Yeah, Rip Van Tinkle over here. You always sleep until it gets to the best part. Then *I* have to take you to the bathroom," Anna reminded her, as she took three clean plates out of the dishwasher and set them on the counter.

"I wanna eat at the table," Em whined.

"Dad?" Anna asked.

"Yeah, why not?" Paul answered, balancing two Corningware dishes covered in foil on his arm, while he lifted the lid of a third.

"All right, girls. What's it going to be? Tuna, taco or spaghetti casserole?"

"Sketti!" Em shouted.

"Going once, going twice... sketti it is. Thank you, Mrs. Cifelli, you goddess of pasta," Paul said, cramming the other two back onto the bottom shelf and closing the door with his foot. He managed to hook the oven door with one finger, pull it open and set the cobalt blue dish with its matching lid on the rack inside.

The doorbell rang as Paul grabbed three glasses from the cupboard.

Anna laughed. "If it's Mrs. Harris, I hope she brought us cherry bars instead of a casserole. Come on cherry bars. Please let it be cherry bars," Anna said in her best *Price Is Right* voice, as she finished folding three cloth napkins and headed for the front door.

Paul walked over to the table and set the glasses down.

"Nice touch, Ann—a real family sit-down meal for a change," he called out.

Anna stepped back into the kitchen and smiled.

"I'll get the door. You go ahead and finish setting the table."

The doorbell rang again. "Cherry bars! Cherry bars!" Em shouted as she hopped down off her stool and danced around the table. "Snowball's gonna eat sketti with us!" She sang, running past Paul and up the stairs.

Anna shouted after her, "You'd better change that cat's name to *Tombstone*, because he's eating dinner with us over my dead body!"

Paul tried to stifle his laughter as he flipped on the light. *Mustn't look too happy or my approval rating is sure to plummet again. Claire's been missing for two months and not so much as a Tic Tac on our doorstep, but Dad dies and it's like we're living amongst the Amish, practically drowning in neighborly love... or casseroles, anyway. They either still think I'm responsible, or that I was in on it. Always will, I bet.*

When he finally opened the door, Jennifer Robles was the last person he expected to see.

"Detective?"

"Sorry to disturb you, but we've had a break in your wife's case."

Paul stepped out on the stoop and closed the door behind him in one brisk move. "Where is she?" He frowned when she seemed to struggle with the answer.

"Cook County... Morgue. I'm so sorry."

Paul closed his eyes and felt the blood drain from his face. He hugged himself and rubbed his arms. There were no words at first, just pain—horrible, mind-numbing pain.

"Should we go inside so you can sit down?" Jennifer asked.

Paul opened his eyes. "No, I'm okay. It's been too long. I knew...."

"You can still have an open casket—some closure."

"Really?" he said, looking up. "Can I see her? I mean, *now*?"

"Of course. I'll need you or someone else close to her to identify her, but it can wait until tomorrow morning... if you can. I'll meet you there. The girls are home, right?"

"Yeah, right. Okay, tomorrow morning at seven? Ann can watch Em. I can make all the necessary calls, but I've got to get the girls out of town for New Year's before we're trapped here by the press again. What time? Seven?"

"Seven's good. Have your attorney release a statement regarding your privacy. It usually doesn't help, to be honest, but it doesn't hurt either. Let me know which funeral home tomorrow."

"Right," Paul said with a shiver. His mind was reeling in ten different directions. He tried to imagine identifying Claire's body, as well as having to break the news to the girls and everyone else.

Snowflakes dusted their clothing and the two of them stood looking up into the evening sky in silence.

"Jennifer?"

"Yeah?"

"What happened to her?"

Jennifer stuffed her hands into her coat pockets. "I believe she was on her way to meet her friend, Collin, at the Starbucks near Union Allied on the morning of the thirty-first. For some reason we'll probably never know, she was crossing the expressway by the El stop on foot, when a drunk driver hit her just a few minutes before Flight 521 went down."

"Oh, Claire," Paul breathed.

"Are you sure you don't want to go—?"

"No," Paul cut her off a little too abruptly, but when his eyes met hers, he knew she understood.

"Did she dress up for Halloween? Because she was wearing

a pair of dirty overalls and a parka with combat boots. They took her for a vagrant—tagged her as a Jane Doe. She didn't have any ID, no fingerprints in the system, and because of the plane crash she went through the morgue with almost three hundred others that day. She just got lost in the system. With the embezzlement the previous day, I'm afraid all eyes were looking in other directions."

"She had nothing to do with it." Paul looked the detective straight in the eye.

"No, not a thing." Jennifer pulled out a clear plastic evidence bag containing a torn up photo. "Not a single thing, Paul. This was recovered from the Volkswagen's ashtray. I don't know how it disappeared from the evidence room or how you got your hands on it. 7:00 A.M. tomorrow."

Paul's brow furrowed as he took it from her. He studied the pieces of Claire and Julia toasting margaritas and nodded. "Yeah, 7:00 A.M."

"I know this is a lot to digest, but try to get some sleep. Tomorrow's gonna be a long one. It's good you're getting away for New Year's." Jennifer turned and walked down the steps.

Paul waited until her tail lights had disappeared before he turned to go inside. He'd locked himself out. For the first time in his life, he knew this was no accident. He was sure it was meant to stop him, to make him think it all through before he went inside and said the things that would change their lives forever. He'd always be grateful the door had latched. He made a deal with himself, as he stood shivering in the cold. *Tell them tomorrow. You don't even know for sure that it's Claire. Tonight, we're going to have a nice quiet meal. Just keep it together... and keep that antenna connected.*

He mustered an apologetic grin, stuffed the baggie in his pants pocket and pressed his finger against the doorbell.

Seconds later, Anna opened the door. "What are you doing

out here?" she asked, looking at him suspiciously and glancing around the empty yard. She stepped back and held the door open.

Paul hurried in. "Locked myself out. Was looking for the paper."

Anna frowned. "Who was it?"

"What?" he said brushing the snow off his shirt and hurrying back to the kitchen.

"Who was at the door?"

"Oh, no one. Just some kids selling stuff." *She knows you're lying. Change the subject.*

"How long before the casserole's done?"

"A while," Anna replied, clearing some mail from the table and setting it on the desk.

"Still?"

"Yeah, it helps if you turn the oven on."

"Oops."

The phone rang and Paul couldn't remember a time when he'd wanted to answer it less. He looked at Anna, and slowly picked it up. "Hello?"

"Hi, dear."

*Lynn. Keep it together.*

"Hi, Lynn. Hey, can you hold on a second?"

"Sure," she answered through a bunch of noise and hammering on her end.

"Ann? You know what would be perfect—Mom's good tablecloth."

"It's somewhere under the stairs in the basement, Dad. Seriously?"

"You don't have to. The table looks so great though, why not really go to town?"

Anna looked at the table. "Yeah, okay. I think I know right where it is," she said and turned to leave the kitchen.

"What's all that racket?" Paul asked Lynn.

"Sal's building a greenhouse. He gave me a hard time about the wheatgrass taking over the kitchen when he and Michael first got here."

"Wheatgrass, huh. How's Michael doing?" *Tell her. Tell her before Anna gets back. Hurry.*

*No, you can't. It might not be Claire.*

*You know it is. Just tell her.*

"Not so great. It's a lot of change for him. Too much, apparently. He's been pretty agitated the past few days. All this noise doesn't help. He stays inside whenever Sal's pounding away out there, but it still bothers him."

"Oh?" *Tell her. Just do it. Hurry up.*

"Well, he's just about worn that old turkey baster out. Morning to night, he's got that thing going. He hasn't found any coins for the past few days, so that doesn't help either. Today, he's got this Mark Grace baseball card in the other hand and he won't put it down for anything, not even to eat. Sal says he hasn't done that since he was a little boy—said he had an Ebba St. Claire card he dragged around until he'd worn the picture off it. I don't understand any of it, but we're managing."

"Huh," Paul said again, his mind a million miles away, visiting morgues, funeral homes, Galena... Collin.

"You okay?" Lynn asked.

"Oh, yeah... I...." *Do it.*

Paul whispered a string of statements in rapid fire succession. "Lynn, they found her. She's at the morgue. I have to identify her tomorrow morning at seven. The girls don't know. I'm not telling them until I know it's her."

"No!" Lynn screamed, "No! Oh, Claire! Where did they find her?" She dropped the phone for a moment and picked it up again.

She'd been such a rock during Christmas. Paul hadn't

expected her to fall apart like this. Now he chastised himself for being so ignorant. *Of course she's going to fall apart. This is her daughter, her only child.*

"I'm sorry I couldn't tell you in person," Paul continued whispering. He could hear her crying hysterically on the other end. He stared at the ceiling, wanting to cry with her, but biting his cheek and digging his fingers into his palm to keep the tears at bay.

"I'll come right down. I'll start packing," Lynn sobbed.

"Just hang on until I call you tomorrow morning, okay? I have to be sure it's her."

"Sure, right. Oh my God. Okay. Tell the girls I love them. Oh God, no."

"I will," he promised and hung up.

He was setting the phone down on the kitchen counter when it rang again. *Here we go. Someone's leaked it to the papers.*

"Hello?" Paul answered brusquely.

"Mr. Cummings? Mr. Paul Cummings?" a man said.

*Damn it! Now I have to tell the girls before all hell breaks loose, and I'll have to deal with a bunch of craziness when I go to the morgue in the morning. So help me, God, if I find out who...*

"Mr. Cummings?"

"Yes, this is Paul Cummings."

"Mr. Cummings, my name is Miguel Vasquez. I'm an attorney. I need to arrange a meeting with you regarding a delicate matter."

"An attorney? Sure you're not a reporter? If this is regarding my wife, I'll advise you to hang up now. I have my own attorney I need to speak with," Paul whispered angrily.

"Mr. Cummings, I'm calling from Venezuela...."

"If you're calling because I've won some cruise or something, you've either got incredibly bad timing or incredibly good timing. Either way, I really can't talk right now."

"Mr. Cummings, please, I assure you that it's nothing of the sort. You and your wife have been appointed legal guardians of an infant born in Sao Paolo, Brazil—a baby girl," the man hurriedly explained.

"Uh... no, you've got the wrong Paul Cummings—never been there. Sorry. I've really, really got to go now," Paul insisted.

"Mr. Cummings, I believe Julia Farelli was an acquaintance of yours."

Paul froze. He could hear the man shuffling some papers.

"Wait, just a minute." Paul quickly walked through the kitchen to the garage door, stepped out into the garage, closed the door and leaned against it. He couldn't breathe. Paul squeezed the phone in the crook of his neck while he loosened his tie and unbuttoned the top two buttons of his dress shirt. He sat down on the step, his heart thumping wildly.

"Mr. Cummings? Are you there?"

"I'm here," Paul whispered. "You know where she is?"

"Ms. Farelli has passed away, Mr. Cummings," the attorney said solemnly.

"Really?" Paul breathed into the phone. He rubbed his forehead and considered taking the conversation to the van, but his legs wouldn't move.

"The authorities have been contacted regarding Ms. Farelli's estate, Mr. Cummings, but there is still the issue of the child," Mr. Vasquez continued.

"Her estate?" Paul snorted. "Wait, Julia had a baby?"

"The embezzled monies and Ms. Farelli's estate are completely separate matters," Mr. Vasquez assured him, "But Ms. Farelli has legally appointed you and your wife as the child's guardians."

"You're serious? Why would she do that? I don't know what

she was trying to pull, but there is absolutely no way on God's green earth that I am the father of that child," Paul said, laughing nervously and trying not to raise his voice.

"You're absolutely right, Mr. Cummings. The documents state that the birth father is deceased."

"I don't understand," Paul said, holding his head in his hand and staring at the cement floor.

"I apologize. I'm sure all of this comes as quite a surprise, but the child has a trust fund which is covering the cost of her care. You and your wife's names are on that trust fund. It will also cover the cost of your family's airfare and lodging. These funds are completely separate from the funds Ms. Farelli embezzled. Those have been seized by U.S. federal agents. How soon can you be here?"

"No, my wife... I can't," Paul said. "I can't *possibly* be expected to raise a newborn I didn't even know existed, five minutes ago. You have no idea the kind of day I've had, Mr. Vasquez. Be serious." He stood up and began to pace with his hand on the nape of his neck as he thought about his father's eulogy and the horribly surreal conversation he'd just had with Detective Robles.

"If you decline to accept your guardianship, Grace will face a lifetime of institutions. It's important that you understand this. She is a beautiful child, Mr. Cummings. I've seen her myself. Ms. Farelli obviously chose you and your wife for a reason. Grace deserves a loving family. She didn't ask for any of this," Mr. Vasquez reminded him.

"Look, neither did I. You've got to understand my position here. I can't just drop everything and fly to South America. I need some time to think. Be reasonable, would you?" Paul was nearly in tears.

"All right, Mr. Cummings. I understand. I know there is a

lot to consider. I'll phone you again tomorrow afternoon," the attorney said and hung up.

"Gee, thanks. I'm sure I'll have it all figured out by then," Paul mumbled to himself as he sat down on the step, pushed the button and set the phone down next to him. *A baby? Julia?*

"Dad?" Anna yelled.

*Ann.*

"Out here," he managed to rasp and cleared his throat. Paul turned, grabbed the door knob and pulled himself up. He picked up the phone, briefly considered heaving it across the garage, but decided against it. *I need to talk to Collin... now.*

"Dad?"

*Quiet family dinner. Focus. Pull it together.* His legs still felt weak, but Paul opened the door and stepped inside.

"Look," Anna beckoned.

He walked into the dimly lit kitchen and when he rounded the corner, he was met by a candle-lit table, complete with a white lace tablecloth and two of Claire's antique crystal candleholders. Gone were the drinking glasses and chipped everyday plates. In their place, she'd set the good china and crystal wine goblets.

"Wow, it's beautiful, Ann."

She looked so pleased with herself, so blissfully unaware of the chaos train headed their way. He was going to do his damnedest to keep it that way for one more night.

*Can I pull this off by myself? No, I need back-up.* "Has Em seen it yet?"

"No, she's trying to put a dress on that cat. I'm sure somewhere, Shadow is laughing her butt off, right now."

Paul smiled, but felt numb with information. He pulled a chair out and collapsed into it.

Anna stood with her hands resting on the back of another chair, her hair still pulled back. She'd changed into a pink oxford and khakis and looked so much like her mother in the candlelight it was unsettling.

The timer on the oven buzzed and they both jumped and laughed at themselves.

"Ta-dah! Ready for sketti!" Em shouted from the doorway, holding up the kitten who'd just managed to pull its front leg out of a little yellow dress.

"We should invite Frank and Collin over. There's enough for everybody," Anna suggested, as she pulled on two alligator oven mitts and opened the oven door.

*Yes! Thank you!* "You think? Okay, I'll give them a call," Paul said, struggling to sound casual while breaking a sweat. He hit *Frank and Collin* on speed dial.

"Frank, it's Paul. Are you busy?"

"Just opening some windows out on the sun porch. Collin's been out here working on Grace all day."

"Grace?" Paul asked, feeling a bead of sweat trickle down his back.

"You know, that portrait of Grace Kelly. He finished Princess Di yesterday—he's on a dead princess kick."

"Oh, right. It's going well then?"

"He's been a painting maniac since Christmas. He's doing so much better since he left the bank."

"That's great. Can I talk to him?"

"He's in the kitchen taking a potato casserole out of the oven. Actually, we were just about to head over to your place."

"Oh, great. I called to invite the two of you to dinner."

"Perfect. Collin hasn't eaten a thing all day."

"Right, okay then. See you soon." Paul hung up the phone. "They're on their way."

"Cool, I'll get two more place settings." Anna had set the spaghetti casserole on the table and replaced the lid.

The kitchen smelled incredible and while Paul was sure

he'd never be able to choke anything down with his stomach in knots, the table looked beautiful, the girls were smiling and he was ready for a giant helping of family time, regardless.

"Can we say grace?" Em asked, jumping up and down.

Paul raised both hands indicating he'd surrendered. Ever since Em had eaten dinner at her friend Kimberly's house, she'd been trying to sell him on the idea every time he so much as dropped a Pop-tart in the toaster.

"Say yes to grace, Daddy," Em pleaded, still jumping up and down next to her chair.

Anna laughed. "No pressure or anything."

"Say yes to Grace," Paul murmured as he shook his head. That was when it flickered through his mind for just a second. He'd heard it before—déjà vu.

The sound of keys jingling in the front door was followed by the sound of stomping boots. A moment later, Collin and Frank walked into the kitchen. Collin carried a casserole dish over to the counter and set it down.

Paul looked around the room at everyone. "Say yes to Grace," he repeated as one of the candles burned out.

Collin frowned. "Who's Grace?"

# EPILOGUE

*COLD, cold, cold and wet. I've been in this box forever. So hungry. If I could just get one arm lose, I'd feel so much better. I can't even roll over.*

"Shhh, okay now. You're okay, Grace," the nurse cooed into her ear as she picked Claire up, cradling her head in her hand and cupping her little behind with her other hand.

Claire settled her cheek against the nurse's shoulder. She felt the woman's warm hand on the back of her head through her little knit hat. Then it moved down, softly patting her back. The nurse hummed a quiet tune as she walked across the room.

*Okay... she's right. I am* okay. *Ahhh, that's good. I still can't believe how incredibly good this feels—pure, unconditional love, warmth and compassion—bliss. I don't need a thing—not a clean diaper, not an arm freed, not a morsel of food—just this feeling, forever and ever.*

The young nurse with the long black braid settled into a rocking chair in the infants' Intensive Care Unit in Our Lady of Saints Hospital in Sao Paolo, Brazil.

At first, it had been odd getting used to the language. Claire had given up trying to read or make sense of anything, since she couldn't seem to properly focus her eyes all the time, anyway. She knew the woman was speaking to her in Portuguese—they all were, but Claire had learned to focus on the doctor's and nurse's facial expressions and voices instead of their words. Once she'd figured that out, she'd begun to understand nearly everything they said to her. She knew she had a lot of medical problems. Not that she cared all that much. *This* was what she cared about, this intoxicating sensation of being so loved for absolutely no reason other than being alive. It was the best. Nothing could touch it.

*I still can't believe I don't have to do or prove a thing... just be. I am finally enough.*

"You were always enough," Nana's distant voice reminded her.

Claire sat up in bed and rubbed her eyes. Traveling between worlds was something she was still getting used to. She never knew when she was going to find herself back in Nana's guest room, but it was such a welcome surprise every time it happened.

"I know I was enough now, but why do we forget that every time we go back?"

Nana laughed as she sat down on the guest bed and tucked a lock of Claire's hair behind her ear. "Because we're human and we go back to learn the lessons we've picked out and to grow. Only animals get to remember they're beautiful and perfect just the way they are, and even then some folks still manage to beat it out of them."

Claire reached out and scratched Ben behind his ear. Shadow whimpered for her fair share as she jumped up and put her two front paws on the bed. Claire pulled her close and kissed the bridge of her nose. "What a crime to steal such bliss from another living thing."

"Misery loves company," Nana reminded her.

"I never could have imagined such a peaceful existence. Between life as Grace there and life as myself here, I never would've believed I could be so ridiculously happy."

"Your loss of power doesn't bother you? Because I was sure that was going to be ten miles of mud road uphill for you," Nana asked.

"Sweep your own porch, first," Claire shot back with a smirk.

"Oh, I know. I've got no room to talk, but that's why *I* stay close to home. You, on the other hand, you bit off quite a chunk, taking your turn as an Egoless Teacher. Who would've thought you had it in you?"

"Not me!" Claire laughed. "But it was much more satisfying watching Paul and the girls and everyone heal themselves, than it was trying to do it for them. Funny, I remember Mom telling me one Christmas that the reason all those Poinsettias die so fast is because they've been forced to bloom. All that trolling... it was like trying to force everyone to grow faster. I was only making things worse."

"Not always," Nana replied.

"Okay, maybe not always. But I was robbing them of their own lessons. I was so worried about them. I couldn't stop."

"I know, hon," Nana said, patting her leg. She stood up and walked around the end of the bed to pull the sheers aside. It had been raining softly for hours. A slight breeze turned the blades inside the old box fan wedged in the open window.

"Someday, maybe I'll give it a whirl. Probably not until I'm missing you like the dickens, though," Nana admitted.

Claire stopped petting the dogs and looked up.

Nana was still staring out the window and sat down, pulling a pillow onto her lap.

Claire pulled the covers back, climbed out of bed and joined her. "How long?"

"What's that, hon?"

"How long do I get to keep visiting you and everyone else here?"

"Little ones enjoy astral travel until they're about two. Then you'll start to come back less and less, in your dreams mostly... until you cross again."

"I wish I could stay this happy forever," Claire said wistfully.

"Nah, you'd get bored I bet."

"How soon before Paul and the girls come to get me?"

"See?"

Claire laughed and covered her mouth.

"Are you ready?" Nana asked, stroking her cheek with the back of her hand.

"Why do you say it like that... so sadly?" Claire asked, cocking her head to one side and reaching out to squeeze Nana's hand.

"Because there's a loud little girl running down a hall with a basket about as big as she is, full of baby gifts. If you think the love of those doctors and nurses felt good, you haven't felt anything yet."

"I'd better go," Claire said as tears spilled down her cheeks. "It's my nature, isn't it? Like that Swallowtail dodging all those spider webs... nothing can to keep me from tending to my wildflowers."

Nana laughed and shook her head. "That's true."

"I'm not going to see you for a while, am I?" Claire asked.

"I'll be around, but you're going to be so drunk on love you won't be able to see straight for weeks. Go on, now. You skedaddle, *Grace*."

Nana turned, looked out the window again and waved to someone below. "Would you look at that? Raining like a cow peeing on a flat rock, but there she stands."

Claire stood up and looked to see who it was.

Wendy stood beneath the giant oak tree, waving.

"I won't be seeing Wendy for a *long* time, will I?" Claire asked, waving back.

"Just take it a day at a time, hon. Go on now... scoot!"

———

"Hi, Grace! Look how pretty she is!" Em said, tapping the glass as she dropped the heavy basket on the floor with a thunk.

"Wow, Dad... she is! Look at her. Look at those teeny-tiny little fingers," Anna gushed, as Paul picked Em up and the three of them peered into the incubator.

"My God, she's little," Paul whispered and shook his head.

"You like to hold her?" asked a nurse.

"Can we?" Anna asked, hesitantly.

"Yes, yes! Best thing for her," he answered, handing them pastel yellow paper scrubs and masks.

In a heartbeat, Anna had hers on and was seated in the rocker holding her arms out.

Paul and Em oohed and aahed over Anna's shoulder, as the nurse placed Grace in her big sister's hands for the first time.

"Mom," Anna whispered, as her tears fell onto the baby's blanket, "Are you seeing this?

## ABOUT THE AUTHOR

Sheri Meshal was born and raised in Iowa. She inherited her lifelong love of books from her father, who sensed she was a writer long before she did, and changed the course of her life by telling her so.

Sheri currently lives in Chicago with her boyfriend, Gabe and her dog, Jebs. She loves to travel, laugh, read, play and explore.

You may contact her at: sheri.meshal@gmail.com

P.S. If you enjoyed this book, please leave a review on Amazon. A review will help more people discover this book and get the word out about her books.

*For more information and to join the mailing list:*
www.sherimeshal.com

Chokecherry

Closet writer Dana Quinn has just lost her Aunt Irma, her last living family member. Dana discovers a letter from her aunt telling her to return to the family farm, Chokecherry. But she's haunted by the accident years ago that killed her parents and three siblings.

For over thirty years Dana believed the farm had been sold and did her best to forget it. But what if everything in the house is exactly as they left it? Nothing can stop her from walking through that door.

She picks up several allies along the way: Slim, the one-eared dog; Stu, the off-Broadway set designer; and Malcolm, the farm's caretaker. Each has baggage to work through, which includes the farm's sordid history and underground passage. Each begins to heal as they try to help the others. Dana and her friends form a tight bond and rise to the challenge of helping Chokecherry realize its true potential, a healing oasis. But in the process Dana's supernatural ability she's struggled to repress for years nearly kills her.

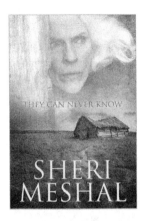

They Can Never Know

For over fifty years, Cleota Ferguson has kept her head down and done as she was told. She managed to outlive her abusive husband, but that's about it and not by much. Time is running out and the money already has, when she accidentally discovers the means to live a completely different life. Her meth-making stepsons are the last people who can ever discover what she's found. Forget putting her in a home. They'll put her in the ground right behind the barn. Sometimes you have to disappear to truly find yourself.

What would you do if your last chance at happiness required you do everything you're afraid of?

Made in the USA
Las Vegas, NV
22 February 2022

44406861R00229